Oct 2014

San Francisco, Paris, New York, Washington, Santa Fe

A Planet called Happiness

R.M. Robinson

firefall^{tm}

First Edition: June 1, 2013

Cover Design & Illustration:
Marcia Repaci, North Creek Design

Editor: Elihu Blotnick

hardcover: 9781939434005

FIREFALL EDITIONS
Canyon, California 94516-0189
www.firefallmedia.com

Printed in the USA

SCIENCE FICTION BY SCIENTISTS-tm

THE SEEDS OF ARIL
Earth reborn, 20,000 CE,
8,000 light years away.

BETRAYAL / BATTLE / STORM
Space mirrors Earth in the warp
of love and weave of war.

A PLANET CALLED HAPPINESS
The sequel to SEEDS

*For my family, without whom I could never
have imagined a world called Happiness.*

Alegria
Beautiful roaring scream
Of joy and sorrow,
So extreme…
A joyous,
Magical feeling,
Alegria

Cirque du Soleil

PROLOGUE

THE GALAXY WAS GETTING SMALLER. The communication system established by the Galactic Space Explorer's Union in the 22nd Century proved to be sufficiently robust and reliable, linking humans across vast distances of interstellar space. Perhaps even more importantly, the customized version of English developed by the Union was still widely spoken, enduring for thousands of years thanks to the diligence of successive generations.

Galactic exploration was made possible by magnetocryogenic technology, where intense magnetic fields allowed humans to be frozen and unfrozen again and again, without causing death or damage to organic tissue. Thousands of space capsules equipped with magnetocryogenic chambers transported humans safely across the galaxy, initiating a new era in exploration and colonization in distant parts of the Milky Way. Supporting this enterprise were seven large supply ships, stationed strategically to provide vital food, water, oxygen, and fuel to the lonely space travelers, who otherwise faced the unknown with no possible chance of returning home.

Human nature being what it was, however, destructive elements eventually threatened the integrity of the GSEU network. Two men, Carl Stormer and Andrew Harding, mobilized a paramilitary army from 22nd Century Earth and attempted to invade a newly colonized planet called Aril. The invaders were defeated by a galactic explorer, Benjamin Mizello, with the aid of a handful of other explorers and a rescue fleet from Earth, led by Admiral Julian Chase. In the victory celebration, the grateful Arilians revealed the discovery of a nearby region of the galaxy that had been seeded by a supernova explosion with elements and molecular structures favorable for the formation of life. The thousands of planets in this region of the galaxy were collectively called the Galactic Garden. The thousand-strong explorer fleet and the supply ships supporting it were relocated to be better positioned for the ensuing exploration.

Another consequence of magnetocryogenic technology was that human lives unfolded on two different time scales. Those in the explorer fleet, who spent thousands of years frozen in their space capsules, aged very little in the time that entire civilizations might rise and fall. New planets could be established by space pioneers in the time it took for an explorer to go from one destination to the next. On the other hand, those who remained on Earth, or any of the colonized planets that humans created, were constrained to live their lives in the time scale of a single century, a blink of an eye in terms of the larger events taking place in the galaxy, yet profoundly critical to the course of those events.

CHAPTER 1
— Century 207 —

A baby born under the light of the aurora would be blessed, the legends said. As Bria gave birth to Benjamin Mizello's child, she looked through tears of joy and pain to see the glowing curtains that foretold good fortune. The baby issued its first terrified cry into the frigid night sky that was graced by a celestial display of unsurpassed majesty, undulating curtains of crimson, green and magenta, a ghostly display that filled the heavens with ephemeral light.

The mid-wife held the baby boy aloft. Bria saw, with mixed feelings of relief and dread, that the child's skin was smooth and without fur. She smiled. It meant that when her son was old enough, he would set off on his own to one of the villages, where the people would take him in and provide him a home, food, and education. The boy would not have to live his life with his mother and the other fur-covered humans called Malanites, who were doomed to live at the ocean shore, spending their days fishing through holes laboriously dug through the frozen surface of the sea.

The Malanites and the people of the villages were descendants of a race of humans who had left Earth in the 64th Century. When they first arrived on the planet Aurora, they enjoyed a pleasant climate with abundant sunshine, mild winters, and spring rains. Their crops thrived and the population grew. The people of Aurora lived a blissfully carefree existence for hundreds of years.

Slow changes are difficult to discern, however. It was centuries before the people of Aurora realized that the climate of their planet had been changing imperceptibly. Scientists of Aurora studied historical records of temperatures and found that the surface had been cooling steadily through the years. The cause, as they soon learned, was that Aurora's sun, the star around which it orbited, was fading. All stars lose energy over time, some more quickly than others. Aurora's star was one of the faster ones. Its radiance decreased by a fraction of a percent each century. No wonder it was hard to detect. Yet over several hundred years, the decrease in its luminosity produced a drastic change in Aurora's climate. In little more than a thousand years after the planet was colonized, it lapsed into a deep ice age from which it would never recover.

The falling temperature forced the people of Aurora to adapt. Some built well insulated, dome-shaped homes that trapped trace amounts of geothermal energy to maintain comfortable temperatures within. The domed structures also protected agricultural crops from the freezing temperatures outside. Others lived by the planet's oceans, where initially the temperatures were milder. They sustained themselves by fishing. As a result, a mutually beneficial trade was established between the people who lived in the domed villages and grew crops and those who lived near the sea and caught fish.

Gradually, though, as temperatures grew colder, the seas froze. The extreme cold led to the expression of a gene causing the Malanites to grow a rich coating of fur, which distinguished them from those who lived inland. Before long, their children were born covered with a fine fur coating and, as the decades passed, this adaptation was favored by environmental factors. Natural selection took over. The number of fur-covered creatures increased. The townspeople grew to fear the Malanites, and communication between the two populations ceased. Out of necessity, they still traded crops for fish, but other than that there was little or no interaction between the two races.

Although furriness became a dominant trait within the Malanite population, every so often one of their children was born with no fur. When that happened, the Malanites raised the child until it was old enough to make his or her way to the nearest village. They knew the townspeople would accept the child as one of their own, believing it to be another refugee from a neighboring village that had finally succumbed to the bitter cold. The Malanites never saw these children again. After being raised in the comfort of the climate-controlled domes, none of the children ever found their way back to the frozen homes near the ice-covered seas. For them, their childhood memories of being raised during infancy by fur-covered beasts were like dreams, distorted by the passage of time and the unbearable cold.

Bria could not help but hope, seeing her new baby held before the flickering auroral light, his unblemished skin adorned by its crimson and emerald glow, that this child would not forget her—that in time they'd be reunited. He was special, she knew. He was the son of a galactic explorer—a child of the stars.

CHAPTER 2

— Century 207 —

Bria named her son Benn, the diminutive form of his father's name. Raising a child was a communal responsibility among the Malanites, but Bria spent every moment she could with her son. As soon as he was able to walk, she brought him with her as she tended to her chores. When she accompanied her brother Albion to deliver fish to the inland towns, she collected wool and other fabrics, from which she sewed warm clothing for the growing boy. Toddling after her through ice storms and blizzards, Benn learned to survive in the brutal conditions of the Malanite fishing village.

In the evenings, Bria sat with Benn. She talked to him almost as if to an adult. In the dim candlelight of the dwelling she shared with Albion and his wife, she drew pictures for Benn, teaching him about the townspeople and the Malanites—why they were so different in some ways and very much alike in others. She also told Benn about his father. As the boy sat gazing with innocent wonder, she related the story of how Benjamin had come from space in a metal capsule. He'd met Bria and they fell in love. During their time together, she learned about his home, a planet called Earth. She drew pictures of Earth for Benn, just as Benjamin had done for her, etching lines into the icy ground with a sharp stick.

After nine years that passed all too quickly, the time came when Benn was old enough to leave his Malanite home and make the journey to one of the domed villages where he'd thrive under the care of the inland townspeople. With a sorrow too great for any mother to bear, Bria said good-bye to her son and set him on the road to a nearby village. As expected, he was taken in by one of the land-dwelling families.

Not a day went by that Bria didn't miss her son. Not a day went by that she didn't curse the life that forced the separation of her from her child. Not a day went by that she didn't dream of seeing him again. Though she wouldn't admit it even to herself, deep down inside, she also longed for the impossible. She longed to be with Benjamin once more.

———————

Seven years later, something happened that had never happened before. Benn returned, urgently searching the Malanite dwellings for his mother. It wasn't easy. The igloo-like homes were moved often to seashores where the fishing was better. Fortunately, word traveled quickly and soon Bria learned of Benn's arrival. When they were reunited, she embraced him, shocked and overjoyed, not believing her son had returned after so many years. He was rail thin, which surprised and upset her because she'd imagined him as a well-fed child enjoying the abundant food of the towns. She sat with him in her brother's ice-home, the light from Aurora's sun filtering through the frozen wall, producing an eerie blue glow upon Benn's pale skin.

"You shouldn't have come back," she told him.

"I don't belong there."

"It doesn't matter. You must stay with the people of the town. You're more like them than you are like us. They have food, schools, warm homes."

"I don't care. I want to stay with you. I'm different from them. You've told me that all my life. My father came from space."

A tear coursed down Bria's cheek. "Benn, you can't stay here."

"I learned something at school."

Bria laughed through her sobs. "You're supposed to learn things at school."

"They found spaceships."

Bria drew in air. "What?"

"Two of them." Benn picked up a stick and carved two shapes in the rime-covered floor. Each was a triangle with a long rectangle extending from one apex.

Bria stared at the pictures for a long time. "Benjamin—

your father—said he came to our planet because two others had come many years earlier. He was visiting Aurora to find out what happened to them."

"The townspeople don't know how the spaceships got there."

Bria stood and paced the small space of the ice-home. She tried to come to grips with the information Benn had brought. What did it mean? Nothing really. Then why did it plague her?

"Do you think they still work?" Benn asked.

"What?!"

"Do you think the space capsules still work?"

Bria sat again, facing Benn, grasping his hands in hers. "What are you saying? What difference does it make?"

"You know what I'm saying, Mother. We can escape in the capsules. We can go to Earth—start a new life there."

"That's nonsense, Benn. It's far too dangerous. We couldn't possibly do that."

Benn was sixteen. He was old enough to understand. His mother had not said she didn't want to go. She was worried about the danger.

"I know where the capsules are," he said.

That evening, Bria couldn't sleep. Was it possible she and Benn could leave Aurora in the two space capsules? Now that she knew about the capsules, could she live another day without dreaming of escape from the planet. One of her dreams had already come true. Benn was back. Dare she believe that another dream might also come to pass? And what was the risk? She and her son might easily meet their deaths attempting to escape the planet on space capsules that were thousands of years old. How could she even consider such madness?

It was Benn whose persistent enthusiasm finally convinced her that they should go. Her dreams were tempered by concerns for the safety and welfare of her son, but Benn had the drive and passion of a sixteen-year-old, unhindered by fear of danger or consequence. In the end, Bria agreed to go, as much for Benn as for herself.

———————

The Malanites' livelihood depended on snow machines, marvelously designed vehicles that could traverse virtually any terrain. Built centuries earlier, they were specially constructed to survive the harsh environments near and upon Aurora's frozen seas. The source of power for the machines was the current that flowed endlessly in the atmosphere above the polar regions of the planet. When all other sources of electricity failed as a result of the icy temperatures that gripped the planet, only those weak currents remained. Any long metallic conductor on the ground would carry electrical currents that mirrored those in the atmosphere overhead. From a single cable, thousands of kilometers long circling the polar cap, wires extended toward the equator, conducting the currents to lower latitudes where the Malanites had set up charging stations. While too weak to heat or illuminate homes, the trickle of electricity was sufficient to gradually energize the batteries that powered the Malanite snow machines. The currents in the upper atmosphere above the polar regions were a result of the interaction between the stream of particles coming from Aurora's sun and the planet's magnetic field. Ultimately then, the power for the vehicles originated from Aurora's dying blue sun.

While being charged, the snow machines were left unattended and could be easily stolen, but that never happened. Where would one possibly want to go? That was true until Bria and Benn resolved to travel to the site where the two mysterious space capsules were buried. One bitterly cold evening, under the dim light of only the stars above, Benn and Bria set out for the nearest Malanite snow machine charging station to find a fully charged vehicle.

Bria didn't have a great deal of experience driving a snow machine and she was unfamiliar with the terrain. They proceeded slowly at first, unable to see beyond the landscape illuminated by the vehicle's four headlamps, which Bria kept low to conserve battery power. Benn was the navigator. Aurora possessed a strong magnetic field and he'd brought a compass from school. He kept Bria on an easterly course even as she turned to circumvent hills and hummocks of ice and snow. It seemed impossible that they'd be able to find two ancient space capsules in that featureless, frozen landscape, but they persevered through the dimly lit blackness.

Their strategy was simple. Eventually, they would reach the next snow machine charging station, where they'd exchange their vehicle for another that was fully charged. They'd move from one charging station to the next until they reached the one closest to where the space capsules had been found. Then, Benn would find the nearest village to inquire about the exact location of the capsules.

They traveled through the night. When the sun rose, they were awed by the vastness of the frozen terrain about them, an endless expanse with virtually no relief save for an occasional mound, the remains of what may have once been a gently sloping hill. They made better time during the day, even though Bria remained attentive for cracks and chasms in the icy surface; they'd be totally invisible until too close to avoid. Occasionally, when the landscape sloped downward, she turned off the engine of the machine and led it slide, often miles at a time, applying the breaks and steering when necessary to stay on course and control her speed. After a while, Benn took over driving. More reckless than Bria and with faster reflexes, he made much better time.

Late that afternoon, on reaching the next charging station, they exchanged their vehicle for another and continued the journey. They didn't stop for the night. As long as they were in the snow machine, Benn would be able to stay warm. If they turned off the engine, the freezing temperatures would quickly penetrate the interior of the vehicle. Bria could withstand the cold, but all Benn had for protection was the long, heavy cloak the people of the inland towns wore.

Finally, after four days, driving continuously, they reached the village near where the capsules had been found. Stopping the snow machine some way off and out of sight, Benn walked the remaining distance quickly. He was greeted warmly by the townspeople. It was common for a visitor from a neighboring village to appear, driven by some circumstance to seek a new home. Teenagers were particularly prone to such excursions, and Benn fit the profile quite well.

Bria remained with the snow machine waiting for Benn's return. She stayed alert, concerned that a group of Malanites might appear, driving to town to deliver fish in exchange for produce. Bria moved her vehicle off the main road, but Malanites didn't always use the roads when approaching towns anyway.

Hours later, Benn returned. He explained that he'd been extremely circumspect in asking about the capsules to avoid arousing suspicion among the townspeople. Following Benn's directions, Bria drove another two hours to where the capsules were. Approaching the site in the dark of evening, they spotted the vehicles, a few tens of meters apart and only partly visible above the ice. They looked just as Bria had imagined from Benjamin's description: conical in shape, with long narrow cylinders extending upward from the narrow end of the cone. The cylinders were the magnetocryogenic chambers that cocooned frozen travelers and prevented aging and death for thousands of years as they moved through space.

Benn and Bria spent the evening in the snow machine, only meters from the vehicles that offered the hope that they'd escape their planet to a new life on Earth. The anticipation of what they'd find with the morning light made it impossible for them to sleep. As Aurora's sun cast its first feeble blue rays across the frozen landscape, they approached the capsules, still partially buried under ice and snow. They used their hands to remove enough to expose the hatches. The flush-mounted handles were embedded in ice. With tools from the snow machines, they were eventually able to swing the hatches open.

Entering the capsules, they were relieved to find both empty. Bria feared the occupants of the capsules had perished while still inside. Apparently, they'd landed successfully. Perhaps they had lived in the nearby town thousands of years ago. Were their descendants living close by?

Benn had learned enough of the Union language in the village school to decipher the words on the capsule's control panel. His first task was to start the computer. Once he had access to the computer, he hoped he'd be able to find information about the capsule's operation.

He spent the next few weeks intently studying the operational instructions resident in the computer's memory. The temperature inside the capsule was freezing. Bria made sure Benn returned to the snow machine periodically to avoid frost bite, but the battery power was waning. If they were unsuccessful in getting the capsules to work and the snow machine lost all its power, they would have to walk back to the town. She was confident that her fur would protect her for that journey, but Benn might die in the cold.

At night they slept huddled together in the snow machine. Out of the wind and in the well insulated compartment of the vehicle, they could survive, but sleep was difficult. Bria worried. Benn was thin and frail, and lack of sleep was weakening him even more.

Each night, Benn recounted what he'd learned from the capsule's computers. He was methodically studying the function of all the ship's systems: propulsion, navigation, communication, magnetocryogenics, life support, and weapons. There was much he didn't understand, but Benn was a tenacious learner. He constantly reassured Bria that he would eventually know enough to launch the capsules, stressing that they were extremely intelligent machines, designed to perform complex tasks without a great deal of human control or intervention. Once the launch sequence was initiated, the computers would take over, firing the rockets and automatically adjusting the direction, speed, and orientation of the capsule until it reached orbit. After they were in space, they could program their course to whichever destination they chose.

Finally, one evening, after 27 long days and nights, Benn said to his mother, "We can leave now."

He said it with such conviction that Bria didn't think to question his certainty. Now it was just a matter of confirming that he really wanted to go.

"Walk with me," she said.

The night was clear and cold. Benn tightened his cloak to stay warm. Bria clutched his arm and brought him closer to her as they ascended a gentle slope. Once they'd reached the crest, she pointed into the distance. Far away, just barely visible against the black night, were the faintly glowing domes of the nearby village.

"Do you see the town, Benn?"

"Yes."

"There is warmth there, and shelter, and food. You could be there now. You could grow up in that town, or one very much like it—grow old in comfort and safety." Bria looked at Benn to make sure his eyes were directed to where her finger pointed. "Now look up. There is only dark space above us—cold, dark empty space. Those are your choices. Do you understand what I'm saying?"

Benn turned his head upward. His pale face seemed to capture the starlight. "I understand you, Mother. I know I'm young, but I understand there are times that choices like this have to be made—choices that will determine the course our lives will take forever after. I understand that. What you don't realize is that I made this choice long ago, when I first learned these capsules had been found. I'm ready to go."

Bria was going to warn him of the dangers—how neither of them could easily fathom the challenges they'd face. But to what end? Benn was determined, and for a young man of sixteen years, little could be done to deter him. She hugged her son and looked skyward. "We'll leave in the morning," she said.

And so it was that almost seventeen years after Bria had watched the father of her child blast into the heavens on an arrow of fire, she and her son were on their way to an extremely uncertain future. To Bria and Benn, however, it was far better than any the cold planet receding below them had to offer.

CHAPTER 3
— Century 282 —

Stephen Nutley was unfrozen when his supply ship detected the approach of two galactic explorer capsules. As was the normal procedure, he'd been frozen in his own space capsule a good distance away from the supply ship to avoid excessive warmth from the star that gave the large vehicle its power. After docking with the larger ship, he activated the computers and was surprised to find that the radar system identified the two capsules as those belonging to the Brinkleys, the couple that had once been the custodians of the supply ship he now occupied. They had apparently survived their attempt to escape to a new planet twenty thousand years ago and were now returning.

Nutley had mixed feelings. The return of the Brinkleys meant that he no longer had to remain as custodian of Supply Ship 2. He'd be free to resume his life as a galactic explorer, but he wasn't quite sure he was ready for that. He could return to Earth, but he had tried that once before and found it unbearably drab and boring, with all aspects of life subject to global scrutiny and control. That was thousands of years ago. How much more tedious would human society be now? He wondered if the Brinkleys would let him remain on the supply ship and help out. It was possible, but would he be satisfied working under them? Clearly, they'd want to take over control of the ship again, and Nutley knew they were far more capable than he was at that.

He stared curiously at the monitor that now displayed the docking station where the Brinkleys would emerge from their capsules. Moments later, the hatches opened and two figures floated into the light of the entry area. What Nutley saw shocked and confused him, for the two figures were not the Brinkleys at all. One was a young, thin male with an ashen face and dark eyes, deep-set in a way that was almost skeletal. The wan skin, stretched over prominent cheek bones, added to the cadaverous look of the youth. The second figure, obviously female from the womanly shape discernible beneath the jumpsuit she wore, stunned him even more because her face was covered with a layer of thick, coffee-colored fur.

The two appeared uncertain about what to do and both floated awkwardly, conversing quietly. Nutley turned up the audio but he couldn't understand the language they were speaking. Switching on his microphone, he stammered, "Who are you? And where are you from?"

The two figures reacted in fear, twisting their bodies in the limbo of weightlessness, trying to comprehend the absence of gravity and ghostly voice emanating from the vacuous space about them. Looking frantically about for a direction to address his words, the boy said in a trembling voice, "We want to go to Earth."

He spoke the Union language, but it was heavily accented, almost Asian in its intonation and crispness. Nutley struggled to come to grips with the bizarre situation. Still suspicious of the strange beings who had entered the supply ship, he spoke again, "How did you get the two space capsules? Where are the Brinkleys?"

"We don't know the Brinkleys," the boy answered with more confidence. "We found the capsules under the ice."

The brief response was sufficient for Nutley to begin piecing together the facts. The Brinkleys must have made it to the planet after all and had remained there. His two visitors had found the capsules, perhaps thousands of years later, and some-how managed to learn how to operate the vehicles. Nutley's con-fusion gave way to curiosity. "Proceed down the corridor to the rotating ladder," he instructed. "Climb down the ladder. I will meet you at the bottom."

Bria was amazed by the gradual return of gravity as she undertook the dizzying descent down the ladder. She felt better when her feet were firmly placed on the floor and there was no further illusion that either the ladder or the room was spinning. Looking about, she saw an elderly man wearing a silver jumpsuit approaching with an uncertain smile and an outstretched hand.

"I'm Steven Nutley," he said, his voice raspy and his breath emitting an unfamiliar odor. He shook their hands as Benn introduced himself and his mother. Although friendly, Bria was wary of the man. He was large and she knew he could easily overpower them both if he chose to. She'd been attracted to Benjamin's quiet and gentle nature, but found Nutley's forward demeanor rude and offensive.

After greeting them, he placed his arm around Bria and guided her through a doorway leading to another room with a table and chairs. As he did, his hand slid to her hip and his body leaned into hers awkwardly. She turned her face and gave him a glare, but he avoided looking at her. He brought out food and drink from cabinets built into the wall, and showed them how to eat the food, chuckling openly at their clumsiness in using utensils and their reactions upon attempting to sip hot beverages.

Bria listened to Nutley and Benn converse, understanding little and vowing to learn Union English as quickly as possible. Benjamin had taught her a few words, but she wasn't able to comprehend even the subject of their conversation. Occasionally, Benn translated for her, and she realized they were discussing Earth. Apparently, Nutley had spent many years on the planet, and although his impressions were not overwhelmingly favorable, Bria learned enough to know that Earth had far more to offer than the planet they'd left. In any case, there was no doubt Earth would be their next destination, and Bria, addressing Benn, told him to ask Nutley to teach them how to navigate the capsules and land them safely on Earth's surface. To her relief and surprise, Nutley agreed, but cautioned that it would take several days of instruction, during which time they would cohabit the supply ship. Bria couldn't help but sense something subtly sinister in his offer.

It happened after Nutley consumed several canisters of the beverage that smelled so offensive to Bria. She refused to drink it, even when Nutley repeatedly offered it to her. Benn, however, tried it and immediately coughed up the first few swallows. Bria warned her son to drink no more, but Nutley chided the boy into trying it again, and soon Benn was finding the liquid easier and easier to swallow. At Benn's age, it wasn't long before he had passed out at the table. Bria shouted in panic at Nutley, but the man just laughed, not understanding a word she said. He walked to the doorway and pointed down the hall, motioning for Bria to help her son.

Benn wasn't a heavy youth, and Bria was strong. She placed her arm around his shoulder and lifted him easily, following Nutley out of the galley and down the corridor to the ship's sleeping quarters. She arranged Benn's delicate frame on the bed while Nutley stood at the doorway. When she was done, Nutley led her to the next room.

Bria entered the sleeping compartment and turned to give Nutley an angry stare before sliding the door closed. She heard him stumble down the corridor back to the galley.

Bria lay on her bed for a long time, unable to sleep, worrying about the extent of the danger she'd exposed herself and her son to. She was encouraged by the conversation between Benn and Nutley, and the man seemed willing to help them, but the more they drank, the more the discourse had deteriorated. She made the mistake of believing that because of Benjamin's easy and kind nature, other galactic explorers they'd encounter would be equally congenial. Nutley seemed to be a different breed entirely.

Just as she was about to doze off, she heard the door to the room slide open. Bright light from the corridor filled the room, momentarily blinding her. She could see Nutley's silhouette filling the entrance, swaying noticeably and getting larger as he stepped into the tiny room. With a swift motion, he unzipped the front of his jumpsuit, but as he attempted to step out of it he tripped and fell backward into the corridor. Bria jumped from her bed and tried in panic to step around him to go back to the galley, but Nutley grabbed her leg and she fell sprawling next to him. Still trying to extract his feet from the legs of the jumpsuit, Nutley thrust himself on top of her, pinning her helplessly to the floor. With surprising agility, he grabbed the zipper of Bria's jumpsuit and pulled it sharply, then tore at the garment and forced it down over her shoulders in a single motion, baring Bria's body completely to the hips. Bria, attempting to squirm from the man, twisted beneath him, but the movement seemed to only intensify his attack.

It wasn't until later, sobbing uncontrollably in the galley, that Bria understood what had happened next. Nutley had raised his head to look down upon her naked body, fully illuminated under the overhead lights in the corridor. Instead of seeing the female body he'd imagined in his drunken stupor, he saw the body of an animal, completely covered in a thick coat of tawny fur. It was enough to bring him to his senses, and he fell back away from her in shock and disgust. Bria kicked out at him then and pushed him away until she could get to her feet and continue her flight down the corridor. Once in the galley, she attempted to lock the door, but it had no mechanism by which it could be secured. Locks were completely unfamiliar to her in any case, as the Malanite dwellings had never needed any. Searching through the galley cabinets, Bria found a variety of odd-shaped tools, whose purpose she could not even begin to understand. She grabbed the most lethal-looking object and stood by the door with it raised above her head. She waited for some time, listening for the sounds of Nutley's footsteps in the corridor. After a while, she opened the door and looked out. He was gone. Bria rushed to Benn's room to check on him. The boy still slept, breathing regularly, but somewhat heavily in the same position she had left him. Bria then returned to the kitchen and sat at the table, the heavy metallic tool lying within hand's reach.

With ever increasing dread and dismay, Bria tried to imagine what life would be like for her on Earth. It would be fine for Benn, she hoped, but what type of life would she have to endure, freakishly covered with a thick coat of animal fur? It had been bad enough suffering the stares of the people of the towns and villages when the Malanites delivered fish. What would it be like on Earth, where she would be the only one of her kind on the entire planet? Even worse to contemplate, what type of persecution would Benn have to suffer as the son of a bizarre creature from another planet. After a while, she dozed, her head dropping to the table, where she noticed tufts of her fur, perhaps pulled out during her struggle with Nutley.

Nutley was contrite hours later when chance eventually forced the three together in the galley. Pretending as if nothing had happened, he went about his business gruffly, saying little to either Benn or Bria. Benn, who remembered little of the first few hours on the ship, engaged him in questions, which he answered in short sentences. At Bria's urging, Benn was able to get Nutley to repeat his agreement to teach them how to land the space capsules on Earth.

Over the next few days, Nutley and Benn spent many hours in the small vehicles, which Bria refused to enter as long as the man was there. She never told her son what had happened while he slept. Thankfully, Nutley largely avoided Bria the remainder of their time on the supply ship.

Benn taught his mother how to operate a computer in the ship's control room, and though the device was totally unfamiliar to her, she was able to execute a program by which she began to learn Union English. She spent many hours studying the language, totally absorbed by the task. She was intelligent and had an excellent memory. Her skills improved quickly. Occasionally, she escaped to the part of the supply ship that contained the greenhouse garden, where she wandered among the rows of food crops, marveling at the warmth and humidity that made the plants thrive. It was no wonder she'd never been satisfied with life on Aurora. Existence in such cold temperatures seemed contrary to life. Bria gazed through the crystalline windows at the universe outside the supply ship and thought of Benjamin. Where was he now? She yearned to see him again and talk to him. She longed to share with him her doubts and fears and dreams. She needed to tell him about their son. In learning the Union language, she'd encountered the word God, which had no equivalent in the

Malanite language. But the idea that there was an immortal being that one could pray to and find comfort with caused her to think of Benjamin in just that way.

Finally they were able to depart. It was a far less dramatic experience than their departure from Aurora. The two capsules separated from the supply ship gently and silently. Benn had already programmed the navigation systems of the two capsules to automatically guide them to Earth. Once free from the supply ship, they both entered their magnetocryogenic chambers and initiated the freezing sequence, just as they'd done after their successful escape from Aurora.

CHAPTER 4

— Century 420 —

Fourteen thousand years later, when Bria and Benn were unfrozen upon reaching Earth, Bria emerged from her magnetocryogenic chamber and donned her jumpsuit in preparation for landing. Looking down at her naked body, she observed with almost dream-like awareness that every bit of fur was gone, exposing glistening white skin of almost supernatural smoothness and beauty. Some combination of warmth from her time on the supply ship and magnetic shock caused by freezing and unfreezing had caused a reversal of the gene expression processes that had enabled Bria and her Malanite ancestors to adapt to the cold temperature on Aurora. She zipped up her jumpsuit with trembling hands, realizing she'd soon be starting a new life on a new planet, without the stigma of being a fur-covered freak of nature.

Bria contacted Benn using the capsule's radio, as he had instructed. She was relieved to learn he was alive and equally excited that they'd arrived. She told him about the miraculous loss of her fur. Benn was happy for his mother. Upon his suggestion they both agreed to adopt new names to use on Earth. From that point on, Bria would be Xyla and her son would be Druix. In the Malanite language, Xyla meant "transformation", while Druix was the name given to a child born from the union between a Malanite female and a male from one of the towns.

The arrival of Xyla and Druix on Earth was accompanied by tremendous excitement. Steven Nutley had sent a message in advance alerting those on Earth that two refugees from the doomed planet Aurora were on their way in space capsules that had once belonged to a pair of supply ship custodians. Though the two arrived seven thousand years after Nutley's message, transfer of information on Earth through the millennia had become routine. When the capsule approached, those who operated the sensitive radio telescopes about the globe detected the beacon signal from the vehicles at the expected time and place. With that detection, news spread quickly. Plans were made to locate a suitable landing spot and arrange for an assembly of physicians, scientists, language experts, and political officials to greet the space travelers.

In specially built structures in the Mojave Desert the earthlings waited for the arrival of the two space capsules. When the parachutes billowed white against the flawless blue sky, cheers rang out and some, unable to contain their excitement, ran from the buildings, jumped into small vehicles waiting nearby, and raced across the desert to be first at the landing site. The plumes of sand rising behind the speeding vehicles obscured everyone's view, especially when the rockets on the two spacecraft ignited. It took several minutes for all the dust to settle, and the greeting party stood uncertainly while the colors of their garments gradually disappeared beneath layers of fine ocher granules. Moments later, the hatches of the capsules opened, and almost simultaneously the two travelers emerged. One was a thin youth around which the gray Union jumpsuit sagged as if unable to find anything within for support. The young man's face was ashen, and his eyes were so dark that his expression was impossible to read. Depending on what was hidden within the deep-set eye sockets, his countenance could have been fearful, curious, or arrogant. But it was the second of the two travelers who invoked the greatest awe. The message from Nutley said the female refugee was a fur-covered humanoid, but the woman who climbed gingerly down from the capsule was stunningly beautiful with the balanced features of timeless perfection. Even the 420th Century men and women in the greeting party were captivated by her universal appeal. Unlike the young man, her expression was easy to read. Her eyes were turned toward her companion with a combination of worry and relief. She lost no time running to him and giving him a long, loving embrace. At that point, both mother and son smiled happily at the crowd, and the resemblance between the two was unmistakable.

Those greeting the travelers included the Director of the Griffith Museum in the hills above the city that was once called

Los Angeles. Dr. Curtis Mendoza was one of the world's few remaining experts on the galactic explorer fleet that had departed Earth in the 22nd Century and paved the way for the discovery and settlement of the planet called Aril. Director Mendoza also knew the history of the planet from which the two visitors had escaped. With little opposition, all on Earth agreed that the two travelers would live at the museum until such time as they were successfully and comfortably integrated into modern day Earth society.

Xyla and Druix became immediate celebrities around the planet. Xyla, in particular, captured global attention, for in the first few minutes the two were on Earth, the whole world fell in love with the exotic beauty whose story cf survival on a frozen planet and escape to Earth left people spellbound. But it was Curtis Mendoza who had the closest access to the woman, because she was shy and introverted and appreciated the museum director's efforts to keep her insulated from the world spotlight.

Xyla loved the museum, and she'd take long walks around the grounds when it was closed to visitors. Mendoza often accompanied her, teaching her about modern Earth, and in the process extracting piece by piece Xyla's incredible tale. With respectful concern for her privacy and shyness, he released to the media only parts of her story. It was a respect and concern inspired by his love for Xyla, which inevitably grew stronger every day. The world was not surprised when six months later, Dr. Mendoza announced that he and Xyla were entering into a formal relationship that was the 420th Century equivalent of marriage.

Druix was as reclusive as his mother, perhaps more so. At the critical age of sixteen, he faced insurmountable challenges dealing with the difference between his appearance and that of his peers on Earth, who were uniformly tall and well-built, with intimidating amber eyes and thick bristles for hair. Dr. Mendoza even had difficulty finding a brush on Earth suitable for Druix to use on his long, thin, straight, ebony hair.

Fortunately, Druix was forever a student, and the interest and dedication he had demonstrated in the schools of Aurora also sustained him on Earth. The museum was an ideal location for him to expand his knowledge, for its computers were linked to every imaginable source of information, not only on Earth, but from space as well. For now more than ever, radio telescopes scoured the heavens for signals coming without interruption from Aril and the Union's galactic scale communication network.

Druix was most intrigued by history. With a well documented record spanning more than 40,000 years, there was endless fuel for his intellectual appetite. He knew as much about the industrial age of ancient Earth as the age of planetary exploration, made possible by the invention of magnetocryogenic freezing technology. He studied intensively the founding of Aril and its emergence as a planet with no wars or lethal weapons of any kind—a planet that had mastered genetics and medicine, yet had the ethical foundation and morality to resist using that knowledge destructively.

Druix wrote a series of treatises on the civilizations of three planets over ten thousand years, studiously comparing them and finding remarkable coincidences and universal truths among the markedly distinctive humanoid races. Had those on Earth, particularly Curtis Mendoza, known that Druix's grandfather was Arthur Mizello, he wouldn't have been surprised at the young man's unique abilities. Druix knew who his grandfather and his father were, and he studied their lives with great interest, inspired by the knowledge of his grandfather's work and how it had earned him a Pulitzer Prize thousands of years earlier.

Druix was happy that his mother had found a fulfilling relationship with Dr. Mendoza, but he himself was plagued by incurable loneliness. He attended college and found a small group of friends, but there was no outlet for his need for female companionship, save his obsession for history. Because of his intelligence and the fame of his short histories, he was respected and popular, but his relationship with others never extended to the physical.

When Druix graduated and became a professor of history, he achieved instant popularity with his students, but it was only because they appreciated his quiet, unpretentious wisdom. He developed a curriculum for teaching a new course that covered fifty thousand years in one semester. This big history approach appealed to the students because it eliminated the need to learn useless facts, dates, and names, but rather treated entire civilizations and societies as unique entities, with personalities, character traits, strengths, weaknesses, desires and dreams.

Though Dr. Mendoza obsessively cared for Xyla and treated her with kindness and respect, only Druix could see that his mother was still not completely happy. Perhaps it was because she didn't have enough to do. Whenever possible though, she found ways to help around the museum, either guiding visitors, maintaining the exhibits, or fixing meals in the cafeteria. But Xyla had been raised from a very young age to work extremely hard in the bleak, frozen Malanite villages. In subzero temperatures, she would unload and haul the fish from the Malanite snow machines and then clean them one by one at the ocean's edge, with the relentless wind blowing slivers of ice in her face. She had to wash Malanite clothing in frigid water and carry the garments dripping wet to special drying shelters. And she'd cook in a small kitchen with minimal heat, trying to achieve variety with the limited assortment of ingredients available. Xyla was undoubtedly happy not to have to work as hard as she had on Aurora, but still the ease and comfort associated with her museum tasks must have produced incurable boredom.

Yet Druix suspected there was another reason for his mother's wistful dreaminess and detachment. She spoke little of his father, Benjamin, but he believed she still loved him. From his room at the museum, he watched her take walks in the evening, disappearing into the darkest regions of the area bounded by the museum's perimeter fence. Outside the fence was a narrow strip of vegetation, the only remnant of the parkland that once surrounded the museum. Beyond that thin ring of shrubs was humanity, a domain Xyla would never enter on her own. She'd stand in the area blocked from the museum lights where the night sky was darkest. Druix followed her one evening and marveled

at the number of stars that became visible, including, on exceptionally clear nights, the Milky Way in all its mysterious glory.
Druix had no doubt that Xyla still thought about Benjamin,
wondering if he was still alive and what he was doing, what kinds
of planets he had found and what type of people he had met.
Radio telescopes on Earth were still receiving reports from the
Union network confirming that explorers were still out there, but
those messages were thousands of years old. What had happened
to Benjamin? It was useless to ponder such questions. He was
impossibly far away in both space and time. That, however, didn't
keep Xyla from the same restless imaginings that had plagued
her on Aurora.

No child ever came from the union between Xyla and Dr.
Mendoza during their time together. It may have been because of
her husband's age, but Xyla suspected otherwise. Her son's birth
in a Malanite ice house, lit only by the dim glow from shifting
curtains of auroral light, had been a difficult one. Xyla had almost
lost her life. The boy, it seemed, would be her only child.

Nine years after their arrival on Earth, Dr. Mendoza passed
away. Xyla was unaware really how old the director was when
they were married. She had no way to calibrate age in a world so
different from her own. Modern Earthlings lived more than a hundred years with remarkably little change in appearance, particularly in the last three decades of life. Medical science enabled
them to maintain vitality and quality of life until the very end.

Xyla was devastated by the death of Dr. Mendoza, and
she fell into a deep depression that only her son could truly
comprehend. With her husband gone, the world attention he had
protected her from returned. To Xyla's dismay, the Board that
managed the museum selected another director who welcomed
the publicity Xyla's presence brought. Even more distressing was
that he acted as though he intended to assume Dr. Mendoza's role
as husband to Xyla as well.

When it finally reached the point that it was no longer
tolerable, Xyla arranged to meet Druix to discuss their moving at
last from the safety of the museum. Druix wasn't surprised, nor

was he at a loss for suggestions about what they might do. Years of loneliness had given him ample opportunity to explore the limited number of realistic options.

One day, the two announced to the new director that they wished to leave for a two-week vacation in the Mojave Desert. The director reluctantly agreed and arranged for them to take an aerial vehicle to a lodge where they could stay. Had the new director understood Xyla and Druix better and paid closer attention to how they had gotten to Earth, he might have realized what the pair intended.

In the desert, in the days it took to prepare their capsules, Xyla's restlessness intensified. One evening Druix followed her to an outcropping of rocks, which Xyla scaled to the highest point by nimbly jumping from one boulder to another. Once at the top, she lay down in an ancient depression caused by erosion of the rock surface, used by indigenous people thousands of years ago to collect water. There Xyla became invisible to Druix until he had climbed up after her. She registered no surprise when he sat down next to her.

"Do you think you'll find him?" he asked.

Xyla sighed. "Does it matter?" she returned. "We can't stay on Earth any longer. We have to go somewhere."

"We should have a plan though."

"We'll go first to Arthur Mizello's supply ship. He can give us advice. Can you get us there?"

"Sure," said Druix. "Will you tell him who we are?"

"No," answered Xyla quietly. The desert was so soundless, she need no more than to whisper. "It wouldn't be right."

"Will you ask him about Benjamin? Where he is?"

"I don't know. If I can do it without raising suspicion. He knows where we came from, and he probably knows Benjamin visited Aurora. It might not seem too coincidental that I met Benjamin during his visit."

"Risky," said Druix. "If he does the math and knows how old I am, he could put two and two together. He's my grandfather."

"You're right. It's better if we don't mention Benjamin."

They were both silent for a while. A slight breeze chilled the air.

"So then, if you're not trying to find Benjamin," Druix said finally, "What are we looking for?"

"A world we can live on," Xyla replied, with no hesitation.

"It may not exist. We've become anachronistic. We can't go back to the world we came from. The humans on Earth are not our kind, nor are those on Aril. Thousands of years of divergent human evolution separate us. There are no others in the entire universe from our time and place."

"So maybe we're doomed to search forever," Xyla said with a heavy sigh.

Druix tried to see his mother's face, but the darkness was too complete. "Except…" he said, and he let the word diffuse into the night.

"Except what?" Xyla turned to him and Druix thought he saw the reflected light from a tear.

"The galactic explorer fleet is still out there—all from Benjamin's generation. Not so far removed from ours. There are more than a thousand still alive at last count, still drifting frozen through space, hardly aging at all."

"How does that help us find a world to live on?"

"It doesn't, but if they've adapted to life without a world, why can't we? Why can't we be like them—nomads of the galaxy, going from planet to planet, exploring, discovering, living almost forever?"

Xyla chuckled. "Sometimes I forget you're still young. At your age, this must sound tantalizing and irresistible—new adventures, the unknown, mysteries and excitement at every crossroad. I'm passed that. I wouldn't know how to be a galactic explorer."

"Nonsense," said Druix. "You'd be a great explorer. You can't fool me. You're not that old."

Xyla didn't respond immediately and Druix surmised that his mother was considering his suggestion. She sat up. "Would you teach me?"

"Of course. Remember I'm a teacher. The data archives on these capsules have all the information we need. We'll learn together how to be explorers, and no one will even know we're new recruits."

Xyla shook her head and her dark hair flowed about her in a graceful arc. With that movement, she shed ten years and was once again the exotic beauty who had stepped out of the capsule to the awed reception of the Earthlings.

"Okay," she said. "We'll start tomorrow. But we can't delay our departure. We don't want anyone figuring out what we're planning and coming out here to stop us."

"Right," said Druix, and he helped his mother to her feet. They climbed down from the rock and started back toward the lodge.

Druix was glad to see his mother happy again, but he knew the real reason she had agreed to his suggestion. By becoming a galactic explorer, she would be Benjamin's equal. It was a small universe really. The Union communication network made it smaller. It was just a matter of time before his mother and father found each other again. Druix was sure that was what returned the youthfulness to Xyla's step.

A week later, two ancient space capsules blasted into the pre-dawn sky of the Mojave Desert, and Xyla and Druix began their 8000-year voyage to Supply Ship 6, leaving behind an Earth wondering why the two mysterious visitors from space had found their planet not worth living on.

CHAPTER 5

— Century 506 —

Arthur Mizello and his partner Krystal on Supply Ship 6 were intrigued to learn that two refugees from the planet Aurora had lived on Earth for ten years and then unexpectedly left the planet for an unknown destination. And now, the supply ship's radar system had just detected two approaching space vehicles identified as those belonging to the previous custodians of Supply Ship 2. Their arrival had initiated an automatic unfreezing of Arthur and Krystal, who watched with growing interest as a man and woman emerged from the docked capsules and floated down the corridor to reach the ladder bringing them to the gravity-controlled portion of the supply ship.

The meeting between Arthur, Krystal, Xyla and Druix was as complex as anyone might imagine involving four people so disconnected on one level and intricately linked on another. Xyla and Druix knew Arthur was Benjamin's father, but knew nothing about Krystal, because at the time Benjamin visited Aurora he was unaware that his father had found a new companion in space. They were confident that Arthur knew nothing about Benjamin fathering a child while on Aurora, but what did Arthur and Krystal know about their lives on Earth and the surreptitious manner they had departed?

In fact, Arthur and Krystal had studied all the information transmitted from Earth about the two refugees and were intrigued that the young man they shook hands with had written prolifically about civilizations and societies, much like Arthur himself had done before leaving Earth. At the same time, Arthur wondered about the controversy surrounding the departure of the two. It caused him to be suspicious, but perhaps unjustifiably so. Even though his immediate reaction was to trust the mother and son in front of him, he was anxious to speak privately to Krystal, who had far keener perception about people than he. Most disconcerting to Arthur though was how the woman, Xyla, looked directly into his eyes as she shook his hand in greeting. Something in the way her eyes locked on his gave him the impression that she recognized him in some bizarrely incomprehensible way.

When the four were comfortably seated in the galley with food arrayed on the table, Arthur leaned back in his chair, feigning a relaxed posture, and said, "We received a message from Earth after your departure. It appears that it was unexpected."

Druix answered, speaking in Union English. "To be honest, we were fearful that we'd be prevented from leaving had we announced our intentions. It's quite a long story."

Arthur nodded. "Please, no explanation is necessary. In space, the past is far away. Krystal will help you with anything you need to continue your journey."

"My mother and I were hoping you could advise us where we might go next. Have there been any new colonies established since we left Earth?"

Arthur hesitated. "As a matter of fact, there has been a successful colonization. It's a planet named Aril. We've received extremely encouraging news about the progress of that society. It's a very advanced civilization that has so far avoided the problems that plagued Earth many years ago."

Druix exchanged a glance with his mother. "Yes, we've heard of Aril. It seems like just what we've been looking for."

"Perhaps," said Arthur. "Except…"

"Is there a problem?" asked Xyla.

"No," put in Krystal abruptly. She gave Arthur a sharp look.

Arthur became nervous. "We know of nothing wrong on Aril." He was watching Krystal as he spoke. "But there have been disruptions in the Union network that may endanger the planet. Our information is too sketchy to influence your plans, but you should proceed with caution upon your arrival there."

"Absolutely," said Druix. "Thanks for the warning. We come originally from a planet in the midst of a miserable ice age. We don't ask for much."

A moment of silence followed. The unasked question

hung in the air. If that was true, why had they left Earth?

Xyla sensed it. "Mr. Mizello, you must understand our situation. We left Aurora in the 207th Century, but the humans we're descended from left Earth 14,000 years earlier. When we arrived at Earth, we lived with people from a completely different race, altered over 30,000 years from the time our people left. They treated us well, but we were hoping to find a society where we'd be able to live normal lives. It might not exist, even on Aril, but we felt we owed it to ourselves to try. We underwent tremendous dangers escaping Aurora and going to Earth. We don't let our fears prevent us from striving for a better life."

"I understand," said Arthur, although his tone was unconvincing. Turning to Druix, he said, "When we have more time, I'd enjoy hearing your impressions of Earth. We know only what we can glean from sporadic messages, sometimes difficult to interpret. I understand that you're a historian. I'm sure this gives you a unique perspective of Earth at the time you left."

"I look forward to doing that, Mr. Mizello. Your work is still widely known and discussed on Earth. You're somewhat of a legend."

Arthur shifted nervously in his chair. "As a sociologist, I know how stories can be distorted through time. In my case, the time has been great enough for a tremendous amount of distortion."

Druix laughed. "You're being humble. Nevertheless, I've read some of your work and find it extremely insightful, even though it was written long ago."

"Thank you," said Arthur. He rose from his chair nervously. "You both must be tired. Krystal will show you to your quarters."

"I understand your son is a galactic explorer," said Druix suddenly.

"Yes, he is," said Arthur, looking confused. "He was here recently."

Xyla stiffened.

"Well, not recently in real time. It was about 10,000 years ago."

"Right," said Druix. "In any case, it must have been incredible seeing your son again."

"It was," said Arthur, looking at Krystal, remembering Benjamin's visit to the supply ship. Benjamin's excitement on seeing his father again had been tempered by his shock at meeting Krystal.

"I suppose he left to continue his planetary explorations."

"Not really," said Arthur. "He's on his way to Aril." Arthur hesitated, glancing at Krystal before continuing. "He was curious about it."

"I see," said Druix. "Maybe we'll see him there."

Arthur laughed. "I'm afraid Benjamin has a head start on you by a few thousand years."

"Of course," said Druix. "I keep getting confused. I continue to be fooled by magnetocryogenics."

"Same here," said Arthur. "Even after all this time."

Later, as she was saying good-night to her son, Xyla confronted him. "Why did you ask about Benjamin?!"

"What's wrong? You wanted to know. Didn't you?"

"No. Yes. I don't know. But now they're going to be suspicious."

"No, they won't. It was a perfectly innocuous question."

Xyla gripped her son's shoulders with both hands. "We're here to find a new world to live on. Let's not get distracted. No more questions about Benjamin."

Druix smiled. "Yes, Mom."

Xyla hugged him and hurried down the corridor, anxious to depart the supply ship and start the journey to Aril. She couldn't account for her own impatience to depart. What difference could a few hours make when she was already thousands of years behind Benjamin.

CHAPTER 6
— Century 650 —

In the years following the failed attempt by Andrew Harding and Carl Stormer to invade Aril, Union explorers converged on the Galactic Garden as if there were a gold rush. The discovery by Arilian astronomers that a supernova explosion had seeded a region of the galaxy with life-favoring atoms and molecules inspired a renewal among the explorers of the curiosity and excitement that had driven them to join the Union so many thousands of years ago. Up to that time, there was general disappointment in the cold and lifeless planets that had thus far been explored.

Admiral Julian Chase, the leader of the Earth fleet that had aided in the rescue of the planet, remained on Aril for several years after the invasion attempt, helping Arilians to organize the reinvigorated galactic exploration enterprise. Together, they carefully orchestrated the destinations of the explorers to maximize the number of worlds they would visit. Each explorer was given precise instructions on how to communicate the outcome of their journeys. If all went according to plan, by the year 100,000, the thousand-strong explorer fleet would investigate several times that many planets.

The Arilians assembled a panel of experts that set procedures for planetary exploration, information handling, and biological intervention. Based on the state of any given planet, explorers were given specific instructions on how to approach, land on, and study the new world. The guidelines were designed to protect the planetary life forms first and the galactic explorers second. Special protocols were established for those planets that harbored alien life. For those that didn't, Arilian biologists created canisters of growth material that could be used to jump-start new biospheres. As was their nature, Arilians were extremely methodical in these planning activities. Explorers were warned not to attempt landing on any planet they might contaminate by inadvertently introducing harmful agents. They were given special suits to wear that prevented the mixing of biogenic materials. After being used once, they'd be released into space to avoid carrying contaminants to the next planet.

The Arilians also created a three-dimensional model of the Galactic Garden that was so large one could walk within its confines as if moving through space. Admiral Chase spent much time in this room, fascinated by the myriad stars floating about him with incandescent luminosity. So real were the images that he felt he would be burned if he attempted to touch one, but when he tried, his hand just passed through them as if they were smoke.

Around many of the stars were planetary systems, with each planet color-coded in a way that indicated whether or not the world harbored life, had once harbored life, or had never harbored life. The Arilians had given the Admiral a hand-held device with a pointer that, when touched to any planet, displayed all the known properties of that world. Admiral Chase was amazed at the thoroughness of the observations made by Arilian astronomers based solely on ground-based measurements. Their study of planets in the Galactic Garden seemed complete beyond all imagination, yet still, Arilian astronomers asserted they'd only scratched the surface in their survey.

Admiral Chase willingly yielded the leadership of the Union's mission to the Arilians because he was convinced they knew exactly what they were doing and how best to go about doing it. He suspected the Arilians were primarily motivated by the idea that the quickest way to rid their planet of the overly explorative earthlings was to help them find compelling reasons to leave. Although their motivation was questionable, it didn't seem to compromise the diligence and dedication with which they led the galactic exploration endeavor.

The Arilians were aided in their efforts by the strength and unity of the Union explorer fleet. Having gone through intensive military training on Earth prior to embarking on the rescue mission, Admiral Chase was impressed that the Union fleet was still intact. The Galactic Space Explorers Union, started by a small group in the 22nd Century, no longer existed in any real sense. It had functioned only long enough to launch the initial fleet of supply ships and individual space capsules, along with the protocols for a robust and resilient communication network linking the components. Other than that, there were no strict lines of authority, no rules of behavior or engagement, and only a very broad mission. Yet the explorers and the supply ship custodians, for the most part, continued to perform their respective functions, even after so many thousands of years. Admiral Chase spent many hours pondering the effectiveness of this very loose organizational structure, and eventually concluded that the Union mission was self-sustaining because it had been so compelling to begin with. Once established, the Union survived because no one sought to disrupt it. Even the transgressions of Andrew Harding and Carl Stormer had turned out to be only a minor disruption, ultimately defeated by forces that drew strength from the communication and data storage systems the Union had developed.

For those who didn't go back, they could either remain on Aril or follow the Union explorers to the uncertain promises the Galactic Garden had to offer. Not trained to explore planets, Admiral Chase decided their best role was to become an emergency response team supporting the galactic explorers. He deployed his fleet strategically throughout the region of the galaxy where most of the explorers would be traveling so they could respond as quickly as possible in the event something went wrong.

This wasn't the only puzzle that occupied Admiral Chase during his time on Aril after the invasion. He also needed to decide what to do with his fleet now that their mission had been successfully completed. He'd told his 500 troops they were free to return to Earth, but not many had chosen that option. The uncertainties of returning after so many thousands of years were not particularly attractive. After all, they'd volunteered to leave Earth, to be part of the rescue mission. No one was aware of any events transpiring on Earth in the interim that would compel them to return.

For those who didn't go back, they could either remain on Aril or follow the Union explorers to the uncertain promises the Galactic Garden had to offer. Not trained to explore planets, Admiral Chase decided their best role was to become an emergency response team supporting the galactic explorers. He deployed his fleet strategically throughout the region of the galaxy where most of the explorers would be traveling so they could respond as quickly as possible in the event something went wrong.

It was a dubious plan, in fact, because with only 500 in the fleet, they'd still be separated by thousands of light-years. If some unfortunate explorer encountered danger while visiting a planet, the odds that any of the members of the Earth fleet would be close enough to help were extremely small. Still, it was comforting to know that there were friendly forces they might rely on if necessary. Admiral Chase instructed his troops to feel free to join the explorers on visits to new planets. That way they'd gradually learn the intricacies of exploration and eventually have the experience to set out on their own.

Arilians abhorred the damage to their environment caused by the landings and lift-offs of space vehicles in the years after the invasion attempt. Seeing no easy end to the resulting devastation, they embarked on the most ambitious undertaking in Arilian history. They began construction of a space launch facility on a nearby planet. The planet was smaller than Aril, with lower gravity and therefore requiring less fuel for takeoffs and landings. It had no atmosphere to be contaminated by the exhaust fumes of rockets. Those toxins were swept away by the stellar wind coming from Aril's sun. Designed with greenhouses like those in the Union supply ships, the launch facility had an artificial atmosphere contained within a huge structure that held living quarters, commissary, entertainment center, conference rooms, classrooms, mechanical shop, warehouse, fuel storage facility, and other infrastructure to minimize the frequency of shuttle flights from Aril. If all went according to plan, the launch facility would eventually become entirely self-sufficient and self-sustaining. In effect, Aril had established a new world for the sole purpose of being its portal to space. Spaceport Aril, or Sparil, as it came to be called, would also eventually become a major manufacturing hub for the construction of space vehicles.

Admiral Chase didn't remain on Aril for the completion of the new spaceport. He returned to his command ship, which he'd left in orbit around Aril, and departed to lead his fleet in their efforts to patrol the Galactic Garden. With the far more advanced communication systems on the command ship, he could better monitor and support his fleet, as well as the galactic explorers already on route to newly discovered planets. When the Arilian spaceport was completed, he'd advise the members of his fleet to visit Sparil and complete formal training to become explorers. Sparil would also become a permanent and reliable location for his troops to reconnect and avert the emotional and physical stresses stemming from many years of isolation in space.

It was on Sparil that two Arilians were trained to be the supply ship custodians to replace Benjamin Mizello on Supply Ship 5. He had taken over as custodian of the supply ship after the invasion, immediately setting off to meet up with Ilsa Montgomery, a woman he'd met before his departure from Earth in the 22nd Century. She was one of the women kidnapped by Carl Stormer and forced to accompany him on his quest to establish his own society on a new planet. After Benjamin and Ilsa were reunited, they escorted the supply ship to its reassigned location in the Galactic Garden. The new custodians rendezvoused with the supply ship and took over, freeing the happy couple to embark on explorations of their own choosing.

When Admiral Chase departed from Aril, he left one chore incomplete. He hadn't fully dealt with the men in Carl Stormer's paramilitary army being held on the planet. After some discussion, he had agreed to leave them to be dealt with by the merciful hand of the Arilians. Fortunately, about thirty members of his fleet had volunteered to remain behind and guard the prisoners during the long and tedious process that Arilian justice demanded.

CHAPTER 7
— Century 650 —

Toro had two pairs and was tempted to raise the bet, but the Ram might have three of a kind. If he raised and lost, Toro would have nothing left. He'd already gambled away almost everything he'd brought from Earth. What did it matter anyway? The loss was only symbolic. The Arilians provided everything they needed, at least for now. After the Earth fleet had defeated Stormer's paramilitary troops during the invasion of Aril, the troops had been placed in a compound, lightly guarded by the formidable warriors of 500th Century Earth. They were so confident in their ability to easily overpower the ancient earthlings, they strolled through the compound unarmed, watching their captives with casual curiosity.

Toro folded. He didn't have much to call his own, but he suspected the little he had left prevented him from falling into deep depression. The Arilians were certainly being remarkably accommodating with Stormer's men, especially considering they had invaded the planet and attacked several villages before being stopped by the Earth fleet. Now, the Arilians were interviewing each of the captives, one by one, and carefully explaining to them their options: transition into Arilian society, return to Earth without their weapons, or become members of the Union explorer force, which was setting off en masse to the Galactic Garden. Whichever option they chose, they understood there would first be an intensive amount of psychological and emotional testing, education, training, indoctrination, and work. None of it was very appealing to Toro, who had lived his life thus far free from such intrusions. Left unsaid, of course, was that if anyone didn't qualify for any of the options, they'd be transferred to one of the Arilian prisons. Toro had no idea what to expect from those facilities and no desire to find out.

As the next hand was dealt, a tall form approached the table, momentarily blocking the muted light from Aril's setting orange sun. Toro knew this guard. She was a grim Earthling with little sense of humor and a perpetual scowl. All the 500th Century Earthlings had the same imposing, amber eyes, but this woman's eyes were cold and lifeless. Toro turned to look at her, but saw nothing but a silhouette. She'd been curious about their card games for some time now. Toro repeated a question he had asked her before, "Care to join us?"

She usually just walked away in contempt, but this time she stepped forward and stood next to the table. Her thumbs were hooked in her belt, which was ringed with unidentifiable gadgets. She said nothing.

"Give her a chair," said Toro.

One of the other men at the table got up nervously and stepped away. The guard sat down, dwarfing the chair with her huge frame. "I'm Stella," she said, in a voice that was raspy, but somehow seductively feminine.

"I'm Toro. That's Ram, Fish, and Scorpio." Toro pointed at his companions with the ace of spades he'd been holding.

"From the Zodiac," Stella said derisively.

"We don't use our real names. They don't have any meaning for us anymore—probably never did."

Stella emitted a guttural snort, not in any way friendly.

"Do you know how to play?" Toro asked.

"Yes. I've been watching."

"You have to bet something to start with."

Stella glared at Toro. Then she grasped one of the items attached to her belt and lifted it off. She threw it on the table where it lay among an assortment of candy bars, utensils, trinkets, and other bric-a-brac the men were gambling with.

"What the hell is that?" growled Scorpio.

Stella turned and looked at him with an amber stare that transfixed the man.

"It doesn't matter," said Toro. "Just deal."

An hour later, Stella had lost almost every item on her belt, but she seemed unperturbed. The men suspected that none of the items had any real value.

"Don't you have any weapons?" Fish ventured to ask. "I'd like to win something useful."

Surprisingly, Stella registered no shock at this statement. Shuffling the deck, which she was already doing with uncanny skill, she remarked, "I doubt you'd know how to use one anyway."

"You're probably right," said Fish. "You have 50,000 years on us in weapon design. The firearms we brought to Aril must be as primitive to you as a six-shooter was to us."

Stella shrugged. "Maybe. There's only so much you can do to optimize a hand-held weapon. You want accuracy, lethality, durability, portability, dependability, stealth, and error correction. All that was achieved thousands of years before my time on Earth. The biggest advance in weaponry during my time on Earth was control. We have smart weapons that read the body language and psychological state of the shooter and the target, analyzing the threat potential and possibility of collateral damage. It was hard to use weapons against another human unless there was a good reason."

"Hah," laughed Scorpio. "It didn't help us that day you and your friends ambushed us. I was one of the ones that got shot. I'll never forget what that felt like."

"We were in combat. All the safety functions were disabled on our weapons. Besides, it didn't kill you."

"So if these weapons are so smart, how come you don't carry any around the compound?" asked Toro.

Stella laughed. "For what? You guys aren't much of a threat."

"I suppose you're right about that," said Toro in disgust.

Stella was a sloppy card player, but somehow she never quite lost everything. She had incredible stamina, and they played for many hours. Several of the others grew weary and excused themselves, replaced by new players. When they got tired, they made mistakes, and gradually Stella began to win more frequently. One by one, the captive men bet the last of their earthly belongings and left the table dejected and defeated.

Finally, only Stella and Toro remained. The compound was

empty except for the two of them. For the second time that night, Toro was down to his last item to bet and once again he had two pairs. He wondered whether Stella had three of a kind.

"If I lose this, I have nothing," he told Stella.

She shrugged. "You'll get used to it."

Toro tossed in a magnifying glass, which he used often because of his failing vision.

"I'll see your bet," he said.

"That's not enough," said Stella.

It was Toro's turn to shrug. "That's all I've got."

"Perhaps," said Stella, drawing out the word.

"Is there anything else you want?"

"I could think of something."

Toro shifted uneasily in his chair. As if she could read his thoughts, Stella added quickly, "Not that. Don't be an idiot."

"Then what?" asked Toro.

Stella leaned forward and Toro saw through the amber in her eyes to the blackness within.

"The Arilians are going to ask you what you want to do. They'll give you a choice. Tell them you want to be an explorer."

"But I don't know that I want to be an explorer," said Toro.

"Yes, you do," said Stella. "And pick out a dozen of your most capable friends. Tell them to become explorers, too."

"Why?"

Stella looked impatient. "Because when you become an explorer, they'll give you back your space vehicles. We'll need them."

"We?" repeated Toro.

Stella sat back in her chair. "Look. I'm in the same boat you're in. Do you think I want to stay here on Aril? It would bore me to death. If I go back to Earth, I'd arrive 20,000 years after I left. I don't want to deal with the shock of that. I could be a galactic explorer, but like you, I don't care for the idea of flying around the galaxy and landing on life-threatening planets just to see what they're like. That kind of romantic adventure does nothing for me."

"Then what do you want?" asked Toro.

Stella sat for a long time, eying the stack of objects she'd won from the men. Finally, she narrowed her eyes and said, "Pretty things." She paused. Then added, "And freedom."

Toro picked up a card from the table and began snapping its edge with his thumb. He slid the card under the four open cards before him and flipped them over. "You win," he said.

Over the next six Arilian months, Toro and his men dutifully went through the training class to become galactic explorers, passing all the exams so convincingly that no one suspected they weren't dedicated to the cause of planetary exploration. When they'd been given their assigned destinations in the Galactic Garden, they instead rendezvoused with Stella at a prearranged location in Aril's debris-filled planetary system. There, Stella told them what their real destination would be. They all set course for Supply Ship 3.

CHAPTER 8

— Century 675 —

Xyla and Druix arrived at Aril almost 2,500 years after the failed invasion attempt on the planet. By that time, Sparil, Aril's spaceport, was a vibrant hub for planetary exploration. Populated mostly by young, adventurous Arilians, the spaceport produced space capsules and trained explorers to pilot them to new planets within the Galactic Garden. It was also a center for processing and analysis of the data streaming back from the original group of explorers who set out for their initial destinations.

The approach of Xyla and Druix's space capsules was detected several weeks before they arrived at Aril. They were contacted by Arilian officials and given instructions in Union English to land on Sparil instead. Confused, but not inclined to disobey the instructions, the two travelers prepared for their landing at the spaceport.

As it turned out, Xyla and Druix were glad they'd been redirected because neither felt particularly odd or out of place at the spaceport, which harbored Arilian astronauts, galactic explorers from 22nd Century Earth, and members of Admiral Chase's fleet. Xyla and Druix, descended from earthlings of the 110th Century, didn't stand out in the way they had on Earth, and they quickly eased into life on Sparil.

Druix was excited by the wealth of data available to continue his studies of galactic history. Not only did the spaceport have all the archived data from Aril and the accumulated data from the Union's planetary exploration fleet, it also received new data from the primary communication nodes in space—the Union supply ships. There was endless fuel for the engine of Druix's mind and, just as on Earth, he stayed sufficiently absorbed in his studies that he had little time to dwell upon his loneliness.

For Xyla, the spaceport was ideal, as it offered all the facilities and instruction necessary for her to become an explorer. She was an excellent student and surprised her instructors with her enthusiasm and commitment, especially since she didn't really fit the profile of those normally drawn to galactic exploration. She wasn't like the young Arilians, who'd left their families on Aril forever, just as their descendants had left Earth 60,000 years earlier. She came from another planet—one that probably no longer harbored life. She'd come to the spaceport after living on Earth for almost ten years. One would have thought her desire to explore planets would have been muted by these experiences, not even mentioning the fact that she had a son, with whom she was extremely close.

Nevertheless, none of her instructors questioned her resolve to become an explorer. Several had tried to engage her in conversations from which they might delve into the factors that motivated her, but Xyla offered nothing by which they might come to understand. How could she, when it was doubtful she understood it herself?

Xyla and Druix hadn't been long on Sparil when Druix approached his mother and asked to speak to her. They went to an artificially-created park under a huge crystalline dome. Children played about them, and soothing Arilian music emerged from hidden speakers distributed throughout the park. The domed enclosure had been designed with vents that created an artificial breeze. The warmth from Aril's sun kept the temperature mild, with the dome providing protection from harmful ultraviolet light. Without an atmosphere, Aril's sun would just be a very bright star in a black sky, but the dome was translucent such that it diffused the light to simulate daytime. At night, the crystalline structure of the dome changed and it became completely transparent, allowing the starlight to shine through. People on Sparil could hardly tell they were on a planet without an atmosphere, where the sky would look the same both night and day.

"I've been reading the accounts of the invasion of Aril," Druix began, as he and his mother settled onto one of the many benches in the park.

Xyla said nothing but knew her son well enough that his tone prepared her for disturbing news. When they'd left Supply

Ship 6, Arthur Mizello had warned them that all was not right on Aril. Now, the account of the failed invasion attempt was ancient history. It had taken place while she and her son were on route to the planet, frozen in their magnetocryogenic chambers. She already knew the outcome of the war, but she had resisted learning of the details. She realized it was just a matter of time before her son, a student of history, would fill in the gaps. She waited for him to continue speaking.

"Benjamin is considered somewhat of a hero in the defeat of the invading force. Because of that, he received a great deal of attention in the weeks immediately following the conflict."

Xyla just nodded. She tried to conceal her anxiety. Her worst fear was that Benjamin had decided to remain on Aril after the war and was now long dead. Would she reconsider her commitment to becoming an explorer if there was no longer any possibility of ever seeing Benjamin again?

"Benjamin left Aril to continue his planetary explorations," Druix continued.

Xyla exhaled, no longer able to mask her emotions. "Then he's still alive."

"As of the most recent accounts," Druix said, and then added quickly, "But, of course, all this information is very old."

"Of course," said Xyla, in a whisper.

Druix sighed. "There's more though. Benjamin left Aril as custodian of Supply Ship 5, the one that Andrew Harding had brought to Aril and used in the invasion. Benjamin was going to pilot the ship to its new assigned location near the center of the Galactic Garden. But he didn't go directly there. He went first to rendezvous with a space capsule that had left his father's supply ship in 55,000. There was a woman on board—a friend he had known on Earth before he left."

Xyla looked down. Almost imperceptibly, her body shuddered. Druix delivered the remaining information. "He will meet her in about 75,000.

"A woman he knew on Earth." Xyla repeated thoughtfully.

"Yes. According to the accounts, Benjamin was surprised.

She wasn't an explorer. Apparently, she'd been kidnapped by Carl Stormer, but had somehow escaped. She provided some key information that helped the Arilians defeat the invaders."

Xyla shuffled her feet in the earth beneath the bench.

"It might just be the Arilians' attempt to romanticize the story, but the tales suggest that Benjamin and the woman will revive their ancient love affair after being rejoined in space. They've even calculated the location in space where the two will meet and named two nearby stars after them: Benjamin and Ilsa. The two stars are in a constellation the Arilians call Serendipity.

Xyla brought her head up and forced a smile, but Druix saw the single tear course down her cheek. She wiped it away and bit her lip.

Druix had run out of things to say. Any more at this point would have been banal and trite. He put his arm around his mother and the smile returned to her face. After some time, she said, "It doesn't matter really. It changes nothing."

Druix didn't believe it, but the statements demanded no response. He changed the subject. "I've requested permission to visit Aril," he said. "All the information I need to continue my research is here on Sparil, but I'd love to go to Aril to visit the sites where everything took place. I want to see the Memorial Garden, where the planet was first colonized, spend some time in the archives at the library, and visit the battlefield where the Earth fleet overpowered Stormer's army. It would be fun to be on Aril for the Festival of Seeds. Do you want to join me?"

"No," Xyla answered, almost too quickly. "I don't want to interrupt my training. How long will you be gone?"

"It makes no sense going unless I stay at least a year."

"When will you leave?"

"It takes a while to get all the permits, and I have to wait for the next shuttle with space available. Maybe six months."

Xyla looked across the park and squinted against the glare of the Sun. After it set, a tiny blue speck of light would appear that was Aril, so far away that it was hardly noticeable against the backdrop of stars.

"I can't wait," she said.

"You mean…"

"I can finish my training in less than a year. I'd be able to leave for the Garden."

"Couldn't you delay until I returned?" Druix asked.

"For what?" said Xyla, with a bitter tone Druix was unfamiliar with. "Wait for you to return and then leave? No. I think it's better if I leave while you're on Aril. That way you won't feel any obligation to return here. If you find you like Aril, you can stay there."

"And if I don't want to live out my life on Aril?"

"Come back here and train to be an explorer. We'll make a rendezvous plan, so we can meet somewhere in the future."

Druix nodded, understanding the rationale for his mother's suggestion. "I'm sorry," he said.

Xyla patted her son's knee. "You've nothing to be sorry for. We're both victims of circumstance. We have to follow the paths that have been laid out for us. Most of the possible paths lead to our parting at some point. Remember, when you were ten, I put you on the road by yourself so that you'd be found and raised by the townspeople of Aurora. I never thought I'd see you again, but now, many years later, we're still together. I feel blessed."

"Me too," said Druix, unconvincingly.

Xyla took Druix's hands and held them between hers. "Let's just enjoy the months we have remaining and hope that fate will bring us together again in the future."

"Fate," Druix repeated. "The original use of that word stems from the name of a legendary myth of planet Earth. It was the name of a Goddess who planned the course of human lives. Fate is the opposite of serendipity."

Xyla chuckled, looking up at the twilight sky. "I guess we're all at the mercy of one or the other."

"Right," said Druix, rising from the bench. He knew his mother needed to be alone. "And odds are neither Fate nor serendipity take into account the possibility of rendezvous plans. I won't leave until we have one."

"Of course," said Xyla. "Of course."

Six months later, from the same bench, Xyla watched the launch of the shuttle that would carry her son to Aril. It was a nighttime launch, so the crystalline dome was clear and the fiery light of the launch vehicle obliterated the surrounding stars as the vehicle ascended. For the second time in her life, Xyla had lost a loved one to the stars.

CHAPTER 9
— Century 724 —

When Union explorers reached the Galactic Garden, news of wonderful and fantastic worlds teeming with plant and animal life spread throughout the network. All the phyla that existed on Earth, plus a few more, were found in various proportions and abundances on other planets. The characteristics that made living organisms different and similar on Earth were also observed in the diversity of species living on the new worlds of the Galactic Garden.

Yet, with all the mind-numbing discoveries, the explorers had encountered no organisms as advanced as homo sapiens of humble planet Earth. Animals of incredible intelligence existed on many of the planets, but like the smart whales of Earth's oceans or the apes of Africa, none had the unique combination of physical and mental capacity that would enable them to develop a civilization in any way comparable to Earth.

That human civilization was unique in this sector of the galaxy was at once reassuring and frightening. It was a tremendous responsibility, the explorers came to realize, that among all the marvelous species so far discovered in the Galactic Garden, only Earth humans were capable of thinking, analyzing, planning, inventing, wondering, and exploring. But it was a double-edged sword, of course, because it meant humans were also capable of mass destruction, mindless evil, pride, arrogance, aggression, greed, vanity, and treachery with unsurpassed efficiency. The supreme mental abilities humans possessed also meant that there was so much more that could go wrong when their brains malfunctioned in various psychological, chemical, neurological, or behavioral ways. The difference between an animal gone crazy and a human gone crazy was vast.

So, as more and more planets were explored, and it became increasingly evident that homo sapiens was far superior than all the millions of other organisms found on the new worlds, humans receiving the information became dangerously over-confident and smug. They had yet to come across one creature that posed any serious threat to the visiting humans—not one plant or animal that couldn't be vanquished by human minds or weapons. Even the tiny alien bacteria, which held the potential to spread uncontrolled through the human anatomy, were quickly understood and controlled with the advanced knowledge of medicine possessed by the galactic explorers of 22nd Century Earth, not to mention what the scientifically, technically, and morally superior Arilians were capable of.

Eventually, word of the remarkable discoveries in the Galactic Garden filtered back to Earth through the Union communication network. Excitement grew to levels not experienced on the planet for thousands of years. Ultimately, it caused a resurrection in fascination with space exploration, and space capsules with magnetocryogenic chambers were reinvented, setting the stage for the next great wave of human expansion from Earth.

At the time, however, the social structure on Earth was in a state of turmoil. It was a pointy planet, in many ways. During the last few tens of thousands of years, it had become stylish to build homes vertically—slender cones and pyramids that were broad at the base and narrow at the top. The height of the structures depended on what the home-owner could afford. Thus, the wealthiest earthlings built tall skyscrapers that dwarfed most of the humbler edifices below them. Hardly an acre of land had not been intruded upon by one of these dwellings. From space, Earth appeared to be one gigantic burr—an object to be avoided lest it attach itself and cause persistent pain and discomfort.

The architecture of the homes on Earth mirrored the overall attitude of the people. They spent most days in the small spaces at the tops of their homes, completely isolated from others. They only ventured to a lower floor to conduct the business of life, which they viewed as an intrusive necessity. Some trauma had occurred to Earth in the past few thousand years that compelled humans to become insular and anti-social. It was overall an un-friendly planet—a grouchy person who'd had a tough life and wanted to be left alone.

Still, there were those among the world's population who continued to monitor the heavens for the radio signals that carried the transmissions from the Union explorer fleet, and it was at just that moment in history when Earth started receiving news of the bio-friendly planets being discovered in the Galactic Garden.

Life on other planets in the galaxy was no surprise to 734th Century earthlings, but the remarkable variety of life forms, and the conditions under which they thrived, provided humans with images that challenged their imaginations and disrupted the isolation they tried hard to maintain. In the restricted spaces at the vertices of their homes, they listened to reports of fantastic worlds being discovered and explored. Their video screens, which provided them the only window to what was happening outside their homes, displayed fuzzy pictures of the unlikely life forms thriving on planets impossibly far way—fuzzy because the data stream carrying the images had been degraded during its long transport through interstellar space.

The discoveries were enough to stir long-forgotten in-stincts in the people of Earth. For the first time in many years, they began to imagine alternate worlds. Slowly but surely ideas reemerged about space travel and colonization. At the end of every day, as men and women all over the world climbed the stairs and rode the elevators to the tops of their houses, they were sud-denly conscious of how their world had narrowed and became more restrictive. Reports from space about the new planets being explored gave them unexpected and much needed release from the tiny prisons within which they spent most of their lives. Once again in the long history of human civilization, people dreamt of colonizing other planets, and the video screens continually re-minded them of all the possibilities for humanity's next home in the galaxy.

Unfortunately, the resources for carrying out such an enterprise were totally lacking. Not that there wasn't sufficient wealth. It was that for many millennia, the concept of wealth had lost its meaning, as the connection between productivity and product became increasingly muddled. Even economists of the day couldn't conceive of the time when commerce had been conducted through the exchange of money or other monetary instruments. All trade was virtual, and the source of value for the exchange of goods and services was so far removed from reality that one might be wealthy just by appearing to be so. Similarly, one might be completely unaware of his or her own true wealth and live unnecessarily in abject poverty, or worse, serving those who were better at capitalizing on nonexistent assets.

It was the perfect climate for the emergence of global corporate empires that dwarfed any previously known in human history—corporations whose only asset was the ability to control information so as to appear to be the most powerful entity on Earth. Though the scale of these corporate empires was unprecedented, like all such conglomerates, each was, by and large, led by a single person. The largest of all was headed by Mr. Beauregard U. Dispasionato. Bud, as he was called by most, believed himself to be above all human laws, restraints, morals, ethics, or any other social construct that might limit what he could do. And like many of the most powerful tycoons on Earth, he was simultaneously responsible for some of the most despicable and most beautiful achievements ever known. Paradoxically, many of his most impressive ideas came at those times he was in the midst of executing his most amoral and misanthropic acts.

At a time when the global impetus to expand humankind into the idyllic allure of a part of the galaxy teeming with other life forms, Bud fell in love with the beautiful wife of a brilliant young man who worked at one of his subsidiaries. In fact, Bud never really fell in love in the usual sense, but one would never guess that from the vigor with which he pursued his passions.

One day the young man disappeared, and his wife was told she would never see him again unless she agreed to yield to Bud's advances. Before long, after unrelenting threats and duress, the woman consented to live with Bud at the top of a tall, slender skyscraper that penetrated the clouds, making Bud feel as if he were a god in heaven. The floors below him were inhabited by Bud's staff, whose sole purpose in life was to serve him and his transient love objects. The young man himself was being kept in a windowless, interior room several floors below. It was no more than a jail cell, and the luckless young man was made to suffer endless days and nights of boredom and sensory deprivation, completely unaware of what he had done to earn such torment. In the ceiling of the room was a video camera, and the images from that camera were displayed on a large screen in Bud's bedroom. That way the man's wife was forced to see her husband go slowly mad as Bud forced himself upon her in the most degrading ways he knew of—and his knowledge of abuse was great.

Eventually, the man's madness was manifested in the development of strange body motions—tics and spasms that were bizarre and unnatural. Gradually, the strange movements drew Bud's attention more than the man's wife did and soon he lost interest in the woman and became obsessed watching the unlikely antics of the insane young man. After several weeks, he sent the woman away, unable to get over his fascination with the display that dominated his bedroom. He could only sleep when the young man slept, which wasn't often.

Finally, Bud's physician, who also lived in the building, suggested that Bud summon experts to analyze the thousands of hours of video that had accumulated and try to interpret the origin of the man's odd behavior. Bud liked the idea. A team of six esteemed behavioral scientists was commissioned to study the video. For Bud to authorize such a plan was unprecedented because he was notoriously disdainful of both science and scientists.

Several weeks later, the team announced they had "cracked the code," as they expressed it. The man had been trying to communicate something, and in his insular desperation had constructed his own language—a body language. The behavioral scientists had used advanced computers with state-of-the-art image processing capabilities to decipher the language. They had translated all of the man's motions and were ready to deliver the message to Bud.

———————————

The six behavioral scientists, three men and three women, who took the elevator to Bud's penthouse in the clouds, knew they were among the very few outsiders ever to be given an audience with the tyrannical corporate mogul. They entered nervously and sat in chairs arranged before Bud's desk. He was alone, but all knew the room was heavily booby-trapped. Bud, who was justifiably paranoid, had nothing to fear from his visitors. For effect, he had ordered a video screen to be placed behind him, so that the six scientists sitting before him were forced to watch their patient performing his insane dance to some imagined rhythm in his demented brain.

Bud jabbed with a thumb over his shoulder at the screen behind him. "So what's with him?"

The six before him exchanged glances. Then one woman spoke, "It's quite remarkable really."

"What's remarkable?" Bud asked impatiently.

"He's created his own language," said one of the men.

"What's so remarkable about that?" Bud actually thought it was extremely remarkable, but he didn't want his visitors to know that.

"Many things," said an older scientist with a goatee, which Bud abhorred because it intimidated him. "It's a very complex language. We've already counted over a thousand words."

"Who the hell cares?" Bud said. "What's he saying?"

There was an uncertain pause from the group as they tried to sort out who would answer.

"Well," started the man with the goatee. "That's really not the point. The interesting thing here is the man's behavioral state and the psycho-social conditions that compelled him to invent his own language. It highlights the fundamental need for expression as an imperative in humans. What is puzzling here is why he doesn't just speak. Why create an elaborate language based on body motions?"

"We think it's some type of defense mechanism," continued another one of the scientists. "He invented a new language to keep himself from going crazy. It's quite fascinating from a psychological point of view."

"I don't care about the psychological point of view!" shouted Bud, rising to his feet. "What the hell is he saying?"

Another long pause ensued. Finally, one of the scientists, who hadn't spoken before, cleared his throat and said, "It's nonsense really—unfortunate given the genius it must have taken to create a new language."

"Quit the crap and just tell me what he's saying," ordered Bud, fuming now.

"He's hearing voices from space. He's telling us what the voices are saying."

"Voices from space," repeated Bud. "You mean the radio signals about new planets?" Like others on Earth, Bud spent many evenings watching his video monitors display the accounts of planetary exploration.

"Not really. He's actually *hearing voices* from space. That's the essential point, we believe. Despite the genius required to construct a language from body movements, the man is crazy. In his sensory-deprived conditions, he may just be converting the information he heard previously about the newly discovered planets into auditory signals to maintain his own sanity."

"If this guy has so much to say, why doesn't he just say it?" Bud asked.

"Efficiency. Speaking is an extremely slow means of communication."

"Bullshit. Was that fast enough?"

"Think about it. It takes many hours to read a book, but only milliseconds to transfer the information digitally in a computer. Ever see a song being played on a musical instrument? Does the musician speak to the instrument and tell it what notes to play? The beauty that comes from it is a result of a complex set of messages the musician transmits to it, none of which entails speaking."

"Do I need this?" said Bud impatiently. "Do I need a lecture on beautiful music? I just asked a simple question."

"Back in the 21st Century, they spent a great deal of time and energy making computers that understood speech. It was incredibly inefficient. Vast amounts of computer time were wasted during the time it took someone to tell the computer what to do. Computers today bypass all that by understanding what people want from all the other hints and cues—muscle tension, body temperature, sweat and other bodily emissions, heartbeat, respiration—equivalent to thousands of bits of data. That's how modern computers work. This man is conveying more, huge amounts of information and we're only beginning to decipher it. We've just scratched the surface. Once we're able to translate his movements, we can program a computer. He'll be speaking directly to the computer at a much faster rate than he could ever speak."

Bud sat back in his chair, disappointment written on his face. "I can't believe I've spent the last few months watching a crazy psychopath who's translating messages from space into body language."

"We're sorry," said the man with the goatee. "May we go now?"

"Yeah. Beat it," said Bud.

They all stood to leave, but in no real hurry. They were almost at the elevator door when Bud said, "Wait. What are the voices saying?"

The woman who had spoken first waved her arm. "Oh, you don't really want to know, do you?"

Bud hesitated. He really wanted to know, but he didn't want to admit to the scientists that he was curious about the mad ravings of an insane man. Finally, he said, "Just tell me what the voices are saying—quickly. Then get out."

"They're calling you to space," the woman answered in a trembling voice.

"Me?"

"Yes, you. Do you want me to show you your name in the man's body language? It took us a while to figure out that it was you."

"No, I don't want to see my name in body language," said Bud angrily. "Why are they calling me to space?"

The woman looked at her companions and nodded to another woman. "She's done most of the translation. Esther, why don't you tell Mr. Dispasionato what the voices from space want him to do?"

Esther stood confidently and looked at Bud with defiant eyes. Her hands were locked behind her back as if she were giving a recital. "They know you. They know you've the power and resources to establish a new world. They want you to build spaceships and bring thousands of people to colonize a planet. They will show you where it is. They've promised to help you, and they want you to call the planet Prosperity."

Bud's mouth dropped. He just stared at the six visitors, speechless for the first time in his life. Finally, he said, "Get out of my sight."

The six scientists left without saying another word. Bud remained staring at the elevator door after it closed. He turned his head toward the video monitor above his desk. The young man was still performing the same strange dance, and Bud wondered which of the movements represented his name.

———————

A year later, Bud's corporate empire announced its most ambitious undertaking ever. It would immediately begin the manufacture of a fleet of space vehicles that would take thousands of earthlings to establish a new planet in the Galactic Garden. The location of the new planet had been divulged in subsequent communications from the voice in space as transcribed into body language by the young man in Bud's skyscraper and translated by Esther. The aliens responsible for the voices from space must have been watching as the project proceeded because they often sent messages remarkably timed to guide the activities being conducted at that time.

After several years, the program was well underway and the voices instructed Bud to release the man from the room, as no more messages would be forthcoming. Bud did as he was told.

Bud watched the progress of the endeavor until he died forty years later. At the time of his death, his corporate empire, which had been founded on virtual assets, was entirely and virtually depleted. Upon his death, the spaceships filled with people began lifting off. In the end then, Bud's artificial wealth had gone from cyberspace into real space.

Some of the spaceships transported passengers, frozen in compact magnetocryogenic chambers. Other more massive ships carried the supplies they'd need to establish the new planet. It was an incredible undertaking, and Bud died too soon to either witness or participate in its successful execution. Bud also died never finding out that the voices from space were only a ruse—a trick conceived by a well-organized group that had been developing plans for space colonization for many years, but never had the resources to implement it. When Bud had summoned the team of behavioral scientists to interpret the motions of his young captive, the six scientists, all of whom were members of the colonization group, devised the body language scheme to trick Bud out of his fortune. It had worked.

The young man was examined when finally released by Bud and found to be truly insane. Fortunately, using the drugs and therapy of 734th Century Earth, he was cured and returned to his pretty wife, who had also recovered from her ordeal through carefully administered therapy. Both outlived Bud and were able to witness the launch of the spaceships, which carried their children and grandchildren to the new world that was to be called Prosperity. They died knowing that the feat would not have been accomplished without both of them making the ultimate sacrifice—the decimation of their pride and dignity, which even with drugs and therapy could never quite be completely restored.

CHAPTER 10
— Century 727 —

Xyla's first assignment was to explore a planet that was suspected by Arilian astronomers to have a breathable oxygen atmosphere. They knew that oxygen in a planetary atmosphere almost certainly means there is animal life present. Some amount of oxygen is released as a planet is formed from the primordial dust cloud out of which it originates. However, oxygen is a light enough gas that it will eventually sputter away into space unless it can be captured and continually recycled. The best process for that is the exchange of oxygen and carbon dioxide that takes place between plants and animals. A stable oxygen atmosphere is evidence for the same wonderfully rare balance that sustained life on Earth for millions of years—a miracle that probably occurs in only a very small fraction of planets. Fortunately, there were thousands of planets in the Galactic Garden, all fortuitously primed with the right organic compounds that are the building blocks of life. The first explorers that set out from Aril to the Galactic Garden were sent to those destinations with oxygen atmospheres, and therefore most likely already blessed with plant and animal life.

As she gazed upon the new world she was assigned to explore, Xyla couldn't help but marvel at the course her life had taken. She remembered very well the despair she'd felt facing every new day on Aurora with the realization that she was living her entire life on a frozen planet, doing no more than cleaning and cooking the fish that were taken daily by the Malanites from the ice-covered oceans.

When Benjamin arrived, he brought a link to a different world, a new existence—like the tiniest sliver of light in the darkest of caverns. Benjamin had departed, but the brief time she'd spent with him stimulated the awareness and determination that enabled her and her son—his son—to escape. Now, it was quite likely that Benjamin had totally forgotten her and had found a new life with another woman. Xyla was grateful to Benjamin. Without him, she would have died on Aurora, never knowing the existence of other worlds. Yet she ached at having lost him forever, because so much of what she felt and experienced since his visit had been inspired by him.

What if by some accident she were to die on the planet she was about to explore? Or worse, what if she were stranded there? Would her life have been any more fulfilled than if she had stayed on Aurora? Not for the first time, she wondered if she would ever find what she was looking for—what she expected from life.

The pre-landing checks completed, she strapped herself into her seat and prepared for entry into the planet's atmosphere. She'd learned her lessons well on Sparil and was confident in her abilities, but this was the first planetary landing she'd attempted alone. The workings of the space capsule remained a mystery to her. She sighed deeply and thought of Druix, then activated the rocket motors to decelerate the capsule and commence the de-orbiting sequence.

Fifteen minutes later, the capsule was on the ground and Xyla was smiling to herself. The buffeting g-forces she'd felt during the landing process had been strangely exhilarating. The violent motions comforted her, reaffirming the physical reality of what was taking place. One couldn't expect to leave one world and enter a new one without some degree of extreme sensation. She prepared to exit the craft.

At first glance, the vista before her was as drab and featureless as the endless ice of Aurora. The planet's surface was a vast desert, almost completely devoid of life. Where was the vegetation crucial to sustaining the planet's oxygen atmosphere? The air must be either a remnant of a well-vegetated ecology of long ago, or perhaps sustained by what little shrubs, grasses, and brilliantly colored lichen covered the stones and boulders strewn about. Hardly a cloud blemished the sky. Whatever moisture was present must reside well beneath the crusted layer of compacted sand and gravel that was home to the sparse vegetation. There was only the slightest hint of a breeze. Without it, the air would have been impossible to sense.

Xyla activated the radio beacon of the space capsule prior to setting out to explore the area around the landing site. It seemed unnecessary, as the surface was so void of relief she felt she could walk for miles without ever losing sight of the capsule. Still, as a back-up system to the beacon, she also placed a high-intensity red lantern atop the capsule, which would be easy to find even in the dark.

Because all directions from the landing site looked the same, she decided to walk toward her own shadow with the sun behind her. From her pre-landing observations, she knew there were still several hours till sunset. She wasn't worried about night-fall. She carried everything she might need in case she had to spend a night away from the capsule. She didn't have to worry about predators. The infrared scan she performed from orbit would have revealed the presence of any large animals in the area.

Xyla enjoyed the comforting grip of the planet's gravity. The ground was firm and the few plants spaced such that it was easy for her to weave among them without disturbing any. Her boots crunched the gravel surface producing a crisp sound that broke the preexisting silence. Her senses became more acute. Each sound, each sight, even the faintest smells were vividly etched into a background that was stark and immutable. To walk upon the planet's surface, Xyla had to resign herself to the utter boredom of traversing a landscape that never changed, never offered a new view or altered aspect. The extreme blandness of the planet's surface should have bored her, but she found herself strangely fascinated by the monotony. There was something palpable in the atmosphere of the planet, as if it was trying to speak without the gift of speech. In its silence, the planet seemed to say so much. Its insignificance was filled with meaning. It was a planet with a secret. It allowed the senses to flourish just by providing so little to sense.

Xyla wondered how old the planet was. It could have

been a very young planet that had still not suffered the ravages of planetary evolution, with moving plates, spewing lava, torrential downpours, and massive floods. Or it could have been a very old planet, where the forces of nature—gravity, tectonics, volcanism, hydraulics—had worn its surface for billions of years, destroying all relief—mountains, canyons, mesas, rivers, gradually eroded to produce the featureless surface that was as infinite as the sky above.

Before long, Xyla felt the unrelenting heat from the merciless sun that penetrated every square centimeter of the planetary surface. Neither the topography nor vegetation offered any possibility of shade as long as the sun was above the horizon. Yet she continued to walk, driven by an enigmatic urge to see if there was more, something else, something hidden, something that would rise up and bestow upon her an unmistakable and profound truth. But it didn't happen. The sun set with a whisper.

At night, the same remorseless sky offered a brilliant vista of the heavens, a view uninterrupted by either nearby hill, distant mountain, unlikely mesa or irregular topology of any sort. Xyla felt as though she were immersed in a vast ocean of shimmering starlight. Heat rising from the surface produced a nocturnal mirage that mirrored the starlight from above. It was as if she was in a dream-world floating through the cosmos, without encumbrance or obstacle. The slow march of the stars across the heavens made her feel she was back in space, on a journey through the universe to an uncertain, or perhaps even inconsequential, destination. Clearly, it was the journey that was important.

In the blackness of night, Xyla realized she was lost. The light she'd left on the space capsule was indistinguishable from the thousands of stars that spotted the sky. She wasn't worried. She could find her way back using the radio wave beacon, but since it was too dark to continue walking, she sat on the ground and enjoyed some of the food and water she'd brought with her. The immensity of the sky above her and the realization of where she was made her feel lonely, but not lonesome. Her isolation was so complete that she defined her own universe. It was a perfect context to evaluate her life—to weigh the importance of all aspects of it with no distractions save for the starlight. In that universe, not surprisingly, her love for Druix and Benjamin took on enormous proportions. Whatever doubts she'd had about her feelings for Benjamin disappeared, which made the hopelessness of the situation even more real. Yet somehow it didn't depress her. It was like one of the stars, a simple truth, distant, undeniable, and strangely beautiful.

When the sun rose again, it did so suddenly, illuminating the stark, featureless desert landscape with rapidly intensifying light. Xyla awoke unable to remember at what point she'd fallen asleep. She felt miraculously revived, as if she'd just emerged from a cosmic bath, cleansed by the rejuvenating properties of the stars.

She started back to the capsule. With the sun at her back again, she felt as if she were leaving her past behind. She'd only look forward now. She'd lift off from the planet a new person. It wouldn't be the first time in her life she had reinvented herself. Her next stop was Supply Ship 2, where she'd refuel and set a course for her next destination. Recalling the stars she'd observed the previous night, she marveled over the infinity of possibilities the galaxy offered.

Chapter 11
— Century 773 —

Max and Sadie had been the custodians of Supply Ship 3 since the ship left Earth in 2152. They'd been in their early thirties when they departed, but now the accumulated time they'd spent unfrozen had aged them by about twenty years. They were steadfast in their dedication to the Union's mission, and both diligently undertook the endless and tedious chores associated with maintaining the supply ship.

Max and Sadie were gracious hosts to the lonely explorers who arrived randomly and unexpectedly through the millennia. Both were jovial beyond all expectation, particularly considering the lifestyle they had committed themselves to. They were also generous with supply ship provisions. Many explorers returned repeatedly to experience the refreshing hospitality of the happy couple.

When he could, Max spent his time at his favorite hobby, making moonshine from the organic residue of the supply ships gardens. He had improved the recipe through the years, and his unique blend quickly became famous within the explorer fleet. Though Max was good-humored and easy going, it was Sadie who sustained their warmth and humanity. She had brought from Earth her entire wardrobe, a vast collection of shoes, clothing, and accessories she had acquired in the months before their departure, spending every last bit of earthly money they had. At odd and unexpected times while unfrozen, Sadie would dress up in the fanciest garments, put on one of the thousands of ancient melodies residing in the ship's computers, dim the lights, and coax Max into a romantic "getaway". Max had one tuxedo, which he donned for these occasions, and broke open a champagne-like beverage he had manufactured in his home-made still. With surprising grace and rhythm, the couple danced for hours on end, liberated by the sparkling alcohol and momentarily setting aside the mind-numbing realization that they were thousands of light-years away from any trace of humanity.

So it was that during one of these happy intervals, Max and Sadie were interrupted in the midst of a Viennese waltz by the ship's alarm, indicating the imminent arrival of a space capsule. Max barely had time to rush to the control room, and Sadie was hurriedly wiping off the excessive make-up she had applied, when the remote camera in the docking chamber showed someone emerging from the iris-like hatchway of a docked space vehicle. Max should have wondered why this visitor had not attempted to contact the supply ship before docking. Perhaps the champagne had dulled his judgment, because he was totally caught off-guard when a man appeared in the control room with an EMP weapon aimed directly at Sadie.

"Who are you?" Max stammered.

"You can call me Toro," the man said. "You're about to receive some visitors."

Over the next several hours, Max and Sadie watched helplessly as a succession of space vehicles docked with the ship. The supply ship only had six docking stations, so after the first arrivals had been emptied of their human occupants, their capsules separated, hovering in the vicinity of the large ship, controlled by their automatic navigation systems. Max counted a dozen men, all of whom were now in the ship's galley, ransacking the storage cabinets for food and drinks. But still one more capsule arrived, and Max and Sadie watched in paralyzed silence as a towering female figure entered the room. Her skin, the parts not covered by a glistening silver jumpsuit, was the color of burnt leather, and her eyes glowed with menacing intensity. A delicate smile floated precariously on her face, like oil on water.

"Greetings from Earth," she said, her voice coarse and gravelly. "I am Stella. This is my ship now."

Max drew Sadie to his side and embraced her tightly. "Don't hurt my wife," he said, more forcefully than he intended.

The smile faded from Stella's face and she strode to the couple in two purposeful steps.

"Your wife," she rasped. "How sweet."

She placed her hand on Sadie's head, and the fist began to close as if to grab the hair that had been tied up in a taut bun for dancing. With surprising speed, Max lifted his hand and grasped Stella's wrist, squeezing it tightly. Stella reacted by trying to pull her hand away, but Max had a tenacious hold, facilitated by the leathery texture of her skin. She glared at Max with anger. "Shoot him!" she commanded to the men behind her, but they and Max knew they wouldn't fire. They were EMP weapons. The pulse of electromagnetic energy would pass through Max into Stella as long as he was holding her wrist.

The two remained in that position for several seconds until Stella lifted her other hand and touched the hem of the red dress Sadie was wearing. "This is pretty," she said. "I want it."

"It's mine," Sadie said.

"It's yours now," returned Stella. "But it will soon be mine." Her Union English was heavily accented, but precise.

"What kind of creature are you?" said Max, still holding Stella's wrist.

Before Stella could answer, a flirtatious whistle came from one of the men behind her. "Wow! Check out Leo!"

They all looked across the room to see a man parading into the galley wearing a burgundy smoking jacket.

"Nice duds," said another of the men.

Stella released her hold on Sadie's hair and pulled away, leaving the couple huddled together. "Where did you get that?" she asked.

"In one of the sleeping quarters. It's filled with clothing," the man answered.

Stella stormed out of the room, completely forgetting her confrontation with Max and Sadie, who both let out sighs of relief. They stood together looking at Stella's men, who appeared to be either puzzled or amused by their leader. Max tried to understand where this unlikely group of humans had come from. Messages they'd received on the supply ship had told of the invasion of Aril and how a fleet from Earth had come to the aid of the young planet. The details included descriptions of the evolved humans who comprised the army from Earth. He suspected that Stella was one of these. He also suspected the men were from Stormer's paramilitary force because they didn't have the uniforms or look of galactic explorers. How had they come together? They'd undoubtedly met on Aril, but why had they come to his supply ship?

His thoughts were interrupted by Stella returning to the room wearing one of Sadie's dresses, many sizes too small. She paraded about the galley to the accompaniment of cat-calls and laughter from her men. Over the next two hours, Max and Sadie were subjected to an entirely different kind of torment than they had suffered upon Stella's arrival. She tried on all of Sadie's clothing, strutting into the room to proudly display outfits that included hats, gloves, shoes, and way too many of the costume jewelry pieces Sadie had brought from Earth. Meanwhile, the men searched the galley until they discovered Max's supply of moonshine. They laughed and hooted and drank with each new display from Stella, and gradually underwent the predictable transition from merriment, to rudeness, to aggressiveness, then depression, and finally stupefaction. Stella, overjoyed with her exploration into the world of earthly fashion, was oblivious to everything and, undeterred, continued modeling Sadie's clothes.

It was altogether a frighteningly bizarre scene. Max and Sadie stood in stunned silence wondering with dread how it would all end. Max considered escaping from the room before the drunken men could react, but he wouldn't leave Sadie's side. Plus, what would he do if he were to flee the room? He could retrieve one of the EMP weapons on the ship, but all of Stella's men were armed. He wouldn't be able to shoot them all before one would fire back at him or Sadie. Max glanced worriedly at his wife, intently watching Stella display her clothing, which fit so poorly on the large woman that it would have been laughable, had it not been so eerily terrorizing.

Finally, Stella settled on a red dress she seemed particularly pleased with. She did several circuits of the room, trying clumsily to get accustomed to high heeled shoes into which her feet barely fit. Stopping in front of Max and Sadie, Stella said, "I'll take this one." Then after a pause, "No, I think I'll take them all."

"Just take what you want and get off my ship," said Max.

Stella laughed. "You don't understand, do you? I'm taking the ship and everything inside it. It is you and your wife who will leave the ship."

She looked at Toro, who was leaning drunkenly against one of the galley cabinets. "Toro, get these two off my ship."

Toro wasn't so drunk that he didn't realize Max and Sadie would put up a tremendous fight to save their ship. He aimed his EMP weapon nonchalantly at the couple and with two short blasts immobilized them both. They slumped to the floor, mercifully unconscious. Toro ordered several of his more sober companions to carry them to their space vehicles, still docked at one of the six stations attached to the supply ship. Once in the gravity-free portion of the ship, they stripped Max and Sadie of their clothes with rude and disrespectful mirth. After they had been maneuvered into the magnetocryogenic chambers, Toro set the navigation systems to automatically pilot the two vehicles to a location so impossibly far, Max and Sadie would never be unfrozen. He set their destinations to a neighboring galaxy, millions of light-years away.

When the two capsules were gone, Toro returned to the galley and found Stella caressing a fur scarf draped around her neck. "What is this?" she asked Toro.

"It's fur."

"Where does it come from?

"A long time ago it came from animals," Toro answered, trying with difficulty not to sound too condescending. "That one is probably fake. It was hard to get real fur in the 22nd Century."

"Why?" Stella asked.

"It was against the law to kill an animal to get its fur. Besides, there weren't many fur animals left by then."

Stella threw the fur aside. "I don't want a fake fur. I want the real thing."

Toro shrugged. "Good luck. There may be fur animals still

on Earth, but I'm sure it's still illegal to kill them."

"I don't care what's illegal," Stella snapped. "Set a course back to Earth. See if you can sober up your friends enough to get them into their capsules. They can experience the pleasures of their hangovers ten thousand years from now when we get to Earth."

"What if you can't get any more fur on Earth? What if all the fur animals are gone?".

"It doesn't matter," Stella said. "There has to be more on Earth than there is here in the middle of intergalactic nowhere."

"Roger that," said Toro, and he began attempting to rouse his companions. It felt good to have a mission again, even if it was being decided by a gigantic female from 500th Century Earth with an obsessive affinity to 22nd Century fashion.

CHAPTER 12

— Century 790 —

The long range radar on the Union supply ships could detect objects as far away as the distance between the Sun and Earth. It required a great deal of power to send out a signal strong enough to reflect off an object at that distance and produce a detectable echo back at the supply ship. The long range radar was only operated under special circumstances, primarily to track asteroids and comets that might threaten the ship.

Now, Arthur and Krystal were using it to detect the nearby passage of Supply Ship 3 on the way to its new location near the Galactic Garden. Seven thousand years earlier, they'd sent the message advising the supply ship to relocate. The custodians of SS3 would have received it about 2,000 years ago. They'd have sent a reply confirming receipt of the message, but it was too early for Arthur and Krystal to have received it. Also, SS6 was already on its way to its new assigned location. The only way they'd have received the message was if it was relayed through the network of space capsules, or from Aril, which presumably would still have large radio telescopes trained on all the supply ships to monitor their radio transmissions.

Direct radar detection of Supply Ship 3 during its closest approach to Supply Ship 6 could confirm to Arthur and Krystal that their message had indeed been received. Furthermore, the echo of their radar pulse was like successfully reaching out and touching their Union comrades from 22nd Century Earth by way of electromagnetic signals. Through the millennia, Krystal had maintained a friendly, long-distance dialog with Max and Sadie and had gotten to know and appreciate their peculiar brand of supply ship hospitality. It would be comforting to know they were okay.

Krystal used all the available power on the ship to transmit the radar pulse at the precisely calculated location of Supply Ship 3. The lights in the control room dimmed noticeably with the electrical power consumed by the signal. There was margin for error in the calculation of expected location because the radar beam broadened with distance away from the ship. Any part of the pulse could strike the other ship and produce a detectable echo. At the distance separating the two ships, the signal would take about 14 minutes to return to SS6. Arthur and Krystal watched and waited. There was nothing. The radar display in the control room showed no echo at the expected position of SS3.

"What happened?" asked Arthur.

"I don't know," said Krystal with concern. "I'll keep transmitting and scan the beam along the estimated trajectory, just in case there's an error in the calculation."

Over the next 30 minutes, they sat with eyes focused on the display before them. Krystal added indicators showing the shape of the outgoing signal, pulse by pulse. In each case, the signal disappeared off the edge of the screen, producing no back-scattered echo.

Arthur shook his head slowly. "Something's wrong."

"Possibly," said Krystal. "But not certainly. They may have changed course for some reason."

"Changing course is risky," said Arthur. "And even if they had to for some reason, they'd return to their programmed route eventually."

Krystal had to agree. Straying off course offered no possibility of rescue should something go wrong. It was against Union protocol. The last time Arthur and Krystal had lost contact with a supply ship, their concerns had been justified. Andrew Harding had moved the ship to Aril to aid Carl Stormer in the invasion of that planet. As far as they knew, both Harding and Stormer had been taken into custody by the Earth fleet and imprisoned somewhere. Both were probably long dead now.

"What now?" said Arthur.

"Not much to do but return to our capsules and continue to our new station. The next time we're unfrozen, hopefully we'll have a message from SS3."

"Better let Aril know that we failed to detect the ship."

"Of course," said Krystal. "And I'll set up an automated routine that will send out a series of signals at regular intervals in the hope we can catch SS3 sometime later. If we get an echo, I'll instruct the computer to unfreeze us."

CHAPTER 13

— Century 791 —

Risto Jalonen was in heaven. He'd been among the first of the explorers to reach the Galactic Garden. The abundance of life-bearing planets was such that he was able to visit a half dozen planets in the 8,000 years since he'd arrived. All were clustered around the new location of Supply Ship 5, the vessel piloted by Benjamin Mizello after he was reunited with Ilsa Montgomery. They stayed with the supply ship until replacements from Aril arrived to take over as custodians, allowing the reunited couple to begin their own planetary explorations.

Risto had become good friends with Hespera and Johanis, the new custodians of SS5. They had lively conversations, marveling over the rich variety of newly discovered planets. Each time Risto visited, the Arilian couple listened with envious excitement to the account of his latest exploit.

One of the worlds he visited was completely engulfed by a single shallow sea, a planetary sized swamp packed with algae and microorganisms, a fantastic soup of life that may have remained unchanging for eons because atmosphere and ocean were perfectly balanced and synergistic. The only solid landforms were two spits of sandy mud barely higher than sea level, almost diametrically opposite one another. They'd been formed over time by soil deposits carried by the sea, where circulation was such that two regions of stagnation remained forever—like planetary cowlicks. The diminished current at these spots caused the particulates in the water to sink, eventually, after millions of years, forming islands of water-soaked earth, barely breaking the surface of the sea.

Risto decided to land on one of the islands for reasons he could never explain. He remained for several days before departing. The many hours spent surrounded by water, all of which was flowing toward him regardless of which way he looked, had almost driven him mad. It was as if he was standing at the center of a black hole, and the weight of the material eternally collapsing in on him became an unbearable burden.

If that hadn't been bad enough, Risto returned a second time, this time landing on the other island, where the water flowed away from him on all sides. Here he had to cope with the opposite sensation—that he could retain nothing. Everything receded from him in all directions as if he were an outcast, a pariah, a perpetually solitary being doomed to eternal loneliness.

The motion of water on the planet at the two stagnation points ridiculed life itself. At one location, Risto watched objects in the water approach with expectation that they would soon arrive, but they never did. At the other location, he waited for objects in the water to recede, but they never did. It was a bitter reminder of the way in which many people live their lives. It was either one way or the other. Some lived constantly waiting for bad elements of their lives to recede. Others lived waiting for the arrival of good fortune. Still others lived their lives waiting for nothing—constantly adrift, trying to get to locations they could never get to, or to leave places they could never escape from. The flow of water on the planet depicted a brutal reality that most humans couldn't accept. Fortunately, Risto was unlike most humans and he was able to depart from the planet with his sanity intact.

Another planet he visited featured a surface covered with massive crystalline blocks, as if the entire orb was a gigantic geode turned inside out. In spite of the glistening crystalline landscape, the planet was nearly invisible from above. All the visible light falling on the planet from its sun was refracted and reflected from the myriad facets so as to be ultimately directed downward toward the planet's interior. At the planet's core, the visible light heated the material, producing infrared radiation that couldn't escape to the surface along the same circuitous route it had entered. It was a black diamond, blending into the blackness of space as completely as if it weren't there. Level landing spots were rare on the upturned crystalline landscape, but Risto had managed to locate a spot barely large enough to accommodate his capsule. After spending nearly twelve hours exploring the planet using all the spare oxygen tanks he carried, he departed in frustration and disappointment, reporting that aside from being spectacularly beautiful, the planet was basically good for nothing.

One of Risto's favorite planets he called the Planet of Small Organisms, or POSO. It had been visited by several explorers already and he knew he'd have to wear the entire range of protective clothing to land there and endure a painstaking process of decontamination before he departed. Some yet to be explained evolutionary process on POSO selectively weeded out the larger organisms. All that remained were millimeter size plants and animals that crawled, slithered, crept, flew, and swam over the entire surface of the planet. There wasn't one square centimeter of the planet that didn't have a thick layer of organic sludge, always in motion, ever shifting and ever changing in uninterruptible metamorphosis.

Had all the large organisms succumbed to the onslaught of the tinier ones, such that the fittest organisms in the survivability contest were those that could destroy others and reproduce themselves most rapidly? Were the organisms that survived simply more voracious than their larger, more sluggish, counterparts? Did evolutionary processes whittle away at life in the same way wind and water eroded rocks into sand? Was it another manifestation of the thermodynamic principle that systems tend to maximum entropy, maximum disorder? Larger organisms represent a form of order that can't possibly last against the forces that create chaos and disorder. Was this the ultimate fate of Earth and other planets that sustained life—the gradual erosion of life forms to smaller and smaller size? Was it a manifestation of the cycle of life that begins with simple, single-celled organisms, evolves into larger, more complex life forms, and eventually devolves back to its basic building blocks—perhaps ultimately to start all over again?

POSO was a dynamic, throbbing, ululating mass of animated living matter. Explorers reported hearing a continuous, audible, monotonic hum—the sum of all the microscopic life processes taking place simultaneously—eating, drinking, reproducing, moving, and carrying out all the other business of life. It was the sound of battles for survival on microscopic scales, teeming with life and death. It was a maddening sound if one were to imagine its origin—the audible signature of organic material in the process of life-sustaining transformation. It was the aria of survival, the concerto of life, death, and rebirth, in notes too numerous to count.

Every now and then, some chance event would cause some to thrive preferentially at the expense of its neighboring species. It created a transient bulge in the strata of organic matter, like a bubble of power and dominance that would eventually burst, the moment of species glory over as quickly as it had begun. With a gurgle and a pop, the brief explosion of life ended, vanquished by the universal and pitiless laws of physics and chemistry.

Another of Risto's favorite destinations was a planet that was rich with so many different varieties of flowers, it was a spectral delight. The shapes and colors were amazingly distinct, and walking among the plants and shrubs that bore these brilliant displays was an unsurpassed joy. It exemplified the beauty that living organisms were capable of achieving. Explorers who visited the planet entertained themselves by inventing names for the different types of flowers they found. Stinkwheels had round, flat petals that, when disturbed, spun about and sprayed a foul-smelling powdery pollen. Frumpies were orchid-like flowers that looked like old men in wrinkled overcoats. Bolerios contained two spherical shaped flowers at opposite ends of slender horizontal branches balanced perfectly on a stem. When picked off the stem, they could be thrown in the same way as the boleros of ancient Argentinean cowboys. Bicuspials had petals that looked like human teeth, and the flowers of the quilliaxes featured featherlike petals that could be used for writing, had there been ink available. Triaxes had three slender petals, each of which extended almost exactly perpendicular from its two neighbors. The petals of the proboscos were perfectly shaped to accommodate the noses of most of the explorers who ventured to try them out for size, and when they did, were rewarded with a delectably sweet aroma.

Bituminees were sturdy flowers with the size, color, and shape of charcoal briquettes. Kite flowers could be plucked and set aloft with little effort, taking to the air with liberating ease.

The one challenge to visiting this planet was that it was also home to an annoying abundance of flying insects, understandably essential to the health and proliferation of the millions of species of flowers. Though the air on the planet was breathable, explorers had to wear helmets to keep the aggressive insects from invading the exposed orifices of their faces. Nevertheless, the stunning display on the planet couldn't be resisted by the explorers, who otherwise hadn't experienced such beauty since leaving Earth.

Of the remarkable worlds that Risto visited, however, one particular planet plagued him more than any of the others, which was inexplicable because it was anything but a remarkable planet. It had a rich oxygen atmosphere and was completely covered by a single type of plant. Somewhere deep in his memory, he recalled hearing about a similar planet whose surface was dominated by just one plant.

After departing, he returned to Supply Ship 5 to refuel and peruse the more extensive archives kept there. It didn't take long for him to learn that in the questioning, after the failed invasion attempt on Aril, Carl Stormer had told about his first attempt at colonizing a planet. It was a planet with a life-sustaining oxygen atmosphere, but like the planet Risto had visited, it was completely covered by a single plant, a prolific vine, with thick, entangled branches spreading horizontally. The large, closely-spaced leaves attached to the branches effectively blocked all light from reaching the ground below, preventing the growth of any other type of vegetation. Extending downward from the branches were slender tendrils that penetrated the soil, probably reaching deep enough to tap into subterranean water supplies. The description matched exactly what Risto had observed on the planet he'd visited.

With Hespera and Johanis, Risto pondered the mechanisms that might coincidentally bring the identical plant to two different planets thousands of light years apart. The plant might be one of many favored culminations of biological evolution, producing a single species that completely overwhelmed all other plant species. Or perhaps the seeds of the plant were so hardy they could spread across the incredible distances separating planets in the galaxy. Or more intriguing was the possibility the vine had actually been planted by a long extinct civilization of cosmic gardeners.

Adding to the mystery was the fact that the vine was similar to plants on Earth in many other ways. Risto brought back samples and as far as they could tell from the simple biological tests they performed on the supply ship, the plant survived through photosynthesis, taking in carbon dioxide from the atmosphere in the presence of light and producing oxygen. If that was the case, where was the animal life that performed the complimentary process: taking in oxygen and expelling carbon dioxide? Was the plant destined to expire once all the carbon dioxide in the atmosphere was used up? Was the plant the remains of a biosphere that had gone out of balance? Was this what had happened to Earth in the first 5,000 years after they'd departed the stressed planet? Had the excess carbon dioxide produced an unstoppable plant, a global kudzu that dominated every other life form?

After Risto departed the supply ship, Hespera and Johanis prepared a message containing everything they had learned about the plant and transmitted it to Aril and all the supply ships. That information would be merged with countless other observations pouring in from the explorers of the Galactic Garden. Somewhere, sometime, the knowledge of the mysterious vine might prove useful.

CHAPTER 14
— Century 829 —

On Supply Ship 2, Alphons Demetriano anticipated the arrival of the next galactic explorer. He'd been custodian of the supply ship since the year 65,000 and had entertained many visiting explorers, but the one that was approaching now intrigued him more than any of the others.

Alphons took over as custodian after the invasion attempt on Aril. Before him, Risto Jalonen had taken over the supply ship from Steven Nutley and used it as a command and control post to neutralize the threat of intervention by Andrew Harding's comrades in the galactic explorer fleet. After the victory, the ship remained in orbit about Aril until a replacement custodian was found. Arilian authorities sent a message to everyone in the fleet, most of whom were still in the vicinity of Aril's planetary system, asking if any would be willing to assume the custodianship of Supply Ship 2. Alphons volunteered without hesitation. He'd wanted to be a custodian even when he was learning to be an explorer at the Union training facility in Florida, but only the most senior members were selected for those few positions, considered at the time to be the most venerable assignments in the fleet. Alphons was a physicist by training, with qualifications that didn't quite line up with those needed to assume the daunting responsibilities of caring for a supply ship. In the aftermath of the invasion, circumstances changed and the authorities were desperate to find someone to take over what everyone now realized was a monotonous and dreary chore: minding the giant ships and hosting the occasional galactic explorer that happened by.

Interestingly enough though, Alphons' personality made him ideal to be a supply ship custodian. He was a busybody. He took nearly voyeuristic delight in learning everything he could about each galactic explorer. The computers on the supply ship put huge amounts of personal information at his fingertips, including medical records and images that were the basis for his favorite pastime. He made virtual scrapbooks of every explorer, using all the data he could assemble.

So involved was Alphons in the lives of the explorers that he found himself experiencing all the thrills, fears, disappointments, loneliness, heartaches, and boredom of that ageless fleet of adventurers. He'd shared in the triumph of Risto Jalonen when he single-handedly orchestrated the neutralization of 600 galactic explorers summoned by Andrew Harding to aid in the invasion of Aril. He shared Benjamin Mizello's frustrations as he traveled from one planet to another searching for that which he could never find—a way to recover what he'd left behind on Earth. He exulted in Ilsa Montgomery's discovery that miracles could happen, and that the seemingly infinite obstacles of space and time could be overcome through courage, perseverance, and love.

Alphons had many other favorites among the explorer fleet. One explorer had never summoned up the courage to land on any of the planets he traveled to, but he made up for it by flying past as many new worlds as he could. Because he never used up fuel in the landing process, he seldom had to divert to supply ships for refueling. Instead, he selected his course to maximize the number of planets he'd visit. The extensive observations he transmitted were used by many other explorers when they considered their next destination.

Another of Alphons' favorites was a young woman who had probably the worst luck of all the explorers. For some reason, her space capsule suffered a succession of failures, and she'd found herself stranded on several planets for weeks at a time until she could make the necessary repairs. Yet she never complained. She undertook each new exploration with all the excitement and energy she had when departing Earth.

Alphons felt much less empathy for explorers who failed to take their assignments seriously. One enjoyed pursuing celestial objects, such as asteroids and comets, and using them for target practice. It gave him twisted enjoyment to obliterate these objects with the combined fire power of his space capsule. For him, galactic exploration was just a very large arcade game.

A pair of explorers had launched a cat and mouse game, where they engaged in interstellar dog-fights using their low-power laser weapons. They boastfully broadcast the results of these contests to other explorers. Eventually, the reports reached Alphons on Supply Ship 2, where he logged with great chagrin the antics of these two explorers.

Several other explorers had challenged each other to a race. They selected a far-off star as the finish line and then plotted separate courses to the destination making use of gravity assists to give themselves an edge over their opponents. The whole galaxy had become their playground. Alphons was irritated that these explorers let boredom drive them to such mindless exploits.

Alphons also kept careful records of explorers who had simply given up. Some went to Aril to live out the balance of their lives. Others went back to Earth. A few stopped on planets with breathable air, bringing as much food and water as they could carry in their capsules. They lived several months, perhaps stretching it out to a year, all alone on these alien planets, until their supplies ran out. Then they found some way to painlessly terminate their existence. This kind of suicide was unfathomable to Alphons, who found so many ways to make his own limited existence meaningful and rewarding.

The depth with which Alphons involved himself in the lives of the explorers over many years on the supply ship gave him great insight. Alphons came to believe that the Union-led enterprise had been more successful as a psychology experiment than as a galactic exploration endeavor. Each explorer provided an opportunity for him to study human behavior absent the influence of society. The behaviors he observed among the galactic explorers were as diverse as those of civilization itself. It also demonstrated why many believed that as a social experiment human civilization had failed miserably.

All of this had taken its toll on Alphons. He spent so much time unfrozen pursuing his interests that he had grown very old. He could barely keep up with his chores on the supply ship and he'd already notified Arilian authorities that they should send a replacement. He wasn't sure how much longer he could perform his duties. He was glad at least that before he succumbed to old age he'd get to meet the next visitor to the supply ship. He had probably devoted more time to her than to any other explorer.

———————

On her last visit to Supply Ship 2, Xyla had been assaulted by Steven Nutley. She knew he was no longer custodian of the ship. This time she negotiated the passageway with much more certainty and confidence. When she entered the galley, the new custodian was waiting for her with food and drink, and a smile that seemed as incongruous to the circumstances as a humming-bird might have been. She was surprised by how old he looked. Stooped, and with a long white beard, he resembled one of the gods earthlings worshiped eighty thousand years ago. In his Union jump suit, however, he looked almost pitiable. On the other hand, there was a liveliness in his step that gave him undeniable presence.

"Welcome to my supply ship. I am Alphons Demetriano. You must be Xyla. Or should I call you Bria?"

Xyla's jaw dropped in surprise. Struggling to regain her composure, she shook the man's hand. Beneath the beard, the angles of his face were invisible, but the creases around his eyes bespoke gentleness and hidden wisdom. Her first thought was that somehow the old man had spoken to Druix and learned the secret of their identities.

"Do you know my son?" she asked.

"It depends on what you mean by knowing," Alphons replied. "Please sit down. We have much to talk about."

Alphons took the seat at the table opposite Xyla and folded his hands upon the ceramic surface. "How are you, my dear?"

Xyla eyed him suspiciously, unsure how to respond. "Do I know you?" she asked.

He must have detected her discomfort. He began again. "I used to be a galactic explorer. In the Union training academy,

I was acquainted with Benjamin Mizello."

Xyla stiffened at the name. Alphons raised a hand to calm her.

"We weren't close friends. We were just close enough that through the millennia I've endeavored to follow his activities. Remember that galactic explorers spend their entire existence in a physical void so absolute, it defies all human instincts. All we have that connects us to reality is the information received from space by our communication equipment. Information is our lifeblood. For me, it means I've spent much of my time exploring the data transmitted through the Union network. When I volunteered to be custodian of this supply ship, I knew the amount of information at my disposal would increase a hundred fold. Instead of remaining frozen in my space capsule like other custodians, I've spent many years studying the data archived in the ship's computers." Alphons smiled. He gave her an apologetic shrug and said, "I learned a lot."

Xyla relaxed. Not knowing what to say, she ate the food Alphons put before her, chewing it slowly. The taste was unfamiliar, but not disagreeable.

"Perhaps you should come with me," Alphons said finally. "It will make it easier to explain."

He led her out of the galley and along the corridor to one of the sleeping quarters for visiting explorers. There he opened the door and gestured for her to enter, but she held back. She remembered how Steven Nutley had attacked her in the room just several meters away, but it was hard to believe this old man was capable of doing her any harm.

"It's okay," Alphons said gently. "I assure you I do not have Mr. Nutley's ill intentions."

Xyla stared at him, still baffled at how much he knew about her. But he was right. He had none of Steven Nutley's gruffness. He seemed kind—and confident. Confidence must come easily, she thought, given his almost supernatural awareness of events so remote in space and time. She walked past his outstretched arm into the room. It was empty save for two chairs against the wall. She took one and Alphons took the other.

"I spend a great deal of time here. I asked the Arilians to help me install a holographic imaging studio for viewing digital renditions of data in the ship's computers. You probably aren't aware that while an explorer is in a magnetocryogenic chamber, tomographic images are made and the data used to monitor the health of the occupant. That data is stored in the capsule's computer memory and periodically transmitted to the Union network for archiving. No one ever looks at the data, but I use it to create holographic images of everyone in the database. Who would you like to see?"

"My son," Xyla answered without hesitation.

"Easy," said Alphons. "Say his name."

Xyla looked confused.

"Either one," said Alphons, laughing. "It doesn't matter."

"Druix."

The lights in the room dimmed and multi-colored laser beams pierced the darkness from numerous apertures embedded in the walls. At the collection of points where the beams intersected, a form appeared in fluorescent brilliance. Several seconds later, an almost exact image of Xyla's son stood before them. He was wearing a navy blue jumpsuit. The rendition of form and color was so exact Xyla half believed Druix had been transported across space to Supply Ship 2.

"Impressive, isn't it?" said Alphons. "Fortunately, I'm able to digitally clothe the image."

Xyla rose and approached the ghostly figure, but as she did so it deteriorated in sputtering luminosity.

"You're blocking the laser beams," said Alphons. "You have to remain seated. I know it looks real, but trust me. It's not."

"Of course," whispered Xyla. And she returned to her seat.

"Think of someone else. Say the name out loud."

Xyla looked at Alphons, barely visible under the reflected glow from Druix's image. "There is no one else," she said.

Alphons returned her glance. "Are you sure?"

"Yes," she answered, but her voice cracked.

"I'll say it for you. Benjamin Mizello."

The image of Druix dissolved and a few seconds later Benjamin stood before her, also dressed in a jumpsuit of sapphire blue, similar to the one he'd worn during his visit to Aurora, except far more brilliant.

Xyla felt a lump in her throat. With Benjamin's image so realistically rendered before her, she couldn't pretend that she'd forgotten about him. Memories rushed back to her of the weeks they'd spent together on Aurora. She recalled their long walks along the frigid shores of the frozen ocean where she and her family lived. She remembered their swims in the freezing cold waters, avoiding the floating blocks of ice, with Benjamin hanging tightly to her for warmth. She looked deep into the eyes of the image before her, but here is where the data failed to replicate what was still vivid in her memory. The eyes were blank and lifeless—void of the warmth and kindness with which Benjamin had gazed at her in the muted blue light of Aurora's dying sun.

Alphons showed Xyla a succession of images of other renowned explorers, but her mind was elsewhere. What had shocked her most was not the image of Benjamin, but her reaction to it. She'd been absorbed for so long in the effort to become a galactic explorer, she was able to bury her loneliness under the rigors of coursework and physical training. On the desert planet, she'd undergone a catharsis—a rebirth that had put an enormous distance between her life on Aurora and her life as a galactic explorer. Now she understood how fragile was the barrier between those two lives. Deep within her, she wasn't ready to give up the dream that motivated her.

"Where is he?" she said into the darkness.

Alphons spoke a single word she couldn't understand. The lights came on in the room and Xyla squinted in the sudden brightness. The old man leaned forward with his elbows on his knees.

"Do you want to find him?" he asked.

"I don't know," Xyla answered, looking at her hands folded in her lap. "No. He's with someone else."

"I know," said Alphons. "But don't give up without seeing him one more time. Failing to do that will make you miserable forever."

Xyla shook her head in denial.

"Think about it," he said, wheezing silently. "At one time I was a physicist. Now, I have little chance to use that knowledge, but every once in a while I see analogies between the laws of physics and the laws that govern the human heart. For example, physics describes the interaction between two moving bodies when they pass near each other. There's a sphere of influence within which the two bodies will be drawn to each other by their mutual attraction and become permanently attached. The size of the sphere is determined by the intrinsic properties of the two objects and their relative velocity. Two people passing near each other may be joined together forever if conditions are right. All you can do is get close to a person and if the laws of the human heart are in your favor you'll be joined forever. That's all you can do. It will close the loop."

Xyla was uneasy with the personal direction the conversation had taken. "And you can get me into Benjamin's sphere of influence?" she asked.

Alphons shook his head. "I analyze data. I can't predict the future, especially when all the data I receive is thousands of years old. However, I can maximize the odds that the two of you will meet again."

Xyla stood suddenly. "I have to go."

They returned to the galley. Xyla took her seat at the table again and forced herself to eat. The food was surprisingly satisfying. She hadn't eaten a great deal on the desert planet, and she was still hungry.

Alphons watched her in silence for a long while. "Information is the only reality for galactic explorers. It takes the place of seeing, hearing, smelling, feeling. It can give them pleasure, or it can give them pain. The radio receivers on space capsules are their spinal cords. By studying the data from the capsules, I can tap into the minds of galactic explorers. I can sense what they sense and, if I understand their individual personalities, I can guess at what they might do."

"What about privacy?" Xyla said. "Shouldn't you have more respect for the privacy of the explorers?" The ethics training she'd received on Sparil had been intensive. The probability that explorers would come upon other life forms in the Galactic Garden was high. What constituted right and wrong when encountering alien life? Humans had struggled with moral issues for tens of thousands of years and couldn't even agree on what constituted ethical treatment of life on Earth. Inevitably, they'd have to apply that imperfect science to the beings of other planets. The Union training could only identify the issues. It was up to the individual explorer how the standards were applied in any particular situation.

"I worry about that occasionally, but not enough perhaps," Alphons said. "Let's face it. We live a bizarre existence that complicates all previous perceptions of privacy and other human rights."

Xyla finished the food and downed the remaining liquid in the ceramic cup Alphons had handed to her. It was warm, a sweet tea, tasting faintly of raspberry. "I need some rest," she said.

"Certainly," said Alphons. "I'll show you to your quarters."

Alone in the darkness of her room, Xyla breathed deeply, trying to relax, but unable to rid her mind of random disconnected thoughts. She should be reviewing the latest data on new planets to select one to explore, but she couldn't put aside her personal thoughts. Her curiosity about Benjamin was overpowering. She knew she'd never be able to function normally until she had spoken to him again. There was a confirmation that needed to take place before she could carry on with her life. Closing the loop, Alphons had called it. But she understood it was much more than that. It was a faint, tenuous pathway that might lead to happiness, and she wasn't yet ready to abandon that hope.

Hours later, after she'd awoken and freshened up, she found Alphons in the control room of the supply ship, sifting through new data being received. She took the seat next to him.

"Where do I go from here?" she asked.

Alphons gestured toward one of the monitors with a thumb. "Go to Supply Ship 5. I'll send further instructions there."

"SS5," said Xyla. "Didn't Benjamin leave Aril with SS5?"

"Yes, he did. Then he met up with Ilsa Montgomery, whom he had become friends with on Earth before beginning his explorations. The two of them took the supply ship to its new station in the Galactic Garden, but they were both replaced by custodians sent from Aril. I believe they then headed for Supply Ship 6 to visit Benjamin's father. They're not there yet. I should be able to find out where they go after that visit. You'll have a message from me when you arrive at SS5."

Xyla smiled inwardly. Somehow, knowing this old man was helping made her feel less alone. It was only after she'd said good-bye to him and boarded her capsule, in the moments before being frozen again, that she realized she'd never see him again. He had very few years left to live and he'd undoubtedly use them up very quickly. It saddened her. She had forgotten to thank him.

CHAPTER 15

— Century 841 —

At first, the message Admiral Chase just received from Supply Ship 6 caused him little alarm. Krystal and Arthur had attempted a difficult experiment to detect the passage of Supply Ship 3 to its new location in the Galactic Garden, but had failed. A quick check through the messages received on his command ship confirmed that the last transmission from SS3 had been in 76,822, prior to the time it would have received instructions to relocate. There was no message confirming the ship had received the instructions. It was possible it had never been received and the ship was still at the location the Union had assigned to it in the 22nd Century. If that was the case, new instructions would have to be sent. A direct transmission from his ship to SS3 was impossible. It would have to be relayed through the explorer fleet, but that was an uncertain link, now that most of the explorers were concentrated in the Galactic Garden. Admiral Chase would have to transmit a message to Earth, hoping the large radio telescope on the moon was still operating. If all went well, the message to relocate could then be relayed to SS3. The whole process would take more than 10,000 years and its success couldn't be confirmed for another 10,000 years after that. Admiral Chase was amazed at how accustomed he'd become to thinking of such long periods of time as if they were no more than days on Earth. It was as if his mind had readjusted and expanded to accommodate the vast spatial and temporal scales of the galaxy, putting events into an entirely different perspective.

More disconcerting to Admiral Chase than the lack of contact with SS3 was the simultaneous disappearance of about a dozen galactic explorers and one of the troops he'd left on Aril. Her name was Stella. The twelve explorers were newly trained recruits from Carl Stormer's army. Having been led into aiding in the invasion of Aril without fully appreciating the legal and moral ramifications, the members of Stormer's army had been treated mercifully by the Arilians. The twelve in question had passed the requisite knowledge, skill, aptitude, and psychological tests to become galactic explorers, but Admiral Chase was suspicious because he knew they'd all been friends while waiting for their release from Arilian custody. That they had disappeared at the same time was sufficient proof to conclude they were most likely still together, and for some reason not communicating their whereabouts to others in the fleet.

Admiral Chase wasn't sure if there was a connection between their disappearance and that of Stella. She'd been a guard at the compound where the men of Carl Stormer's army were being held. Admiral Chase knew Stella and was reluctant to believe she was involved in anything nefarious. Her record as a member of the Earth fleet was flawless, and she was a highly skilled and well-trained soldier. Unfortunately, she was quiet and introverted, with no real friends among the other troops. All those he spoke to after her disappearance could offer little information about what may have motivated her to depart without communicating her flight plan or destination.

The only hint of where Stella and the twelve explorers might be heading was from one of the other guards, who had overheard the group talking a great deal about Earth. It was marginal information, but enough for Admiral Chase to order a change of course for his command ship. Instead of moving to fill the gap in the distribution of supply ships left by SS3, he directed his ship toward Earth. The other supply ships, along with his 500 troops scattered throughout the Galactic Garden, could provide support to the explorer fleet if it was needed. Instinct told Admiral Chase that Earth faced more immediate danger.

CHAPTER 16
— Century 850 —

Sparil had become a thriving hub for space commerce, tourism, and science. No one on Aril could have predicted the irresistible attraction space would have on its population. Aril was a planet founded upon the philosophy that both science and art existed to serve society. Science for the sake of science wasn't sustainable; nor was art solely for its esthetic value. Both had to be balanced with the pressing needs of the general population—a balance that had been established early in the history of the planet and reinforced by socio-economic forces through the millennia.

However, balance is never maintained without continuous adjustment. For Aril, the relentless drive to understand, the curiosity that fueled questions, and the exploration that led to discovery, all had to be siphoned off lest they upset the traditional order. Sparil was the outlet for those inclinations, and over thousands of years, the spaceport had attracted the greatest scientific and engineering minds the Arilian educational system produced. Sparil was a magnificent monument to the imperatives of curiosity and knowledge.

Sparil was governed by a hierarchy of committees and subcommittees that permanent residents claimed were uniquely critical to the seamless operation of the facility. In fact though, the committees accomplished little. At the head of the committee structure was a Board of Directors—about a dozen or so members selected for their proven records in contributing to the mission of Sparil. Each member chaired one or more committees, and those committees in turn convened a number of subcommittees to aid in fulfilling the functions they'd been charged with. It didn't stop there, however, because the subcommittees were constantly forming task groups assigned with carrying out specific responsibilities. If the task groups were successful, they'd be eliminated, but that seldom happened. Few of the task forces ever reported that their work was complete, and so the number of such groups grew continuously. The Board of Directors consequently formed another committee whose sole purpose was to keep track of the entire organization. That committee, predictably, couldn't perform its function without assigning it to a subcommittee, which, to avoid forming more task forces, organized working groups instead. Some residents of Sparil were on several of the groups, while others turned down such opportunities because they were too busy. When they refused, it was necessary to recruit others less qualified for the work. Thus, members on the committees, subcommittees, task forces, and working groups were either overworked or under-qualified.

It was Sparil's cumbersome committee structure that resulted in the amazingly long time it took for the spaceport to call the first ever Galactic Exploration Conference. About 50 centuries earlier, Sparil had received a transmission from Earth saying that a massive corporation had launched an expedition to locate and colonize a new planet in the Galactic Garden. It was an old story, but this time it was given far more credibility because of the scale of the undertaking. News of the expedition was received with great interest at the time and documented by the Interplanetary Relations Committee, which reported it to the Board of Directors through the Committee Chair. When the Chair passed away, the record of the expedition from Earth was put into archive and forgotten about.

Over the next few thousand years, huge amounts of data were sent to Aril from the galactic explorers describing the planets discovered. The disposition, dissemination, and storage of the data were handled by the Data Task Force under the Planetary Exploration Subcommittee, which was formed by, and reported to, the Galactic Science Committee. At one point, the Subcommittee became extremely excited over reports that the same alien plant form had been found on several of the planets, and a new task force was formed to investigate the ramifications of the discovery. Unfortunately, the findings of the task force never received high level attention and the results were forgotten.

Now, in the 850th Century, Sparil had just received a

message from Admiral Chase expressing alarm that twelve galactic explorers, once members of Carl Stormer's army, had disappeared, along with one of his own troops. Admiral Chase was also concerned because there was evidence that Supply Ship 3 had never received the directive to relocate to the Galactic Garden. No message from that supply ship had been received for many thousands of years.

The disconnected events occurring over the last 5,000 years surfaced at last during a meeting of the Committee on Communications, whose primary responsibility was producing a newsletter that few residents of Sparil read. The newsletter was displayed on monitors scattered about Sparil's recreation center, usually during those hours when most of the residents and visitors of the spaceport were asleep. Paradoxically, the meetings of the Communications Subcommittee were closed to only its members, but for this particular meeting they had invited a member of the Subcommittee on Exobiology, who suggested that a workshop on galactic biology would provide a means for all the collected data on new planets to be discussed and studied. Communications Committee members worried that such a workshop was too limited and would not attract a sufficient number of attendees to make the assembly worthwhile. One member suggested that the workshop be expanded to highlight habitable planets in general. That statement jogged the memory of another Committee member, who had a distant recollection of a fleet from Earth that was on its way to the Galactic Garden to start a new planet. This started a cascade of memories from the members present, who together brought to light the poor effort expended through the millennia to assimilate the vast quantities of data being collected. This was the primary message that was reported by the Chair of the Communications Committee to the Board of Directors. Fortunately, the idea to convene a Galactic Exploration Conference was well received and adopted unanimously by the Board. The earliest such an assembly could take place was 20,000 years in the future, because that was how long it would take for explorers to receive the notification about the conference and travel to Sparil.

They agreed to send out a message to gather as many of the galactic explorers as possible, along with the dispersed members of the Earth fleet, in the year 108,000. Perhaps the reason the idea was so overwhelmingly accepted was that all the members on the Board knew they'd be long dead before the meeting took place. Nevertheless, the Board immediately charged the Communications Committee with developing an agenda for the conference, which it undertook by establishing a new task force. Unlike other task forces, the Galactic Exploration Conference Agenda Task Force wouldn't last forever—only 23,000 years, when the conference was held, after which it would morph into the Galactic Exploration Conference Report Task Force. In this case, the extended charter of the task force worked well because Sparil never lost track of the future gathering of galactic explorers. The responsibility of developing, maintaining, and updating the agenda was diligently handed down from one generation to another through the millennia.

CHAPTER 17
— Century 854 —

More than 20,000 years after leaving Aril, Benjamin Mizello visited his father and Krystal on Supply Ship 6 for the second time. On this occasion, he brought with him Ilsa Montgomery, who was also visiting the ship for the second time. The four had much to talk about. Arthur and Krystal were anxious to hear a first-hand account of the invasion of Aril from Benjamin. Ilsa and Benjamin looked forward to learning more about the planets that had been discovered in the Galactic Garden. The reunion was also a celebration of how nicely everything had turned out despite the hopelessly desperate circumstance of Ilsa's kidnapping by Carl Stormer.

After the initial festivities, the four settled into routines that came as close as possible to replicating what they remembered family gatherings to be like on Earth. They all got along extremely well considering the unexpected routes by which they'd arrived. The supply ship was large enough and its living spaces varied enough to offer each of the four a comfort zone to enjoy solitude when he or she needed it.

When he first met Krystal during his previous visit to Supply Ship 6, Benjamin had reacted guardedly to her, not ready to accept the idea that his father had a new partner, seemingly so soon after his mother's death. Now, however, Benjamin and Krystal spent much time together poring over the data received on the supply ship from the explorer fleet. After all, they both trained as galactic explorers, equally fascinated by the incredible richness of the environments and habitats of the life-sustaining planets being discovered on a regular basis.

"It's a regular zoo out there," Krystal told Benjamin with excitement. "Every variety of planet you can imagine, and some you could never imagine—all teeming with life. It's a testament to the ability of living cells to emerge spontaneously, provided the right elements are around. Apparently, it's not even important what type of atmosphere the planet has. Once living organisms get established, there seems to be a natural process that establishes and stabilizes a benign atmosphere—one within which they can survive."

Both recalled fellow explorers they knew from the Union training academy, and laughed and joked about the twisted irony associated with the planets they'd come upon. One explorer everyone disliked mistakenly found himself on a particularly hostile planet from which he barely escaped. The experience made him a new man. Two explorers, who had liked each other at the academy but never gotten together, found each other exploring the same planet at the same time, an impossible co-incidence. Benjamin was particularly interested in the exploits of Risto Jalonen, who had figured so importantly in preventing Aril from being invaded by Harding and Stormer.

"I've heard directly from him," said Krystal. "He sends his regards."

"I'm glad to hear he's still in the business," said Benjamin. This was explorer lingo meaning Risto had not given up on galactic exploration.

"He's explored more than a half dozen planets in the Garden so far," reported Krystal.

"Anything interesting?" asked Benjamin.

"Risto wouldn't bother with a planet if it wasn't interesting to begin with."

"Right, but Risto has a unique idea of what's interesting."

Krystal told Benjamin about Risto's visits to two planets that harbored the same kind of verdant vine covering the planet Alpha, which Stormer and his paramilitary army had accidentally destroyed by a carelessly started fire. When surviving members of Stormer's army were interrogated by Arilians during the months after the failed invasion attempt, they described the prolific vine in considerable detail. The Arilians dutifully relayed the information throughout the explorer fleet. Risto noted the similarity between the plant on Alpha and the one he'd found growing abundantly on an entirely different planet. He wouldn't have reported the similarity except several thousand years later, he explored another planet and found the same vine growing there as well. This time he transmitted the discovery fully to his Union colleagues.

Benjamin and Krystal puzzled for long hours over the coincidence. The best explanation they could come up with was that the hardy vine represented a favored evolutionary life form, the most likely end product of natural selection processes acting over millions of years. It was hard to believe, given the richness and diversity of the life forms found by the explorers, that the dreary vine was the culmination of random mutations and natural selection through the ages. Typically, evolutionary forces led to greater diversity, not less.

Whereas Benjamin and Krystal delighted in reviewing the planetary observations, Arthur and Ilsa found common ground in studying the human side of the exploration enterprise. They were fascinated by the culture of Aril, about which there were volumes of information proudly supplied by the Arilians. Benjamin and Krystal embarked on a long discourse comparing and contrasting Aril with 22nd Century Earth. That there was any basis for comparison at all was remarkable in itself considering the amount of time and distance that separated the two civilizations, but Arthur and Ilsa were both skilled at identifying the essence of humanity linking them.

Ilsa's interests weren't confined to Aril and Earth, however. Having been a victim of Carl Stormer's malevolence, she was curious about what had motivated him and Harding to embark on their invasion, as well as the mentality of the paramilitary troops who had joined them on their misguided adventure. As an investigative journalist on Earth, such anomalies of human nature were her sustenance. Unfortunately, she couldn't interview her subjects as she would have done on her home planet. But she did have access to transcripts of conversations between the Arilians and Stormer's troops. These were extremely revealing, and Ilsa used the information to document what she was hoping would give her a better understanding of people and all life. Arthur, a sociologist, was perfectly willing to be a sounding board for her ideas, tempering Ilsa's often bitter interpretations with his unique brand of optimism.

One conclusion Ilsa reached as a result of her studies was that hostile elements remained among Stormer's troops, and the Arilians had been far too trusting in dealing with these men. She believed they were entirely too confident in their ability to rehabilitate the soldiers through nothing more than kindness and compassion. Arthur was amused by Ilsa's indignation, but had to agree that evil was deeply rooted in some people and would often resurface without continuing intervention. A society where people are in close contact might be successful in damping these dispositions, but in the emptiness of space there was far too much freedom for human psyches to travel down deviant pathways.

When Ilsa heard about the possible disappearance of Supply Ship 3, she immediately suspected it had been hijacked. She still remembered how Harding had secretly moved his supply ship to Aril, and it took many thousands of years before Arthur and Krystal even became suspicious about the ship's disappearance, and many thousands of years more before they could even guess what happened to it. Too much damage could be done in the impossibly long times it took to get information across the galaxy.

Arthur performed a quick calculation, later confirmed by Krystal, that enough time had passed since the invasion of Aril for those responsible for the aggression to have traveled to every corner of the Galactic Garden and then some. If they harbored evil intentions, it would be like a disease spreading through the system, extremely difficult to control once released. This caused all four a good deal of uneasiness. They were reminded of how fragile their existence was and how alone they were in space and time.

By far the highlight of Benjamin and Ilsa's time on Supply Ship 6 was the information they received from the fleet of spaceships that had left Earth carrying thousands of frozen humans along with everything needed to establish a new planet. The fleet, on route to the Galactic Garden, was only about a thousand light-years away from SS6 at the time of Benjamin and Ilsa's visit. Krystal reported that she was receiving regular communications from the leaders of the expedition now that the fleet was so close. Although they were prepared to create a favorable atmosphere on any suitable planet, they still solicited the latest data from the explorers that would enable them to make the best decision on where to establish a colony.

Reviewing the messages heralding the arrival of the corporate fleet from Earth was like watching a parade. Krystal had compiled the data received during the previous thousand years. Now she displayed the results of that communication in graphic splendor on the ship's control room monitor.

"The corporation that launched the expedition was extremely strategic, diligent, and thorough. It was undertaken in phases that took place over 1,500 Earth years. That Earthlings could execute a long-range plan over so many years is by itself testimony to how much has changed since we left," Krystal explained.

She moved her hands deftly over the controls of the ship's computer to bring the monitor to life. The backdrop was a myriad of stars showing the characteristic spiral arms of the Milky Way galaxy. She added symbols showing the locations of Earth and Aril, then more indicating the current positions of Union supply ships. She animated the display and the supply ships moved across the screen, tracing the paths taken from their original locations around Earth to new stations about the Galactic Garden. She zoomed in to that sector of the galaxy and added new symbols, color-coded according to a convention only she knew.

"These represent the corporate fleet from Earth. The ships are spread out over a line because they left Earth at different times. The first group of ships carried the scouts, the ones that we've had most contact with. They're responsible for selecting the planets the fleet will eventually colonize, prepared to either land on a planet with an existing atmosphere and take the steps necessary to make it safe for human occupation, or to send drones with organic material to land on barren planets and seed new Earth-like atmospheres. They have a thousand-year head start on the others so the atmosphere is fully stabilized by the time the others arrive.

"The next group of ships carries tiny construction robots and small nuclear power plants. The colonists bringing these are responsible for building the initial infrastructure on the planet: homes, buildings, roads, bridges—everything that will be needed to house and shelter the other colonists when they finally arrive."

Krystal was adding symbols as she spoke, zooming in to show the different groups of ships in more detail. She had assigned icons to more easily distinguish them.

"Remember that many of the human occupants of our ships will remain frozen near the selected planet while all the preparatory work is being completed. Everything is done autonomously. They'll unfreeze themselves periodically, just as we do, to make sure everything is proceeding according to schedule."

Benjamin, Arthur, and Ilsa watched and listened silently. Their imaginations struggled to believe that the luminous dots on the monitor were symbols of a much larger reality—thousands of humans streaking through the galaxy on route to starting a new civilization.

"The next group to arrive will be the farmers. They have seeds and equipment needed to initiate a thriving agriculture more than sufficient to sustain the colony. Unlike the others, they'll land on the planet and live there while nurturing the crops. This is a task that can't be automated. The success of the colony depends on the ability to develop a thriving agriculture."

"Hmm," murmured Arthur, breaking the silence in the room. "These farmers will be there for centuries before the others even start arriving. After so many generations, how will they feel when thousands of other colonists come popping through the clouds to live on their planet and gobble up their crops?"

"Hard to tell," replied Krystal. "Living on the planet will be marginal until others arrive. The farmers and their descendants have to believe that sometime in the future the other colonists will arrive bringing all the other elements of life they've been missing—medicine, music, art, science. They will look at it as if it's some kind of celestial blessing from space."

"Maybe," mused Arthur. "But in a thousand years they may have developed all that on their own. The raining down of humans may be viewed as an apocalyptic nightmare from the heavens."

"Ironically though," argued Krystal, "the next group that arrives will not be humans. They're animals. At the time the corporation was planning the expedition, they knew all about Aril, and how it was founded without all but the simplest life forms—other than humans. They considered that a mistake. They've frozen every type of animal Earth had to offer at the time and put them in specially equipped space capsules."

"Like Noah's Ark," ventured Benjamin.

"A distributed ark," corrected Krystal. "The animals will travel in separate capsules that will land on the planet, and then pop open on the surface to release some very surprised beasts."

"Well, I'm sure the farmers are looking forward to that," commented Ilsa. "Rhinos dropping from the sky and running amok through the cornfields."

Krystal smiled and added pictures of animals to the monitor. Now the march of objects across the monitor really did resemble a parade.

"What's next?" asked Arthur. "The clowns?"

"Politicians," said Benjamin, and they all laughed.

"According to the plan," said Krystal, still moving her hands over the console, "all the others arrive next. Several space capsules per planetary day will land. Can you imagine what that will be like? They will have left Earth thousands of years earlier and arrive on a new planet in what will seem to them like an instant. They'll have places to live, food to eat, and new homes."

"Assuming all goes according to plan," reminded Arthur.

"There always has to be a plan," said Krystal, the engineer.

"I suppose so," said Arthur, unconvinced.

"One more thing to note," said Krystal. "It's not necessarily true that there will be a finite number of colonists arriving at the planet. Up to the time of the information we have from the advance party, Earth continued to launch space capsules carrying colonists. So what they have is a continuous stream of humans heading away from Earth to a new planet that hasn't even been formed yet. It's like a highway in the galaxy for evacuees from Earth." She added symbols to the display, which now showed a line of luminous dots stretching all the way from Earth toward the Galactic Garden.

"When do they expect to start landing colonists?" asked Benjamin.

"It's hard to say. They don't know themselves where the planet will be or how long it will take to condition it. My guess is anywhere between five and ten thousand years from now."

Benjamin said no more. He was looking toward Ilsa. As if feeling his gaze, she turned to look back at him. After a moment, she said, "I know what you're thinking."

Benjamin smiled. "Yes?"

Ilsa returned a smile, which was the same one she'd given him in 2,149 at the IGET conference in Washington. "We still haven't had our honeymoon."

"How many brides can say they spent their honeymoon on a brand new planet?" said Benjamin.

"I'm game," said Ilsa.

"Krystal, can you calculate a course for us to join the corporate fleet from Earth?"

"No problem," said Krystal.

"Wait," said Arthur. "The planet hasn't even been colonized yet. What if the expedition fails?"

"They can always turn around and come back here," Krystal said. "Or go somewhere else. I don't see that there's much risk."

"No, just lots of uncertainty," argued Arthur.

"That's different," returned Benjamin. "I can deal with uncertainty."

Arthur sighed in resignation and Ilsa patted his arm reassuringly. A moment later, Krystal added two symbols on the monitor, one for Benjamin and one for Ilsa. They all watched as the two glowing dots executed a smooth trajectory that intercepted the Earth fleet near the center of the Galactic Garden.

CHAPTER 18
— Century 911 —

Theonius Appleby was a big man, even by 911th Century Earth standards. Always somewhat of an outcast, the 8-foot tall giant landed his ideal job overseeing a living museum, the one fragile outpost for the ancient species of endangered animals on Earth. The vast reserve covered an island roughly the size of the ancient nation of Greece, artificially constructed off the western coast of what used to be Central America. Building a new island to protect the creatures was the only guarantee that the reserve would not impinge on territory already claimed by some segment of Earth's teeming population. The island was designed to offer a variety of climatic and physiographic conditions suitable for animal life needing protection.

Theonius took his job seriously, even though it didn't necessarily entail much effort. Access to the island by other people was prohibited, but enforcing its isolation was not his responsibility. That was taken care of by sophisticated, automated surveillance systems and perimeter defenses. More importantly, no one really felt strongly disposed to enter the reserve. It was instrumented with an array of state-of-the-art audio and video recording devices by which everyone on Earth could observe the animals in far more detail and reliability than they'd enjoy if they were physically present.

Nor was it Theonius' responsibility to ensure the animals on the reserve didn't harm each other. That was largely taken care of by the design of natural barriers preventing one species from wiping out another. Not that predatory behavior was completely absent from the island. The designers of the reserve realized that the predator-prey relationship was a natural process that ensured a proper balance of animal populations. The approach had been to construct habitats as favorable as possible for the animals and then let nature take its course. The strategy had worked for several centuries and every animal species survived to various degrees of success with little intervention from humans.

All Theonius really needed to do was observe the animals, which he did from atop a lookout tower perched on the island's highest peak. He could have sat in a room and watched an array of video monitors displaying the images captured by the hundreds of cameras distributed about the island, but he preferred to observe more directly. Occasionally, he traversed the reserve in a hovercraft to check on the regions that couldn't be seen from the tower. Now and then, one of the audio-visual sensors would be damaged and he'd have to fix it. He also inventoried his charges at regular intervals and recorded the changing population levels as accurately as possible. Natural fires and floods occurred rarely, but when they did, he monitored their location and progress to ensure one of these disasters didn't threaten the entire reserve.

Big as Theonius was though, and easy as his job seemed to be, he was totally unprepared when twelve objects descended from the sky onto the island, landing on the ground beneath billows of glistening white parachutes. Theonius then made perhaps the only mistake he'd ever made as overseer of the reserve. Instead of contacting mainland authorities to notify them, he boarded his hovercraft and glided at full speed to the site of the landings. Had he communicated with his supervisors, they would have told him that a large spaceship had recently arrived at Earth and was now orbiting the planet with unknown intentions. As it were, Theonius was the first to learn its intentions, or at least one of them. When he arrived at the landing site, twelve very primitive humanoids were slaughtering every animal they could find with ancient, but extremely lethal weapons.

Toro strolled about, eying the landscape, while his colleagues enthusiastically scoured the area in search of more animals to shoot. They were all elated to be back on Earth, breathing the familiar air and enjoying the comforting embrace of normal gravity. Toro had done his advanced research well, and there was no opposition to their arrival on this island, which was ideally suited to their purpose. That purpose, as Stella had explained, was, "Go down there and bring me back pretty things."

Stella's power over Toro and his companions was simple. She ordered them to perform tasks they were naturally disposed to do anyway. They were like children, and all she had to do was tell them to go outside and play. They reveled in their charge and excitedly set about killing every animal they could. Toro understood they could hardly bring back all the animals they were destroying. Later, they'd collect the bounty and decide on the most precious commodities they could extract from the carnage—skins, teeth, bones, tusks, antlers, and other body parts Stella would treasure, not to mention the meat, which he was less sure she would enjoy.

Toro's eyes fixed on the reflected glare from an object moving across the sky in their general direction. He took shelter behind an outcropping of boulders and propped his weapon on one, aiming it at the moving object with its power set on full. He waited calmly as the craft approached and executed a gentle landing several hundred yards away. Seconds later, an enormous creature emerged from the vehicle, larger even than Stella, and with no hesitation charged at the nearest of his men with a weapon in each hand firing what looked like thunderbolts erratically in their direction. Toro fired his weapon and watched with satisfaction as a blue streak shot from it and struck the creature in mid-stride. The thunderbolts ceased and the large form that had seemed so terrifying a moment before lay lifeless on the ground. The ensuing silence was absolute as Toro and his men held back, almost expecting the creature to rise up again. But it didn't. Approaching their victim, they saw that it was a man, somewhat similar in appearance to Stella, but larger, with a slightly different skin color and texture. Toro kicked the lifeless form. To his surprise, the man moved. Groaning, he turned over on his stomach and attempted to rise up on hands and knees. Toro heard the sounds of weapons drawn by his men, but he motioned with a hand for them to hold off. His weapon had been set on full power, yet this man had apparently survived the blast. It was unbelievable.

"Pisces is dead," said one of his men.

Toro nodded. "Get something to tie this guy up."

"What for?" someone asked.

"We're bringing him back," answered Toro.

As he expected, all the men objected. He let them voice their indignation, then turned to face them. "I said to find something to tie him up with. If he doesn't cooperate, blast him again. He can take it. Stella told us she wanted us to bring pretty things, and that's what we're going to do. When you've got him tied up, strap him into Pisces' capsule and get it ready for lift-off."

They spent the next several hours extracting the parts of the animals they'd killed. By the time they lifted off, their capsules were filled with booty. The skins would need cleaning and curing, but Toro supposed that could be done on the supply ship. The men couldn't take a chance staying on the planet any longer. As night fell, the twelve capsules blasted off, leaving behind Theonius' empty hovercraft and dozens of carcasses.

When Theonius regained consciousness, he blinked in astonishment and confusion. He was bound tightly to a chair in a room constructed entirely of metal. He sensed an unusual lightness, not unlike the feeling he experienced when his hovercraft descended quickly. What was most incredible, however, was the woman standing before him, not more than two meters away. She was smiling.

"Welcome to my ship," the woman said in a raspy voice. "What's your name?"

Theonius didn't answer.

"Never mind. If you don't tell me, I'll give you one. I am Stella. You work for me now."

Again, Theonius didn't answer, but this time he responded by popping his arms and legs out of their bonds as if they didn't exist. He rushed at the woman, but totally overestimated the force needed in the diminished gravity. Stella dodged his attack gracefully and watched him strike the bulkhead with full force. Before he could turn and charge again, she grasped his arms and locked them behind his back in a bone-crunching hold. Theonius cried out in pain. At the same time, three men entered the room carrying weapons that were aimed directly at him.

"Put away your weapon, Toro," said Stella, hissing through gritted teeth. "I've got him. He's not going to do that again. Right?" she asked, tightening her grip.

Theonius said nothing.

Stella used her hold on Theonius to force him down to the floor. She placed a knee on his back and Theonius moaned in agony. "I'm going to teach him to talk to me," she said.

"You'd better teach him the language first," said the man named Toro.

"What?!" cried Stella.

Toro chuckled. "This guy is from 911th Century Earth. Why would you assume he could understand Union English?"

Stella released her hold on Theonius. She turned to glare at Toro. "Why would you bring back an Earthling who I can't even talk to?"

Toro shrugged. "I thought you'd like him. He'll learn the language eventually. If you don't want him, we'll just shove him out the airlock. He's tough. Maybe he'll survive reentry."

"Idiot!" Stella screamed. "Get him out of here. Lock him in one of the sleeping quarters."

The two other men lifted Theonius to his feet and cautiously led him to a small room where they left him, securing the door behind them.

Theonius sat on the edge of the bed organizing his thoughts. In fact, he understood Union English. He'd been raised in one of the few remaining families on Earth that still tried to hold onto the ancient language. It was widely known that the galactic explorer fleet still populated the distant parts of the galaxy, sending back information on new planets, all in Union English. In addition, Earth was in constant communication with

Aril, and those messages were also in the old language. Yes, Theonius had understood every word Stella said, but for now he didn't want his captors to know that.

"How do you like them?" Toro asked Stella as she ran her palms over the skins his men had brought back.

"They're wonderful," replied Stella. "You did good, except…"

"Except what?"

"No shiny stones."

"Ahh," replied Toro, remembering how much Stella had admired Sadie's jewelry. "Well, we didn't go to the right place on Earth to find any gems and precious stones."

"Why not?"

Toro sighed. "That would have been much riskier. Earthlings are more protective of their jewelry than they are of their animals."

"I don't want to hear excuses. I just want shiny stones."

Toro shook his head. He didn't want to refuse her. For him, it wasn't about the jewels. He didn't want to admit there was something in the galaxy he and his men didn't have access to. It was a matter of pride. Still, he understood the need to be practical. "We can't go back now. They'll be waiting for us." He paused. "But I have another idea."

Stella stood and wrapped one of the skins about her. "What's your idea?"

"Satellites," said Toro.

"What about them?" Stella asked absently.

"We steal some."

"What for?" Stella became attentive.

"Back in the 22nd Century, precious elements were used to construct satellites—gold, platinum, silver, even diamonds. The space around Earth is filled with satellites with tons of valuable metals."

Stella smiled slyly. "I knew there was a reason I like you, Toro. Get your men busy collecting satellites. Bring them onto the ship. We can take them apart and extract the valuable material once we've left Earth. Maybe we can teach our guest to help out—after he learns the language.

Over the next several weeks, Stella's ship scooped up more than three dozen satellites orbiting Earth. All had been operational before being hijacked. Satellites that performed Earth observations, communications, and navigation disappeared unexpectedly. Toro's men jettisoned much of the supplies on the ship to make room for the stolen satellites. So poorly prepared was Earth to defend itself from this space-based piracy that Stella and her crew were completely unopposed, stopping only after they had filled all remaining space on the supply ship with the prematurely decommissioned satellites.

Theonius forced himself to cooperate in the capture of the satellites because he felt it was the best way to find out what Stella and her crew were up to. As he gradually gained their trust, he came to understand that they were motivated only by a petty and primitive obsession with material things, one of the most basic of human instincts he believed had been suppressed ages ago. Once he had calibrated his captors' intelligence, he devised a plan.

While eating with Stella and Toro in the ship's galley, he waited until the conversation turned, as it always did, to the amount of gold they had collected.

"You're wasting your time here on Earth, you know?" he said in perfect Union English, a spoonful of meaty soup hovering before his lips.

"You see. He does understand!" shouted Stella, slapping her hands on the table.

Unperturbed, Theonius continued eating in silence.

Toro stood, gripping his weapon, but not raising it from his waist. "Why are we wasting our time?" he asked.

Theonius finished the last of his soup and, still chewing, wiped his mouth with the sleeve of his jump suit. "The real valuable stuff left Earth more than 20,000 years ago."

"What stuff?" demanded Toro.

"Jewelry, gold, diamonds, art, artifacts, anything you can imagine."

Now Stella was standing above him too. "Why didn't you tell us that before?"

Theonius shrugged. "I didn't know what you were looking for. Makes no sense to me."

"Why was it all taken away from Earth?" Stella had circled around to stand in front of him.

"Read your history," said Theonius. "Back in 72,000, a big corporation organized a mass exodus from Earth. People left by the thousands. In fact, they're still leaving, even now, taking all the wealth of Earth with them. What's left down there is nothing. It's all gone."

"Where are they going?" asked Toro.

"Beats me," answered Theonius. "But you can find out easily enough. It's no big secret."

Stella looked from Toro to Theonius, not saying anything for a long time. Then she placed her fists on the table before Theonius and said quietly, "I hope you don't think we're going to let you go back to Earth."

Now it was Theonius who smiled. "Nope. I was hoping you'd take me."

Stella's eyes narrowed. "Why?"

Theonius did his best to sound convincing. "I'm ready for a change. I've had the same job for more than 20 years. The idea of going to a new world is appealing."

Stella's eyes were locked on his. He couldn't tell if they registered belief or suspicion. He played his last card. "Besides…"

"Besides what?" Stella asked impatiently.

"They've got animals."

"Animals?"

"Right. The ones your men killed on Earth were just the leftovers. All the more exotic and valuable animals were removed 20,000 years ago. The others are either extinct or on the game reserve your men just devastated."

Stella let out a breath of air.

"If you don't believe me, check it out," Theonius said, now more confidently. "They took animals with them—animals with fur."

Stella straightened and looked at Toro. "See if you can find out where that fleet from Earth ended up. Then get your men to prepare the supply ship. We're through here."

During the entire time Stella and her crew were at Earth, the only action Earthlings took in response to the pillaging of the game reserve and theft of its satellites was to send an SOS message to Aril about the crimes taking place. The message was accompanied by graphic video of the slaughter on the game reserve, because the entire event had been captured by the hidden audio-visual equipment and broadcast live to shocked families across the globe, who had tuned in expecting to view a far less harsh reality.

CHAPTER 19

— Century 924 —

The large corporate conglomerate from Earth succeeded in establishing a new society on a planet they named Prosperity. The success of the enterprise was a tribute to the careful planning and preparation that preceded it. With sufficient resources and time, the elements necessary to start a new world had been launched from Earth. All that was needed beyond that was good fortune. They'd relied upon the certainty that by the time they reached the Galactic Garden, there'd be plenty of potential sites to start their colony. It was a gamble that paid off because they found the ideal planet on the first try.

Prosperity was similar to Earth in so many ways it was uncanny. Its sun was very much like Earth's sun, its light fully compatible with the plants and crops the settlers had brought with them. When the fleet arrived, everyone wondered whether they'd gone anywhere at all. Had they just gone around in a cosmic circle and arrived back at a future, unpopulated Earth? Like Earth, Prosperity had copious amounts of water covering nearly 70 percent of the planet's surface. Unlike Earth though, the land mass was concentrated in one continent spanning the planet's equator and fully navigable along its entire shoreline. Two ice caps permanently covered the polar regions, alternately shrinking and expanding with the seasons.

By and large, the effort to establish Prosperity succeeded because the original population arrived with a single-minded work ethic that was rigid and unforgiving. From a very early age, every citizen of the planet was trained to appreciate the importance of industry and success. In just two thousand years, the inhabitants of Prosperity enjoyed a quality of life equal to that of the most affluent regions of Earth. As one might expect from a planet founded by a corporation, Prosperity meant business. No enterprise was undertaken that wasn't in some way profitable.

By design, Prosperity mimicked a living cell. What could

be more efficient than the life sustaining processes selected and validated by millions of years of evolution? The vast ocean that dominated the globe was like the cell cytoplasm, the medium within which all the cell's organelles existed. The primary land mass of the planet was like the nucleus of the cell, where life functions were controlled and information stored. The continent was aptly called Nucleanis. The many islands that dotted the oceans performed life-supporting functions. Those that created and stored energy for the planet were the mitochondria. Others performed tasks related to food production and storage. Still others contained the chemical and pharmaceutical plants that manufactured the products critical to maintaining the health and quality of life of the population. A network of computers connected the islands with Nucleanis, ensuring pathways for information that kept the planet united.

The process established to feed the population was a thriving enterprise, beginning with the farms that covered the islands and produced a variety of life-sustaining crops, and ending in the food storage areas scattered about Nucleanis. The transportation, communication, and power systems were modern and efficient, with little waste or duplication of effort. The educational system produced a continuous supply of well-trained, energetic youths ready to join the workforce and make their mark on the planet. The government was hierarchical and efficient, with the upper levels filled by those with demonstrated success and personalities commensurate with their elevated responsibilities. If there were self-help books for planets, Prosperity most certainly would have read every one. It didn't miss a beat. It was bred for success. Prosperity was an engine—an engine fueled by the industry and energy of its people.

If there was anything missing in the society of Prosperity, it was arts and entertainment. Unprofitable by nature, arts were not encouraged, and those that exhibited a penchant for such skills were redirected to more profitable pursuits. Still, the absence of such frivolities was recognized, and after a couple of millennia of uninhibited growth, the population of Prosperity at last decided it was time to invest in fun. To ensure it didn't interfere with the machinery of commerce so carefully implemented on the planet, the hub of arts and entertainment was constructed on a neighboring planet. They called the planet Happiness. The only enjoyment the people of Prosperity allowed themselves was to take vacations of three to six months every few years on their planetary neighbor. When discussing their intention to take a vacation, the people of Prosperity would say, "It's time to find Happiness", because other than that, their lives were dominated by interminable drudgery and work.

Happiness was a theme park, designed like those that originated in the 20th Century on Earth, except on a global scale. The different domains of Happiness gave visitors an opportunity to experience the most amazing eras of human civilization. In constructing those domains, the creators of Happiness took advantage of the knowledge and data passed down through the eons from the galactic explorer fleet.

One part of the planet featured the wonders of ancient Earth. Full-scale replicas of the tallest skyscrapers, longest bridges, largest space vehicles, and most gargantuan sea-going vessels were constructed—all tributes to that bygone era when humanity strove for god-like grandeur. The government even built small-scale versions of Earth's greatest cities—New York, Tokyo, Paris and Rome.

Another part of the planet displayed modern Earth—or as modern as the builders of Happiness knew of, given the thousands of years that had passed since they left. This area highlighted the miracles of microrobotic technology, demonstrating how whole cities could be constructed with a cup full of invisible worker molecules. Though lacking any artistic or stylish accents, and blandly uniform in color and architecture, the thousands of rooms, hallways, alcoves, and passageways offered unending possibilities for exploration and discovery. They also provided lodging for the thousands of visitors who came to Happiness for leisure and relaxation.

On an island in one of the larger lakes, the designers of the park created a model of the continent of Nucleanis. Here they constructed three large pyramids, memorials to the solidity and permanence of the power and industry of Prosperity. The designers had fashioned the three pyramids after those of the Egyptian, Mayan, and Aztec empires of ancient Earth. From the apexes of the pyramids, visitors were graced with a magnificent 360 degree view of the core of the amusement park and all it had to offer.

In addition to the attractions that highlighted the most glorious aspects of Earth's civilization, the creators of Happiness had deemed it important to remind visitors of the days long ago when, driven by bizarre primeval rules of engagement, humans took opposite sides in battle, attempting to slaughter as many of their opponents as possible. Perhaps it had made sense once when the population of Earth was such that it was conceivable one side could completely annihilate the other side, but those days had passed. At some point, all on Earth acknowledged that such goals could never be achieved, nor could one group of combatants ever really bring the other group to the point of submission. Once the futility of war was widely accepted, other means were used to resolve differences, unsatisfying as the outcome might be to one side or the other. Real dirt from some of Earth's most deadly and memorable battlefields had been brought across the light-years and spread reverently over the area on Happiness to awe people into the sobering realization that the blood of ancient warriors had once flowed into that soil.

Farther from the center of the park, in regions accessible by magnetic levitation railways, some of the more remarkable planets discovered by the galactic explorers were replicated in miniature. There was an attempt to reproduce the tremendous geyser from a towering volcanic peak, like the one that had produced a flash flood almost drowning Benjamin Mizello during his first planetary exploration. At predetermined times of the day, the fountain of water emanating from the geyser produced a stunning rainbow that encircled a distant, snow-capped mountain peak. Try as they might, however, the engineers of Happiness were unable to simulate the aurora borealis that had accented the scene during Benjamin's visit.

There was also a full-scale reproduction of the Arilian Memorial Garden, commemorating the establishment of the first successful extraterrestrial colony. Even the statues of Captain Warner and his three companions were duplicated at the center of the park. On a daily basis, hot air balloons floated over the park and seeds would rain down on spectators, providing all a rare opportunity to share in the thrill of the renowned Arilian holiday, the Festival of Seeds.

Predictably, there was a zoo on Happiness, which contained the wild animals that had survived the voyage to Prosperity from Earth. Those exotic animals with entertainment value had been shipped to Happiness, and placed in a special compound that was created to enable visitors to view them in environments similar to their natural habitats. The creators of the amusement park hoped that in the future the zoo would harbor animal species from alien planets, but at the time the park was constructed and for thousands of years after, that had not happened.

Interestingly enough, the construction of Happiness had a secondary result its creators failed to foresee. As attractions were added and the park grew, so too did the workforce needed to sustain them. Predictably, the most artistic and talented people from Prosperity were the ones drawn to Happiness. Those who came enjoyed their jobs so much that they stayed permanently. They married and had children, and the resident population of the planet blossomed. New infrastructure was necessary to provide the homes and services for the expanding staff. Park employees and their families lived in well manicured residential areas with shops, schools, hospitals, libraries, and all the other services a thriving population depended upon. They even had their own police force, though it was seldom needed. Crime was virtually nonexistent on Happiness. People came to Happiness for the purpose of having fun and enjoying themselves. That seemed to make all the difference in the world insofar as crime was concerned. In some inexplicable way, the attitude of the visitors, which seemed to improve the moment they emerged from the shuttle, made all malevolent and destructive thoughts disappear. On Happiness, it was understood that people weren't supposed to be unhappy, and so they weren't.

For those who resided on Happiness, there was no distinction between work and play. One did not wake up in the morning, go to work for a certain number of hours, and then return home to family and personal activities. People on Happiness worked and played throughout the day seamlessly. They carried the tools of their trade with them at all times. Just as a photographer always carries a camera, a dedicated artist on Happiness always toted a brush and paints, a rolled-up canvas, and a collapsible easel. Natural writers carried pen and paper, musicians carried blank musical scores and whatever musical instrument they preferred. Gifted sculptors carried balls of clay, and whenever the mood struck them, they'd mold the pliable masses into miniature statues, busts, or other forms. Gymnasts and acrobats might spontaneously perform dazzling feats of grace, dexterity, and gravity-defying courage. Artistic performances were staged with no preset plan. Several people might be standing in line at the grocery store when one would begin tapping a beat with whatever percussive object was in reach. Someone nearby would begin dancing to the beat, and still another would begin a chant that would be picked up by others. And on it would go.

As more and more planets were discovered and explored, additional regions were constructed on Happiness. It wasn't necessary for those on Prosperity who wanted to experience the universe to freeze themselves for thousand of years. To enjoy the excitement and thrill of planetary exploration, they needed only to get to Happiness, less than a one-month space journey from Prosperity. Happiness became as integral to society on Prosperity as the principles of ambition and industry that had helped establish the planet in the first place.

CHAPTER 20
— Century 932 —

Xyla was unfrozen several hours before her arrival at Supply Ship 5. She sat at the control console waiting for the automated routines to prepare her capsule for docking with the supply ship. She'd been unfrozen once since leaving Supply Ship 2 by a priority message from Aril. It was an announcement of a conference to be held on Sparil in the year 108,000. She hadn't thought much about it at the time, except to feel inconvenienced at having been unfrozen prior to reaching her destination, but now she wondered whether it might be interesting to attend the assembly. She herself didn't have much to report, having gotten a later start than others in the planetary exploration enterprise. However, she was intrigued by the discoveries others had made and considered the conference a good way to learn about them. Also, she suspected that Druix would attend the conference. This was an opportunity to see him again if he was still alive. They'd agreed that if at any time one or the other of them decided to settle down on a planet, they'd let the other know immediately via a priority message. That was the first thought that came to Xyla when she'd been unfrozen en route to Supply Ship 5. To her relief, there wasn't a message from Druix. She looked at the date display on the console and calculated whether there was enough time to explore one more planet before heading back to Sparil. There was, but she first stopped at SS5 as Alphons had instructed her.

Like most Arilians, the two custodians of Supply Ship 5, Hespera and Johanis, were older than they looked. Warm and bubbly, the couple displayed almost clown-like gaiety, accentuated perhaps by the shocks of yellow hair adorning both their heads. They bustled about, fussing over Xyla and trying all too vigorously to draw her into their happy world. Xyla, whose life thus far had made such cheerfulness rare, struggled not to offend them. Over food and drink in the supply ship's galley, she feigned a false weariness to shield herself from the couple's excessive attentiveness.

"How is Alphons?" Hespera asked. "We were trained to be custodians on Aril at the same time he was."

"He's fine," said Xyla. "He's getting old."

"Yes, he is," agreed Johanis. "But still going strong as of our last communication. Of course, much could have happened since then. We can only hope he hasn't remained unfrozen for too long. None of us can afford that luxury."

Xyla nodded sadly.

"He told us you'd be coming here," said Hespera. "We're glad you did. We'd like to help you."

"That's very nice of you," replied Xyla, slightly disturbed, wondering what the couple had been told about her.

"We've prepared a video sequence of the explorers who've visited the supply ship," said Johanis. "I'm sure you'll find it fascinating for your study."

Xyla was confused. What had Alphons told them she was studying, and why make up any kind of story at all? She found out soon enough, after they brought her to the control room to view the video. It began with the couple's arrival on Supply Ship 5, when they'd taken over as custodians from Benjamin and Ilsa. That was in the year 74,501. The ancient tradition that a captain of a ship could legally marry two people was still observed. Johanis had married Benjamin and Ilsa before they departed to visit Arthur and Krystal on Supply Ship 6.

Xyla hardly paid attention to the remainder of the video. The shock of seeing and hearing Benjamin again stunned her. Even though she knew about the marriage, witnessing it on the supply ship's monitor reinforced the hopelessness of her desire to see him again. How often was she to receive the same message before it no longer upset her so deeply? Alphons had known she needed to see it, and he'd arranged a way to accomplish that through his friends on Supply Ship 5. Mercifully, he'd done it in such a way that Hespera and Johanis had no idea what the real objective of the video was. It wasn't until the video was almost over that Xyla began to pay attention again. The last visitor to the supply ship was a member of an advance party assigned to scout out potentially habitable planets where a massive corporate-based expedition from Earth might establish a new planet. Xyla was amazed at the scope of the undertaking and marveled at the course human civilization had followed. She and Druix were descended from people who had attempted a similar escape from Earth, at the time equally ambitious in scale, but ultimately to fail because of the vagaries of stellar evolution. Quite likely, she and Druix were the lone survivors of that race. She sincerely hoped this latest expedition from Earth would have greater success.

"Perhaps that should be your next destination," said Hespera.

The words snapped Xyla from her reverie. She looked at the Arilian couple sitting beside her with a puzzled expression.

"We know where the Earth fleet went to establish the new colony," Johanis said. "It's only 2,000 light-years from here. They were fortunate to find a planet with a preexisting oxygen atmosphere, a vast ocean, and vigorous biosphere not unlike Earth's. They probably arrived there about a thousand years ago. Hopefully, by the time you get there, the new planet will be well established."

"You'll find it fascinating," said Hespera, clapping her hands together as though announcing dessert at a dinner party.

"I was thinking of attending the Galactic Exploration Conference on Sparil," said Xyla, not sure she was prepared to deal with a mature civilization comprising humans with 50,000 more years of evolutionary progress under its wing.

"You have time to visit the new planet first," encouraged Johanis. "You might as well. What else are you going to do until the time of the conference?"

"What are my options, in terms of other planets close by to explore?" Xyla asked.

"None that will allow you time to visit before going to Sparil," continued Johanis. "The interesting ones are too far away."

Xyla sighed. She wondered briefly where Benjamin and his wife were. They might also decide to visit the new planet, but it was extremely unlikely she'd arrive there at the same time they did. "What if the fleet from Earth failed to establish a colony?" she asked.

"You'll know as soon as you arrive. If they don't send out a beacon to guide you in, you should assume that something has gone wrong and return here. By then, we'll know what happened. Odds are, if the expedition fails, the news will be communicated quickly through the Union network."

Xyla acquiesced, and told Hespera and Johanis she'd follow their suggestion. Once again, she felt uneasy with the way she'd lost control of her own destiny. On the desert planet, she'd been alone, and had drawn on her own strength to generate the will to keep on living. She'd resolved to make her own destiny, but after that, Alphons, a stranger with a bizarre obsession, had talked her into going to Supply Ship 5. Now, she was letting a happy couple from an alien planet decide her next destination. It didn't sit well with her, letting herself be continuously influenced by others, but what else could she do?

Benjamin and Ilsa now looked forward to their honeymoon on Happiness. News of the incredible planet spread quickly through the Union communication network. Given the bizarre route the couple had taken to reach that particular time and place in the galaxy, the existence of a nearby destination that was rather ideal for their budding romance was almost miraculous.

The landing site on Happiness was a large spaceport, dominated by an extensive tarmac peppered with a variety of space capsules and shuttles, all sparkling in the brightness of Happiness' sun. Benjamin and Ilsa's capsules were ancient compared to the other vehicles—not surprising as they were more than one hundred thousand years old and were pockmarked by numerous impacts with infinitesimal debris particles in interstellar space.

Benjamin and Ilsa were met by a warm, young woman, who introduced herself as Gabriana. She spoke Union English with no perceptible accent. Benjamin and Ilsa were obviously not the first visitors from the galactic explorer fleet. This was a relief, as they both preferred not to receive special treatment. The account of the invasion of Aril must certainly have spread to Happiness. Benjamin and Ilsa had figured so prominently in that historic event, they'd been worried about drawing too much attention.

They were also concerned about whether any form of payment might be expected during their visit to the park. They'd been assured in advance that no payment was necessary, but they didn't know whether that was because of their celebrity status, or because no one was expected to spend any more upon arrival. The logistics of calculating fees and taking payments in a theme park that encompassed an entire planet undoubtedly made it simpler to just exact the cost up front.

The four travelers rode with Gabriana in a car that ascended from the ground to a height of 30 meters and then soared smoothly and quietly over the landscape below. Other cars moved ahead of and behind them, keeping a constant distance while an oppositely directed line of cars whizzed past them precariously close. Benjamin was amazed at how accurately the cars stayed on course with little effort by Gabriana, who sat before a control panel at the front of the car, doing very little.

"How do these cars keep from hitting each other?" he asked.

Gabriana laughed. "They're on tracks. How could they collide?"

Benjamin looked outside through the windows that surrounded the vehicle. "I don't see any tracks."

"Of course, you don't. They're electromagnetic—invisible lines of force, used by the car's propulsion system to control the lateral and vertical motion of the car. It's impossible for the vehicle to move off course."

"And the power source for the cars?" Benjamin asked.

"Also electrical," said Gabriana. "The electromagnetic tracks carry energy that's tapped by the car's engine as it moves."

"Wouldn't that eventually extract all the energy from the track and cause it to fail?" asked Benjamin.

"There's plenty to spare. The absence of friction between the car and the tracks makes the vehicle very energy-efficient. Most of the energy is needed to levitate the cars, but they're cleverly aerodynamic. Once moving, they're more like gliders than cars. They stay in the air with minimal energy consumption."

Gabriana helped Benjamin and Ilsa check into a hotel in the area of the theme park constructed using microrobotic technology. Bland, but functional, the hotel was clean and efficient. In minutes, they were comfortably settled in a small room with a view overlooking a large lake. In the distance, on an island in the middle of the lake, they saw the peaks of three pyramids standing out above the horizon. Exhausted from their travel, Benjamin and Ilsa ate a satisfying meal in the room, seated at a small table set before the window. They were unable to suppress the awe they experienced, not just at the vista, but at the realization that somehow they were at an amusement park on a planet thousands of light-years from Earth. It left them speechless and numb.

That night, they made love on a bed constructed from a foamy material that was simultaneously firm and yielding. They'd made love in the reduced gravity of the supply ship, and also had tried sex in the weightless conditions of their space capsules. The lack of control and unexpected rotations and drifts their movements had caused detracted from what otherwise would have been ecstatically wonderful sexual experiences for both. Afterward, in their erotically resilient bed on Happiness, Benjamin and Ilsa had agreed in giggling whispers that their love-making had captured the best of both worlds. It was like being weightless with weight, uncontrollably controlled, and captivatingly free.

The next day, they spent several hours in a visitor center that provided guidance on how to navigate the reconstructed worlds of Happiness. Ilsa was amazed to see that Benjamin still carried the same camera equipment he had with him when they'd first met at the International Galactic Explorers Technology Conference in Washington DC, almost a hundred thousand years ago. There were no time constraints on their visit. They decided they'd take as long as they needed to see every sight the park had to offer. With the advanced air and ground transportation of the planet, they could see all the thematic areas in three months or so. They learned that it was unnecessary to carry any luggage, as every place they went they'd be staying in rooms that provided all the clothing and toiletry articles they'd need. Clothing was selected on a computer screen and produced in seconds, made from entirely recyclable material. They wore it for a day, and then deposited it in special recycling containers to be remanufactured according to the next guest's needs and preferences.

The memories of those few months on Happiness were as perfect as one might imagine given the circumstances. They were delighted by the miraculously accurate depictions of the times and places captured in the different regions of Happiness. Strolling along the Left Bank of the Seine with the brightly lit Eiffel Tower before them, they shivered with excitement and disbelief. Music played everywhere on Happiness, so pervasive that it seemed to emanate from the air itself.

In 20th Century New York, they dined in elegant restaurants, eating cuisine that was indistinguishable from what they remembered on Earth, even though they knew it couldn't possibly have come from the same meats and vegetables available in that far off era. They saw musical shows that captured the grandeur and excitement of Broadway, an experience that must have been as distant and mysterious to the humans who created Happiness as Stonehenge had been to Benjamin and Ilsa.

Then they climbed the pyramids on Nucleanis, enjoying the expansive view of the attractions the elevation provided, and musing over the fascination so many human civilizations had with pyramids. Always mysterious and enigmatic, and invariably linked to the religious beliefs of the civilization that constructed them, pyramids were the symbol of humanity striving to be something bigger than it was, to rise above the mundane and mediocre to new heights of majesty. However hard humans strove for greatness, the fundamental laws of gravity—of human nature—prevented achievement without a base or foundation. The pyramid was simultaneously a symbol of that greatness and the sacrifices that had to be made to accomplish it.

With some trepidation, Benjamin and Ilsa traversed the recreated battlefields of ancient Earth. They puzzled over the rationale for including this grim reminder of the death and destruction humans were capable of. It was a memorial to that which should neither be memorialized nor remembered. It was a monument to humanity's cruelty and barbarity. Perhaps it was to show the absurdity of such events—that seen from afar, many thousands of years in the future, the zealousness with which one group of humans strove to annihilate another group was ridiculous beyond all comprehension—a very poor, sick cosmic joke.

Benjamin and Ilsa concluded their visit to Happiness on a small cruise ship that stopped at famous Caribbean ports of ancient Earth. Guests disembarked to shop, dine, swim, and party at miniature versions of San Juan, Cartagena, Aruba, Dominica, and San Maarten. Music and dance were everywhere, and so mild and benign was the climate that Benjamin and Ilsa spent much of their time outdoors. Whether they were eating at one of the seaside restaurants, basking in the sun at the beach, or strolling the avenues of the shopping districts, they embraced the simple pleasure of being on a planet with the reassuring grasp of gravity and comforting shroud of breathable air. It was difficult to imagine that they'd soon end their visit and depart Happiness in the artificial confines of their space capsules. They had to convince themselves that the bliss of Happiness was artificial, and that there was no place for them either there or on Prosperity. Too many mysteries still remained and the Galactic Garden seemed to hold the answers. If that weren't enough, they received a message forwarded from the space communication system that Arilian authorities were organizing the first Galactic Exploration Conference to be held at its spaceport in the year 108,000. Benjamin and Ilsa had just enough time to return to Aril to attend the assembly.

CHAPTER 22
— Century 977 —

Xyla was unfrozen upon reaching Prosperity. She reviewed the capsule's data archive and the many messages transmitted from the planet recounting all that had taken place in the 4,000 years since she'd left Supply Ship 5. As Xyla read the updates from the planet, she became less and less willing to land there. Although she was happy to hear of the success of the new civilization, she wasn't sure she was ready to witness these futuristic earthlings living in uninhibited bliss on a manufactured planet; they'd even created their own vacation world and named it Happiness. How would visiting such a planet make her a better person or help her achieve a more meaningful existence?

She'd almost made up her mind to abort the landing and return to Supply Ship 5 when she read a series of messages from the 976th Century, five thousand years after the creation of the two planets. Astronomers on Prosperity had observed an asteroid on a direct path toward Happiness. The asteroid was watched for centuries and after several near misses was projected to collide with the planet on its next pass. Fortunately, the prediction gave them a lead time of about 75 years during which the entire population was evacuated to Prosperity. It was a devastating loss—the theme park that had been lovingly built up over many centuries was destroyed in the blink of an eye. All the lives that had been built around the creation of a place where the people of Prosperity could relax, have fun, and enjoy the sights and sounds of unfamiliar places were irreversibly altered. By the time the asteroid struck, Happiness had been completely abandoned, its simulated environments void of human presence, the sounds of music and merriment silenced, and its gardens, fountains, and statuary fallen into disrepair. Happiness had become a ghost planet.

Reading subsequent messages, Xyla learned that those who had fled from Happiness tried to assimilate themselves into the society of Prosperity, but most of them made their livelihoods in arts and entertainment. They found themselves unable to thrive in the fast-paced world of business and commerce. This led to a succession of social conflicts ultimately culminating in a major upheaval of the well organized structure of Prosperity. This last bit of news was several hundred years old, after which there were no more updates from the planet.

With renewed interest, Xyla attempted to contact Prosperity by sending radio signals according to standard Union procedures. She was surprised when she received a response. She'd expected the breakdown in society would have affected Prosperity's ability to support space travel, both from the planet and to it. Fortunately, this was not quite the case. After her successful landing, she found the infrastructure of the planet still in place. Other than that, however, there was little left of the glory the planet had known in the past.

A delegation of officials greeted Xyla—slender beings with amber eyes, closely resembling the members of Admiral Chase's fleet she'd met on Sparil, except paler and less imposing in stature. Those that met her spoke Union English and all were anxious to demonstrate their linguistic skills by engaging her in conversation as she shook their hands and returned their enthusiastic greetings. The receiving line ended at what appeared to be a middle-aged woman with reddish hair and a forced smile. She introduced herself as Heronia. Taking Xyla by the arm, she escorted her to a motorized vehicle unlike any she'd ever seen before. It was sleekly designed and constructed from a stunning metallic substance that sparkled in the bright glare of Prosperity's sun. Inside were seats of contoured plastic that adjusted to the curves of her body, and when the vehicle moved the material yielded in response to the shifting weight.

"We will take you to a hotel where you can freshen up," Heronia said. "Later, you will join us for dinner and we will talk."

The streets of Prosperity were neat and clean, but with a drabness Xyla found disconcerting. On Sparil, the functionality was accepted as an inevitable consequence of limited supplies and cost-effective design. On Prosperity, the suppression of anything beautiful or unique seemed to be embraced. No attempt was made to improve the appearance of anything beyond what was necessary or expedient. More astounding was that no one seemed to care about or take notice of what was missing. Even the hotel held little in the way of luxury or excess—not that Xyla needed it, but certainly the quality of the establishment was inconsistent with the enthusiasm of her reception.

Xyla showered and dressed in clothes that were laid out for her. Then she sat on the edge of the bed looking out the window at a limited view of the city. She hadn't been told its name, except that it was the largest city of Prosperity's only continent, Nucleanis. It could have been a city from any time on any planet, efficiently designed with simple geometric shapes, lacking any frills or adornments that might distinguish one structure from the other. It depressed Xyla, especially after all she'd read about Prosperity's success. What had happened? Or had the stories of Prosperity's grandeur been distorted and exaggerated? Had everything changed after the demise of Happiness?

Over dinner with Heronia and three other officials, Xyla learned more than she wanted to know about the internal strife and petty squabbles among Prosperity's people.

"Things haven't been the same in Nucleanis since the elders relinquished control of the chemical plants," one of the officials was saying. "The younger generations don't respect the knowledge and experience we have. All they're interested in is manufacturing substances that will make life easier. They've forgotten the value of hard work and sacrifice."

"I see," said Xyla, not sure if she did.

"It wouldn't be so bad," said another at the table, "but some of those chemicals are used in medicines. Using those chemicals for frivolous purposes is driving up the price of medication. Insurance rates have risen, which is affecting bank loan rates."

"I see," said Xyla again.

When dessert finally arrived, Xyla couldn't wait to leave. She'd tried to follow the conversation, but her fellow diners used terms she didn't understand and mentioned people she couldn't possibly have known. She wondered why her hosts felt the need to bring her in on their complaints and criticisms. Did they somehow think she could or would help them? Did they view her as a representative of some higher power, so that when she relayed their dissatisfaction all the injustices would be remedied by an external influence?

While her companions were talking excitedly, about some topic Xyla had lost track of long before, a young man approached the table to help clear the dirty dishes. Purposely bending down and reaching in front of her, he momentarily blocked Xyla from the others at the table. He turned to her as if to say "Excuse me," but instead said, "Ask to use the restroom."

Xyla was confused, but when the young man finished removing the dishes from the table she asked to be excused. Before she'd gotten to the restroom, he intercepted her, but now accompanied by a young woman, who took Xyla's hand and pulled her out of the restaurant through a rear door. In an alley behind the restaurant with not a speck of dirt or debris, the two backed her up against the wall and regaled her in a discourse she couldn't begin to follow.

"Don't listen to them," the woman said. "It's not our fault. Their whole future is tied up in the bond market. Any redirection of priorities in the chemical industry will cause them to give back the huge profits they've enjoyed for years. But the food processing industry is suffering. Unless new chemicals are developed, the market for produce will decline and food prices will soar. Those people in there don't mind because they're set for life with the food subsidy program grandfathered in by the new government."

"I see," said Xyla, "But what can I do about it?"

"Talk to them. They'll listen to you."

"I don't see why." Xyla fidgeted. Then reconsidered. "Okay, but I should get back inside."

The two guided her back, seemingly satisfied with Xyla's willingness to help. Xyla returned to the table and endured the remainder of the meal, saying little and hearing even less. It had been a mistake to visit Prosperity. There was too large a gulf between her life experience and the issues plaguing the planet. She resolved to avoid visiting any planets with advanced societies. What could she possible learn from their experiences?

Her hosts left her off at the hotel where she attempted to negotiate the lobby without being seen. At the elevator door, two men in military uniforms confronted her. "The Magistrate would like a word with you."

Xyla acquiesced, but with rising irritation at the imposition on her time. She understood their need to inform her of what was happening on the planet, but she was perplexed that at no point so far had anyone asked her about what news she might have from the rest of the galaxy. Obviously they knew she was an explorer, with knowledge of the latest discoveries, but no one displayed the least bit of curiosity about what was happening outside the limited world of Prosperity.

After another ride through the darkened streets of the city, she arrived at a building much like the others except it stood alone within a gated area surrounded by military guards. Inside, she was escorted through a sparsely furnished marble hallway to a room containing a desk, a few scattered chairs, and a bank of computer monitors covering one wall. She was shown to a hard chair and told to sit.

Several minutes later, a well dressed man entered, tall and slim, with a proud and confident demeanor, reeking arrogance and snobbery.

"You are Xyla," he said, as if telling her instead of asking.

Xyla didn't answer.

"I am Mr. Ames, the Magistrate of the city." He waited for a response, but Xyla remained silent, unimpressed.

"They didn't tell me you had arrived. What have they been saying about me?"

"Nothing," said Xyla.

"I find that hard to believe. They've been against me ever since I took office."

"Really. They said nothing. Anyway, it's none of my business. Can I go now?"

Mr. Ames snapped his fingers and an aide entered with a glowing tablet. "We put together an agenda for your day tomorrow. You will first be briefed by members of our Executive Team. They'll bring you up to date on the status of the various programs we've implemented since I took office. Then you'll tour our administrative offices and meet our Director of Communications, who is in charge of information dissemination. He is key to ensuring the benefits of our new programs are widely appreciated among the populace. Tomorrow night you'll have dinner with industry leaders from across Nucleanis. I think by the end of the day you will appreciate the strength of our society."

Xyla cringed, already thinking about how she might escape the planet. Then, inexplicably, she said, "I'd like to learn more about what happened to Happiness."

Mr. Ames looked at her sharply. "We don't talk about that. It was destroyed by an asteroid. End of story."

"What about all the people who were evacuated?"

"What about them? That was hundreds of years ago. They're all dead now."

"I imagined that it may have had some lasting impact on Prosperity—having to accommodate refugees from another planet."

Mr. Ames walked to his desk and sat down behind it. Holding the glowing tablet before him, he studied it, tacitly indicating to Xyla that her interview had ended. "Those times are behind us now. Good night," he said. "I will see you briefly tomorrow, but unfortunately will be too busy to accompany you on your tour."

To Xyla's dismay, it was not just one tour she was scheduled to take. Over the next fifteen days, she was taken on tours of every aspect of society on Prosperity, schools, law enforcement agencies, businesses of every type. She even visited the islands where food, chemical, and energy were manufactured and processed. Everywhere she went, she was forced to listen to the proprietors of those enterprises complain about other people and other institutions. Everyone, it seemed, carried a gripe or grudge against at least one other person or entity. Everyone blamed someone else for their troubles and the problems of the planet. The amount of blame far outnumbered the people and institutions upon which it could be placed. Thankfully, there were no wars on Prosperity, but the level of aggression among the various organizations that claimed to be critical to the economic and social well being of the populace was just as depressing, and in some ways equally damaging.

At the hotel the evening before she was to leave Prosperity, Xyla was too worked up to sleep. She did something she'd never done before. She went to the hotel's lounge and sat down at one of the tables. Having no idea what to order, she asked the waiter for a glass of water. The water came, but next to it was another drink, amber colored with an alcoholic aroma that Xyla found strangely irresistible. She looked around the lounge and saw an elderly man sitting at the bar, his back to her. Without turning, he said, "I thought you might need that."

"Thanks," said Xyla. She took a sip.

The man slid from his chair and walked to her table. He was extremely thin, with shallow cheeks and a stubble of a beard. "May I join you?"

Xyla sighed, but nodded her approval. It was one of the times she was thankful she'd lived on Earth for ten years. It was the only experience she had that prepared her for these awkward social situations. She hadn't had many opportunities to drink in bars during that time, but she'd done it often enough to know that it could lead to enlightenment or tedium. In the first minute of contact, it was impossible to tell which way it would go.

"What's it like in space?" the man asked. It was a good start.

Xyla considered her answer. "Rich," she said finally. "Diverse, unexpected, surprising, unpredictable. Thanks for asking."

"Glad to oblige," the man said.

Xyla sipped her drink. "Why is everyone on this planet fighting with each other? And what do they expect me to do about it?"

The man laughed. "Some would say it's human nature. Put people together anywhere—a city, an island, a planet—eventually they'll find something to disagree on. You drop down from the sky and they all see you as the only person who can be objective. They all want you to be on their side."

"They're wasting their time," Xyla said. "I'm not taking sides."

"Very wise," said the man.

Xyla shook her head. "Nucleanis has made discord an obsession. There must be other topics to talk about besides the things people disagree on. Why the need to dwell on the negative aspects of life?"

"I can't answer that, but I can tell you it wasn't always like this. Historians tell us it began after the destruction of Happiness."

"But why?"

"For centuries the people of Prosperity relied on Happiness for their enjoyment. When the planet was destroyed, they didn't know any other way to relax and have fun. The refugees from Happiness tried to introduce arts and entertainment to Prosperity, but they were marginalized and persecuted. After a few generations, even they gave up."

"Very sad," said Xyla, beginning to feel the effects of the alcohol. She'd never drunk before and had a low tolerance. "They shouldn't call this planet Prosperity. They should call it Negativity instead."

The next day as she prepared to leave Prosperity at last, she wasn't sure she accurately recalled the full conversation.

"Prosperity is dying," the man had said. "All cells die eventually. It's programmed into their chemical make-up. It was a great idea to design the planet after a living cell, with a nucleus and an ocean of cytoplasm, but with an overblown concentration on the operational and functional aspects of society, the population lost sight of the meaning for its existence. It existed only to continue its existence. Happiness had given the people something external to connect to, a meaning beyond mere survival. Happiness gave them all something to strive for. Without Happiness, they were all just spinning wheels. The loss of purpose led to lack of excitement. The wheels of industry slowed. The organic processes that kept the cell alive were grinding to a halt, and the life of Nucleanis began to fail."

When her capsule blasted off from Prosperity at last, Xyla felt a tremendous burden lifted from her. Had she stayed any longer, she would have suffered utter depression from the continuous bombardment of negative energy from all the people she encountered. Other than the man she'd met at the hotel bar, no one had asked her the purpose of her visit, nor inquired about what new planets had been discovered in the Galactic Garden. So completely were the people of Prosperity absorbed in their own problems that they failed to open their minds to the universe that existed everywhere. She felt sorry for them.

CHAPTER 23

— Century 987 —

The automated radar system on Admiral Chase's command ship detected echoes of an unusual nature. That had initiated unfreezing of Admiral Chase and two of his officers. When they reviewed the data, they confirmed that the ship's long-range radar had received echoes from a group of objects 432 million miles away, moving at high speed, half the speed of light, in the opposite direction from where Admiral Chase's ship was heading. The high speed alone was ample evidence that the objects were not of natural origin. In addition to that, the trajectory of the objects was exactly what would be expected if they were moving from Earth toward the Galactic Garden.

Admiral Chase suspected that the echoes were Stella and her twelve cohorts from Stormer's paramilitary army. The calculations made by his ship's computers confirmed that the intensity of the echoes was consistent with the presence of a much larger vehicle, which he believed to be the missing Supply Ship 2.

He ordered his officers to change course immediately and initiate a pursuit of the source of the echoes. Distressingly, at the speed they were moving, it would take hundreds of years to execute the turn. That meant a significant delay in his effort to overtake Stella, even at the faster speed the Earth command ship could travel. He feared the danger and destruction Stella and her gang could do in the relatively brief time, enabled by her lead over him. Because of that, Admiral Chase sent a warning message to the remainder of his fleet patrolling the Galactic Garden. He also sent similar messages to the Union supply ships in the area and to Aril. He hoped that someone would receive the warning in time to intercept Stella before she did more damage. Admiral Chase had heard the news that a large corporate fleet had left Earth thousands of years earlier to establish a colony on a planet in the Galactic Garden. He suspected that this was Stella's next destination.

CHAPTER 24
— Century 1080 —

Benjamin and Ilsa arrived at Sparil several weeks before the first Galactic Exploration Conference was to begin. After the splendor of Happiness, the sleekness and functionality of Sparil held little appeal to them. The order and regimentation that underlay all activities at the spaceport unnerved them and forced them into a formality that made them edgy and argumentative.

Then Ilsa learned that she was pregnant, and such irritations were quickly forgotten. She'd been carrying the child when they arrived on Sparil, which meant the baby had been conceived on Happiness. Remarkably, to the best knowledge of the physicians on Sparil, the fetus hadn't been harmed by the thousands of years Ilsa had been frozen while traveling from Happiness. Still, Benjamin and Ilsa worried obsessively about the normalcy of the pregnancy, and after discussing it for a long time, they decided it was best if they went to Aril where the medical facilities and physicians were far superior. Rather than risk traveling in their space capsules, they booked passage on one of the shuttles that regularly transported people and supplies between the two planets. The next shuttle wouldn't leave for several weeks, so there was plenty of time for them to relax at the spaceport and attend the Galactic Exploration Conference.

Ilsa and Benjamin were among the earliest to arrive for the conference. They spent much of their days in the multi-purpose room, a large expanse that served as reception area, cafeteria, lounge and entertainment center. They watched with intrigue and amusement as, over the course of several days, the room filled with arriving travelers—members of the original Union fleet, new recruits from Aril and Stormer's army, and even a few representatives from Admiral Chase's fleet. The commotion in the room was soon overwhelming and the roar of the multitudinous conversations made it necessary for Benjamin and Ilsa to shout to hear each other. Eventually, they retreated to an outlying dome covering a park with trees, gardens, fountains, and benches. They weren't alone. Others had the same idea, but it was still better that the din and hubbub of the multi-purpose room.

Soon the day arrived when the meeting was to start. The multi-purpose room had been arranged with several hundred chairs, all facing a massive 3-D display monitor that dwarfed the speakers podium set off to one side.

The meeting began with an animated travelogue of Aril. The lights dimmed and the planet appeared on the screen, gradually coming to life in a reconstructed reality that left the audience spellbound. They were swept away by the rapidly changing images showing Aril's impeccably beautiful landscape from a height of several hundred meters, as though from a balloon drifting smoothly and silently above the planet's surface. Music played in the background, a perfectly pitched melody that sounded as if it were emanating from a thousand string instruments set into the walls of the auditorium. Even the galactic explorers, who had experienced the exhilarating thrills of landing on alien planets, were rendered speechless by the majesty of the music and imagery that kicked off the Conference.

After sitting through the initial presentations by galactic explorers, describing the results of their expeditions in varying degrees of detail and entertainment, Ilsa grew tired and retreated to the park. Benjamin endured the morning sessions and then ate a bland, banquet lunch while attempting to make friendly conversation with the other explorers he was seated with. Even after so many years, he still felt like an outcast among them, though they treated him with great respect because of his achievements in helping save Aril from invasion.

The afternoon was more of the same. It was remarkable that a conference, featuring presentations on the first explorations of planets bearing alien life forms, could actually grow tiresome. The dreariness could be attributed to the quality of the presentations. None of the explorers had experience or training in public speaking, and holding the audience's attention, even while describing truly wondrous discoveries proved beyond their abilities.

Dinner entailed another banquet meal. Fortunately, Ilsa rejoined the meeting and sat with Benjamin, but the dinner and conversation were still dull and tedious. They were both anxious to leave, but this wasn't to be a short affair because the organizers had invited an after-dinner keynote speaker.

The audience applauded perfunctorily as the speaker was introduced—an historian, who had come to Aril from Earth and specialized in studying the history and evolution of civilizations and planets over time spans of tens of thousands of years. This piqued Benjamin's interest. It made him think of his father and how he'd devoted his life to examining the similarities and differences among diverse cultures on Earth. The title of the talk, "The Fate of Happiness", intrigued Benjamin.

The speaker was introduced as Professor Druix. He was a tall, lean, young man, with cadaverous features and a pale complexion. He would have seemed ghostlike except for the dark intensity of his eyes and the liveliness of his movements. His voice was strong, mellow, and deeper than his youthful appearance suggested.

"I'm here tonight to tell you a sad story with an ambiguous ending," he began. "It's about a planet called Happiness, created by the people of a nearby planet called Prosperity. Prosperity was founded by a powerful corporate entity from Earth, which executed a plan for colonizing a planet in the Galactic Garden on a scale unprecedented in human history. Thousands of spaceships were launched carrying all the people and materials necessary to create a fabulous new home with all the best Earth had to offer."

Professor Druix activated the video monitor with barely perceptible motions of his hands. The screen showed a planet from afar and then zoomed closer, revealing the towers and spires of a magnificent city.

"The organization of Prosperity was based on that found in living cells, with a nucleus surrounded by a protective and nurturing medium called cytoplasm. It was a successful design that was efficient and functional. The population thrived for thousands of years until an unexpected cosmic event caused an upheaval on the planet. The nearby planet Happiness, which had been a vacation spot for Prosperity's people, was struck by an asteroid. It was no surprise. The exact date and time had been predicted a hundred years in advance and the unfortunate planet was completely evacuated before the event. Still, no one could have foreseen the effects the collision would have on the collective psyche of the people on Prosperity, safely watching from ten million kilometers away.

"Happiness was only a faint point of light in the heavens above them, but telescopes all over the globe observed the collision with great magnification and clarity. At the moment of impact, they saw a diffuse puff of glowing dust rise slowly into the previously empty space about the planet. It took a full minute for the dust to rise to its maximum extent, fully half the planet's radius. It appeared to be a slow ascent, but was in fact incredibly fast and cataclysmic when the volume of space being filled was taken into account. For several days thereafter, those on Prosperity watched as the dust cloud diffused around the planet's circumference. Eventually, Happiness was shrouded by a hazy aura, that lasted for many decades.

"Perhaps the people of Prosperity should have predicted the effects the collision would have on their planet. The glory days of Happiness were legendary, and for decades after, people looked back fondly on the time when shiploads of vacationers took the four-week space trek to the spectacular theme park.

"Why did the collision on Happiness have such profound effects on the lives of the people and the fate of their planet? Had they been shocked into realizing their own fragility in the universe? Had the doom of Happiness reminded them of their own mortality? Or had there been an invisible bond between the two planets that had been suddenly and catastrophically severed?

"Whatever it was, a great feeling of gloom overcame the population. As if overnight, the enduring work ethic that had sustained the planet for many millennia suddenly was no longer sufficient to keep the machinery of life going. Prosperity had lost its will to live and strength to survive.

"Over the next thousand years, one devastating event after another weakened the backbone of the planet. The global economy collapsed, producing unprecedented conflict and strife. The planet's vast infrastructure failed. Buildings and bridges collapsed, water supplies were compromised, and electrical power systems became erratic and undependable. Communication was disrupted and mass transportation halted. Finally, and most devastating of all, food supplies were cut off. Crops wouldn't grow, food processing plants were shut down, and decades of starvation thinned the population.

"Why had the spirit of Prosperity been so broken by the impact of the asteroid on Happiness? Had it just been coincidental that the downfall of Prosperity followed the destruction of Happiness? Had the people of Prosperity always been subconsciously strengthened by the awareness that Happiness was there above them, twinkling faithfully in the night sky? Or had the planet been doomed from the beginning?

"No one will ever know for sure, but the best guess is that invisible linkages connected the destiny of the two planets. The asteroid had struck one, but the devastation had spread to the other, as surely as a plague might spread from one nation to another.

"How does a planet die? At what point does one know that its civilization is on a downward spiral from which there is no hope of recovery? Despair leads to greater despair, handicapping the people from taking the very steps needed to arrest the momentum of descent. First to go are the arts and sciences that typically thrive when a culture is in its prime. Not that Prosperity had ever excelled in the arts, as very early all those with artistic talents moved to Happiness, where there were many more opportunities for them to exhibit and exercise their talents. Science was limited to only that needed for practical applications. Purely curiosity-driven science was discouraged by the citizens of Prosperity, who expected immediate and unambiguous return on their investments.

"Also contributing to the global funk that encompassed

the planet was the proliferation of boredom. Prosperity's population had never learned how to be content doing nothing. So when businesses failed and people found themselves idle, they became depressed. Depression led to stagnation, which led to greater idleness.

"A social scientist might have been able to predict the chain of events that imposed collective gloom on Prosperity after the asteroid impact. However, no one could ever have predicted that this global psychological disease would eventually couple into the planet's food supply. How could the despondency of the population inhibit the growth of crops?"

An eerie stillness filled the room following Druix's remarks. He peered out at the audience almost as if he expected a hand to go up—a student who had done the homework and could answer the teacher's questions.

He began again. "Unfortunately, it takes 5,500 years for information from Happiness to reach Aril. We don't yet know for sure what has transpired in the last five millennia. We can only speculate."

Druix changed the image on the screen behind him. It now showed a jagged line running horizontally across the screen. It was clearly some sort of chart or graph, but there were no labels by which one could tell what the data were.

"There is more, however—something I haven't told you about. Arilian radio telescopes have acquired data during the past few thousand years that add to the mystery of Prosperity and Happiness. The data shown here are measurements of radio transmissions from the direction of the two planets. It's difficult to see in the graph, but mathematical analysis reveals that the intensity of the transmissions decreases drastically on a regular basis. This is not unusual. Radio signals from a planetary source disappear when the object is eclipsed by its sun. We know the orbits of Happiness and Prosperity very accurately. We can calculate when the eclipses should occur and compare those predictions with the observations. We know Prosperity had many radio transmitters and probably still does. However, we didn't expect the intensity of the radio signals to fall off when Happiness was eclipsed by the sun it shares with Prosperity. We assumed that Happiness was completely evacuated prior to the asteroid collision and that no one was left on the planet. This is unambiguous evidence for a source of radio signals on Happiness. The nature of the transmissions is unlike any natural sources, like lightning, for example. The source is clearly artificial and the conclusion is undeniable. There was life on Happiness when the signals originated. Perhaps there is still life on Happiness. Perhaps, the survival of civilization on Happiness gives hope for Prosperity as well, except..."

And here Druix paused again. The young man had a talent for adding drama to his words solely by the subtle intonations in his powerful voice. The audience waited for the exception that prevented Happiness and Prosperity from regaining their previous grandeur.

"Arilian astronomers have analyzed the radio signals received during those times when Prosperity is eclipsed. After subtraction of the natural signals from the star eclipsing the planet, the residual signal represents only those transmissions coming from Happiness. After studying these carefully for many years, Arilian scientists have concluded that the transmissions are of alien origin. They are being generated by alien intelligent life forms. There can be no doubt about this."

These words produced a profound silence in the room as each attendee struggled to assimilate the information. Most of the attendees were galactic explorers. They'd grown accustomed to encountering all manner of life forms on the planets they visited. It was difficult to produce wonderment in them, yet Druix had made the one announcement still able to stun them all.

"Ladies and gentlemen," Druix concluded. "It is time to return to Happiness. What we find there may transform us far more than its creators on Prosperity ever imagined."

Druix waved his hand and the screen went momentarily dark until the 3-D image of Aril reappeared. The audience burst into applause and Druix bowed his head in thanks before stepping down from the podium.

The keynote address complete, the attendees began to exit the room. Some remained and wove their way toward Druix, who was already shaking hands and conversing with a group of admiring explorers. One strode confidently up to him with arms outstretched. He smiled and they embraced. It was a woman, somewhat older than Druix. She kissed him on both cheeks and, as she drew away, her face turned toward Benjamin. Looking directly at her, Benjamin sensed a hint of recognition in her expression. He searched his memory wondering where he might have seen her before. She was quite beautiful in a darkly exotic way. He was sure he'd have remembered her, had he met her in the past. The woman became agitated at Benjamin's return glance. She withdrew from Druix and disappeared into the crowd. Ilsa tugged Benjamin's arm, and they followed the rest of the crowd out of the room.

———

"He looked right at me and didn't recognize me," Xyla said to Druix later, as they walked through a long corridor, enclosed by the same crystalline structure from which the domes of Sparil were made. The sun had set many hours ago. The crystal had become transparent, allowing the glittering light from thousands of stars to illuminate their path. The corridor led to an outbuilding of the spaceport used primarily for storage, intentionally located several kilometers away, so the pathway could be used by those desiring long walks.

"That's a good thing, I suppose," replied Druix.

"Yes," said Xyla wistfully. "I didn't really expect he'd remember Bria."

"You know it has nothing to do with memory, Mom. How could he possibly connect you with the person he knew on Aurora?"

"It doesn't matter anyway. Benjamin has someone else now. It would just create unnecessary disruption in his life. Better to leave things as they are."

Druix put his arm around his mother. "You're an amazingly strong woman. He'll never know what he missed out on."

Xyla smiled, but said nothing.

"Where will you go from here?" asked Druix.

"I don't know. I haven't given it much thought."

"Can I make a suggestion?"

"Of course."

"Come to Happiness with me."

Xyla stopped and turned to look at her son. "You're going to Happiness?"

"Yes. I've been working closely with Arilian scientists all along. As soon as they speculated that the radio signals may be coming from an alien intelligence, I offered to go there. If I suggest you go with me, they'll agree."

"I'd like to go to Happiness," said Xyla. "It intrigues me."

"You sound hesitant. Don't you want to come?"

Xyla shook her head. "I'm not sure."

Druix grasped his mother's shoulders. He could have been the parent and she the disobedient child. Druix had gained several years of age on his mother. During the thousands of years that had passed since they parted, he'd spent more time unfrozen, continuing with his research and teaching history courses on Aril.

"I know why you're reluctant to go. You think Benjamin will go there. You don't want it to seem as though you're following him."

Xyla shrugged this off and resumed walking.

"There are two reasons why you shouldn't let that deter you. Even if Benjamin goes to Happiness, the odds that he'll get there at the same time we do are very small. We'd take a different route to the planet. The difference in travel time could be decades—or centuries."

"True," said Xyla. "So what's the second reason?"

"Benjamin may not go there at all."

"Of course, he will," said Xyla quietly. "Alien intelligence fascinated him. He never stopped talking about it."

"Things have changed," said Druix, becoming the parent again. "There's something you don't know. Benjamin's wife is

157

pregnant. They're both going to Aril where she'll have the baby."

Xyla didn't seem to register any surprise at this. It was as if she'd already known. She smiled. It was a smile of resignation. "So you'll have a half-sibling, Druix. How do you feel about that?"

Druix hesitated, clearly considering how best to answer his mother's question. Finally, he said, "To be honest, I like the idea of having a relative. I don't have many, and the galaxy is huge. In a funny way, I feel less alone."

Xyla nodded. "I'm sorry. I often think I should have never taken you from Aurora."

"Don't be sorry," said Druix. "You've given me a life unimaginable for someone who grew up on Aurora. Maybe I would've been happy there, but only because I wouldn't have known any other life. You've given me greater awareness and knowledge, and even though it may not be complete I don't regret it at all. To have knowledge without regrets is to be truly blessed."

"You shouldn't give up," said Xyla, knowing what he meant by not having a complete life. "You may still meet someone."

Druix laughed. "I was going to tell you the same thing."

"Right," said Xyla, and she threw up her arms in surrender.

"I'm excited about going to Happiness. I have a feeling history will be made there. Not often are historians able to witness history in the making. I want to be there."

It was difficult for Xyla to conceal her delight that she'd be able to accompany Druix. She clung to that thought, temporarily warding off the depression she knew would descend upon her when she was alone and imagining Benjamin on Aril with his wife raising their child. Regardless of what they found on Happiness, she couldn't help but envy the woman who was sharing a life with Benjamin.

CHAPTER 25

— Century 1080 —

Something had changed in Benjamin since the evening of the banquet. Ilsa suspected it was the news that alien intelligence had at long last been found, which must have given vent to long dormant emotions in Benjamin that had subconsciously driven him to leave Earth more than 100,000 years earlier. With the discovery, Benjamin was probably anxious to go to Happiness and investigate. He was undoubtedly torn between this excitement and his desire to stay with Ilsa on Aril and raise their child. Would he ever explore the galaxy again after becoming a father? It was no surprise to Ilsa that Benjamin was distant and detached.

Ilsa had to admit that she herself was captivated by the banquet presentation. The young professor who gave the talk was intriguing and clever. He'd artfully drawn the audience into the plight of two planets thousands of light-years away.

After the conference, amidst the pomp and fanfare typical of most Arilian festivities, Benjamin was invited to attend a meeting of the Committee on Galactic Exploration, which was charged with developing a strategy for continued exploratory activities. Not surprisingly, the meeting was dominated by the possible existence of alien intelligence on Happiness. Benjamin was surprised to learn, however, that the Committee was also interested in Prosperity and what was happening there. The Arilians received a message from Earth that a band of invaders had arrived in galactic explorer space capsules, terrorized a wild game reserve, and abducted the warden of the park. The gang was accompanied by a Union supply ship, believed to be the hijacked Supply Ship 3. Before departing Earth, the invaders had stolen dozens of satellites out of orbit for reasons no one could really fathom, other than the thrill of shear mischief. Information received, subsequent to their departure from Earth, suggested the band was now on route to plunder Prosperity, an attack that would certainly add to the woes of the doomed planet. If the situation wasn't bad enough, now the population of Prosperity faced pillaging by space pirates.

Ilsa sat with Benjamin trying to tease from him everything that had transpired at the committee meeting, a subject Benjamin seemed reticent to discuss.

"So what strategy did the committee decide on?" she asked.

Benjamin took a sip of a beverage from a sleek pewter canister. It was a juice the Arilians had created, reminiscent of wine, but with more alcohol. Benjamin seldom drank it, which was a sure indication to Ilsa that something was amiss.

"The Committee decided nothing. Everything was tabled until more information is available. This is typical. Arilians, to a fault, refrain from action until all the options have been worked out and considered ad nauseum."

Ilsa waited several moments, then asked, "What are the options?"

Benjamin sighed. Clearly he didn't want to discuss this with Ilsa—another sign of the changing fabric of their relationship since the banquet. Ilsa couldn't repress the sinking feeling of dread deep within her.

"Do nothing. That's always an option, especially considering that it'd take thousands of years to send help to Prosperity. By that time, the damage would be done."

"As deliberate as the Arilians are, I'd be surprised if they did nothing," Ilsa said. "After all, their planet was rescued from space marauders; they must empathize with the plight of another planet in a similar situation."

"They've already relayed the message to Admiral Chase. He's on his way to Earth with a large part of his fleet chasing down these bandits. He probably doesn't know they've left Earth already and are following the corporate fleet to the Galactic Garden."

"It's crazy," Ilsa said. "How can there be any law enforcement in the galaxy, when it takes so long to find out that a crime has even been committed?"

"Right. The Arilians recognize this. The strategy is not to

stop the crime or catch the criminals, but to mitigate the damage done after the fact. They have to anticipate the impact to a society decades or centuries later. The objective is to send people with the right training and experience to address the potential problems."

"After so much time, there may be no lasting effects on a society or civilization."

"Exactly. And that may be the case in this situation. After all, we're only talking about a dozen men in space capsules with limited capabilities."

"Don't forget the supply ship," Ilsa added.

"True. Which is why the Arilians are treading carefully. Also, they're worried about the galactic explorers. After the keynote address, many of them are probably thinking Happiness will be their next destination."

"Without a doubt," said Ilsa, wondering whether Benjamin was one of those.

"The Arilians are concerned that a flock of explorers descending on Happiness might not set well with the aliens. They'd like to approach the planet more diplomatically—whatever that means to an alien civilization."

Ilsa had the distinct impression Benjamin's exposition was leading somewhere. She attempted to change the direction of the dialog, fearing where it might lead. "How can they be so sure the signals they're detecting are from aliens?"

"That question came up at the meeting today. It has to do with the coherence of the radio transmissions. Mathematical calculations indicate that the variations in intensity are not random. Natural sources of radio emissions have certain recognizable characteristics. The fluctuations in these signals are neither natural nor random. They're distinct from any previously observed."

Benjamin took another sip of his beverage. He seemed ready to say more, but held back.

"So what did the Arilians decide to do?" Ilsa's voice was husky, as though the words were forced. She didn't want to hear the answer.

"Professor Druix has volunteered to go to Happiness with just one or two others. Another group will go to Prosperity to meet up with Admiral Chase's fleet. They'll deal with Stella and her pirate gang, or whatever aftermath occurred in the wake of their attack."

Ilsa was suddenly tired of skirting the issue. She sat back in her chair and fixed him with an accusatory stare. "They want you to go. Right?"

In the brief instant that followed her words, Ilsa knew the answer.

"I'm not going," said Benjamin.

"But they want you to go. Right?" she said again. And before he could answer, she added, "You should go."

If this were chess, Ilsa could have predicted the next several moves and the outcome of the game. She would lose. Nevertheless, they finished their game.

"I won't go," said Benjamin again. "I'm going to Aril with you."

"You should go," Ilsa repeated. "They need you to be in the group that first contacts the aliens. It has to be you."

"They don't need me." Benjamin finished off the last of the liquid in his canister. "Professor Druix is going. He's worked most closely with the Arilians analyzing the data. His mother is going, too. She's been trained as a galactic explorer. They'll find someone else to go with them."

Ilsa rose from her chair and bent over to hug Benjamin. "Listen to me, Benjamin. I know how much you want to do this. Encountering intelligent aliens is something you've dreamt about since you left Earth. This is an opportunity you can't pass up."

"It's not all I dream about," Benjamin said, smiling. Ilsa forced herself to smile back.

"I'll go to Aril alone and have our child. As soon as he or she is old enough, we'll leave and meet up with you on your father's supply ship. He and Krystal will love to see the child."

Benjamin shook his head. He knew it wasn't good for humans to undergo the freezing process until they're past puberty.

The risk of disturbing the development of the reproductive organs was too great. "I'm not going to miss the first thirteen years of my child's life."

"It's not that risky. I'll wait ten years and then we'll leave. Remember, this fetus has already been frozen and is doing fine." Ilsa rubbed her hand over her stomach. "Let's make a rendezvous plan—just like the one we bought at the IGET conference in DC. In case anything goes wrong, we'll have multiple meeting places. It'll be fine."

Benjamin stood and put his arms around her. "I love you," he said. "I can't believe you'd make this sacrifice for me."

"It's for us," Ilsa replied. "You, me, and the baby. As soon as I heard about the aliens, I knew it had to be this way."

She took Benjamin's hand and led him back to their room where they made love. Afterward, in the silent darkness, when she knew Benjamin was asleep, Ilsa wept.

––––––––––

"What?!" Xyla shouted, after Druix explained what happened at the committee meeting.

"I couldn't help it," Druix explained. "They were discussing who should go with us to Happiness. I had no idea they'd want Benjamin."

"Of course, they'd want him," Xyla cried. "He's a hero. What were you thinking?"

"I was thinking exactly what I told you—that Benjamin won't go because his wife is pregnant."

"But he's going. Right?"

"That's what I understand," answered Druix quietly.

"I'm not going," said Xyla.

Druix shrugged. "Suit yourself, but if you drop out now, it will cause suspicion. I don't think you want to be subject to that much scrutiny."

Xyla sighed and covered her face with her hands. "How is this happening?"

"Fate," said Druix. "Remember what that is?"

"Yes. A mythical being. I also remember that I'm still in love with one half of a constellation in the Arilian sky, but the other half is not me."

Druix laughed. "It should be, Mom. Let's just go to Happiness and meet the aliens."

———————

Xyla's heart was pounding as she entered the pre-mission briefing room. She was upset with herself. She'd been born and raised on a frozen planet, had cleaned fish in a frigid Malanite ice house, successfully escaped the planet with her son on space capsules buried in the ice for thousands of years, lived a decade on Earth as the wife of a museum curator, and crossed the galaxy to a new world where she learned to be a galactic explorer. Why then did she feel so weak and helpless in the presence of a man she'd only known for a few weeks? Sure he was the father of her child and they had shared a close connection during Benjamin's brief visit to Aurora, but how could that account for her inexplicably dysfunctional behavior when he was nearby?

Benjamin and Druix were already seated at a large table when she walked in. She looked down and mumbled an apology as she took a seat next to Druix. A goup of Arilians sat at the table facing the three travelers. Druix spoke to them in quiet conversation. Not surprisingly, he knew them all, being fellow scholars. For Benjamin and Xyla's sake, they introduced themselves in turn as Arilian experts in various aspects of Happiness. Each spoke in succession about the results of their studies.

One, an historian, focused on Happiness during its construction and subsequent popularity as a vacation spot for Prosperity. The information he provided was confirmed by Benjamin, who'd been there with Ilsa during the planet's glory days, prior to its evacuation. He showed detailed maps of all the attractions of the amusement park, along with photographs. In some cases, these were three-dimensional holographic images, of the incredibly lifelike renditions of monuments and landmarks, representing the stages of human civilization on Earth and other planets. If there was a general theme to the theme park, it was a celebration of homo sapiens and everything the species had achieved during its brief existence on cosmic time scales. While Happiness also exposed some of the darkest and most tragic eras, they were depicted in a way to illustrate the challenges that had been overcome in humanity's remarkable quest forward. The success of humankind as a lasting force on Earth, and now in the galaxy, was undeniable.

Another expert had studied the effect of the asteroid impact on Happiness. Because there was little real data, either from remote observations or communication with the planet, these conclusions were more speculative. For several decades after the impact, amateur astronomers on Prosperity continued to observe Happiness from afar, but given the limited capabilities of the instruments they used, all they could conclude was that the physical state of the planet had been indelibly altered by the catastrophe. A thick layer of dust, blasted into the atmosphere after the impact, completely obscured the planet's surface. Depending on the thickness of the layer and the nature of the particulates comprising it, the effect would be either a drastic cooling or heating of the planet's surface. Arilian astronomers also observed the planet, but from that distance, and all they saw was the light from the star about which both Happiness and Prosperity orbited. The miniscule variation of that light caused by the periodic eclipses of the two planets was the only information gained. Speculations about what happened after the asteroid impact were model calculations based on measurements of the size of the asteroid, its trajectory, and its probable impact point on the planet. Benjamin, Druix, and Xyla watched computer-simulated images of the impact, the explosive plume of debris that rose into the planet's atmosphere, and the spreading of the resulting cloud to encompass the entire globe. The settling of that dust took hundreds of years. Because the impact occurred more than ten thousand years earlier, the Arilians were fairly confident that Happiness was no longer concealed by atmospheric dust, especially accounting for the 5,500 years it took for light from the planet to reach Aril.

Unfortunately, even the amateur astronomers on Prosperity had lost interest in their neighboring planet by then, and no new observations were available.

The next Arilian to speak was a biologist. She expressed the opinion that survival of any humans on Happiness after the impact was extremely unlikely. The historical records from Prosperity were unclear about whether all humans on the planet had been evacuated, but if any had chosen to stay for some reason, the atmospheric conditions after the event would be deadly even if they survived the explosive impact itself. Other life forms on the planet—and there was known to be a rich biosphere introduced by the creators of the theme park—could have survived. It was possible the planet recovered and the atmosphere returned to its well oxygenated state. Life and breathable air on Happiness was still within the realm of possibility. Nevertheless, she warned the travelers of all the precautions they'd have to take upon landing on the surface. All three nodded their understanding. That was perhaps the most thorough aspect of the training needed to become galactic explorers.

Another biologist attempted to prepare them for what to expect in terms of the appearance of the aliens. An elderly Arilian, he was methodical and deliberate in his presentation, gesturing with professorial authority.

"Symmetry is a common feature of most life forms," he began. "I'm fairly certain you won't encounter alien life with two eyes on one side of their bodies and one on another. The requirement of mobility limits the nature and form of organisms, alien or otherwise. Sea creatures will undoubtedly be aerodynamic and sleek. Land animals will have legs or similar appendages that will allow them to walk, climb, turn, and stop. Two-legged and four-legged beasts have thrived on Earth, so we expect they'll do well on other planets. And two legs are better than four if the organism is going to develop intelligence because the two appendages thus freed up mandate increased brain capacity.

"Sensory organs are important. It's tempting to think that humans have a full set, but there's no reason aliens might not have senses that allow them to see ultraviolet light, detect radio waves, or respond to other disturbances in the ether caused by objects and events that might affect their ability to survive. Communication must be universally important because it allows organisms to interact, establish relationships, warn each other of dangers, and learn. Means of communication would have to be strongly tied to the being's sensory organs. It doesn't help an animal to have vocal cords if it doesn't also have ears to detect the vibrations in the air created by others.

"Let's consider the placement of the brain, which any advanced life form is likely to have. Evolutionarily advanced animals on Earth have centralized brains. Though we might imagine creatures with brain functions distributed throughout the body, that approach has certainly not gained traction on Earth. And does the brain have to be encased within a skull-like enclosure? Probably. Brains are extremely important. An organism wouldn't last long if the brain could be easily damaged or destroyed. Does the brain have to be far from the ground and near the front of the organism as it moves? I suppose not, but just about every animal on Earth I can think of is constructed that way.

"How about digestion, respiration, circulation? Millions of years of evolution on Earth have produced a vast array of diverse organs to perform these functions, but the same basic principles apply. One might suppose that some chance mutation long ago started life on this path and evolutionary processes have not permitted organisms to stray from these early functional mechanisms. Perhaps some other approach, started long ago, might have produced an entirely different method for distributing nourishment and life-giving atoms and molecules to the cells that make up the body, but I don't think so. The process of evolution is a great experiment, and my guess is that many different approaches were tried through the eons. That we now have this particular physiology is living confirmation that the solution we represent worked on Earth better than all the others. Why should we expect the evolutionary process on another planet to result in anything different?

"The size of aliens shouldn't surprise us. The laws of physics and biology dictate the stature of an organism able to achieve reasonable mobility under the influence of gravity. Anomalously large animals haven't fared well on Earth, though whales and elephants have achieved admirable intelligence, perhaps owing to the mass of brain tissue they carry around. Nevertheless, a large alien will have to nourish its immense volume and that requires a good amount of effort, energy, and time, which otherwise could be devoted to more intellectual enterprises. I expect that alien life forms capable of advanced thought won't be towering over us, nor will they be tiny, top-heavy creatures sporting huge crania on delicate necks.

"Skin type and color is interesting to contemplate. When one considers the tremendous variety in Earth's animal kingdom, we should really have no expectations about what outer covering might protect alien beings from their environment. Clearly though, skin type and color are probably the aspect of animal physiology that is most dependent on external elements. Witness the chameleon, which actually changes appearance in response to its surroundings. So, even though the external appearance of our alien friends may be subject to an infinite range of possibilities, given knowledge of the aliens' environment, we may be able to narrow down the options substantially.

"Finally, there is no doubt that no matter how bizarre the aliens you encounter may be, they will certainly have their own mechanism for reproduction. In the animal kingdom there are two main types of reproduction. If we include the plant kingdom, then many more means of reproduction are possible. Our aliens may drop like fruit from trees, fully formed and ready to go about their alien business. Or they may sprout from seeds in the ground, reaching a certain age after which they grow legs and set off on their way across the fields of Happiness. Perhaps the alien civilization has advanced to the point that they reproduce themselves artificially by cloning their DNA, choosing the complexity of that process to the complexity of the interactions inherent in human reproduction and its many associated nuances. In any case, we shouldn't have any expectations, or be surprised by, the manner in which aliens might procreate their species. Anything is possible."

The last two experts talked about the evidence that had been compiled leading to the suspicion there was alien life on Happiness. They reviewed the radio telescope data, explaining again how the time variations of the received transmissions could only be interpreted as being from a source on Happiness. They described the scientific basis behind their conclusion that the transmissions could not be of natural origin. The complexities of phase and amplitude modulation of radio signals, as a means to encode and transmit information, baffled all three of the explorers, but it gave them confidence in the scientists' assertions. They were shown a graph that illustrated the difference in the frequency distribution of radio noise from all possible natural sources, compared to those being received from Happiness. It was extremely convincing, even if the science and mathematics behind the data were largely incomprehensible.

"But how do we know those transmissions are coming from aliens?" Benjamin asked. "Isn't it more likely that some humans survived the asteroid impact and are now trying to communicate with us?"

"That's possible," answered one of the Arilians, "but if that was the case, they'd most likely be sending signals to Prosperity, which is much closer. In the messages we've received from Prosperity, there is no mention of radio signals from Happiness. We sent them a message a few thousand years ago asking them specifically about whether they've detected radio transmissions from the planet, but it's too soon to expect a reply from them." The man shrugged. "Such is the problem with interstellar communication."

"Have you tried to translate the signals you're getting from Happiness?" asked Benjamin.

"Of course," answered the scientist. "But we've had no luck with that. The biggest problem is that the signals we're receiving don't appear to be coming from a single source. If they were, we might be able to decode it through the repetition of certain patterns. The signals we're hearing are more like a jumble of superposed transmissions from many sources at many different frequencies. Taken together, it's similar to noise in a room filled with people where everyone is talking. That's the nature of the signals we're hearing."

"In fact," added the other Arilian scientist, "We believe it's possible these aliens communicate with each other via radio waves, and what we're receiving are the signals escaping into space. We're hearing the roar of the crowd, so to speak."

"It's also possible," said the biologist, "that the radio wave transmissions among our alien friends on Happiness are not being generated artificially."

"What do you mean?" asked Benjamin.

"I mean these aliens might actually have physiological organs that allow them to transmit and receive radio signals without needing external electronic devices."

"So these aliens might have antennas on their heads?"

The biologist smiled. "That's the classic image of aliens, but it certainly isn't essential for them to have external antennae. Even our bodies are transmitting electromagnetic signals continuously—without antennae. Remember, the brain and nervous system function using electrical pathways built into our physiology. With sensitive enough instruments, these electrical signals can be detected. It's the basis of modern medicine—or at least modern Arilian medicine. When you left Earth in the 22nd Century, it hadn't been perfected yet."

"In case this hypothesis is true," said one of the scientists, nodding respectfully toward the biologist, "We'll give you all radio devices to help you communicate with the aliens. They'll detect whatever transmissions the aliens are emitting and turn them into auditory signals you'll be able to hear. The antennas and filters in these devices will allow you to focus on one particular individual so the audio rendition is not muddled by multiple signals. You'll still have to learn their language because the audio equivalent of their words will be completely unintelligible to you. Hopefully, in time you'll build up a vocabulary by which to communicate with them."

"Will we be able to speak to them?" asked Xyla.

"Yes. The devices we'll give you are very clever. Once you've associated a word with a specific radio transmission, then you'll be able to speak the word into the device and it will transmit the matching radio signal back to the aliens."

"This is all assuming they don't just kill us as soon as we show up," said Druix.

"Yes, there's that. But we can't help you with that," said the biologist. "You should use all possible care in your approach."

Xyla asked, "Is it just coincidence that these aliens appeared after the asteroid impact?"

The Arilians exchanged glances. Then one of them said, "That's an excellent question. The impact and the time we started receiving the radio signal are only about a thousand years apart. On galactic time scales, the two events are nearly simultaneous. It's very possible they're connected. That's why we feel your mission is extremely important." The man paused and looked at his companions for encouragement before continuing. "Frankly, we can't really say how many more asteroids are out there heading toward other planets. This may not be a lone incident. We need answers."

Xyla looked at Druix, who smiled back at her. "It beats cleaning fish on Aurora," he said.

When the briefing ended, Druix approached the Arilian scholars to engage them in further discussions. Xyla paused, wondering whether to join them. She decided not to, and turned toward the door. She hadn't taken two steps before she heard Benjamin's voice behind her.

"Excuse me."

Xyla stopped, but remained facing the doorway. Her heart was racing again and a debilitating lump trapped her voice.

Benjamin stepped around to face her, his right hand raised.

"I just wanted to introduce myself. I'm Benjamin Mizello."

Xyla hesitated a moment, then grasped his hand tentatively. Her eyes remained downward. "My name is Xyla," she said. Her own voice sounded far away. There was a pounding in her ears. She knew she was blushing, and she hated herself for it.

"I was interested to learn you've been to Prosperity," Benjamin said. With the last word, he released her hand.

Xyla only nodded.

"Perhaps before we leave for Happiness, we can chat. I'd like to find out more about it."

It suddenly occurred to Xyla that Benjamin in no way recognized her. With new found confidence, her eyes locked on his, and she said, "Sure. And perhaps you can tell me about Happiness. You were there with your wife. Right?"

Now it was Benjamin's turn to blush. "Yes," he stammered. He seemed to be searching for more to say. "It was an amazing place."

"I'm sure it was," agreed Xyla. And with that, she stepped around Benjamin and walked away.

They missed having that conversation about their respective experiences on Prosperity and Happiness. Both were too occupied with the preparations for their galactic voyages. When the day came for them to leave, Xyla and Benjamin only nodded to each other in silent greeting from across the small space of the boarding area. Ilsa was there as well, looking very pregnant and wearing a look of sad resignation. She hugged and kissed Benjamin before retreating into the crowd of others who came to see the party off. Druix placed his arm around Xyla's shoulder and squeezed her. She smiled weakly back at him. All three then entered their capsules. The next time they would see each other would be on Happiness. Xyla looked forward to the oblivion of the magnetocryogenic chamber, where she'd be temporarily free from the conflicting thoughts racing through her mind.

Chapter 26

— Century 1140 —

When Ilsa and her ten-year-old daughter Elsenia arrived at SS6, Arthur and Krystal had already received a full report from Aril about the outcome of the first Galactic Exploration Conference on Aril's spaceport Sparil. Though disappointed that Benjamin had not also come, they were overjoyed now to meet Elsenia.

It hadn't been easy to explain to little Elsenia why they had to leave Aril. Although different from the other children in outward appearance, the child was in all other ways just like any of her Arilian friends. She thrived in the Arilian schools, both socially and academically. When she was old enough to understand, Ilsa told her about her father, and prepared her for their eventual departure from the planet. Unfortunately, that wasn't enough to prevent Elsenia from feeling extreme distress and resentment over having to leave her home and blast off into a very uncertain future in space. She left Aril a very angry and bitter young lady, and when she arrived on Supply Ship 6, she had every intention of making sure the adults around her paid for this intrusion on her life.

Ilsa had often questioned the wisdom of taking Elsenia away from Aril. She even considered returning and trying again when the girl was older. Perhaps at another stage of her life, she'd be more excited about seeing her father for the first time. She explained to Elsenia that when Benjamin showed up, they'd return to Aril and she could resume her childhood there. But Elsenia was smart enough to know that there was no way her life could pick up where it left off after so many thousands of years. The suggestion just made her angrier. Ilsa was tempted to return as quickly as possible to their magnetocryogenic chambers to wait for Benjamin's arrival, but she felt it would be better if Elsenia were in a better mood first. Otherwise, Benjamin, upon his arrival, would be greeted by a hostile daughter and distraught mother. Arthur and Krystal agreed to help, but the shell into which the irate and antisocial Elsenia withdrew defied all attempts by Arthur and Krystal to penetrate it.

Elsenia was an avid reader and spent most of her time perusing the extensive digital library on the supply ship, mostly searching for news from Aril. Krystal sat with her at times, showing her how to navigate the database, execute search routines, and download the documents she was most interested in. Elsenia was more tolerant with Krystal because she made no attempt to draw her out and cheer her up. In fact, Krystal's natural cynicism and introverted tendencies appealed to Elsenia. Unfortunately, this did little to change her mood or improve her attitude.

Arthur gave her a few chores caring for the greenhouse gardens, which Elsenia did grudgingly. That was until one day, while the two of them were walking among the rows of plants, she uttered a cry and stooped suddenly to peer beneath one of the long tables that held the soil. She scooped something off the floor and held it protectively within the confines of her two palms.

"What is it?" asked Arthur.

"A frog," she answered, turning away from him.

"Can't be," said Arthur. "There are no animals on the ship."

Elsenia opened her palms so Arthur could see the object she held. It was a frog, unmoving.

"Impossible," declared Arthur, as if saying so would make the amphibian cease to exist.

"It may not be alive," said Elsenia.

"Bring it under the light," said Arthur, moving toward the end of the row.

Directly under one of the halogen lights that illuminated the greenhouse, Elsenia opened her palm again. The frog was dark green with pale yellow spots. It was no bigger than Arthur's thumb.

"Damn," muttered Arthur. "How could it possibly have survived for this long?"

"I'm not sure it did. It hasn't moved."

"Let's give it some water," said Arthur. "See if it revives."

He went to a cabinet and took out a ceramic dish he used to get seedlings started. From a nearby spigot, he drew a small amount of water. Elsenia carefully lowered the inert amphibian into the water and waited. In the next instant, the tiny frog jumped directly toward Elsenia and she caught it, shrieking with surprise and delight. "It's alive!" she cried, and burst into laughter. It was the first time Arthur had heard the girl laugh.

"I'll be darned," he said.

Arthur called Krystal and Ilsa and the four bustled about preparing a home for the frog—a large basin made from galvanized steel. They added a layer of dirt and embedded the dish of water into it, such that it was flush with the surface. Reluctantly, Elsenia released the frog into the confines of the basin.

"What can we give it to eat?" she asked.

"We have insects," Arthur proclaimed. And from another cabinet he extracted a jar of mealworms that were used to ensure the soil maintained the right balance of nutrients for the plants. He released some into the basin. The frog ignored them.

They covered the basin with a screen so the frog couldn't escape. Elsenia remained in the greenhouse watching her new friend. She wouldn't leave it alone. Ilsa had to bring her dinner. The three adults were surprised to see this new aspect of Elsenia's personality, which she had done such a good job of concealing. Over the next several days, the girl spent most of her time in the greenhouse. To fill the hours, she offered to help Arthur with his chores. Nurturing the plants came just as naturally to her as caring for the frog. She tended the young seedlings and they grew better than they had under Arthur's care. As she went about her activities, she continually looked for more frogs, but found none. She worried and fretted over the tiny animal she'd saved. She also, for the first time, took interest in the stars that swirled in circles outside the crystalline windows of the greenhouse. She sat at the bench that Arthur and Krystal had installed to watch the spectacle, with the basin next to her. She gazed for hours in thoughtful wonder. Her ten-year-old mind was trying to assimilate the scale of the universe, unable to comprehend where she fit between the diminutive amphibian from Earth and the cosmic infinity outside the supply ship.

After several months, the frog died. Elsenia cried, and Ilsa feared she'd retreat into the angry world she'd occupied since their departure from Aril. Happily, that didn't happen. Elsenia remained obsessively interested in living organisms of all kinds, and she devoted herself to the nurturing of the plants in the greenhouse. She was disappointed when Arthur announced that it was time they all returned to their magnetocryogenic chambers to wait out the next hundred-year interval, when it would be time again to perform routine maintenance on the supply ship. Eventually, however, she got used to the routine, and each century, upon being unfrozen, she rushed to the greenhouse to resume her duties. Each time, she conducted a thorough search around the tables that held the crops to see if another tiny refugee from the past appeared. She also spent an enormous amount of time perusing the ship's archives, studying all the knowledge available on biology—and there were many lifetimes worth of information on that topic.

CHAPTER 27
— Century 1153 —

When they first left Earth, the troops of Admiral Chase's fleet accepted the reality that they were leaving their homes forever. Each dealt with it in his or her own way, but for Stella it was easy. She was an insular being and the population of Earth was such that few places on the globe offered the kind of isolation she craved. Socially, she'd been an outcast from childhood, and her ostracism caused her to become bitter and resentful. Stella longed to be surrounded by the emptiness of space, the vacuum of nothingness, the absence of the attitudes, opinions, and scorn she'd been subjected to all her life. Stella was a freak of nature, or at least as nature was defined in the 57th Millennium. She was huge by Earth standards, a giant really. Even as a child her enormity was obvious. It was an abnormality that could not be remedied, finessed, masked, or ignored. It just had to be dealt with, and it wasn't long before Stella came to the realization that she'd be forever alone in that struggle.

Toro and his men learned very quickly to give Stella her space. They could tell when she'd had enough of their rowdy garrulousness. Inferior to Stella in many ways, the men dared not impose on her need for solitude. During their attack on Earth, they had a brief respite from her, but upon arriving at Prosperity, she proclaimed she'd go along with them to pillage the planet. They dreaded her presence because they'd learned that being around Stella had a way of ramping up the drama, suspense, danger, and unpredictability of any situation.

Stella was a dreamer, but not in the sense of a visionary who imagines astounding achievements and remarkable events. When she slept, she dreamt incessantly. Anyone who witnessed her asleep was terrorized by her convulsions and contortions. At first, Toro supposed this to be some type of post-traumatic stress disorder, but he soon learned that her dreams were self-induced by a pipe she smoked every night before going to bed. When he summoned the nerve to ask her about it, she explained her belief that dreaming was the mind's way to exercise neural pathways that otherwise would go unused and deteriorate. As a soldier, she knew she had to condition herself to sudden perils and unexpected danger. It was difficult to stage such surprises except in sleep, when the mind itself creates the extremes of stimuli that one wouldn't ordinarily experience. When awake, she was in a nearly continuous state of déjà vu. She always felt as though she had experienced situations before, because she probably had—while sleeping. Toro believed that Stella's technique worked because she had incredibly sharp reflexes and was seldom caught by surprise. All the neurons in her brain were so well exercised, her response to any stimulus was immediate and precise. Stella was as taut as a tightly coiled spring.

During their pursuit of the fleet from Earth, Stella had periodically monitored the transmissions among the thousands of vehicles comprising the expedition. What she heard excited her, for Theonius had been right. The fleet contained enormously valuable treasures. She and her men were intrigued on hearing of the successful colonization of Prosperity, as well as by the transmissions boasting of the thriving metropolises and wealthy societies covering the planet. Later, Stella heard the subsequent messages, telling of the hardships that befell the new world, after its sister planet Happiness was struck by an asteroid. The information Stella received about the downfall of the economy and drastic weakening of the social structure overjoyed her and her men. The vulnerability of the planet played perfectly into their plans.

Stella wanted to land on an island, of course. That was the only way she'd feel comfortable—knowing that a good quantity of water separated her from the prying eyes of Prosperity's populace. Never mind that every island on Prosperity's cytoplasmic ocean was used for some type of life-sustaining activity, particularly those requiring vast amounts of water. Thus, Toro and his men had to choose from among possible landing sites that were either fish farms, nuclear power plants, desalination facilities, or shipyards. They selected a shipyard, one specializing in the manufacture of boats designed with state-of-the-art propulsion technology. These were slender, subsurface vessels with hulls made of a flexible composite material embedded with thousands of actuators that allowed the ships to mimic the motion of fish in the sea. The occupants were housed in a control room suspended on gimbals protecting them from the dynamic, convoluted motions of the hull as it raced cleanly through the water. With their own nuclear power systems, these ships could traverse Prosperity's only ocean with uncontested speed. Their target was the continent of Nucleanis.

After overcoming the shipyard workers and setting them adrift on powerless barges, Toro and his men helped themselves to four of the fish-like speedboats. While Stella remained on the island, they plundered as many seaports on Nucleanis their speed and stealth allowed. Like vultures swooping down upon the carcasses of dying animals, Toro and his men terrorized the continent while stealing its most valuable treasures. The ease with which they committed their crimes, and the lack of resistance on the part of the people they stole from, surprised them. It was almost as if they enjoyed being robbed—as though being victims of crime confirmed their impotence and failure.

The wealth of Earth had become a serpent, winding and hissing its way through space-time. Those who tried to catch it and contain it could only do so for a short time, on cosmic scales. It always wriggled away and slithered into the undergrowth, feeding on its victims and growing larger and stronger. Once trapped by the corporate fleet, that had launched the expedition to establish Prosperity, the serpent went skyward in a long line of space vehicles stretched out over many light-years, writhing its way toward its new home. Prosperity was the perfect place for the serpent to hide, camouflaged amidst the affluence and extravagance of a self-absorbed, industrious society. Everyone on the planet owned a piece of the serpent, at least until Stella and her cohorts rescued it from its owners.

Stella's loud, cackling laugh could be heard across the island as shipload upon shipload of treasures arrived under the escort of Toro and his men. It was all stored in a warehouse on a dock, in piles crudely sorted according to the nature of the wealth. Gems and stones occupied one area, precious metals another, fine ceramics and glassware were thrown among the piles, along with works of art, haphazardly reclining along any available wall space, with statuary lining the curving aisles like a bizarre army. Toro's men also brought back racks and racks of exotic clothing. They had no eye for fashion, but it didn't matter to Stella, as long as it was outlandish and loud.

The only treasures Stella had no affinity for were modern technological devices and gadgets. She stormed at Toro's men when they presented her with marvelous inventions with capabilities far beyond any their minds, still stuck many thousands of years in the past, could ever imagine. But that mattered little to Stella, who despised technology and the transient gratification it brought. The only item she was inexplicably drawn to and kept was a robot—a human-shaped mechanical contraption that could mimic the behavior of a real person with an eerie reality. Such androids had been around for a long time. Toro couldn't understand Stella's particular attraction to this one, which followed her around everywhere. She spoke to it as if it were human, and it responded in kind. It never argued with her. Perhaps this was the attraction, although Toro never argued with her either, but somehow he didn't receive the same level of respect the robot enjoyed.

In the end, Toro was glad he didn't receive the same treatment as the robot, because before her departure from Prosperity, Stella nonchalantly drew her EMP weapon and with the power setting on high, blasted the machine into an inert mass of electronic rubbish.

Stella wouldn't let Theonius go out with Toro's men on their raids. She still didn't trust him. Besides, she needed someone to harass, and Theonius' stoic tolerance of her tantrums and tirades made him the perfect companion. To keep busy, he worked in the warehouse, sorting the stolen goods as they arrived. He kept a tally of all the property on a digital tablet strapped to the sleeve of his jump suit. Stella admired his size and strength, but never let her admiration for the game warden show. She ridiculed him and abused him, especially when Toro's men were nearby. They taunted him endlessly, secretly relieved that Stella's temper had a different outlet. Theonius seemed to be just as immune to this heckling as he was to Stella's insults. He had a quiet dignity that was imperturbable.

Toro returned from a raid one day and approached Stella, who was sitting on a pile of clothing, caressing a string of pearls that barely fit around the circumference of her neck. Each pearl was the size of a robin's egg, and exquisitely perfect in shape and color. Toro knew Stella well enough to recognize the menacing look she wore when disappointed or upset.

"Why are there no furs?" she asked.

Toro looked around the warehouse hoping he'd see some furs piled on the floor somewhere, even though he knew there were none. He shrugged. "There are no fur animals on this planet."

Theonius passed between them just then, carrying a porcelain goblet the size of a watermelon. Stella glared at him as if wondering whether to direct her growing rage in his direction.

"No animals," she repeated, drawing out the words.

"Well, there are animals," said Toro. "Just no animals with fur. Only animals raised for food—like chickens and cattle." He said this uncertainly. The animals he'd seen during his raids on Prosperity bore little resemblance to those he remembered from 22nd Century Earth.

Stella seemed to be processing the information. Her eyes peered about the room and found Theonius again, now depositing the goblet in a box filled with other similar objects.

"Theonius," Stella shouted. "Why are there no fur animals on this planet?"

If Toro could have slipped away then, he would have. He knew Theonius never answered direct questions from Stella, and her attempts usually ended up with some sort of physical violence.

Theonius straightened to his full height, turned and walked casually back toward them. When he was standing before her, he turned his head and spit on the floor. It was his one bad habit, one he had obtained while watching over the animals in the game reserve on Earth. He believed it established his territory, which the animals indeed grew to respect.

"How the hell should I know?" he said quietly.

In terms of mass, Stella and Theonius were about the same size, but Stella had a bad temper and warrior instincts that gave her a tremendous advantage over the game warden. Nevertheless, Theonius was strong enough that Stella refrained from physical attacks unless absolutely necessary. In this instant, she manifested her rage by walking past him to the box he'd been filling. Grabbing the goblet he had just deposited there, she propelled it across the room where it shattered against the wall. Then, picking out other smaller objects she began throwing them at the two men. They tried to dodge the projectiles but were unsuccessful.

"Find me furs!" Stella shrieked. Still removing fine pieces of pottery from the box, one by one she smashed them to the floor—one for each word as she shouted, "Find! Me! Furs!"

Toro turned immediately and hurried away. Theonius stood his ground, thumbs tucked into his belt. He was rolling something around in his mouth, as if getting ready to spit again, but Stella didn't give him the chance. She stormed away, leaving him amid the rubble of broken pottery shards.

Day after day, Stella's riches grew, until finally, she entered the warehouse and saw the serpent. It was huge now, and strong, and it wanted to be free. Stella posted guards about the warehouse, but there weren't a sufficient number of Toro's men to ensure the serpent wouldn't escape. She stood on the beach for many hours and watched the sea, knowing that before long others would arrive to steal the serpent away from her. It was time to leave Prosperity, taking the serpent with her.

The authorities on Prosperity finally mustered sufficient anger and indignation at the robberies occurring over the globe and, after much delay caused by bureaucratic red tape, assembled a team of law enforcement officers to defend what remained of the planet's wealth. When Toro reported this to Stella, she ordered them to cease their raids and begin transporting the stolen goods to the supply ship. This was a tedious task because each of their capsules had to be loaded with as much treasure as it could carry and still take off. After delivering the goods to the supply ship, they'd refuel the capsules, return to the planet, and start loading again.

Stella soon bored of the process and returned to wait on the supply ship while the rest of the treasure was transferred. Toro left two of his men with her, along with Theonius to help on the receiving end and keep Stella happy. Only occasionally did Toro wonder why he and his men were risking their lives to help Stella in her greedy enterprise. The wealth had no meaning for any of them. The best explanation he had for their devotion to Stella and her larcenous ways was that somehow or other it felt good to steal. The act of stealing was an end in itself. For Stella, it was simply a way of demonstrating her contempt for the galaxy and all humans who occupied it. With the serpent transported to the supply ship, Stella should have been contented, but she wasn't. She still didn't have any furs.

CHAPTER 28

— Century 1153 —

Risto Jalonen arrived at Prosperity just a few days after Stella and her gang. While still in intergalactic space he had received Admiral Chase's priority message about a band of space pirates heading for the planet, with an expected arrival time during the 1153rd Century. Risto knew he'd get there well before them. He navigated his capsule into an orbit far from the central star of Prosperity's planetary system, then returned to his magnetocryogenic chamber to wait for Stella's fleet to show up. He programmed the surveillance systems on his capsule to unfreeze him upon the detection of multiple space capsules in the vicinity.

His plan had worked. With the approach of Stella and her comrades, he was automatically unfrozen, after which he set a course to follow them to Prosperity. Since that would take several more years, Risto had re-entered his magnetocryogenic chamber to wait out the time in frozen oblivion, his vehicle remaining a sufficient distance behind Stella's ship to avoid detection. It was only after they entered an orbit around Prosperity that Risto was unfrozen again, but by that time the space capsules accompanying Stella were gone. Apparently, in the few extra days it took Risto to get to Prosperity, they'd already landed on the planet—all except two capsules which remained docked at the supply ship.

Risto contacted Prosperity by radio with a certain degree of dread, expecting to hear of ruthless attacks by well-armed mercenaries. However, the person he spoke with reported no anomalous events on the planet and reassured him that no alien spacecraft had landed on the planet.

Risto lost no time. He resolved to dock with the supply ship to gain control of it before it could be used against the planet. As his capsule approached the ship, Risto pointed the vehicle's telescopic imaging system on the supply ship's weaponry, prepared to accelerate rapidly away if they should turn toward him during his approach. His greatest fear was of the EMP weapons, which used an array of antennas flush with the exterior of the ship. The destructive beam was aimed by phasing the electrical pulses emanating from the antennas, in such a way as to produce constructive interference of the wave fronts at the location of the target. There was no way to know where the beam was pointed until after it was fired, but by that time all evasive maneuvers were impossible.

Risto might not have been able to approach undetected were it not for the fortuitous passage of a small asteroid fragment that obliquely intersected the supply ship's orbit just astern of the large vehicle. He navigated his capsule to mirror the trajectory of the object. The proximity of the two objects confused the ship's automated identification systems. To observers in the supply ship, his vehicle and the asteroid fragment looked identical.

Nevertheless, as soon as Risto docked his capsule, he knew the pirates would be aware of an unexpected visitor and they'd initiate all their defensive systems. For that reason, Risto did something that was highly unusual and risky. He donned a spacesuit and crawled through the magnetocryogenic chamber into the empty space outside, sealing only the inner door to the chamber behind him. Then he carefully removed a plate attached to the exterior hull, exposing a handle that was used in emergencies to open the magnetocryogenic chamber from the outside. With one hand grasping the handle, he waited, breathing slowly and listening carefully for sounds from within the capsule. He knew the occupants of the supply ship would enter the capsule, heavily armed against the intruder. Not seeing anyone in the vehicle, they'd assume the traveler was still frozen in the chamber and open the inner door, an action Risto had executed many times and was thoroughly familiar with.

When he heard the unmistakable sound of the inner door opening, Risto rotated the emergency handle. The exterior door exploded open, responding to the pressure difference between the interior of the capsule and the vacuum of space. An instant later, one of the pirates was propelled through the chamber by the blast of air and was probably dead, before he'd even exited the vehicle. His body shot through the opening and in seconds was a diminishing spot against the blackness of space. A second man was suspended in the chamber. He'd had sufficient warning to grab the edge of the hatch and was exhaling air trying to equilibrate the pressure in his body to the vacuum around him. It just meant it took him longer to die in a slow and painful way. Risto looked away until the corpse floated freely in the chamber. He grasped a leg and pulled the body out, sending it adrift in space.

Risto pulled himself back into the capsule. Sealing both doors of the chamber, he waited until the capsule filled with air again. Then he floated quickly into the supply ship's docking area and down the cylindrical corridor that provided access to the rotating segment of the ship that simulated gravity. Once there, he entered the control room and was just able to glimpse a very large 540th Century human female with a diabolical face, her EMP weapon pointed directly at him. She fired. As he collapsed to the floor, Risto heard her cackling in victorious delight.

When Risto recovered, he found himself immobilized, a drug-induced paralysis that blocked all neural connections between his brain and his body, save for those necessary for basic life functions. He was fully conscious of his helplessness, which for someone like Risto represented the worst kind of terror. It should have been some relief that his paralysis also prevented him from feeling any pain if he was physically tortured. However, that was small consolation, as it meant he could actually witness himself being maimed by his adversary. He'd only be able to see, hear, and perhaps smell the consequences of the torture, or worse yet, observe, as if from a distance, his own body bleed to death. The drug that had been administered to him was so diabolical, it had been universally banned back in the 22nd Century, but that was a long time ago. Obviously, it hadn't been completely eliminated.

Of course, he might not be tortured at all. Perhaps even more terrifying was the possibility that he'd be left alone with no food or water. He'd be forced to wait until the absence of nourishment gradually caused his organs to shut down. It would be an agonizingly long wait until the moment his consciousness succumbed to the absence of blood flow to the brain—a truly pitiful way to die, particularly for someone who had survived so many perils throughout the galaxy.

Minutes passed with agonizing slowness for Risto, knowing he was completely helpless as long as the drug was in effect. He could drive himself insane imagining the physical insults the creature that captured him might carry out, but those thoughts weren't helpful. He tried to consider all the possible situations he might find himself in when the drug wore off. He'd read that the paralysis disappeared over about a half hour, during which time he'd feel an uncomfortable, almost painful, tingling sensation throughout his body. This was good: it would give him time to prepare for his eventual mobility. When that happened—if it happened—where would he be? He had to comfort himself with the supposition that if the creature wanted him dead, she would have killed him already. He suspected she meant to use him as a hostage in case she was confronted by Admiral Chase and the Earth fleet. That would be her only insurance against a direct attack. Did she know that Chase was on his way to Prosperity? There was no way for him to tell.

Risto's thoughts were interrupted by the door to the room opening. A giant entered. He was even larger than the female creature who'd shot him. The leathery skin and amber eyes indicated he was another earthling from Stella and Admiral Chase's time, but not quite the same. Risto noted some differences in posture, complexion, and hair texture.

The large man approached Risto slowly, stooping to get a better look into his eyes. Risto tried to read the expression in the man's face. Was it aggressive, threatening, or evil? Not obviously so. In fact, it was more an expression of curiosity, and perhaps compassion. The man seemed to be struggling to comprehend what had happened to Risto. He was half a meter away, staring into his eyes, perhaps looking for signs of life, but Risto couldn't even blink—could respond in no way that required muscular activity. The man remained for several minutes, then appeared to be startled by something. He turned and hurried back to the doorway. Before leaving the room, he looked both ways down the corridor, as if ensuring no one was there. Just as he closed the door, he gestured to Risto with one hand. It was a vertical motion with palm downward, repeated several times. Risto couldn't be sure, but the man seemed to be telling him to relax.

Toro sensed something was wrong the minute he exited from his capsule, onto the supply ship. He had brought the last of the treasure, which he now pushed ahead of him through the corridor that led to the gravity-controlled portion of the ship. He shoved the package downward and then climbed the ladder after it. It moved away from him, or appeared to. He was gaining angular momentum from the rotating hull of the ship, while it was left behind, weightless in free space.. One of his men would catch it later and move it to the cold storage area of the ship.

He found Stella in the control room.

"We had a visitor," she said, downing a packet of food that smelled like hamburger.

"Who?"

"A galactic explorer. He killed two of your men."

Now it was Toro's turn to be enraged. "Where is he?"

"I shot him. He's still alive, but completely immobilized, thanks to a drug I gave him."

"Where is he?" repeated Toro. "I'll kill him."

"No, you won't," said Stella. "We may need him."

"For what?"

"In case anyone else tries to interfere with us. We know Admiral Chase is looking for us. Perhaps our little trick with the android didn't fool him."

Toro saw the sense in what Stella was saying. He was disturbed that Stella wasn't as angry as he'd have liked her to be. Two of his men had been killed. He'd seen her blow up over far less serious circumstances. Why was she so complacent at this intrusion?

"Where is he?" he said again.

"In one of the rooms down the hall."

Toro turned and stormed out of the control room. One by one he checked the quarters set aside for visiting explorers. They were empty.

Back in the galley, he confronted Stella. "All the rooms are empty."

Stella finally displayed concern. She hurried from the galley with Toro following and went to the room where she'd left the explorer. Seeing it empty, she hissed, "Find Theonius!"

She ran back to the control room to activate the ship's surveillance cameras. Toro went to the galley, where his eight remaining men were lamenting the loss of their two comrades.

"Find Theonius. He's taken the explorer."

The men scattered. The supply ship was large, but there were only so many places one could hide. The long planting tables in the greenhouse garden offered some likely places. The cold storage area had even more options. The engine room was the best place. The complex array of machinery, pipes, wiring, and computer banks was like a jungle. Eventually, Theonius and the explorer would be found, but how much damage might they do to the ship before then?

———————

Risto had never felt so powerless. The giant had entered the room where he was being held and lifted him like he was a baby. Now he was carrying him along a catwalk in the supply ship's engine room. Risto knew the inner workings of the ship well enough. The catwalk led nowhere. The giant would reach the entrance to a supply closet that offered no exit. They'd have to turn back.

To his surprise, the giant opened the door of the room, carried him to one corner, and set him down, arranging his limp arms and legs into something resembling a comfortable position. Then, from the closet, he extracted a spare jumpsuit. Filling it with other items he found in the storage area to give it bulk, he lifted the mass in the same way he'd been carrying Risto. With that, he exited the storage room, closing the door behind him.

Stella scanned the surveillance cameras, waiting for the inevitable image that would show where Theonius was. Every part of the supply ship, both interior and exterior, was in view of a camera. The ship was designed so that someone sitting at the control console could monitor the entire vehicle. Unfortunately, this meant there were hundreds of such cameras, and without knowing exactly where to look, one had to cycle through all the images until the object of the search was found. Thus, it took a better part of an hour before an image appeared showing Theonius with the drugged explorer huddled beneath one of the planting tables of the greenhouse. Somehow, they'd managed to elude Toro's men, who had conducted a thorough search of that part of the ship.

Stella bolted from the control room and headed for the greenhouse, calling to one of Toro's men to follow her. She strode directly to the location Theonius had been hiding, but the big man must have heard her enter. He jumped from his hiding place and charged at Stella. With incredible calmness, she drew her weapon and fired at Theonius, stopping him as if he had run into a wall.

Stella turned to the man behind her. "Find Toro. Tell him to get these two to their space capsules. I want them both frozen."

Sometime later, Toro, found Stella in the galley. "The explorer is still missing," he said.

"What?!" cried Stella.

"Theonius is smarter than you think. He was carrying a jumpsuit filled with junk. He must have left the explorer somewhere else in the ship."

Risto began to feel his legs first. The giant had bought him some time to recover, but to what end? What did he expect Risto could do on the supply ship in the minutes he'd have before they found him? He was in the engine room. With what he knew about the supply ship and sufficient mobility, he could sabotage the ship's propulsion system. But how would that help—unless the giant hoped that Risto would be able to destroy the ship and everyone in it as an alternative to whatever transgressions Stella and her gang were intent on executing?

As he considered his options, the feeling in his arms and legs returned, and he was soon able to stand. Risto exited the storage room and walked unsteadily back along the catwalk, holding the railings that helped prevent accidents under reduced gravity conditions. Carefully, he negotiated a series of intersecting catwalks that brought him to the communications electronics room. This contained the transmitters and receivers that enabled the supply ship to continually send and receive messages. They were connected through the ship's hull to the exterior antennas, arrayed in various shapes and sizes to span the frequency range over which the radio instrumentation operated.

Risto wondered what he could do to disable the ship's communication, and what possible benefit it might have if he did. It might not be worth the time and effort it would take to do any real damage. The bank of computers and electronics was so extensive, he'd only be able to eliminate one tiny fraction of the ship's full capability. Farther down the catwalk was the room that contained the electronics for the ship's weapons systems. That seemed a more promising target for sabotage.

As he was leaving the communications room, he spotted a glass cylinder filled with blue smoke. He stopped before it, searching his memory to recall the purpose of this piece of equipment. Then he remembered. The hulls of supply ships were constructed of a composite material that made them less vulnerable to EMP blasts. An electromagnetic wave striking the exterior surface of the ship wouldn't easily penetrate the hull and couple into the ship's electronic systems. The only parts of the ship vulnerable to EMP blasts were the external communication antennas. After all, they were designed to receive electrical signals, and an electromagnetic pulse was nothing more than an extremely powerful burst of electrical energy. Because of its susceptibility to EMP, designers had taken great care to isolate the antennas from the ship's electronic circuitry. If an EMP blast struck the exterior antennas, it had to be prevented from entering the ship's systems. The blue gas was the medium that electrically isolated the communications electronics from the antennas—a customized surge protector. Without the blue gas, isolation would be compromised. Risto grabbed the largest metal tool he could find and smashed the thick glass of the cylinder. The blue gas escaped in a rush of warm, moist vapor. Risto knew that somewhere in the ship's control room, a red indicator would light, alerting the occupants that the surge protector was not functioning. They would eventually replace it, but until that time, the ship was vulnerable to an EMP blast from space. Risto hurried from the room, realizing how unlikely it was that the ship would be fired upon by an EMP weapon. Perhaps he'd done nothing more than alerted his captors to where he was. He continued his passage to the weapons control room.

The catwalk that led there was on a different level of the ship. Risto negotiated a flight of stairs to get to it. Near the top of the stairway he looked both ways along the catwalk and saw no one. Moving faster, he reached the door that led to the weapons room. Twisting the metal handle he stepped inside. Before him was a bank of computers and electronic equipment even more extensive than the one he had just left. He was disappointed because there was no access to the actual weapons systems; only the remote computer interface was accessible, but without a security password, there was little he could do to compromise the equipment. He scanned the indicators and controls and found nothing that might be easily damaged or destroyed.

He'd been wrong to try to access the weapons systems through the computerized controls. However, just on the other side of the bank of computers was the direct interface to the actual weapons. That was where he needed to be. He hurried out of the room and back down the catwalk. A locked metal gate provided access to the area behind the control room. It was a magnetic lock. If he was to compromise the ship's weapons, he'd have to break the grasp of the magnetic force that secured the gate. But what could he do, if he were to accomplish that? He might be able to disable the weapons to prevent the ship from any violent or aggressive actions, but if Stella and her gang were already on the planet, how would that help? The other option was not to disable the weapons, but to use their destructive power on the ship itself, killing himself in the process. Perhaps that was the soundest approach because, if nothing else, the loss of the supply ship would greatly hinder Stella's capacity to inflict injury on anyone else. The capsules on the ground would have no way of refueling after leaving the planet. They'd have to drift in space, prisoners in their magnetocryogenic chambers, until they reached another supply ship where they could refuel. By that time, all the supply ships would be alerted and none would allow Stella and her gang to dock and resupply. Eliminating the supply ship would be like taking the queen in a chess game.

Risto still held the heavy metal tool he'd used to break the glass cylinder containing the blue gas. He struck the gate with it, using the slowly returning strength of his limbs. The magnetic lock was tremendously strong, but he knew that if the door could be displaced a little, the magnetic attraction holding the gate would weaken drastically. After every strike with the tool, he shoved against the gate with his shoulder, providing a one-two impulse he hoped would soon force the gate to yield. Finally, the door budged a little and he quickly inserted the metal tool into the narrow opening. Using the tool as a lever, he was able to break the magnetic hold. Risto was about to pass through the gate, when he heard a noise behind him on the catwalk. Had he not looked back—had he moved forward letting the gate close behind him— he might have been able to move to safety. Standing in the corridor was Stella, with her EMP weapon raised and pointed at him. Risto had a momentary feeling of deja vu, but it lasted for only an instant. The bolt of electrical power from Stella's weapon struck him and he collapsed unconscious to the floor. This time, he was spared the misery of hearing Stella's joyful cackling as he fell.

CHAPTER 29
— Century 1153 —

Admiral Chase landed on Prosperity with a platoon of his most skilled soldiers just 52 years after the departure of Stella and her gang. The ability of this group to deal with any conceivable foe was wasted though, because the crime, committed half a century earlier, was hardly even remembered by the authorities he spoke to on the planet. All the information about the events following Stella's arrival had been archived in a digital storage medium. The decoding algorithm was obsolete and had to be recreated by irritated and ill-tempered software experts, who couldn't understand why it was so important for Admiral Chase to access these old records.

Fortunately, the crime reports were written in Union English. Once decoded, Admiral Chase and his men reviewed them without needing translators, who might not share his keen interest in finding Stella. She was long gone from Prosperity, and the people of that hapless planet had bigger issues to deal with. Nevertheless, they left the visitors from space to the questionable task of perusing old records of a long forgotten theft of treasures no one missed.

Because Admiral Chase's team reviewed the reports in chronological order, it wasn't until the very end, hours later, that one of them read about how a damaged robot was found in the abandoned shipyard warehouse where Stella and her gang had stored the stolen goods. The robot's electronic circuits had been fried, probably by a blast from an EMP weapon, but investigators had easily extracted the data residing in the robot's solid state memory. The audio recordings from the robot took another few hours for Admiral Chase to review, but it was well worth the effort. The bizarre conversations he listened to gave him new insight into the mentality of the people he'd been pursuing. They now knew the number of members in the gang, their nicknames, and, to his delight, their plans as to where they were going next. It was an obscure planet, orbiting a star 1,800 light-years away. That was extremely valuable information. Admiral Chase could transmit the coordinates to other members of his fleet stationed closer to that star, and they'd be able to intercept Stella upon her arrival. Admiral Chase, only fifty years behind Stella, might still be able to overtake her, taking advantage of the superior speed of the space vehicles in his fleet. Unless Stella abandoned the supply ship, she'd be constrained to move at only the speed made possible by 22nd Century propulsion technology. And he suspected she'd never abandon the supply ship because he knew, from the audio recordings extracted from the defunct robot, that all the treasure was on the ship.

Admiral Chase and his team spent only another couple of days with the perplexed citizens of Prosperity before blasting away to continue their pursuit of the galactic pirates. The people of Prosperity never comprehended the importance of the Admiral's mission. He became a joke, quickly spreading over the planet, which had little else to be amused about. Very few humans of any planet were fortunate enough to witness an encounter with travelers from space. Rather than bringing profound messages of cosmic truths, instead Admiral Chase had been totally absorbed by dated information stored in a damaged android, and had quickly departed to chase down a band of interstellar pirates led by an oversized, female sociopath from the 500th Century.

CHAPTER 30

— Century 1170 —

Stella and her comrades, along with Theonius and Risto, were more than a thousand light years away from Prosperity when Toro was automatically unfrozen to perform one of the regularly scheduled status checks on the supply ship. It was Toro's responsibility because Stella hated the freezing and unfreezing process, and she endured it only when absolutely necessary. Not only did she dread the lack of control while frozen, she also viewed the process as a completely useless waste of time. For the thousands of years she was unconscious, she'd be completely incapable of dreaming. For Stella, sleep without dreams was like being dead, and she loathed the thought, and the near reality of it.

So it was Toro who'd been assigned the chore of checking every one hundred years to make sure all the systems on the supply ship were working properly. He docked his capsule with the larger vessel and, after verifying that all systems were functioning normally, sat down at the computer console to begin the tedious task of reviewing the messages received by the supply ship's radio receiver since the last status check. There was a huge volume of data, of course, because the vehicle was still performing one of the key tasks it had been designed for: being a hub for the Union communication network. Its sensitive receivers continuously scanned the heavens for signals from other supply ships, galactic exploration vehicles, and from Earth and Aril, the two planets with transmitters powerful enough to send signals into deep space. The only function Stella disabled was the transmission of data from the supply ship because that would let others know their location.

To more expeditiously search through the messages, Toro spoke a series of keywords into the ship's computers. Any messages containing those words were flagged for his review. As usual, the keyword "Stella" produced many messages, but upon scanning them Toro satisfied himself that there was no new content—only the familiar sensationalized reports of her crimes on Earth and Prosperity. The keywords "Admiral Chase" produced virtually the same set of messages, since every news report on Stella also included mention of Admiral Chase's determined pursuit of the interstellar bandits. Toro knew there'd be no messages directly from Admiral Chase or any other member of the Earth fleet. For security reasons, all those messages were encoded using a new encryption scheme—changed because Stella knew the old one that was originally used by the rescue fleet from Earth.

All the other keyword searches Toro performed produced equally humdrum results until he pronounced the word "Happiness". The computer displayed a message that immediately caught his attention. It was a report that Benjamin Mizello was on route to the planet with two other travelers, on a mission to establish contact with alien life forms suspected of being there.

Toro hated to do it, but he didn't hesitate. He transmitted the signal to Stella's space capsule that would unfreeze her. She would have to see the message.

———

"Why can't the Union and its silly minions mind their own damned business?!" Stella yelled, upon reading the message.

Toro didn't answer. He sat next to Stella before the console, looking glumly at the screen before them.

"When will they get to Happiness?" Stella asked.

"In 119,453," answered Toro, glad that he'd performed the calculation already while Stella was going through the unfreezing process.

"Damn," hissed Stella, peering at the date display, calculating how long it would take for them to return to Happiness.

"He may not find the treasure," offered Toro, regretting the words as soon as he'd said them.

Stella glared at him. "I'm not taking that chance. Here I was feeling comfortable that we'd fooled Admiral Chase into believing the information we left in that stupid robot. Who would have thought that some other galactic explorers would show up on Happiness?"

Toro nodded. It had been an elaborate trick. He hadn't understood Stella's affinity for her robot companion until he realized she'd done it purposely to leave misleading information for the investigators on Prosperity, who she knew would be able to extract all the data stored in the robot's memory even after she destroyed it. The ruse had worked, but now Toro and Stella had to deal with the unexpected visit to Happiness of Mizello and his two fellow travelers. They wouldn't be as difficult to deal with as Admiral Chase and his troops, but something would have to be done. If not, and they found the treasure, everyone in the galaxy would converge on Happiness to recover it.

"There were no aliens on Happiness," Toro said.

"Of course not," said Stella. "These galactic explorers are just a bunch of silly idiots, zooming around the galaxy hoping to find God sitting on a planet somewhere waiting for them."

Toro thought about Happiness. They'd landed there, searched for a suitable hiding place for the treasure, and found many options. Quite a few of the amusement park's attractions were still standing after the asteroid impact. There were artificial volcanoes, pyramids, mountain peaks, sea grottoes, and ice caves. In addition, some of the monuments of human engineering were still standing: the Statue of Liberty, the Taj Mahal, a 13th Century castle, the Saturn V rocket, a luxury cruise ship, and miniature versions of the tallest skyscrapers, still large enough to easily accommodate Stella's treasures. How long would it take for Benjamin and his companions to stumble on the stolen goods? Toro and Stella had selected the most improbable and inaccessible place on the planet, but Stella was right. They couldn't take the chance.

"Is there any way we can intercept them on their way to Happiness?" Stella asked.

Toro shook his head. "They're coming from Aril. By the time we reverse course and head back in that direction, they'll have reached the planet. The only thing we can do is get there as quickly as possible. We don't know exactly when they'll land. We could get lucky and beat them."

"Okay. Calculate the fastest way to Happiness. Let's get turned around. No need to unfreeze the others. Just override all their navigation systems."

"Right," said Toro. "Are you going back to your space capsule now?"

"Not yet. I'm going to smoke, and then sleep. Real sleep, with real dreams. I'm not ready to be dead again yet." With that she left the control room. Toro sighed with relief. It could have been much worse.

CHAPTER 31

— 119,480 —

Once close to planet Happiness, Benjamin, Druix, and Xyla were unfrozen and, after taking their seats in the control rooms of their capsules, communicated via radio while making the requisite pre-landing observations.

They were relieved, and to some extent surprised, that the oxygen concentration in the atmosphere was ideal, and they wouldn't need artificial breathing equipment during their visit. They were even more excited when the infrared images showed evidence of warm-blooded life forms on the planet, although confined to one area roughly the size of the ancient country of Mexico. The rest of the planet was heavily vegetated, except for several good-sized oceans, spotted with small, barren islands. The general topography of the planet was consistent with the maps the Arilians had provided, except that the various thematic areas of the amusement park, which had once dominated the surface, weren't visible—at least not from space. For their landing, Benjamin selected a large, flat area near the region where the infrared emissions were seen. The three travelers prepared their capsules for entry into the atmosphere.

By chance, the spot he'd selected was one of the ancient battlefields the creators of Happiness had seen fit to include in the park. Had Benjamin realized the significance of the open field upon which they landed, he might have chosen a different location. The battlefield soil that had once been soaked with human blood was blown into massive plumes by the roaring rockets of the three descending vehicles.

At Benjamin's advice, they waited a full ten minutes for the dust to settle before exiting their vehicles. When they emerged, squinting in the bright glare of the planet's sun, they were amazed to find themselves surrounded by a crowd of angry people, shouting at them and waving fists in the still-dusty air. Benjamin recognized them as earthlings, very closely resembling those he'd met during the thwarted invasion of Aril. Though he had learned some of the language from his time with Admiral Chase and the Earth fleet, that was from tens of thousand of years earlier. Xyla and Druix's time on Earth was even farther in the past, but fortunately both had studied more recent versions of the language during their stay on Aril. More importantly, the language was very similar to that spoken during Xyla's visit to Prosperity. She'd learned enough during her limited time there to understand the shouts from the crowd.

"They're telling us to leave—calling us names. We've interrupted something important." Xyla translated, though it was difficult to pick out individual words and phrases from the general melee.

The three huddled together awkwardly as the crowd surrounded them. Oddly though, none felt particularly concerned or frightened by the display. Somehow, they sensed that the intent of the agitated crowd was only to make noise and threaten. Finally, from the rear of the throng, a loud voice boomed what sounded like a single word. The crowd silenced immediately. The man who had shouted pushed his way through and advanced to the visitors. In Union English, he asked, "Are you immortals?"

Benjamin stepped forward and answered, "No. We're space travelers."

The man just nodded. "Yes. That's what I meant. Why have you come?"

Benjamin hesitated, glancing at his companions uncertainly. "We're here to learn about your planet."

The man peered suspiciously at them, then relaxed. "I am Ostinia. Please, follow me."

"But why are these people so angry?" Benjamin asked.

"You interrupted their performance."

"Performance?"

"Yes. Their reenactment. You're on a battlefield where we re-enact the famous war that took place on Earth in the 38th Century."

"But why?" asked Benjamin.

"We do it every day. It's one of the shows."

Benjamin looked again at his colleagues, a look of incredulity on his face. "I knew this planet was a theme park very long ago, but I'm surprised nothing has changed even after thousands of years—especially after the asteroid struck."

Ostinia looked paralyzed. "I know nothing about an asteroid or a theme park. We know there was an ancient civilization that constructed buildings and roads here, all of which are ruins now, except for those we've rebuilt. We do not concern ourselves much with ancient history. We know the planet is named Happiness from the signs we find in the ruins. We are a civilization of artists, actors, singers, dancers, musicians, writers, entertainers of all kinds, and skilled craftsmen of every trade imaginable. We all do what we do best, and for these folks here, it is battlefield reenactment."

At this, Ostinia gestured for them to follow him, and the crowd that had been so aggressive moments before yielded respectfully to the travelers. "I'll take you first to a place you can eat and rest. Then I'll show you other amusements."

It was a long walk across the open field they'd landed on. Along the way, the travelers saw no visible evidence of any motorized transport of any kind. The land about them was dominated by rolling hills, dotted with shrubs and patches of dry grass. It was only after they'd crested one of the hills that they saw the skyline of New York City as it looked in the 22nd Century. The tall skyscrapers sat upon what must have been an artificially created island similar in shape, but not in size, to Manhattan. The entire city lay before them in eerie and unimaginable grandeur. Even with its diminutive size, it was still sufficient to leave the visitors from space breathless and awestruck.

Ostinia led them along a series of paths that simulated the streets that had once criss-crossed New York. There were no vehicles in the city. Remarkably, the residents walking along the pathways largely ignored the three visitors, even though their appearance stood out in many ways.

They checked into a hotel that replicated one of the old

luxury establishments in New York, were shown to their rooms, and given clothes and instructions on how to make use of the few amenities the hotel offered.

Several hours later, the three were waiting in the hotel lobby for their tour to begin. They appeared to be the only guests there. They stood awkwardly in stunned silence trying to understand the disconnect between what they'd expected to find on Happiness and what confronted them now. They had little chance, however, because Ostinia showed up promptly with several helpers to guide them on a tour of the city.

"You are the first visitors from space in many centuries. We only know about such visits through the data archives, but time has made these tales the stuff of legends. A few of us think Happiness was created by people from another planet, but most of us don't believe that."

"Actually, it's true," said Benjamin cautiously. "But that was long ago."

They exited the hotel and were walking again through the streets of New York. "So your data archives say nothing about an asteroid hitting the planet?" asked Druix.

"No, but gaps in the record exist, of course. It's ancient history, after all."

"Yes," said Xyla. "And you shouldn't let it concern you or your people. What's important is that somehow your society has survived. We're looking forward to learning more about it." Xyla looked at both Benjamin and Druix sternly, as if reprimanding them. They both nodded their agreement.

"Wonderful," said Ostinia. "Please follow me. I've planned our route to enable you to see some of our most entertaining shows."

For the remainder of the day, Benjamin, Xyla, and Druix were delighted by an astonishing array of exceptional entertainment. Many of the acts were performed in the open, on the street corners and parks throughout the city—musicians, singers, dancers, mimes and many more, all executed with incredible skill, grace, and precision. Each performer was a virtuoso in his or her specialty. Even the street venders, where the group stopped to shop or eat, provided their wares with pride and enthusiasm far beyond what one might have expected from the seemingly insignificant nature of those tasks.

In addition to the street entertainment, the buildings held other enjoyments for the visitors. Most of them had false facades, meant to duplicate what New York had looked like in the 22nd Century, but, in fact, all had been converted to different types of art studios. Each displayed a unique array of paintings, sculpture, pottery, jewelry, wood products, glassware, and other unique and magnificent works. After two hours, Benjamin, Druix, and Xyla had hardly traveled more than two blocks. One could easily spend many weeks exploring the endless collection of galleries and studios throughout the city.

As the sun was setting, Ostinia hurried them along to their next destination. It was a large stadium at the middle of the Central Park replica.

"This is where we have our shows. You've missed today's performance, but we will come back tomorrow to see it. I'm sure you will enjoy it."

That evening, after dinner, Druix suggested they meet in his room to discuss the events of the day. He and Xyla insisted Benjamin sit in the only chair in the room, while the two of them sat on the edge of the bed.

The proximity of Benjamin in the intimate space of the hotel room unnerved Xyla, but she tried to keep her mind on the issues at hand. They'd only been on Happiness a few hours and already their expectations had been overturned completely. There were no aliens on the planet—only descendants of survivors who had escaped the immediate death of the asteroid impact and the subsequent effects caused by the shroud of dust that had covered the planet. In the 22 thousand years since the collision, the people had restored many of the buildings, gardens, landscape, and infrastructure of the theme park, and even resurrected the entertainment and attractions that had once captivated visitors from Prosperity. But to what end? There were no visitors anymore.

Entertainers and artists performed before scant crowds of people, most of whom were their neighbors. They respectfully cheered for and supported each other, but that was the only reward their efforts engendered.

"It's bizarre," said Druix, chewing on a sliver of wood he'd been given after dinner to use as a toothpick. This whole society has been sustained for the sole purpose of continuing activities initiated thousands of years ago without anyone even questioning why."

Xyla wanted to say that it reminded her of the Malanites on Aurora, who had continued to fish in the seas of the planet even after they'd been covered by ice. Though other means of survival were possible on Aurora, none of the Malanites ever considered doing anything other than what their ancestry had programmed them to do. Xyla didn't verbalize these thoughts because, as far as she knew, Benjamin still didn't know she and Druix were from Aurora. If he knew, he might make the connection between her and the furry Malanite female he'd loved during his visit in 20,000.

"I've been trying to piece together what might have happened after the asteroid struck," Benjamin said. "Obviously enough people remained and survived the catastrophe and its aftermath to reestablish a society."

"The historical records say that all were evacuated," added Druix. "But, of course, there's no way to tell for sure if everyone did leave during the evacuation."

"That's right," agreed Benjamin. "And a sufficient number must have stayed to bear children and grow the population."

"There could have been enough food and water in the theme park to sustain a small number of people until they could grow their own crops." Druix stood and paced the room. "Aril was started with far less. It must have taken remarkable fortitude and persistence."

"Don't forget the atmospheric conditions after the impact," said Benjamin. "The dust cloud covering the planet caused runaway heating or cooling of the atmosphere. Either way, they must have suffered incredibly adverse weather conditions."

"It doesn't matter," put in Xyla quietly.

The two men looked at her.

"What doesn't matter?" Benjamin asked.

"Adverse weather conditions." Xyla recalled her home planet, with its freezing temperatures, blowing snow, and ice-covered seas. "People don't just die when the weather changes. They adapt and endure. The Arilian scientists got it wrong. The climate on Aril hasn't changed in thousands of years. How could they understand how humans survive in adverse weather conditions? They were wrong to assume the asteroid killed everyone on the planet. They survived and these people are their descendants. It's no surprise really."

Druix smiled, amused at his mother's assertiveness, and pleased with her willingness to draw on her experiences living on Aurora. Benjamin seemed impressed, as well. "You're right, of course. When I was on Earth, I visited some of the most blighted places in the world. Even in the face of insurmountable threats to life, people managed not only to survive, but also enjoy their existence. It's human nature."

"Or the nature of life," Xyla corrected. "Not just human life."

"Speaking of which," Druix said. "So far we've seen no evidence of alien life here."

"Do you think we should try the translators the Arilians gave us?" his mother asked.

"What for?" asked Druix.

"They said the devices would pick up radio signals from aliens. Maybe they're nearby," said Benjamin.

"Yes, it's worth a try," said Xyla, extracting her translator from a pack she'd been carrying.

She powered up the device and waited. Almost instantly, it emitted a continuous stream of static, dissonant crackling sounds with no pattern or coherence. Xyla pressed a button on the device that automatically scanned in frequency, searching for a signal of any kind. All they heard were the characteristic changes in pitch as the frequency varied, but the static remained. Artificial or otherwise, it was just the random crackling caused by the movement of electrons in the instrument's circuitry.

"No signals," said Druix decisively. "No aliens."

"The survival of these people after the asteroid impact is a remarkable story," said Benjamin. "But other than that, we have little to report from our trip here. We'll stay a few more days and then leave." He was looking at Xyla as he spoke, almost asking her approval. She stared back at him, her face impassive and unreadable.

Druix nodded. "I'm curious to see the show they've promised us, to learn more about their society. I think I'll stay longer."

Xyla glanced at her son. "I'll stay with you."

Benjamin smiled. "Of course. I didn't mean to say we had to leave together. As soon as I return to space, I'll send a message back to Aril reporting the outcome of our visit.

"What about the radio emissions they detected?" asked Xyla. "Won't they want an explanation about the source of those signals?"

Benjamin shrugged. "Perhaps, but it could well be that they're not hearing them now. Eleven thousand years have passed since we left Aril. Whatever was producing those signals may have disappeared."

"Interesting thought," said Druix. "Maybe there were aliens here once, but they've left."

Xyla was still adjusting the controls of her translator. "If that's true, maybe we'll find residual signs of an alien presence."

"Right," agreed Druix. "It wouldn't hurt to stay here a few more days and look around."

Benjamin nodded in agreement and left the room.

The next day they attended the show. Although the audience was sparse, it didn't diminish the enthusiasm of the performers. There was a troop of clowns engaged in zany acts of bizarre unpredictability. A marching band stepped smartly around the stadium, filling the space with toe-tapping rhythms. Monocyclists twisted their way among performers walking on stilts, barely avoiding catastrophic collisions. A line of actors filed in, wearing garish costumes. They were supposed to look like circus animals, emitting ferocious roars and beastly screeches. Given there were no animals other than humans on the planet, that was the best the people of Happiness could do.

The high point of the day was a full length theatrical production called "The Day the Sun Came Back", complete with music, dancing, stunning costumes, and elaborate set designs and special effects. It was a story set amidst the gloom and chaos of ancient Earth, when climate change and nuclear holocaust produced a layer of clouds that blanketed the planet for thousands of years. The show ended when the first rays of light from the sun emerged through the cloud layer, auguring hope for the struggling population. The humans of Happiness who staged the show used smoke and mirrors to simulate the returning sunlight. What they lacked in mechanical and electronic technology they made up for in the clever ways they manipulated light with reflecting surfaces, lenses, and prisms. The show was a rousing performance that left the audience uplifted and joyful.

The last act of the day was an incredible demonstration of acrobatic prowess performed by a group of entertainers called Tattoo People. They were scantily dressed, with bodies covered by so many tattoos their skin color was predominantly the distinctive blue-green tone of blood vessels painfully teased into spectral transformation. For most of them, it was difficult to discern where one tattoo stopped and another began. Close up, one could hardly identify any characteristic shape or form, but at a distance the jumble of lines and curves revealed subtle images— faces mostly, but occasionally patterns and designs of leaves and foliage, twigs and berries, waterfalls and fountains.

The Tattoo People performed astounding feats of acrobatics and aerial skill. They walked effortlessly on tightropes, swung on trapezes with ease and grace that defied imagination. The Tattoo People were thin—not in girth in the usual sense, but in depth. It was as if they were designed to be templates on which their dermatological artwork would be most effectively displayed. On a windy day, they'd have to turn sideways to avoid the aerodynamic lift that was an inevitable consequence of their physiology. One had the impression that with any reasonable set of wings they could take to the skies.

When the performance was over, the Tattoo People bowed to the crowd, then waved and cartwheeled off the stage amid scattered applause. The enthusiasm of their exit didn't seem the least bit muted by the feebleness of the audience's response.

One female performer, wearing a brightly colored and heavily ornamented hat, caught Xyla's eye. They exchanged smiles and Xyla waved. The woman acknowledged the gesture by removing her hat and presenting it to Xyla before bowing graciously away.

The performance ended with a fanfare of rousing music, which signaled the start of a parade of all the entertainers. After assembling at the center of the stadium, they linked arms and hands and sang a vibrant song that compelled Xyla, Druix, and Benjamin to stand also and link arms, Xyla in the middle. The three attempted to follow the words of the song, but failed miserably. It didn't matter, as their voices were inconsequential compared to those of the people around them.

The song ended precisely when a ray of light from the setting sun struck an elevated crystal sphere that stood at the entrance to the stadium. The reflected light produced a brilliant display of rainbow colored luminescence that fell upon the entertainers. It lasted for less than a minute and disappeared as quickly as it had begun. Then, the last rays from the setting sun struck mirrors ringing the far side of the stadium. Beams of light reflected from the mirrors to torches that lined the pathways leading out of the stadium, lighting the exit routes for the departing crowd. Although the people of Happiness had lost the knowledge of electricity, they'd successfully harnessed the energy from their sun and used it in remarkably clever ways.

After sharing another feast with Ostinia and other leaders of the city, Benjamin, Xyla, and Druix met again in Druix's room.

They were tired, overwhelmed by the sensory overload of the day's events. No one spoke for several moments until Xyla, who was sitting on the bed closely examining the hat she'd been given, said, "Interesting."

"What?" asked Druix, standing by the window looking out over the replicated New York skyscrapers.

"This hat."

"What about it?" asked Benjamin. He rose from his usual spot on the chair and sat next to Xyla, who moved over to make room for him on the bed.

"I'm no expert," she said, "But when we lived on Earth, I owned jewelry—some very rare and valuable pieces. They were gifts from my husband. These stones along the rim of the hat look like rubies. The medallion on the front could be a diamond, a very large diamond, surrounded by emeralds, mounted on gold."

She handed the hat to Benjamin, who studied it for several moments. "I think you're right," he said. "It's beautiful. And beautifully made."

"Yes," agreed Xyla. "Feel the fabric. I can't identify it." The hat was made from a coarsely woven fiber, each fiber brownish in color, but with sinews of green twisted through it.

"We should ask Ostinia tomorrow how the hat was made and where the gem stones come from," said Benjamin.

"Yes," Xyla repeated, absently.

Druix approached them and looked down at his mother. "Is something wrong?" he asked, seeing her absorbed in thought.

"No," Xyla answered, unconvincingly. "I was just thinking about the Tattoo People." She looked up as if to see whether Benjamin and Druix were paying attention. "They don't speak."

"They don't have to," Benjamin said. "They're acrobats."

Xyla smiled. "They don't even speak to each other. At least, I didn't notice them talking. Not once." She stopped, giving her companions time to consider her words.

Druix spoke first. "Are you wondering if the Tattoo People are aliens?"

Xyla didn't answer. Benjamin stood. "You're thinking that

the reason they don't speak is that they can't. They communicate in some other way—perhaps by radio waves, as the Arilians suggested."

Benjamin reached into his backpack and brought out one of the translating devices. "We tried it yesterday, but the Tattoo People weren't around. We never thought to try again today during the show."

"No," said Xyla. "We didn't."

"Is it too late to try now?" Benjamin asked.

"Probably," Druix said. He returned to the window. "All the torches lighting the city are out. The streets are empty. We'll try it first thing in the morning. And while we're at it, we'll ask Ostinia about the hat."

None of the three visitors to Happiness slept much that night. They were all too excited about the possibility that the Tattoo People were aliens. Their minds were occupied going through the arguments for and against the hypothesis Xyla had raised. Would aliens get tattoos to perform at an amusement park for humans? Could an alien civilization have enough in common with humans, that they could coexist with no one even suspecting their extraterrestrial origin? Both conjectures were possible, but if so, what were the evolutionary and life forces that produced an alien civilization so similar to that which had been created on Earth? Or had humans even been created on Earth? Was it possible humans and these alien creatures shared a common origin that bound them? How much did the aliens know and understand about their origin and connection to the humans for whom they did backflips and cartwheels?

Morning found Benjamin, Xyla, and Druix blurry-eyed and unable to make the transition from the fantasy world of their thoughts to the reality of a new day on Happiness. They left their rooms and met in the hotel reception area, all anxious to find Ostinia. They walked the streets of the city back to the stadium, guessing that Ostinia was there preparing for the day's show. They hoped to encounter a Tattoo person along the way, to try out the translating devices, but there were none to be seen.

"You will seldom see Tattoo People in the city," Ostinia explained, after they'd found him. He was overseeing the repair of some of the set decorations used in the show. "The Tattoo People live in the forest."

"All of them?" asked Benjamin.

"All of them," confirmed Ostinia. "They only come to the city to perform. Then they go back."

"Can we visit them?"

"That would be difficult. The forest is impenetrable. Only the Tattoo People know how to enter and leave it."

"We'd like to try," said Benjamin. "Is there someone who can guide us to the forest edge?"

"You don't need a guide to get there. Any of the streets out of the city will take you. I suggest you use Broadway though. Where it ends, at the edge of the forest, is a small house. My friend Hovar lives there. He knows as much about the Tattoo People as anyone. Please give him my regards."

"Thank you," said Benjamin, and he turned to leave, but Xyla held back.

"Ostinia," she said holding out the hat to their host. "Can you tell us about this hat? How is it made?"

Ostinia hardly looked at it. "The Tattoo People make those hats using the leaves of the plant that grows in the forest."

"Which plant?" asked Xyla, looking around to see if Ostinia might point to it among the shrubs and trees of the park landscaping.

"There's only one kind of plant in the forest," Ostinia said. "It's more of a vine than a tree. Very hardy. It chokes out all other plants."

The impact these words had on Benjamin stopped him short. A vine that was so dense and so prolific that it inhibited the growth of all other plants reminded him of the one discovered by Carl Stormer during his failed attempt to start a colony on planet Alpha.

Benjamin was absorbed in thought as the three made their way down the ersatz Broadway in a direction that would have been northward had they really been in Manhattan. Was the plant that surrounded the amusement park on Happiness the same one Risto Jalonen and Carl Stormer had encountered on three other planets? Each of those planets featured a breathable, oxygen-rich atmosphere. Was it a coincidence that the presence of the plant also ensured an atmosphere conducive to human habitation? Was there a connection between the plant and the Tattoo People, who apparently lived within the vine's embrace? He wanted to discuss these questions with Xyla and Druix, but they both seemed immersed in their own thoughts.

Continuing along Broadway, they eventually exited the city. Here the roadway was flanked by shattered and abandoned structures, the untouched remnants of the ancient amusement park—jumbles of broken concrete and metal, twisted into impossible shapes. The travelers were awed by the forces that must have produced the destruction. Ahead of them was the forest, its vivid greenery standing out in sharp contrast to the lifeless rubble they'd been walking through. Where the roadway ended was a crumbling, wood-framed house, patched together with debris scavenged from the surrounding ruins. A man was sitting in a rickety chair on a porch-like structure, that may have been the sturdiest part of the shack.

"You must be Hovar," said Benjamin, offering his hand. "Ostinia said you might help us find the Tattoo People."

Hovar shook Benjamin's hand with an amused expression. Gesturing to equally shaky chairs lined along the porch, he said, "You three might want to sit down. There's no way to find the Tattoo People. You just have to wait till they come out."

Benjamin, Xyla, and Druix sat with Hovar and waited, looking at the devastated buildings stretched out before them. Benjamin and Druix tried to engage the old man in conversation, but his responses were curt and it soon became clear he didn't care to talk. Not that he was unfriendly; he just seemed to enjoy the silence, and soon, they did as well.

After about thirty minutes, which seemed like much longer, a group of Tattoo People appeared before them. They'd come from the forest behind the house. Benjamin stood and approached one who appeared to be the leader of the group. He held out his hand and when close enough stopped. The Tattoo man stared down at Benjamin's hand for several seconds, then offered his in return. Benjamin took the translating device from his pocket and turned it on. The Tattoo man stared at the device suspiciously, but didn't appear to be afraid. Benjamin heard a modulated hum come from the translator, very different from what they'd heard the previous night. He pressed a button on the device to select the output mode. It transmitted a frequency very close to that of the signal it was receiving. Benjamin pointed to himself and spoke his name into the translator. Immediately, the face of the Tattoo man lit up in amazement. In turn, Benjamin pointed to his two companions and spoke their names, first Druix, then Xyla. At the moment Benjamin pointed to her and said her name, Xyla felt an inexplicable flutter of excitement, which almost matched the thrill manifested by the alien being, when he'd heard the names of the three humans, translated into a unique pattern of radio waves that his mind could identify and interpret.

With uncertain, hesitating movements, the Tattoo man pointed to himself. Immediately from the translating device came an audible word that sounded like "Katru". He had transmitted his name as radio waves, which the Arilian translating device rendered into the closest audible equivalent detectable by the human ear.

Benjamin pointed to the man and spoke the word "Katru" into the device. This time the man not only smiled broadly, but he executed a clean, smooth backflip, landing gracefully in the position from which he had begun the movement. It was a gesture of uninhibited joy. Hurrying back to his companions standing some distance behind him, he ran from one to the next pointing to each, and as he did, the translating device pronounced a different name, clearly and unambiguously. Xyla seldom had occasion to laugh in her troubled life, but this time she did so. It was unrestrained, delightful, and melodious. She wasn't sure how the translating device turned sound into radio transmissions, but whatever it did caused the Tattoo People to do excited flips and jumps and other gestures that were clear indications of the joy they were feeling when finally, after thousands of years, they could communicate with humans, their neighbors.

Benjamin made gestures to indicate their desire to enter the forest. Katru hesitated a moment, then waved them forward. The three humans held back, not sure where exactly Katru wanted them to enter the foliage, which seemed dense and impenetrable. Katru noticed their hesitation and motioned for them to watch carefully. One of his colleagues walked to the edge of the forest, stood before it with his body pressed tightly against the foliage. Then, sliding to the right, disappeared from view. Benjamin stepped forward and followed the example. Sure enough, when close enough to the edge of the foliage he saw a narrow opening that he could enter by moving sideways. Once inside, he almost panicked at the cramped space within which he found himself, but he continued to move sideways. At some point, he met an obstruction and became confused because he could see no way to proceed. Only very dim filtered sunlight penetrated the foliage. He was about to slide back from where he came, but then realized there was another narrow path to take. It was a switchback, which he followed until it ended at another sharp turn. With each turn he penetrated deeper and deeper into the forest. He wondered whether his companions were following him. He waited and before long felt someone bump into him. It was Xyla.

"Benjamin, is that you?"

"Yes. Are you alright?"

"Yes. A little claustrophobic, but I'm okay."

Benjamin took her hand and began moving again. When he reached the end of a switchback, he had to release her hand, move to the side, and then grab her other hand. They continued on, making their way farther into the compacted mass of branches, leaves, and twigs of the alien vine.

At last, and with no forewarning, they broke through the tangle and found themselves standing in a broad corridor molded through the foliage itself. The walls of the corridor had not been formed by cutting and trimming vegetation. Instead, it had been trained back, leaving a densely packed tangle of leaves and branches that was not only impenetrable, but also gave the appearance that it was one continuous surface. The lattice of brown and green looked very much like the coarse weave of the hat Xyla had been given. The overall impression was that the walls of the corridor were carved through a single block of mahogany-like, multi-colored wood.

The group followed Katru along this path, which periodically opened to allow light from the sky above to illuminate their route. They passed other Tattoo People, all of whom politely yielded to the three human visitors, intrigued but not surprised. Almost certainly, Katru was transmitting a message of explanation as they walked, and before long they were being followed by a growing assemblage of curious Tattoo People.

Xyla left her translating device on and, as the crowd behind them grew, the jumble of sounds from the speaker became more garbled and complex. She scanned the frequencies to no avail. The interference from so many nearby sources of radio transmissions overwhelmed the device.

They made several turns at intersecting pathways, and

before long Xyla realized that without the help of the Tattoo People, she'd never be able to find their way out of the thicket. When she recalled the images of the planet that she, Benjamin and Druix had viewed from space, it was clear they were at the margins of a network of paths that probably covered most of the planet's surface. There was no telling how many Tattoo People occupied the forest.

At random locations along the walls of the corridors, Xyla noticed slender, vertical openings through which the Tattoo People could easily pass. She suspected these led to other paths, and perhaps homes. The habitat of the Tattoo People had been cut from the foliage in the same way ants carved out a habitat in mounds of sand.

Finally they stopped at an opening before which stood a Tattoo man, who bowed to them and executed a clean backflip. Katru did the same, and a moment later the man disappeared inside the opening. Katru pointed to the man and then to Xyla's translator, which emitted the audible version of the man's name, Gmobo. Katru gestured for his three guests to follow the man inside, where they found themselves in a room that had been formed by training the branches of the surrounding vine into a tight lattice that made up the walls of the dome-shaped space within. But perhaps more remarkable was what the Tattoo People had stored inside the room. There were signs of varying shapes and sizes, made of metal or plastic, and all obviously very old. They'd been scavenged from the ancient amusement parks of Happiness. Among the many signs were ones that said "Restrooms", "Food", "Water", "Welcome", "Caution", and tens of others one might expect to find in any place that catered to the general public. Some were written in Union English, others in the language of Prosperity, and a few in both languages.

Gmobo waved Xyla over to a sign that said "Closed". He pointed to the translator and Xyla understood that she was to read the sign out loud. After she'd done that, the man moved to the next sign, and again Xyla read the word into the translator. What the man was doing soon became apparent. The Tattoo People knew what the signs said, but they couldn't connect the words to the language spoken by humans because they couldn't hear the words. The translator allowed them to associate a pattern of radio waves with the human words on the signs. As Xyla read the words on the signs, the Tattoo People began to build a limited vocabulary. It made them very happy, and they showed their excitement with grateful bows and graceful flips.

The Tattoo People must have had excellent memories because when Xyla finished, Gmobo pointed at each sign in succession and from the translating device came an amazingly accurate rendition of the word on that sign.

Druix and Benjamin watched this display with amusement and curiosity. They kept their devices turned off, so as not to create interference with Xyla's. When the exercise was over, Katru escorted his visitors back out onto the pathway where a small crowd of Tattoo People had gathered. Almost immediately, they exhibited similar excitement. News of what was happening in the room spread very quickly. It was no surprise. Information communicated by radio waves is far more efficient than speaking. What might take a person one minute to verbalize could be transmitted in seconds when coded in the language of radio. Also, radio waves travel at the speed of light—orders of magnitude faster than the speed of sound. It was quite possible that every Tattoo person on the planet had already received the word that human visitors were now helping them communicate with other humans at last.

In the declining hours of the day, Katru led Benjamin, Xyla, and Druix back to Hovar's house. Before he returned to the forest, Katru pointed to Xyla's translating device and from the speaker came the words, "Tomorrow. Come back. Please." He'd already figured out how to put words together to express a thought. His three human guests all smiled and nodded their heads, waving at Katru as he departed.

They sat with Hovar on his porch as the sky darkened. They related to the old man their success in establishing a means of communication with the Tattoo People. Hovar was impressed, but not surprised.

"Smart people—the Tattoo People. I always knew it."

"Did you know they were aliens?" Benjamin asked.

"I don't know what you mean," said Hovar.

"They come from space."

"Like you?" asked Hovar.

Benjamin smiled. "Yes, like us. Except we're humans. They're not."

"Never gave it much thought," said Hovar. "It's none of my business. Don't see where it makes much difference."

"I suppose not," said Benjamin.

There was no more to say, so the four sat quietly. The silence was absolute. The edge of the forest loomed behind them. Memory of their time with the Tattoo People was taking on a dream-like quality. It was hard to believe in the fading light of day that within the forest an entire civilization of alien beings lived out their bizarre existences in a planet-sized habitat carved from a prolific vine.

The next day, they returned to Hovar's house and found Katru and two other Tattoo People waiting for them. Their excitement was evident as they led their human guests again through the tangle of branches to the pathway they had traveled the previous day. This time they took a different route and ended up at another slender entrance almost invisibly embedded in the side wall. What they found inside amazed them even more than the room filled with amusement park signs. There were stacks of books, the old fashioned kind with pages bound in hard covers, all perfectly preserved and complete. Benjamin picked up one of the books. Upon closer inspection, the pages were made of a thin plastic material, not paper, which explained their perfect preservation in spite of their obvious age. Perusing the titles, he noted some of the most famous books ever written.

It was obvious what the Tattoo People wanted their human friends to do. They wanted the books read to them so they could learn the human language. That day, all three read to separate groups of Tattoo People from books selected from the library. They read till the sun began to fade. Then they were escorted back out to Hovar's house. The next day, they did the same, except that Benjamin and Druix tired of it and ventured off on their own to explore more of the Tattoo People's world.

Xyla enjoyed reading to the Tattoo People—so much that eventually they allowed her to stay overnight instead of returning on the arduous route through the tangled vegetation. She insisted that Druix and Benjamin return without her in spite of their hesitation. Secretly, she was somewhat afraid to stay overnight among the aliens, not because of any fear they'd hurt her, but because she was afraid of the darkness she knew would descend upon the forest when the sun set. The Tattoo People possessed no form of artificial lighting that she could tell, and certainly wouldn't burn fires amidst all the flammable foliage about them. To her unexpected delight, however, she had nothing to fear because with the darkness, the Tattoo People began to glow. Their skin was bioluminescent. She could see all of them moving eerily about in the darkness, and if there were a sufficient number nearby, they produced collectively enough light for her to read by. This worked out very well because there seemed to be a line of Tattoo People waiting to join her in the library just to listen to her read through the translating device. She read until she was too tired to go on, at which time they showed her to a bed made from young, tender leaves of the vine, where she slept soundly until the sun shone through the branches around her the next morning.

The Tattoo People grew extremely fond of Xyla and saw to her every need. They fed her a variety of dishes made with berries from the ubiquitous vine. Xyla savored the meals. Having grown up on Aurora where the main diet was dried fish, she wasn't fussy. During her years on Earth, she'd never grown accustomed to the rich foods served on that planet. The simplicity of the food the Tattoo People prepared was comforting to her.

They also showed Xyla where to bathe. The forest was filled with small ponds, ideal for swimming as well. They made clothes for her, freeing her from the confines of her Union jumpsuit. The fabric, like most everything else in the Tattoo People's forest was made from vines. That single vine was the source of all the materials the Tattoo People needed to live—not just building material for homes and furniture, but also hemp for rope, fibers for cloth, long, sturdy twigs for weaving baskets and other containers. Whatever race engineered the vine had been extremely clever to combine so many of life's necessities into a single living organism. In Union English the word plant had two meanings: a biological organism and a place where products are manufactured. The vine of the Tattoo People was both.

The ease with which the Tattoo People learned English solely from having books read to them was remarkable and uncanny. They couldn't have known what the books were about in advance, but somehow they decoded the language using the few words they'd already learned from the amusement park signs, combining that with what they could glean from the position and repetition of words used in the books. Also, each of them seemed to be able to quickly communicate to others what they'd learned, so that the knowledge was shared almost instantaneously among all. The task would have been daunting for the most advanced computers humans had ever constructed, but the Tattoo People possessed logical capabilities far superior. They didn't need computers for in many ways the Tattoo People were computers—organic computers that used neurons instead of silicon chips. They processed, stored, and shared data in much the same way 22nd Century cloud computing was accomplished on Earth, but with much greater efficiency. The Tattoo People didn't so much think as compute—by reconfiguring their internal software as needed. They created customized applications to perform whatever tasks needed to be done. Their ability to transmit and receive radio waves was just another manifestation of their amazing capacity to self-manipulate the electrochemical pathways in their bodies to perform multiple functions.

One of the more astounding demonstrations of their capabilities was seen when they asked their human friends for one of the translating devices. Benjamin surrendered his, and the next day Katru appeared with a small wooden medallion hung around his neck. It was disc-shaped and smoothly polished on all sides except for the front, which contained a circular patch of fabric made from a greenish colored cloth. Katru smiled proudly as the words "Good morning, Benjamin" emerged from the disc in electronic precision. The Tattoo People had replicated the functionality of the translating device. Before long, all the aliens carried identical discs around their necks, each rendering the radio waves generated in their bodies to audible voices that were as distinct from one to the next as human voices.

The precision with which the Tattoo People could control the electrochemical processes in their bodies was also the origin of the tattoos they all wore. By mentally adjusting specialized cells embedded in their skin, they could alter the pigmentation, producing finely etched images of varying colors—some even luminous in the dark. It was almost an art form for the Tattoo People, and whenever possible they proudly displayed the images they'd created. It was what had enabled some of the Tattoo People, who craved to perform in the theme parks of Happiness, to design their skin in such a way that they looked sufficiently like humans to be indistinguishable among the other entertainers.

The Tattoo People were excellent boatmen also. The vine had overgrown many rivers, lakes and ponds, which were connected with artificial and natural waterways, part of a vast complex network that enabled them to move freely and quickly over large distances. A series of locks and canals allowed them to travel expeditiously upstream, and levees and dams permitted them to move swiftly and safely downstream. In some places the vine had been trained to completely enclose the waterways in the same way the roads had been constructed. In other places, the space above the waterways was left uncovered. Thus, the boats sometimes passed through dark tunnels formed from the foliage that suddenly opened up to the blue sky above. The waterways were also punctuated by small ponds and lakes, often fed by waterfalls. Sandy beaches had been made by training back the vegetation. These were popular spots for Tattoo People and their children. They were used for recreation and bathing, as other than that there were no other means by which Tattoo People cleaned themselves. During the weeks that Xyla read to them, the Tattoo People had taken her to one such pond, an exceptionally large and beautiful one, fed by a broad cascade and with several secluded beaches. Xyla bathed there, marveling at the cleansing quality of the water, and luxuriating in the tingling coolness as she lay drying in the sun.

While Xyla lived among the Tattoo People, reading to them as often as she could, Benjamin and Druix found their own pastimes. Druix spent much time with Gmobo. He was the librarian of the Tattoo People. As Gmobo's English improved, they spoke endlessly about the history of the Tattoo People and the planet upon which they lived.

Benjamin took long walks, exploring the many paths the Tattoo People had constructed through the forest, taking thousands of photographs. Fortunately, Happiness had a weak magnetic field and Benjamin's navigation device was able to guide him back from wherever he roamed by recording the magnetic path he had taken and reversing it. During one of his walks, Benjamin stumbled upon the pond where Xyla happened to be bathing. He greeted her and she waved back, submerged to her neck in the sparkling water.

"Do you mind if I watch?" asked Benjamin.

"No," answered Xyla, and she continued her swimming.

Benjamin sat on one of the thick trunks of the surrounding vine. It probably had been trained to grow in that spot to provide a seat by the pond. Benjamin watched Xyla, shielding his eyes from the sun's glare. She was an excellent swimmer and something about the way she moved through the water struck Benjamin with an eerie feeling of familiarity. She was wearing a snug-fitting swimsuit the Tattoo People had made for her out of leaves from the vine.

"Why don't you join me?" Xyla asked.

Benjamin smiled. "Not today. I can't imagine it would be very comfortable swimming in my jumpsuit, and I don't think you want me taking it off."

"No, I don't," laughed Xyla.

"How's the reading going?"

"They can't get enough of it. I can't get enough of it."

"Have you read the books before?"

"A few, but not many."

"You didn't read much growing up on Earth?"

Xyla's face darkened and she turned to swim away.

"I'm sorry," Benjamin called after her. "I was just making conversation."

Xyla returned with a few graceful strokes. "Life is not always conducive to reading. In some cultures, in some societies, in some situations, it's a luxury."

"Yes," agreed Benjamin. "And certainly Union training did not offer much time for leisure reading."

"No," Xyla said. She shivered.

"Can I help you out?" Benjamin asked, rising and walking to the edge of the pond.

Xyla swam to him and extended a hand. He took it and pulled her up. Benjamin looked into her eyes and again felt a twinge of familiarity. Xyla was stunning. He was afraid to look down at her body, which dripped glistening drops of water. "I guess the Tattoo People didn't give you a towel."

"No," said Xyla. She was looking intently back at Benjamin. He stepped to her side and put an arm around her shoulder, trying very hard to make it seem a friendly gesture and nothing more, but Xyla leaned into him and their bodies touched. It was at that moment Benjamin knew who Xyla was. Or was she? How could she be?

After several weeks of being read to almost continuously by Xyla, the Tattoo People could carry on easy conversations with their human visitors. They had mass-produced the translating devices and all wore the medallions, never missing an opportunity to show off their knowledge of not one, but two human languages. Little by little, the conversations they had with human guests revealed the secrets of their origin. They had come to the planet via the asteroid, which was no asteroid at all, but a space transportation system that carried the biological information needed to start a new civilization of Tattoo People. The process began with the seeding of the fast-growing vine, which served multiple purposes. The hardy plant spread voraciously wherever it took hold, not only destroying other competing plant species, but also transforming whatever atmosphere was present. The photosynthetic processes of the plant produced the oxygen necessary for the survival of the Tattoo People. It was biologically programmed such that when atmospheric conditions were favorable and stabilized, it bore fruit. In this case, however, the fruit contained not plant DNA, but the DNA to replicate the Tattoo People. The pod-like fruit that grew on the vine were wombs within which the first batch of Tattoo People were cloned. Once mature, the fruit fell from the branches and the new beings emerged into an atmosphere already perfectly adjusted for their survival. Once that initial yield of fruit was produced, the vine no longer cloned more individuals. Subsequently, it produced edible berries, which were the primary food source of the Tattoo People. And, of course, the vine was also used to bioform houses, streets, bridges, and other infrastructure the new civilization would need.

Even though the asteroid had collided thousands of years before, and the original Tattoo People had died long ago, all the knowledge about their origin was flawlessly passed on through many generations. So efficient was the mechanism by which information was communicated through time that nothing was lost. The Tattoo People possessed a collective knowledge and awareness that extended back to the first generation. They enjoyed a unified soul, making all of them feel as though part of a larger being. The capacity to transmit, receive, and relay messages at the speed of light connected all the Tattoo People of Happiness so efficiently that they thought and acted as a single entity. Be that as it may, none had any knowledge about the beings that originally launched the space vehicles carrying the biologic material from which their civilization had started. They were surprised when Benjamin told them that it was likely that large vehicles carrying their DNA had crashed into other planets and started similar civilizations. When Benjamin expressed this idea to Katru, the Tattoo man replied, "If you're right, then there may be more of our people on other planets."

"Almost certainly," said Benjamin. "It's quite probable your creators made the plant extremely hardy and adaptable." Benjamin was thinking about the planet Alpha that Carl Stormer had set on fire during his brief visit. He had not only destroyed a plant. In the process, he had stopped the birth of a new civilization. Benjamin decided it was best not to tell the Tattoo People about that particular disaster.

"I suppose we will never know how many worlds were created by our ancestors," mused Katru.

"What intrigues me," said Druix, "Is why your creators endeavored to plant vines on so many planets throughout the galaxy."

"To propagate the species," answered Benjamin. "To assure the survival of their race."

"But why would that matter to them?" persisted Druix. "I can see it would be important to ensure that your children and descendants had a secure place in the universe, but in this case there's no real connection between those born from the vine on distant planets and the aliens that launched the vehicles carrying the DNA. Why bother creating homes on other planets for unborn beings who don't even remember who you are or where they came from?"

"I wouldn't say there is no connection," put in Katru.

"What's the connection?" asked Druix.

Katru paused. He was searching his vocabulary for the right words to answer the question. "The connection is who we are. We possess an awareness of being part of something greater. It is difficult to explain, but you can ask any of us. We all feel a connection to this greater truth. It defines us and gives us our identity. That, I believe, is what our creators were trying to sustain and propagate—who we are. Do you understand?"

Benjamin and Druix looked at each other with blank expressions. Then Benjamin said, "Not really. Not so much. For humans it's more about the individual. There's no group connection that we all strive to be part of."

Katru processed this for several moments. "That makes me sad. It must be lonely being human."

Benjamin and Druix said nothing. They had to agree: it seemed that humans were doomed forever to live on a planet called Loneliness.

Another time, Benjamin and Druix questioned Katru about whether he was the leader of the Tattoo People, and Katru laughed. He told them the Tattoo People had no leader. They were ruled by the collective will of the people, which was easy to measure at any particular moment. Whenever a sufficient number of them felt strongly about any issue, they'd transmit their feelings to the rest of the population. In the 22nd Century, that was done through surveys and electronic tabulation methodologies, which was a flawed and inefficient process. In any case, it was unlikely the people of Earth would have a unified collective will. Unlike the Tattoo People, civilization on Earth suffered from multiple personality disorder. Even if it were possible to measure the collective will of Earth's population, there'd be no convergence by which decisions could be made. Earth's population was too divergent going in, and any hope of getting billions of people on the same page on any issue was slim to none. Katru was a local leader only as long as he was recognized as such by the Tattoo People in the region.

Benjamin was still amazed at the ability of the Tattoo People to communicate with each other instantaneously over the entire planet. Although the signal from an individual Tattoo person wasn't strong enough to traverse the globe, they'd relay messages to each other with split-second efficiency. Tattoo people were continuously bombarded by radio waves from all others in their vicinity, but they had the uncanny ability to filter out all but the signal they were most interested in, much like humans could do when trying to hold a conversation in a very noisy room.

"We're fascinated by the human psyche," Katru said to Benjamin and Druix one day. "In many ways, it represents a primitive form of our civilization. We have individual minds and free will, but we're also part of a larger whole that takes intelligence and cognizance to a higher level."

"It could be the next step," mused Druix.

"The next step in what?" asked Benjamin.

"In human evolution. Perhaps homo sapiens has gone as far as it can go with humans acting individually. The next great leap in evolution is a species where the individuals communicate and interact in such a way as to create a single super-being."

"I could see where such a species might win in the survival contest," said Benjamin.

"Very true," said Druix. He sighed. "All we have to do is figure out how to communicate with each other by radio waves."

"We know how to do that already," said Benjamin. "We just can't do it in our heads."

"Makes all the difference in the world," concluded Druix.

Katru nodded and smiled knowingly.

One day, Katru offered to take Benjamin, Xyla, and Druix on a trip to see other sights on the planet. They agreed without hesitation, anxious to explore the world of the Tattoo People and confident there was much more to be seen. They weren't disappointed. They traveled by boat with a crew of a half dozen Tattoo People who navigated the waterways with utmost ease and skill. The three humans relaxed to the gentle splashing of the water on the boats bow and marveled at the way the vine had been trained to construct the waterway. The spirals and curves of its interlaced branches were never quite the same, and each displayed an esthetic balance and grace that was unique and special.

After several hours, the waterway broadened and merged into a very large lake. The distant shore could barely be seen, but the sight that caught their attention was a prominent island in the middle of the lake. Benjamin immediately recalled it as the replica of Nucleanis, Prosperity's only continent. Now it was covered with vegetation. Only the triangular peaks of the three pyramids stood out above the greenery. When he and Ilsa had visited the theme park, they'd climbed one of the pyramids together. It was an eerie feeling, seeing the structures again after so much time.

Now the group landed on the island and set out to explore it. The native vegetation surprised them. The vine hadn't been able to spread across the lake to the island. The vegetation that remained was part of the original landscaping designed thousands of years earlier. Hardly any evidence remained of the walkways and buildings that had been part of the theme park, but the Tattoo People had carved out new routes through the shrubbery. They walked along these trails and visited each of the three pyramids. At the last pyramid, the Tattoo People led them on a circuitous trail that led to the far side of the structure. There they found an entryway into the base of the pyramid, blocked by a large wooden door, which looked far too new to have been part of the original construction. It took three of the Tattoo People to push the door open. They entered and walked along a corridor toward the interior of the pyramid, the darkness growing deeper with every step. When it was no longer possible to see, Katru stopped the group. They stood and waited. Several seconds later, the Tattoo People began to glow, and soon the room was illuminated by the diffuse blue light emanating from the exposed parts of their bodies. Before them, stacked in disordered heaps was a vast assortment of jewelry, gemstones, precious metals, paintings, tapestries, books, glassware, pottery, and other valuables from the great civilizations of Earth.

Awestruck, Benjamin, Xyla, and Druix strolled among the piles of treasure, occasionally caressing the precious items in reverence. The tattoo men followed, providing continuous illumination as they went deeper into the darkness of the chamber. Benjamin stopped at a large mass of crumpled gold foil, easily as tall as two men.

"What is that?" asked Druix.

"I'm not sure," said Benjamin. "It appears to be gold. Back in the 22nd Century, gold foil like this was used to insulate instruments on spacecraft."

"The pirates," said Druix. "Remember the report that they'd stolen satellites from orbit around Earth."

"They stole them for the gold. Such incredible madness," pronounced Benjamin.

The group completed one circuit of the room and then wordlessly walked along the corridor to exit the pyramid. They stood blinking in the glare of the sunlight. Benjamin spoke first. "Do you know that this treasure is extremely valuable to humans?" he asked Katru.

"Yes, we surmised that. These are beautiful objects to us as well. We enjoy coming to look at them, and occasionally remove some—temporarily, of course."

"Do you know how the treasure got here?" asked Xyla.

"We don't know who brought the treasure, but it was relatively recent. The door of the pyramid is not as old as the amusement park, and its construction is not the same as other doors in the park, most of which have disintegrated. It had to be added later. We believe it was installed at the same time the treasure was put inside the pyramid."

"Do the humans in the city know about the treasure?" asked Benjamin.

"We don't believe so. We've never asked because until now we haven't been able to communicate with humans. In any case, none of the humans ever come here. As far as we know, they don't even know the pyramids exist."

Benjamin shuffled his feet nervously in the sandy ground. "Katru, if you don't mind, I suggest you not tell the humans about this treasure. These kinds of valuables have a way of changing people."

"We understand. We've learned more than language from the books Xyla has read to us. Wealth of this kind caused much grief to humans on Earth. We find it interesting that humans allow things of beauty and value to cause such destruction."

"Yes, it's an enigma," said Benjamin. "I'd like to say that humankind has progressed since the days when treasure caused so much evil, but I'm not sufficiently sure to feel comfortable letting too many people know about this."

"Thank you," said Katru. "We will heed your advice. I have the feeling you may offer similar advice when we take you to our next destination."

Benjamin, Xyla, and Druix looked at each other. They realized they were being trusted with secrets the Tattoo People had kept to themselves for hundreds of years. It was a burden they hadn't anticipated. In all the scenarios they'd considered and discussed prior to landing on Happiness, the possibility that they'd be trusted with preserving the secrets of an alien civilization had not been one of them.

They returned to the boat and continued their traversal of the lake, exiting into the channel of another river. Here they moved upstream. The current was weak but they still made good progress. Katru had warned them they would have to spend the night somewhere, because their next destination couldn't be reached the same day. That night, Benjamin and Druix had their first sampling of just one of the many foods the Tattoo People created from the berries produced by the ubiquitous vine. Benjamin asked if there were fish in the rivers and streams they'd been traveling on. Katru believed there were, possibly introduced at the time the theme park was created. Since the Tattoo People couldn't conceive of eating fish, they'd never thought of catching them as a source of food. Katru was even more adamant when Benjamin mentioned that fish were normally cooked before being eaten. Tattoo people avoided fires at all cost. They couldn't risk starting a fire that might easily spread and destroy the vine so important to their survival.

They slept on a sandy beach next to the river, all lost in their own thoughts, listening to the gentle lapping of the water against the boat's hull. The glow from the Tattoo People, which had been sufficiently bright to illuminate their camp in the early evening hours, gradually faded till they were left in complete darkness. Above them, they saw a brilliant display of stars, all completely unfamiliar. Later in the evening, a particularly bright object rose above the line of vegetation that surrounded them. They knew it to be the nearby planet of Prosperity. The people of that planet had created the theme park on Happiness, but then abandoned it because of the impact of a large object from space. To this day, they'd never entertained the notion that some on the planet survived the collision and started a new society. Or that the object from space had carried the ingredients for the birth of an alien civilization, which now coexisted and shared Happiness with its human neighbors. What other bizarre possibilities did the universe admit?

The next day, they boarded the boat again and resumed their trip upstream. The current strengthened as the stream narrowed and the Tattoo People worked hard to maintain the forward motion of the vessel. Benjamin, Xyla, and Druix felt guilty that they weren't helping, but the Tattoo People seemed to accept their task with little complaint. Considering their thin frames and small size, they were incredibly strong. When they tired, they guided the boat to the shoreline where narrow inlets allowed them to rest without the current drawing the boat downstream again. These inlets weren't natural; they'd been created by training back the surrounding vegetation producing a notch in the shoreline within which the boat fit perfectly. It was like a ratchet in a gear that prevented the backward movement in response to an opposing force.

Later in the day, the stream widened again and they made better time. Along with the broadening of the stream, the vegetation that had been growing right up to the shoreline receded, leaving open, flat areas on each side of the watercourse. Before long, they found themselves in the middle of a large meadow upon which grasses and shrubs grew. For some reason, the vine that covered most of the planet had not grown over this area, and the natural vegetation remained.

"Why hasn't the vine grown here?" Benjamin asked.

"It did once," answered Katru. "We've trained it back to leave this meadow. The meadow is very large. It took a great deal of work to teach the vine not to grow here."

"Then why have you done it?" asked Druix.

Katru smiled. "You will see soon."

Sometime later they rounded a bend in the stream, and the full extent of the meadow opened before them. It wasn't a meadow at all, but the entry to a large plain, so vast that it disappeared into a hazy horizon. It appeared flat, but low hills and shallow valleys could easily be hidden within the topology. The vegetation consisted of the same grasses and shrubs, except that dotting the landscape were larger bushes and trees, black against the muted yellows and greens of the surrounding plants. Or were they bushes and trees? As the three humans tried to focus their eyes on the expanded scale of the new vista, the dark spots moved, changing position against the inanimate backdrop.

"Animals," Benjamin was the first to pronounce.

"Where did they come from?" Druix asked.

"They've always been here," answered Katru. "We discovered them living among the vine—or barely living. The vine is engineered so that its leaves and branches are inedible. Only the berries can be eaten, but they aren't produced until after our initial population was born. As the vine grew, the animals migrated, trying to find the remaining grasses before they were choked out. Many species probably didn't survive. The carnivores were more successful."

"There are predatory animals here, too?" asked Xyla.

"Yes. We've made no effort to select the animals that live here on this plain. When we realized there were animals on the planet, we trained the vine back to leave space where they'd have a chance of survival. It has worked. The population of the animals is fairly stable, as far as we can tell. We try not to interfere."

"The theme park had a zoo," said Benjamin. "It was filled with animals brought from Earth by the same fleet of vehicles that established Prosperity."

"What types of animals are here?" asked Xyla.

"You will have to help us with that," said Katru. "We've tried to compare them to pictures in the books we found in the pyramid, but there weren't enough of those. And the pictures we found bore little resemblance to these animals."

"Thousands of years have passed since the pictures in those books were taken," said Druix. "The animal species could have changed significantly in that time."

"Yes," agreed Katru. "They are mostly mammals, but reptiles and amphibians are also present. There are a few species of birds—only those that can live off small animals or the berries. There are few insects on the planet."

"How about domestic animals?" asked Druix.

"They are not domestic anymore. The feral cats and wild dogs may be descended from domesticated animals. It's difficult to tell now."

"Can we get closer?" Benjamin asked.

"Certainly. We will walk from here." Katru signaled the

other Tattoo men to steer the boat to a landing. "We must explore the plain while the sun is up. Before dusk we need to return to the boat. Many of the predatory animals are nocturnal."

Benjamin, Xyla, and Druix spent the remaining hours of the day hiking over the gently rolling hills of the plain, trying to observe the animals up close. Benjamin had brought his camera, which could zoom in on far away objects with remarkable precision, displaying the image on a plastic sheet that unfolded to a size that could be comfortably viewed by the whole group. Even the Tattoo People were amazed by the technology. It seemed ironic that aliens, who had crossed the galaxy and established a new civilization on a biologically engineered planet, didn't possess even the most rudimentary electronic devices. Why should they, when their anatomies provided all the same capabilities without exterior contrivances?

Benjamin's familiarity with animals was limited to only those still around in the 22nd Century. The population of North American and European mammals had diminished substantially. Their habitats couldn't be sustained with the rise of human populations and the increasing encroachment of urban areas into the few remaining open spaces. Africa, Australia, and to some extent South America still had a tremendous diversity of wild life. The animals brought to Happiness came from a time 50,000 years later. How many of those species had survived the environmental and climatic disasters that had taken place in the intervening years? Xyla and Druix were acquainted with some of those species from their time on Earth in the 420th Century.

Exploring the region the Tattoo People had protected and kept isolated for thousands of years was a lesson in what animal traits were important for survival. Herd animals did well, but only the smaller ones needing minimal vegetation to thrive upon. There was evidence that many mammals lived in subsurface dens and dry tree trunks, but most were probably nocturnal, as Benjamin and the others saw only a few rodent-like creatures, scurrying away into the underbrush. There may also have been reptiles, but neither snakes nor lizards were seen. As far as they could tell, no birds or flying insects existed on the planet, but they found worms, slugs, and other crawling animals dwelling in the soil. The Tattoo People asserted that there were carnivorous four-legged creatures who preyed upon the herds of plant-eating animals, but they were unable to come upon any. It would take many weeks to discover all the species that existed in the area. Benjamin wondered whether they'd ever have the opportunity to return and see more, perhaps bringing supplies and gear that would allow them to stay overnight.

The return trip was faster, as they moved with the current over much of the trip. Nevertheless, when night fell, they were still moving along the dark waterways. The bodies of the Tattoo men glowed, providing enough light for them to complete their journey. Exhausted by the day's exertions and mentally striving to assimilate all they'd seen, Benjamin, Xyla, and Druix had little to say. Benjamin broke the silence. "Katru, don't you think it's time your people met with the humans from the city?"

"Yes," Katru answered without hesitation. "Now that we can communicate in the language of the humans, we will meet with them. There is much that we can learn from each other."

"That's what I was thinking," said Benjamin. "They know nothing about your people. They believe you're humans who live in the forest and possess special acrobatic and gymnastic skills. That's all. They should learn the truth." Benjamin's voice was critical, as if he was embarrassed by his fellow humans.

"It's not their fault. We made no attempt to inform them. We were just happy they let us perform in their shows. Our people have learned a great deal from them. We have only limited capacity for artistic expression, mostly confined to what we can display by controlling the pigmentation of our skin. We control the glands that produce the pigmentation in the same way you control muscles in your body. Just as your brain sends messages to nerves to activate muscles, our brain can control both muscles and pigmentation. However, we never thought to use our brains to express as your brains do. By watching humans, we've learned that our minds are capable of other art forms as well:

music, dance, acrobatics, drawing, sculpture. There was a time when those were incomprehensible to our people. The humans awakened our awareness. This happened long ago, of course, but with our people, any knowledge or skill that is learned becomes permanently engrained in our nature. What began as something that needed to be learned now comes naturally, instinctively to us. We owe that to your human friends."

"I'm happy to hear that," said Benjamin. "But it's also true that they have much to learn from you. I believe there's good synergy between your people and the humans. It's time to realize the interconnections."

"Yes," agreed Katru. "Synergy. I understand the word. We will do as you advise."

CHAPTER 35

— 119,480 —

To celebrate the new alliance between the Tattoo People and the humans of the city, they arranged a show that surpassed any previously performed, even in the glory days of the Happiness Theme Park.

The festivities began with the entry of the Tattoo People. The humans sat scattered about the oval-shaped stadium, barely filling half of the available seats in the massive structure, which had been built long ago for the many visitors from Prosperity. The crowd was silenced with the peal of a large bell and, in the stillness that followed, a distant flute was heard, playing a gentle marching melody that gradually grew louder. The audience strained their necks to see the source of the music, but it was from outside the stadium. They waited in anticipation, and soon the sound resolved itself into not one, but many flutes, playing in remarkable unison. It was too perfect to be many people playing the flute separately. It was more like one person playing many flutes. The crowd stood, eyes fixed on the arched entryway at one end of the stadium.

Then, Tattoo People entered in pairs and parted to parade before the spectators on each side of the arena. The humans had no conception of how many Tattoo People lived in the forest that surrounded them. And this was the first time they saw the children of the Tattoo People—lively and energetic little sprites, just as excited at being in the stadium of the humans as the humans watching them. They were equally light on their feet and flexible in their movements as the Tattoo People who had been entertaining the humans for many years. They did flips and cartwheels and exhibited a freeness of spirit inspiring to all. The line of Tattoo People seemed never-ending. They continued to file along the inner perimeter of the playing field to the inspiring cadence of the flute music.

When the stream of Tattoo People entering at last came to an end, the music abruptly stopped. With incredible precision they turned in unison to face the stands where the human spectators watched and waited expectantly. Then, as one, they all bowed to their hosts, which evoked unrestrained applause from the humans. With that approval, the Tattoo People jumped nimbly into the stands and ran among the humans, bowing, shaking hands, doing flips, and, incredibly, bestowing on each a marvelous gift—stunning pieces of jewelry—bracelets, necklaces, watches, and rings of all shapes, sizes and composition. Thus, the timeless and irreplaceable treasures of Earth were returned to its descendants by the aliens of Happiness in a gesture of interstellar solidarity and goodwill. The aliens then took seats among their new friends. After many thousands of years, the stadium was again filled with an audience breathlessly waiting for a new show to begin.

The bell rang once more. There was a collective hush in the massive arena, and from the archway came an unprecedented parade of entertainers. First, a line of youngsters carrying flags—the flags of the different regions of the Happiness theme park—appeared. Behind the flag bearers was the band, marching proudly and playing a rousing circus tune. The clowns were next, several hundred at least, both human and Tattoo People, whose antics thrilled and amused the audience, still standing and clapping to the tune of the marching song. The acrobats then entered, mostly Tattoo People, but some humans as well, performing impossible kinetic feats as if gravity didn't exist for them. The acrobats were followed by other entertainers, walking in a neat phalanx, waving at the crowd, blowing kisses, and bowing. These were the actors, singers, dancers, and musicians who would be entrancing the crowd with a show that lasted the entire day and transported the spectators, both human and alien, into a new world defined by the physical domain of the stadium, the artistic talents of the performers, and the universal need, desire, and will to just be happy.

In the days following the show, the remainder of the treasure was handed over to the humans by the Tattoo people. The art, ceramics, sculpture, books, precious metals, and glassware were distributed among the galleries and museums of the replica of

New York City. Even the gold foil was turned over to the humans, given to one of the art schools, where it was used to add brilliant coatings to sculptures and statuary.

CHAPTER 36

— 119,480 —

With mixed feelings of anticipation and regret, Benjamin took the long walk back to the battlefield where they'd landed the space capsules months before. He needed to check out the capsules and prepare them for their departure. Their mission was complete, successful beyond anything he could have imagined. They had not only found the aliens, but they'd been able to communicate and connect with them in a way that surpassed all expectation. They had learned much from the aliens, and it was good knowledge, heartening to the human spirit—a secret that elevated the human condition and gave it profound importance, purpose, and hope. It was a message that had to be conveyed to Benjamin's fellow humans across the galaxy.

The triangular silhouettes of the three space capsules grew larger before him. It was only as he approached within a hundred meters that he discerned odd irregularities in their profiles. He hadn't seen the vehicles since the landing, but he didn't recall any damage sustained during their descent or impact. His pace quickened and with every step his feeling of dread heightened. The hatches of all three capsules had been removed. Much of the exterior hulls of the vehicles had been removed as well, exposing the interior spaces that contained the wiring and control electronics. Entering the first of the three capsules he came to, which was Xyla's, he found the interior gutted. All the metal panels of the control console, storage areas, and electronics racks had been torn out, leaving the skeletal remains of the naked support structure.

Benjamin's heart sank. If all three capsules were in similar condition, then there was no way any of them would ever leave the planet. Glumly, he extracted his ever-present camera and recorded images of the remains of the three capsules. Then he started the long walk back to New York.

"It was to make the bell," Ostinia explained apologetically.

"But why would you destroy our space capsules?" Benjamin's voice was high pitched. He hated himself for it.

"How else? We don't manufacture metal here. Everything you see made of metal has been retooled from objects left in the amusement park, much of it unusable because of deterioration through the years."

"But our space capsules!" cried Benjamin. "Didn't you realize we wouldn't be able to use them again?"

"We didn't think you wanted to return to space? How could we have known? Why would you want to leave Happiness?"

"You could have asked first," said Benjamin, calming down somewhat after considering the simplicity of Ostinia's question.

"I would have, but those that removed the metal from your capsules did it without consulting me. It was too late by the time I learned how they had constructed the bell." Ostinia paused. "Besides, it's a beautiful bell."

———————

That evening, Benjamin explained to Druix what had happened, and the next day they both went to the forest to tell Xyla. As usual, they found her reading to the Tattoo People, but now she was also teaching them to read. When they'd told her about the destruction of the space capsules, she smiled in resignation. "I'm very sorry. I'm sorry for both of you. As for me, to be honest, I've been thinking that I'd rather stay here than return to space."

Benjamin felt an inexplicable limpness come over him, as if his body was suspending activity until it could determine how to respond to Xyla's statement. "What do you mean?" he asked, knowing very well what she meant.

Xyla ignored the question. "Do the radios on the capsules still work? Perhaps you can call for help."

"I don't know, but it doesn't matter. Any explorer vehicle is probably many light years away. And it's not clear what they could do anyway."

Xyla shrugged. "I'm sorry, Benjamin. I don't know what to tell you." Her voice trailed off at the last words, as if she were finally realizing how devastating the truth was to him.

"Is there any hope the capsules can be repaired?" asked Druix.

"I don't have the skills to repair them. Even if I were able to, can you imagine how dangerous it'd be to return to space in reconstructed galactic space capsules?"

Druix nodded in agreement. Then he said, "You'd have to make sure the launch capability was intact. Presumably they didn't remove the rocket engines and there's still fuel in the vehicles. Once you get to space, the most important system is the magnetocryogenic chamber. Even without the intergalactic propulsion system working, you could just remain frozen until someone came along to rescue you. You'd have to get the radio working to send out a distress signal. They know where we are. They'll be listening."

"Or you could get to Prosperity," offered Xyla. "They could help you."

Benjamin didn't know when the conversation had shifted to him leaving Happiness instead of all three of them. "Are you both staying here then?" he asked.

Xyla looked at Druix. "I can't speak for my son. He needs to decide how he wants to spend the rest of his life. I'd love it if he stayed, but there's very little for him here."

"I'm not even thinking about it," said Druix. "Unless we have the means to return to space, I don't have to make that choice."

"Those space capsules are incredibly complex machines," said Benjamin. "What about the defense systems for protecting the capsules from collisions? Without those, traveling through space will be incredibly risky."

"Maybe," said Druix. "It would depend on the interstellar environment you're traveling in. You could pick a route where the probability of encountering other objects is almost negligible."

Benjamin looked from Xyla to Druix. They were both examining him, trying to read his thoughts, unnerving him. "I'm taking another walk out to the capsules to check them out again. Do either of you want to come along?"

Xyla shook her head. Druix hesitated, then said, "Sure. I'll go along."

On his second visit to the capsules, the destruction didn't seem as bad. It was certainly true that large amounts of material had been removed from all three, but it might be possible to scavenge bits and pieces to repair one of them. Fortunately, most of the electronics was still operational, even though the metal housing, and in some cases the cabling, had been removed. Only one of the three computers worked. Benjamin decided to make that capsule the one he'd try to repair.

Over the next several weeks, Benjamin spent all his time working on the capsule, stripping pieces off of the other two when he could. When he couldn't, he'd ask for help from Ostinia, who, feeling responsible for the demise of the vehicles, was very willing to assist. As it turned out, the humans on Happiness were excellent metal workers. Their existences had depended on the ability to salvage from the rubble of the ancient amusement park and use it to rebuild infrastructure. Without electricity or other forms of motorized technology, they had to do everything by hand, forging the metal in blazing ovens and pounding it into shapes with hammers. Yet their skills had been honed through the years such that little was beyond their capabilities. Before long, the capsule looked as though it had never been touched. But the most difficult task still had to be completed successfully—repairing the mechanical, electronic, and propulsion systems. The motors of the rockets used for launching were particularly critical, but this was the one system that couldn't be tested ahead of time. There was little fuel on the capsule to spare.

Finally, Benjamin completed the repairs and performed the tests he could. There was nothing left to do except board the capsule to see if it could be launched. Only one attempt could be made and it had to work. Benjamin sent messages to Xyla and Druix, asking that they meet him for lunch at one of the small restaurants in the recreated New York. Benjamin was the last to arrive. Druix and Xyla sat at a table set well apart from the other guests, as the restaurants and other establishments in the city were never full. Benjamin took the seat next to Druix, facing Xyla. She was wearing a sleeveless smock made from the fabric the Tattoo People wove from the leaves of the vine.

"One capsule is fixed," he said. "I've run all the tests I can run on it without wasting fuel. It's ready to go."

"When will you leave?" asked Xyla, with a hint of sadness in her voice.

Benjamin took a sip from the water glass in front of him. "I'm not leaving."

"What?" Druix and Xyla said together. They looked at each other in confusion.

"I'm not leaving Happiness," repeated Benjamin. Then he looked away, fixing his eyes at a window at the front of the restaurant. After a long moment, he returned his glance to Xyla. "I should be angry," he said.

Xyla let out a long slow sigh. "You know," she said.

Benjamin just nodded, his eyes locked on hers.

"When did you find out?"

"It doesn't matter," said Benjamin. "What's more important is why you didn't tell me."

"Benjamin, I couldn't. When I found out you were married, I thought it best if you didn't know who I was."

"Druix is my son," said Benjamin, through clenched teeth. "You didn't think it was important for me to know that?"

"Benjamin, I'm sorry." Xyla's voice was breaking. She looked at Druix.

"It was a joint decision," Druix said. "We both agreed it would be best. We needed new lives. Benjamin, think of what we went through. Think of how far we've come."

Benjamin nodded, angry creases lining his face. "There's

one capsule that's operational. I am not leaving. You two should decide which of you will leave." He rose, turned, and walked out of the restaurant.

Druix walked with Xyla through the sunlit streets of the little New York City. Her steps were slow and heavy. "You should leave," she said. "There's more for you out there than here."

"I won't leave you alone," Druix said.

"I'll be fine. The Tattoo People accept me. I'll have a home with them."

They walked in silence. The streets were empty save for a few groups of teenagers on their way from school. Xyla and Druix no longer attracted attention as they had in the weeks after their arrival. That fact led credibility to Xyla's words, but there was a larger issue that hung over them.

"Why do you think he's not leaving?" asked Druix.

"I don't know. I'm sure he'd like to. He just knows he can't."

"Why can't he?"

"Think about it, Druix. If he leaves, he's doomed us to live out our lives on this planet. He's taken away our choice. He may be angry and upset, but he's still the Benjamin I came to know on Aurora."

"He won't stay angry. He just needs time to adjust—to accept."

Xyla grabbed Druix's hand and stopped him. She turned him around to face her—a mother addressing her son. "Druix, I think you should go. You have a career. You're an historian and a professor. You need to tell others what has happened here—about the aliens. But I have to do one thing before you do, and I hope you understand."

"What?"

"I have to try to convince him to leave. He has a wife and a child waiting for him. They need him. He has to return to them."

"I do understand," Druix said. "And I honestly hope you're successful. I'm prepared to stay here with you. I can continue my work just as well on Happiness."

"Thank you," said Xyla. With a shake of her head, she gave a short laugh. "Druix, we've led strange lives and I think it's about to get even stranger."

Druix smiled and hugged his mother. "No regrets, Mom. It sure beats what we had on Aurora."

"Yes," said, Xyla. "It certainly does."

Xyla found Benjamin sitting with Hovar on the rickety porch where the old man spent much of his life. When he saw her approach, he offered her his seat next to Benjamin. Then he disappeared into the house.

"Benjamin, you have to leave Happiness." Her voice was stern.

"I won't," he answered without hesitation.

"Why?"

"Don't ask me that. I just can't leave you and Druix here."

"We're fine here."

"I have no doubt. But you have to realize that even if…" Benjamin paused, searching for the right word. "Even if the situation were different, I still couldn't leave. It's not a choice really. I messed up by not making sure the capsules were protected. We're all caught in that mistake. Do you think I'm going to save myself and make you and Druix the victims?"

Xyla reached out and touched his arm. "But Benjamin, you have a wife and child waiting for you. Druix and I have no one waiting for us. No one will miss us if we stay here. We understand that you have to leave. It's okay."

Benjamin said nothing. He looked down, shaking his head. He took Xyla's hand. "Thank you. I appreciate that. Can I be honest with you, Xyla?"

"Of course."

"I've just learned recently that someone I loved a very long time ago is alive and here with me. And now I also have a son. There's no hurry for any of us to leave. I, for one, would just like to get to know you and Druix better. You're both way ahead of me on that score. You've known all along. I need to catch up."

"Benjamin, I'm so sorry."

"It'll be okay," Benjamin said. He released her hand, patted her on the arm, and left. It was the most hurtful thing he could have done to her. She sat in stunned silence and watched him walk away.

The next day, Benjamin asked Katru if he could visit the miniature continent of Nucleanis alone. Katru provided Benjamin with a small rowboat, which Benjamin effortlessly propelled across the calm surface of the lake. The island was used as a getaway spot for Tattoo People, but there were never more than a few there at any time. Benjamin noticed with amusement that one group was practicing acrobatic movements on the beach where he landed his boat. Benjamin waved to them and then set off with a small backpack. He spent the remainder of the day hiking around the island, enjoying the quiet solitude, lost in his own tumultuous thoughts.

Just as the sun began to set, he climbed the steps of one of the pyramids. At the top, he ate a packaged meal under the last vestiges of daylight. By the time he was done, it was pitch black, and he was blessed with a completely unobstructed view of the star-studded heavens. He lay down with his hands folded under his head and watched the stars in their slow, silent transit across the sky. He thought of Ilsa. He knew very well the star grouping within which his father's supply ship was located. Ilsa was there with their child, frozen in time, waiting for him. His father and Krystal were there as well, impossibly far away and infinitely unreachable. How could he remain on Happiness and ignore the grief he'd cause them when they learned that he wouldn't be coming back? In what universe would it be right to cause so much sorrow to loved ones? It was the universe he was in—the universe that created the unexpected and irreversible circumstances that trapped him on a planet called Happiness.

The pyramid was a replica of one that had been used to sacrifice humans in a time when it was believed such actions would be looked upon with favor by ancient gods. Would the gods smile on him for the sacrifice he was about to make? It was an awful analogy. The sacrifice he was making in no way compared to those gruesome exhibitions. For him it would mean spending his life on a planet with humans, whose primary goal in life was artistic expression and entertainment, and with aliens, who lived simple lives in symbiotic harmony with a prolific vine that provided all they needed, and with a woman he'd loved on a distant planet, who somehow had ended up with him, and her son, their son—all three imprisoned by fate and circumstance. In what way was it a prison at all? What had he sacrificed? The stars floating in black space above him had no answers to these questions.

———————

Xyla suffered severe depression in the weeks following her conversation with Benjamin on Hovar's porch. Benjamin's curt dismissal of her attempt to apologize had left her completely uncertain about his state of mind. She had no solid ground on which to sustain hope that her relationship with him would be repaired. Nor was there sufficient rationale for totally giving up on winning back his admiration and respect. That, at least, would have allowed her to close the door on that part of her life.

She worried about Druix. She didn't believe he'd ever find fulfillment while stranded on Happiness. He had devoted his life to studying the history of human presence in the galaxy. That all the knowledge he had achieved would die with him on this planet was a deplorable thought.

If it weren't for her work with the Tattoo children, the depression would have made her life unbearable. She spent many hours each day reading to them and teaching them to read and write. Writing was a source of great amusement to the Tattoo children. The ability to communicate via radio waves made writing unnecessary. Nevertheless, they took great delight in learning the new skills that Xyla taught them. They were naturally adept at large motor skills, but the delicate art of penmanship challenged them. With stubborn pride and persistence, they practiced diligently until they could duplicate even Xyla's graceful lines and letters.

Living in the forest and spending much of her days with the children, she didn't see Benjamin again. Druix visited her occasionally, bringing her food, clothing and other necessities from the city. He kept himself busy exploring the galleries and shops of the miniature New York. He described with great excitement the rare pieces of art he found during these expeditions. Xyla knew her son and she could tell he wasn't happy. He was trying very hard to keep engaged in life and avoid boredom, but how long could he do that? How long could Xyla herself fight off the oppression of hopelessness, as each day followed the previous day with little new to offer? It was no better than being on Aurora.

Then one day, Druix visited Xyla and told her that he had been meeting regularly with Benjamin. They'd drink coffee together in one of the small cafes near Central Park that served coffee grown and prepared with the utmost of artistic care and exactitude. Benjamin had started a journal describing their experiences on Happiness. They had long discussions about the Tattoo People, trying to solve the puzzle of why they were so much like humans. If it was true that humans and Tattoo People were the result of evolutionary processes in different parts of the galaxy, why did they have so many similarities? They each offered conjectures on the functions that are essential to all living organisms and what factors might lead evolution to a common solution to meet those requirements. They agreed it was possible that human physiology might in fact be an optimum design that evolutionary processes will eventually lead to, regardless of where in the universe they took place. Xyla was pleased to hear that Druix and Benjamin had a friendly rapport, but it also made her sad that she hadn't achieved an equivalent status.

Some time later, she went to the small pond fed by the sparkling waterfall surrounded by walls formed from the meticulously manicured alien vine. She removed her clothes and jumped in, enjoying the liberation the water offered. The world of water was one where gravity was more merciful, and she could almost convince herself that even the weight of her problems was alleviated.

She swam two laps around the pond and stopped. Looking up, she saw Benjamin, standing on the small beach at the side of the pond. The sun was behind him and even shielding her eyes with her hand, she could only see his silhouette. In the next moment, he jumped into the pond, disappearing beneath its surface. She watched his form move through the clear water beneath her. He came to the surface next to her.

"It's warmer than the water on Aurora," he said.

"Yes. No floating chunks of ice."

"Right. The ice kept getting in the way," Benjamin said.

"That's not good," agreed Xyla, but the inflection in her voice made it sound almost like a question.

"No, it's not. Except…"

"Except what?" Xyla asked, and she felt an inexplicable burst of joy.

Benjamin reached out and pulled Xyla to him. "Except it was the ice that brought us together."

They kissed, and for Xyla they could have been back on Aurora, drawn together by inescapable need and profound desire. They swam together back to the shore, falling onto the beach and rolling in the sand, reestablishing a link that had never weakened.

Later, lying with Benjamin on the side of the pond, Xyla thought of Alphons, wondering whether this was what he meant by sphere of influence. Was it this small pond, formed by an alien vine, that had finally bound her and Benjamin? Or had it been the remnant fishing hole in the ice she and Benjamin had swum in thousands of years ago? Perhaps it was the moment she and Benjamin landed on Happiness that had sealed their fate. Or was it when she became a galactic explorer and joined Benjamin's sphere, the Union network? Or maybe it was the entire galaxy. Had her union with Benjamin been ordained by a sphere of influence that couldn't be explained by any laws known to man? She'd never know. She was just happy. At least on this day, the answers to those questions no longer mattered.

———————

Two weeks later, Druix decided to leave Happiness. It was the obvious thing to do now that his mother and Benjamin had been reunited. He might have decided to depart eventually in any case, but seeing his mother so happy made it unnecessary to delay any longer. During his last few days on the planet, he spent as much time as possible with his mother and father. They knew they'd never see their son again, but they also understood the circumstances that compelled him to leave. Benjamin was more devastated than he ever could have imagined. He had just recently learned he had a son and now all too quickly he was losing one. His other child was with Ilsa, impossibly far away. He and Xyla would have no more children, in all likelihood. It was difficult for him to conceal his disappointment. Druix was having difficulty enough dealing with his mother's remorse and regret. The cruelty of life, which created circumstances that would inevitably lead to heartache and grief, was incomprehensible to him.

On the day Druix was to leave, Xyla doted on her son as if he were a five-year-old, getting ready for his first day at school.

"Go right to Sparil," she said, grasping both his shoulders in her hands. "Don't go off looking for a supply ship. You can resume your planetary exploration later, if that's what you want to do. You'll need a new space capsule anyway."

"Yes, Mom. Where else would I go?"

"Be careful who you talk to about the Tattoo People. Societies and civilizations can change a great deal in the thousands of years you've been away. Make sure the Arilians are still as peaceful and well meaning as they used to be before you tell them about Happiness."

"Of course. Don't worry, Mom. Everything will be fine. I'll do what's right."

"I know," said Xyla, wiping tears from her eyes.

Benjamin hugged his son one last time. He removed the necklace that he'd worn ever since he'd met Ilsa back in the 22nd Century at the International Galactic Explorers Technology Conference. The medallion had once carried a rendezvous plan of an old woman who was looking for her son. When he left Sparil, he and Ilsa had reprogrammed it with their own rendezvous plan. He wouldn't need it anymore.

"I've replaced the rendezvous plan on this medallion with a letter to Ilsa. Ask the Arilians on Sparil to give it to someone who might end up on Supply Ship 6. Please."

"Will do, Benjamin," Druix answered, taking the necklace in his hand. Then after a pause he said, "Dad."

They embraced again and then Druix boarded the capsule. The launch was a great spectacle for both the humans and aliens of Happiness. It was one of those rare occasions when the show in the stadium was cancelled so all could watch. Neither the aliens nor the humans of Happiness had any type of advanced technology, so when the rocket motors ignited they were filled with fear and awe. To see an object as massive as a space capsule lift vertically from the ground with such an incredible expulsion of heat, light, and sound astounded them, and when it had climbed far enough into the air they all applauded, as if it was a performance in one of their shows.

For Benjamin and Xyla however, it was no show at all. It was the closing of a door to a part of their lives they didn't want to lose, and they didn't clap.

The humans and aliens of Happiness arranged a ceremony to celebrate the union of Xyla and Benjamin. It was held at the time of the harvest, when the vine produced a sea of brilliant pink blossoms before yielding the berries that were the primary food source for the Tattoo People. For a wedding present, the Tattoo People constructed a house for the couple, formed by training the vine to create a living space adjacent to the lake where the replica of Nucleanis was located.

In the coming years, Xyla and Benjamin became the primary links between the aliens and the humans. They forged a union between the two species built on trust and respect. Commerce between the two civilizations blossomed, each benefiting from the strengths of the other. The humans learned how to work with plants to create furniture, clothing, and a host of other useful products. They also discovered a new food source in the vine's crimson berries. The Tattoo People learned from the humans how to make and use metal tools. They also learned from their human neighbors the creative art of growing crops and garden plants. They had natural instincts in nurturing plants, but previously only had the opportunity to practice their skills with the alien vine. The diversity of plant life in the world of the humans amazed them, and they became extremely useful partners in caring for and harvesting the agricultural products upon which the people of Happiness thrived.

Benjamin continued to visit the pyramids of Nucleanis through the years. He sat for hours looking across the lake at the distant horizon, now dominated by the alien vine but for the diminutive skyline of New York. He'd stay there until the sun set, after which his gaze turned upward to the stars. At one time, the sight of so many stars filled him with awe and wonder. Now it was a reminder of the life he'd left behind and could never return to. He watched the traversal across the sky of the cluster of stars where his father's supply ship was located. On these occasions, he thought of Ilsa and their child. He didn't even know if it was a boy or a girl. He loved Xyla, but knew he had to give vent to these suppressed feelings of regret and resentment that plagued him at various times. He had willingly traded a god-like existence as a galactic explorer to one of a mere mortal. Benjamin wrote much of his journal during the hours he spent atop the pyramids of Nucleanis.

Toro wondered if Stella was ever happy. No matter how much he and his men tried to satisfy her demands, she always seemed to find something to rage about. He often thought about collecting his friends and setting off on his own, finally free of her tyrannical control, but he never did. It wasn't fear that prevented him from leaving her. It was a sentiment in many ways more sadly pitiful. He and his men needed the control that Stella provided. She gave them a sense of focus and purpose. Without her, they were lost—22nd Century men a thousand centuries out of touch with the galaxy. The thought of that crippled them. Stella gave them no time to dwell on such imaginings. They were men of action, and she told them what form their action should take. It was that easy.

When they'd all been unfrozen upon their approach to Happiness, they convened in the galley of the supply ship—except, of course, for Risto, who remained frozen in the magnetocryogenic chamber of his space capsule. Theonius was there, somewhat dazed, still not accustomed to the staggering advance of time that took place while he was frozen.

Toro found Stella in the control room, scanning the data recently acquired by the observing instruments on the supply ship. Whatever she was looking at invoked such wrath in her she could hardly remain seated.

"What's wrong?" asked Toro, not sure he wanted to know.

"My island is covered with plants!"

Toro looked at the monitor, which showed an image of Happiness. It was one of those false color renditions that Toro could never understand. Stella obviously did, because she was pointing at it with an angry finger. "My island is covered with plants!" she repeated.

Toro just shrugged. "It's been thousands of years since we left. It's no surprise that it's covered with vegetation."

"We need to check on my treasure!" Stella shouted. "Just where are we going to land?"

Toro blinked uncertainly. "Are there any clear landing spots?"

"Yes, but not on the island. If we land somewhere else, how are we going to get to the treasure?"

Toro could see the problem now. "We should have hidden it someplace that wouldn't be overgrown with plants."

"Brilliant!" screamed Stella. "Thank you for that information. Now, tell me what we're going to do, to get my treasure out of that pyramid."

Toro cringed. For a moment he wanted to suggest they abandon the treasure, but then thought better of it. "Maybe we can try landing in the vegetation. If it's not too thick, the capsules will be okay."

"Idiot!" roared Stella. "The rockets will ignite the vegetation. The whole island will go up in…" She stopped. Slowly, she returned her massive body into the chair before the console. "Of course," she mused. "How silly of me not to think of it."

"What?" asked Toro meekly.

"We'll start a fire. We'll burn away the plants before we land."

"How?" asked Toro.

"The ship's laser weapon should do it. A few pulses will start a nice, toasty fire down there. The treasure is safe inside the pyramid. When the fire burns out, we'll have plenty of clear landing sites."

Toro was nodding. "Do you think there's anyone living there—on the island?"

"Who cares?" said Stella. "They'll just get in the way anyway."

Toro continued to nod, dumbly.

"Don't worry," added Stella. "The infrared cameras show no life forms on the island. The place is just vegetated."

"That's good," said Toro, genuinely relieved. "When will you start the fire?"

"The next time the supply ship passes over the island."

Two hours later, Toro looked on as Stella sat before the weapons console of the supply ship. On the monitor before her, an image of Happiness appeared, executing a slow rotation, which was in fact an apparent motion caused by the progress of the ship in its orbit. Stella waited until the supply ship was directly above the large lake containing the island with its three pyramids.

"Ready," Stella announced, moving a lever on the console that delivered power to the laser weapon.

"Aim," she said, and placed her outstretched index finger on the island where it was situated on the touch-sensitive screen.

"Fire!" she shouted, and her open palm crashed down on a large red button before her with far more force than was actually necessary. She cackled with delight and the overhead lights in the room dimmed perceptibly.

Some 200 km below the supply ship, the laser beam ignited the dry foliage on the island replica of Nucleanis..

CHAPTER 38

— 119,502 —

Benjamin was woken by electronic voices outside the home in the forest he shared with Xyla. She was still sleeping. He couldn't see her in the absolute blackness of the room carved out of the alien vine, but he could hear the steady, relaxed breathing he'd grown used to through the years. It was a natural and comforting sound, like the gentle splashing of the waves from the lakeshore outside their home. He seldom thought of Ilsa anymore. When he did, it made him feel guilty and sad.

The electronic voices outside were from the translator boxes of the Tattoo People, unusual at this time of night. He walked carefully through the dark house to the door leading outside and emerged to see the silhouette of a group of Tattoo People standing on the shore of the lake looking out at the distant island of Nucleanis. It was ablaze, and the orange glow and billowing smoke plumes filled the sky with a crimson pall.

"What happened?" Benjamin asked as he joined the crowd. Over the years, he'd become well known and liked by his neighbors.

"No one knows," came the electronic reply in the dark.

"Where is Katru?"

"He is organizing a team to surround the lake and watch for burning embers that might cross the water."

"Please tell him I'm on my way," said Benjamin.

"It is done," said the voice.

With the imminent danger of the fire raging on the island, the collective fear of the Tattoo People was real and complete. A spark landing on any part of the life-giving vine could be catastrophic.

Benjamin found Katru with a group of other Tattoo People. Many weren't wearing their translators, so Benjamin couldn't hear the discussion taking place, but soon they dispersed.

Conversations at the speed of light didn't take long. Benjamin approached Katru, who wore his translator.

"Fire is our biggest fear," said Katru to his long-time friend.

"Is there anything I can do?"

"I've dispatched teams to circle the lake and watch for burning embers blown by the wind. They will extinguish them with water if any should happen to land on the vine, but it is difficult. They may land on a part of the vine that is inaccessible. Also, we're worried about daylight. It is easy to see the glowing ashes now at night. With daybreak, it will be much more difficult."

"Have you asked the humans for help?"

"No, but that would be good. From the tall buildings in the city, they can watch for signs of fire."

"I'll alert them," said Benjamin.

"Thank you," said Katru.

Though the humans and Tattoo People worked together, and a productive commerce had been established between the two societies, the aliens were still reticent to impose on their human neighbors, and they still tried to maintain their self-sufficiency.

For three days, both humans and Tattoo People watched the conflagration on the island of Nucleanis, continuously alert for smoke or flames that might indicate the fire had spread. Life went on to the extent possible, but with the looming threat the overall mood of the people was muted. All shows were cancelled in the stadium in a gesture of mutual respect and concern. The humans flocked to the highest floors of their mini-skyscrapers and scanned the horizon day and night, watching for the telltale signs of fire in the vast domain of the Tattoo People. When the crimson glow from the island waned, all sighed with relief, knowing that the worst was over. Or so they hoped.

That evening, Benjamin was woken again, this time by a distant roar, like thunder only more prolonged. Leaving the house, he found himself alone on the lakeshore, looking out at Nucleanis.

The diffuse red glow of the fire was gone now. Instead he saw tiny specks of light descending from the sky above the island. He recognized them immediately as the glow from the rocket engines of space capsules executing their landing sequence. Grimly, he watched, trying to count the number of vehicles that were landing. If it was one or two, he might have believed that Druix was returning, perhaps with someone else, another galactic explorer. He counted nine vehicles. And the fact that they'd landed on the island after all the vegetation was burned away led him to believe that whoever hid the treasure in the pyramid was returning to Nucleanis to claim it. He went back into the house to wake Xyla.

"We have company," he said.

"Who?" asked Xyla. Her voice came from the darkness, heavy with sleep.

"Space capsules. They've just landed on the island." Benjamin sat on the bed, close enough to feel her warmth.

"Explorers?" she asked.

"I doubt it. There were nine of them. Explorers don't travel in packs. They don't set fire to islands either."

Benjamin felt Xyla sit up in bed. "Are you saying they started the fire so they'd have a place to land?"

"That's my guess," said Benjamin.

"Why not just find someplace else to land?"

"I think it has to do with the treasure."

Xyla let out a gasp. "You think it's the pirates?"

"Yes. They must be coming back for their spoils."

"What will they do when they find it's gone?"

"There's no way to tell."

They sat in silence. The roar of the rocket engines was gone and they could hear the movement of the water on the lake again.

"I'm going over to the island in the morning," Benjamin said.

Xyla found his hand in the darkness. "I'll go with you."

"It's better if you stay here. Tell Katru and Ostinia what's going on. I'll be back before noon."

"It could be dangerous, Benjamin. You shouldn't go alone."

Benjamin patted her hand. "They won't hurt me. I'm an old man now. I'm just going to talk to them."

Xyla sighed. "At least take one of the Tattoo People with you—to help you row."

Benjamin shook his head, but she couldn't possibly have seen the gesture. "The last thing I want is for them to see the Tattoo People. Believe me, it will be less threatening if I show up alone."

When day broke, Benjamin boarded one of the small rowboats that ringed the lake. Settling in, he grabbed the oars and started out. As usual, the wind was calm in the morning and the boat cut cleanly through the glistening surface, reflecting the first rays of the rising sun. Benjamin squinted. He'd be looking at the sun the entire way. His back was to the island, blurred in the moist air that hung over the lake.

The calm surface of the lake made it very easy for him to be seen. By the time he felt the bow of the boat strike the shore, he turned to see a group of men standing among the blackened remains of the plants that had once grown prolifically. The air smelled like wet ash.

He pulled the boat far enough onto the shore that it wouldn't float away, all the time knowing the eyes of the men were upon him. Turning to face them, he saw that they carried EMP weapons, every one aimed at him. Benjamin wiped a hand across his brow, which was damp with sweat. He was out of breath. He took several steps closer to the men. One moved forward. "Who are you?" he asked, gesturing toward him with the muzzle of the sleek weapon.

"My name is Mizello. Benjamin Mizello."

The man looked at him suspiciously. "You're old."

"Good point. Who are you?"

"They call me Toro. I knew you when you were young."

"Have we met?"

"Not really. We worked for Carl Stormer during the attack on Aril. I saw you at the victory celebration. You were younger."

Benjamin shrugged. He looked around, taking in the scene before him. The entire landscape was blackened with ash. All that stood out from the charred surface were the pitiful remains of the trunks of the larger trees. Everything else alive on the island had been leveled. The three pyramids stood out, starkly reflecting the first rays from the sun, their lower portions also darkened by soot. Scattered about among the blackened ground were smaller triangular shapes, their metallic exteriors shining brightly. Benjamin knew space capsules when he saw them, even now after so many years.

"What are you doing here?" Benjamin asked.

"We're looking for something that belongs to us."

"Really," said Benjamin. "Where was it when you saw it last?"

"In the pyramid."

"And it's not there now?"

"No. You wouldn't happen to know where it is."

"No."

"Don't you want to know what it is?"

"Doesn't matter. I don't know where it is."

Toro turned and looked at his men, as if to remind Benjamin of their presence.

"Did you start the fire?" Benjamin asked.

Toro hesitated. "Guess so. We needed to clear out a place to land."

"How did you know there weren't people on this island?"

"It didn't matter," said Toro.

"Maybe the thing you're looking for was burned in the fire."

"No. We think someone took it from the pyramid."

"That's too bad," said Benjamin. He looked toward the space capsules. "Maybe you should look on some other planet."

"Yes, I suppose we should," said Toro.

"Good bye," said Benjamin, and he started back toward his boat.

After several moments, Toro called to him, "Hey, Mizello!"

Benjamin turned.

"Any animals on this planet?"

"No."

"Are you sure?"

"Yes," Benjamin answered. Then added, "Only aliens."

"Aliens?"

"From space. Maybe they took whatever it was you were looking for."

Toro snorted. "Yeah, maybe."

Benjamin resumed his walk to the boat. He took a seat and grabbed the oars. Before departing, he said, "By the way…"

"What?" said Toro.

"My guess is the aliens don't like that you set fire to their island. You might want to leave soon."

"Thanks for the advice," said Toro.

Benjamin was about to start rowing when he saw Toro approach the boat. At the water's edge, he bent down and drank, using his hand to scoop the liquid into his mouth. "In case your alien friends are too upset about the fire," he said, wiping the remaining drops from his chin. "You might want to know that an old friend of yours is with us."

"Who might that be?"

"A galactic explorer, like you—like you used to be. His name's Risto."

It was no use for Benjamin to pretend he didn't know who Risto was. He recovered from the shock of hearing the name and said, "Give him my regards."

"I will," said Toro, "If we decide to unfreeze him. He's at our mercy, if you know what I mean."

Benjamin nodded. "I know what you mean."

When Benjamin had crossed the lake and landed the boat, he sat on the shore and watched the island. An hour later, the nine space capsules lift off amid a plume of fiery red smoke. He listened to the roar of the rockets until the capsules had disappeared above him. They were gone, but Benjamin was fairly certain he hadn't seen the last of them.

After the capsules had disappeared into the pale blue sky, Benjamin returned to Xyla, who was waiting anxiously for him on the porch of their home. Benjamin sat beside her on a wooden bench, exquisitely crafted from twisted branches of the alien vine."

"They're gone," said Benjamin. "At least for now."

"Was it them?"

"Yes. They were looking for the treasure."

"Did you tell them what happened to it?"

"Not really. Sort of."

"You think they're coming back for it?"

Benjamin sighed. "I can't be sure. They may be back, but perhaps not for the treasure."

"Then what for?"

"They asked if there were any animals on the planet."

"You didn't tell them. Did you?"

"Of course not, but they don't need me to tell them. If they're part of the group the Arilians told us about, then they have a Union supply ship. That will tell them all they need to know about the presence of animals on Happiness."

Xyla rested her head on Benjamin's shoulder, as if suddenly it had become too heavy a burden to bear. "What are we going to do?"

"There's more. They have Risto Jalonen."

Benjamin and Xyla had discussed Risto often in conversations about the invasion of Aril. Risto and Benjamin had never met, but they'd communicated often after the defeat of Carl Stormer and Andrew Harding.

"How do you know?" she asked.

"He told me. It was a threat—not to interfere."

Xyla sat forward on the bench, turning her head to look at him. "Benjamin, we have to help him."

"I know, but I can't think of any way to do that. They're in orbit around Happiness. They said Risto is frozen."

Xyla rested her chin on her hands. "We need to go to where the animals are. That's where they'll end up."

"And then what?"

"We have to talk to them—find out what they want and see if we can make them set Risto free."

"Yes, we'll do that, but first I wanted to try something else."

"What?"

"I want to try one of the radios on the two remaining space capsules. If one is working, I can send a message to Risto's capsule."

"What good will that do if he's frozen?"

"I was custodian of a supply ship for a while. Remember? Supply ship custodians know the codes that can be added to radio transmissions that automatically trigger the unfreezing of explorers in their capsules."

"Of course," Xyla said excitedly. "You could send a message to Risto with that code. Once he's unfrozen, he might be able to deal with Stella and her gang."

"That's what I was thinking."

"But, Benjamin, what's the likelihood you can get one of the radios to work? The capsules were stripped many years ago and have been exposed to the elements for too long."

"Not very likely. And even if we do get one transmitting, we have no idea where Risto's capsule is. We'd have to transmit the same message continuously for many days and hope that his capsule passes through the signal. And we won't even know if we're successful or not."

Several hours later, after Benjamin returned to the site where the two remaining space capsules had been sitting for more than thirty years, his fears were confirmed. Parts from both radios had been removed long ago, and what remained was corroded by age and oxidation. It was hopeless to think they could be repaired. Benjamin returned to Xyla with the burden of worry written into his countenance. Risto was their one hope of dealing with the threat from space, but there was no way to contact him.

"Gone!?" Stella screamed.

"Everything," said Toro.

Toro would have feared the outburst to follow, but he had an ace in the hole he would play at the right moment.

"Gone where?" Stella asked through gritted teeth.

"Removed by someone," said Toro. "There's no way to tell who has it or when it was taken."

"Was anyone there? Did you try to find out?"

"There was only one person to ask. Benjamin Mizello."

"So he got here before us. I was afraid of that. He knows where the treasure is. Why didn't you bring him to me?"

"For what?"

"So I could ask him where the treasure is."

"Why? The treasure is gone. There's no way to get it back. Too much time has passed."

"That's not acceptable!" screamed Stella. "It belongs to me!"

"Forget about the treasure," Toro said.

"I will not forget the treasure!" Stella took two giant steps toward him and thrust her face into his. He could feel her breath.

"There are animals," he said quietly.

Stella let out a deep breath that was almost a snarl. "What?"

"There are animals on Happiness."

"How do you know?"

Toro shrugged. "Just a hunch."

"Did you see them?"

"No."

"Then how do you know?"

"I asked Mizello."

"And he told you there were animals on the planet?"

"No. He told me there weren't, but he was lying."

Stella turned away and began to pace. "You should have brought him here. I have ways to get him to tell the truth."

Toro waited before responding. "My guess is that would've alerted the entire planet that we're here. I thought it better that they think we're leaving."

Stella stopped pacing and turned to look at him. "Come with me," she said. Toro followed her into the control room.

Seated at the console, Stella commanded the computer to display the images of Happiness. These were visible light images that showed the surface of the planet as it would look to the human eye—no false colors with incomprehensible meaning. Like Earth, the blue oceans covered more than two-thirds of the planet. Unlike Earth, with high mountains and arid deserts where plants grew only sparsely, the land surfaces of Happiness were completely covered by plant life. Only upon closer inspection, which Stella did by zooming in on selected regions of the image, could they discern breaks in the greenery. There weren't many, and most were small regions that couldn't be more than several acres in extent, perhaps created by some anomaly in the planet's topography—an outcropping of rock or water-soaked swampland. Here and there were the remnants of the ancient amusement park, crumbling buildings and torn roads, jumbles of broken concrete and twisted metal. Stella and Toro studied a replica of New York City, in better repair than the other infrastructure of the planet. When she commanded the computer to switch to an infrared image, they could clearly see that the city was home to thousands of people. Stella grunted with satisfaction, then resumed her search until she found an anomalously large expanse of land relatively free from vegetation. In infrared, isolated spots were apparent, of different sizes and, under further inspection, changing location.

"Here," Stella said with satisfaction.

"Can you zoom in any closer?"

"It won't help. This is the best resolution we can get, but without a doubt there are life forms down there. Some are too large to be human."

"Too large," Toro repeated, trying to process the implications of this statement.

"Get your capsules refueled. We're going down there."

"You're going too?" Toro said, unable to hide his dread.

"Yes," Stella answered, in a tone that dared him to argue.

"Who will take care of the supply ship?"

"Leave two of your men. I'll give them instructions on what to do. If anyone interferes with us, they'll use the lasers to start fires all over the planet."

They'd been staring at the images so intently they hadn't noticed the presence of another person in the control room. Instinctively, Stella turned and eyed Theonius standing in the entryway, peering at them strangely, his entire body tense. Stella pulled out the EMP weapon she carried on her belt and without hesitation fired it at the enormous man. Had Toro imagined it, or had Theonius just started to charge at them before the electromagnetic pulse stopped him short? He fell to the floor paralyzed, shaking with spasmodic motions.

Toro was amazed at the speed, accuracy, and ease with which Stella fired her weapon. Her lethality was heightened by the absence of any hesitation in using the firearm. Toro supposed that she'd been trained with the philosophy that it was better to kill a dozen people by mistake than allow hesitation when faced with a real threat. Stella had explained that the smart weapons of 500th Century Earth could sense the shooter's intent and automatically adjust the lethality of the emitted EMP pulse, in some cases even not firing at all. Supposedly, she had disabled that function on her weapon, which would have made the pulse fired at Theonius sufficient to kill any human instantaneously. Fortunately, Theonius was anything but a normal human and somehow he survived the shot from Stella's weapon.

"Put him in his capsule and freeze him," Stella ordered. "He heard what we're planning to do. We can't leave him here unfrozen and he's too dangerous to take him with us. Put him in one of the spare capsules. He and Risto can keep each other company."

"Why don't we just kill him?" asked Toro.

"He's been useful," Stella said. "Just do what I tell you."

Toro left to get his men to carry the big man to a capsule. They had to work quickly while the giant was still incapacitated. Toro didn't quite understand why Stella tolerated having him around. She was right. The giant was too dangerous and too unpredictable.

While Toro's men were refueling their capsules and preparing for their second landing on Happiness, Toro selected two of them to remain on the supply ship. They were to wait for instructions from Stella in case it was necessary to create fires on the planet using the laser weapon. Before they departed, Stella demonstrated the operation of the laser weapon to the two men. With the same indifference as she had started the first fire, Stella started a second one.

"That should keep them occupied and out of our way," she said.

This time the fire was in an area of the planet covered by the alien vine. Her last instructions to the two men were, "Keep monitoring the ship's radio. If we give you the command, repeat what I just did all over the planet."

Chapter 40

Word spread immediately among the Tattoo people when the fire broke out in the vine. They responded quickly, executing procedures they'd probably practiced often to extinguish any fire that threatened their life-giving plant. Those were fires ignited by the errant lightning strike, highly localized and easily dealt with if caught soon enough. With the instantaneous communication system of the Tattoo People, getting to a fire quickly was never a problem.

The fire started by the laser beam from space was a different story. The beam ignited an entire acre of combustible material and by the time the Tattoo People converged on it the fire had spread to many times its original size.

The Tattoo People had no equipment to fight fire, but what they lacked in machinery they made up for in personnel. The speed with which they could mobilize fire fighters and the efficiency of their command, control, and communication made it possible for them to surround the area quickly and begin the task of creating a firebreak. Although they were highly skilled at training the vine to suit their purposes, they had little practice cutting it. The vine had almost spiritual importance, and hacking away at it with various tools didn't come naturally to them. Plus, the tools they used were made from the vine itself,   so they weren't particularly effective. While many of the Tattoo People worked at the firebreak, others formed teams to carry water from the rivers and lakes, which they used to soak the surrounding vegetation.

Benjamin was of little help in these endeavors. Instead, he went to seek the aid of Ostinia and the humans in the city. He hoped they were better prepared than the Tattoo People. Fires were rare on the planet, and Benjamin knew little about how effective human methods were here.

Ostinia responded immediately to Benjamin's alarm and hurried from the stadium where he'd been working. He ran through the city streets with Benjamin following closely behind, until they came upon a building with two large doors. It was an old-fashioned fire station. Benjamin had passed it before, never imagining that it might contain real fire-fighting equipment. Ostinia pulled a chain next to one of the doors. It rolled upward. Light slanted in, illuminating a brilliant red fire truck. Next to it in a similar bay was a second vehicle. Proceeding farther into the building, Ostinia found a single cord extending upward through a hole in the ceiling. He pulled on it and a bell rang. Several minutes later, people in various states of dress appeared.

"Our volunteer fire fighters," Ostinia explained.

Benjamin smiled at the primitive state of their approach. When he departed Earth in the 22nd Century, fire fighting was far more sophisticated. The equipment, fire extinguishing chemicals, and communication technology were such that fires resulted in little destruction. Here on Happiness, fire fighting was no better than it had been in the 20th Century.

"There's a problem," he said to Ostinia, trying to be as polite as possible. "The fire is in the middle of the forest. None of this equipment can get close enough to the flames to be of use."

"Ahhh," said Ostinia. "Follow me."

Continuing through the building, they exited out a rear door. There, occupying the better part of a vacant lot, was the largest bulldozer Benjamin had ever seen. At the front was a massive plow, which looked fully capable of destroying or moving anything in its path.

Benjamin stared at the vehicle for several seconds. Then looked at Ostinia and said, "Fuel?"

"It's steam powered. It burns wood. With the forest on all sides of us, wood is easy to come by. We haven't had to use it for a long time, so we have a lot of wood stored up. In any case, the machine is designed to remove wood and feed it into the engines. It's a perpetual motion machine, in some sense, designed long ago by our ancestors who struggled to keep the vine away from the city. We don't have to worry about it anymore, because the Tattoo People keep it under control."

Benjamin strolled around the object admiring its design. Once he'd seen a picture of a dredging machine used long ago for mining purposes. They floated on rivers and moved slowly upstream, scooping up dirt and gravel ahead of them, processing the material to extract the precious metals, and then depositing the leftovers out the back. The vehicle before him was similar in design and size to those gargantuan machines.

Ostinia saw the amazement in his expression. "It'll work. We'll clear a path with this machine. The fire trucks can follow."

Benjamin nodded. "We should get started."

It took several hours for the engines to start up and then more time for the gigantic vehicle to make its way through the streets to the edge of the forest. In the meantime, Benjamin returned to tell Katru about the human machinery to help them fight the fire. When the three vehicles arrived, Katru, Benjamin, and a group of Tattoo People stood at the outskirts of the forest to meet the human fire-fighting team.

Katru was just as amazed as Benjamin when the bulldozer appeared. He walked around it, trying to understand how it worked. He stopped at the front of the vehicle where the huge plow had been lowered into position to mow away the vegetation in its path.

"It will hurt the vine," he said to Benjamin, through the translator hanging around his neck.

"What?" said Benjamin.

"The parts of the vine that extend into the soil are sensitive. We never cut those branches because they connect to the subterranean root system of the plant. It hurts the plant when we do that."

"How do you know?" asked Benjamin.

Katru looked confused. "We just know. It is knowledge that's been passed down through generations. We cut branches and wood from the vine above the surface, but we do not damage any part directly connected to the root system."

Benjamin was frustrated. "But the fire," he said. "It's destroying the vine. Surely that must hurt it."

"Yes," said Katru. "That is why we must first isolate the part of the vine that is under attack. We cut away all the branches that connect to the part that is burning. We're doing that now, before we start making the firebreak."

"That will take too long," said Benjamin. "This machine will make a firebreak much more quickly."

Katru sighed with resignation. "You are right, but before we allow the machine to enter the forest, we will cut the branches on either side of its path. That way the vine will not be hurt so much."

Benjamin and Ostinia exchanged glances. They seemed to understand the futility of arguing with Katru.

"What are you using to cut the branches?" Ostinia asked.

"We have tools."

"Do you have metal tools?"

"No, they're made of wood."

Ostinia walked to one of the fire trucks and opened a panel on its side, revealing a set of axes and picks mounted firmly within. "Can you use these?"

"Yes, of course," said Katru.

"We'll get more." And with that Ostinia turned to his firefighting team and instructed them to collect all the metal tools from the city that could be used to clear vegetation.

Katru must have communicated this plan to other Tattoo People because in minutes they were emerging from the forest, grabbing the tools that were offered to them and starting immediately to work severing branches from the vine in parallel paths, sufficiently separated to allow the wood-fueled bulldozer passage between.

An hour later, Katru gave Ostinia the okay to begin moving the machine into the forest. With great puffs of steam rising from its engine, it moved forward. In no time, the plow in front was filled with broken branches, twigs, leaves, and stems. It pivoted upward and back, depositing the detritus into a large chute which funneled the material into the machine's steam engine. There followed more smoke, an incredible din of massive pistons firing, and the plow clattered to the ground again, after which the bulldozer lurched forward to restart the cycle. Benjamin estimated the time it would take them to reach the fire. It was a sobering thought. How much more would the flames spread, before they'd be able to construct an adequate firebreak? The longer it took, the greater distance the machine would have to travel to circumvent the area in flames. It seemed hopeless, but the slow, rumbling motion of the bulldozer was encouraging and certainly better than doing nothing.

Benjamin stood next to Katru, who grimly watched the machine's progress.

"Benjamin, do you know how this fire was started?"

"Yes, I think I do. It was started by intruders from space using a weapon fired from an orbiting spaceship."

Katru nodded. "Then they are able to do this again?"

Benjamin sighed. "Yes."

"Is there no way to stop them?"

"As long as they're in control of the vehicle in space, they can start fires anytime they want."

Katru saddened visibly at this pronouncement. Benjamin felt embarrassed by his own species—a species capable of so much destruction and violence.

"I believe we have a friend in space—someone who could help us. I tried to contact him with the radio on one of the space capsules, but it didn't work."

Katru looked at Benjamin. "What didn't work?"

"The radios from our space capsule. They're too old and have been damaged."

"And your friend could help us if you could communicate with him?"

"Almost certainly."

"There's another way to contact him," Katru said.

"How?"

"It's the same way we communicate with others who are too far away."

"I thought your people relay messages from one to another to communicate over large distances."

"Yes, we do that most of the time, but sometimes when there aren't enough of our people between us and them, we use a different technique. We transmit together at the same time, producing a signal much stronger than any one of us can generate alone."

"The signal needed to reach my friend in space would have to be very strong. How many Tattoo People would be needed to transmit a strong enough signal to reach a space capsule?"

"I don't know, but we will use as many as we can spare."

"It has to be sent at the right frequency and coded in the same way our communication signals are transmitted."

"We can do that," said Katru. "Remember, transmitting radio waves for us is like speaking is to you. You control the organs in your body that produce the sound waves by which you communicate. In the same way, we possess organs that transmit radio waves. They are just as versatile as yours. Transmitting in unison at the same time is the same for us as when humans sing together."

Several hours later, in the dark of evening, four hundred Tattoo People assembled in the replica of Central Park at the heart of the miniature New York City. They stood in a square grid, with the spacing between each Tattoo person equal to the wavelength of the radio wave they were about to transmit. With that spacing, the signals from all the Tattoo People would constructively interfere, concentrating the power into a beam. On a signal from Katru, they all began to transmit, exactly in synchronization. It was like four hundred violins playing in an orchestra, or a choir of four hundred voices, reaching upward to the heavens. Benjamin suggested they should transmit for as long as possible to ensure the space capsule they were attempting to communicate with passed through the transmitted beam. In its orbit about the planet, it would only pass over them once every two hours. They had to hope that it would receive the message on one of those passes. It was likely the supply ship that carried Stella and her gang would also receive the message, but Benjamin had coded the transmission so that only Union exploration vehicles would be able to decipher it.

They continued transmitting for six hours. Then, with clear regret, Katru explained to Benjamin that the fire was still spreading rapidly, and they needed all their people in the forest assisting with efforts to control it. The act of transmitting required energy, and the four hundred Tattoo People were exhausted.

Benjamin returned to Xyla, who was helping to care for the children of the Tattoo People. As usual, she was reading to them. They never tired of hearing the bizarre stories of ancient Earth. It simultaneously defied and inspired their imaginations.

"I'm going to the plain where the animals are," Benjamin said when he finally got her attention.

"Benjamin, it could be dangerous."

"I'm almost sure they've returned. The question they asked me about animals was just too random to be a coincidence."

"I'm sure the Tattoo People can deal with it. They've protected the animals for many years."

"Maybe they could if they weren't fighting a fire. But I don't think they've ever had to deal with this kind of threat."

"If you're right and the pirates are there, what will you do?"

Benjamin smiled. It was the one he used often—a delay tactic while thinking of an answer. "Talk to them," he said finally. "I'm an old man. What else can I do?"

Xyla grimaced. "Will you at least take some Tattoo People with you?"

"If they can spare any. I need them to get me out there to begin with."

"I can arrange that," said Xyla, and she gave him a hug as if reassuring a small child.

Later that day, Benjamin departed with two boats and a

group of Tattoo people. Katru had been puzzled by Benjamin's request to go to the plain, but Xyla intervened and explained that Benjamin was concerned about the safety of the animals. The shrubs on the plain did not have the flame retardant properties that were built into the genetic make-up of the vine. An errant spark that reached the plain might ignite a secondary fire that could spread frighteningly fast. It was a stretch of the truth that Benjamin was continually reminded of as the boats made their way through the night. He looked up into a sky that was black except for the red glow of the fire emanating from the distant horizon, the brilliant pin-points of starlight, and the occasional shooting stars. Or were they floating embers streaking across the sky that would soon alight?

Chapter 41

Once on the plain where the animals of Happiness roamed, Stella was transformed. She'd always looked out of place amid the metallic confines of the supply ship, and even more incongruous crammed into the tight interior of a space capsule. No one had ever seen her in her magnetocryogenic chamber, of course, nor had anyone even wanted to. The image of Stella frozen naked within the confined space of the cylinder was one neither Toro nor any of his men could comfortably fathom.

Once on the ground, however, amid the rolling hills and open spaces of the plain, Stella regained the vigor, athleticism, and deadly grace that made her feared and respected. Even with the increased gravity on the planet relative to that on the supply ship, there was still a spring in her step and Toro's men struggled to keep up with her. The ground was uneven, with rivulets caused by differential erosion and clumps where patches of grass stood up from the surrounding terrain. Stella negotiated these obstacles as though it were second nature, traversing the surface in impossible leaps and turns.

Before long, she was far ahead of the men and they only saw from a distance the speed at which she raised her EMP weapon and fired it. Catching up with her, they found her standing over an antelope, still writhing on the ground, panic-stricken, terrified, and pitifully devoid of any intelligence by which it might understand what had just happened. Toro drew a pistol from his belt, on old-fashioned model that fired bullets, and he shot the tormented creature in the head.

"Why did you do that?" asked Stella. It wasn't a question asked in anger, but with innocent curiosity.

"It was suffering. Didn't you have the intensity of your weapon set high enough?"

"It was on automatic," said Stella.

"What does that mean?"

"It means the weapon senses how much I want to kill the target and adjusts the intensity automatically."

"What kind of worthless piece of crap weapon is that?" said one of Toro's men.

Stella glared at him. "One that could kill you right now," she said.

"Well, obviously you didn't want to kill that antelope," said Toro, trying to diffuse the situation. "Otherwise, it wouldn't have been still moving."

"Let's look for more," said Stella, turning away.

"Can we take this for food?" asked one of Toro's men.

"Do what you want," called Stella, already well way from the group.

Toro moved off tangentially from the rest, seeking higher ground. He felt better being able to see farther in all directions. He realized they were in strange territory and should proceed cautiously, despite Stella's lack of concern. Her recklessness could easily get them into trouble.

While climbing the nearest rise, he examined the ground carefully. Signs of animals were abundant—feces, clumps of fur sticking to branches, the occasional hoof print, and narrow tracks worn into the ground by repeated passage of animals on the move. Once at the crest, he looked about, shielding his eyes from the sun's glare. The plain was really quite beautiful—an endless sea of grasses and low shrubs as far as the eye could see—excellent horse country, if one were around to be had. Stella and his men were tiny specks now. He would have worried about losing sight of them, but the featureless topology left few spaces for conceal-ment. With relief, he noted that in all directions he could see no signs of anything that might endanger them, human or otherwise. It was only after he descended from the crest that he came upon a deep footprint in a sandy watercourse that was unmistakably produced by either an extremely large bear or feline animal. He couldn't tell which. He quickened his pace to catch up to the oth-ers, his hands gripping his EMP weapon tightly and his finger fixed upon the trigger.

He caught up with them just as they came upon a herd of animals that looked very much like the buffalo of ancient America. Toro was taken aback by the shock of seeing these animals, knowing how many millennia had passed since they existed on Earth. How had they survived the passage of time and the voyage from their home planet? He wanted to get closer, but before he could, he saw Stella drop on one knee, take aim with her weapon, and fire. An instant later, one of the larger buffalo in the herd dropped. Three of Toro's men followed Stella's example and then the others. In no more than a half a minute, seven buffalo lay dead among the remaining herd, which had not moved. Had they been using old-fashioned weapons, the sound of the shots would have scared the others, but the EMP weapons made no sound. The seven buffalo had just fallen in silence, alive one moment and dead the next.

When they walked among the grazing animals to view the carcasses, the surviving buffalos trotted away with neither panic nor fright. Their minds couldn't make the connection between the humans and their fallen friends.

Up close, Toro saw that the hides were great jumbles of dry, twisted hair. Stella ran her hand through the hair and pulled it away in disgust. "This fur is not nice," she declared.

"It's wool," said Toro. "Not fur. We haven't seen any fur animals yet."

Stella pointed to the animal's head. "What are those?"

On each side of the mouth were long, curving tusks, yellow tinged and bluntly pointed. "Those are tusks," Toro explained.

One of his men crouched with a knife and started the tedious process of cutting away a tusk.

"What are you doing?" asked Stella.

"Taking the tusk," he answered.

"What for?"

"They're good luck."

"Ridiculous!" said Stella, and she moved away.

Just then, from off in the distance came a long, deep, menacing roar. The group looked about to see where the threatening sound came from. It was impossible to tell. The buffalo heard it as well and began to move, chaotically at first, and then, when a sufficient number had gathered, finally coalescing into a mass movement. The rapidity with which the situation evolved from stagnation, to chaos, to ordered mass motion took everyone by surprise. They found themselves caught in a current of unyielding force.

Toro and his men scrambled away, trying to escape from the primary path of the herd. Once safely aside and on relatively high ground, they watched the spectacle. Hundreds of buffalo careened across the plain, escaping from some imagined or real peril, guided only by their mutual panic-stricken ignorance. In the midst of the moving herd, barely visible through the dust and debris kicked up by the pounding hooves, stood Stella, looking about in stunned curiosity, but in no way frightened. By some miracle, the beasts parted before reaching her, letting her stand her ground.

The herd passed and without hesitation Stella strode purposefully in the direction from which they'd been fleeing. Toro and his men hurried to catch up to her. She stopped, peering down at the ground before her. Toro got there first and saw the target of her attention. It was a pool of blood, now churned into a muddy, crimson mixture. It was the beginning of a bloody streak that trailed off into the distance. They followed it about two hundred meters until it ended at what was left of a partially eaten buffalo carcass.

"Did you see what happened?" asked Toro.

"It was white," Stella said. "A white blur."

Toro pointed to bloody paw prints in the ground, as large as the one he'd found earlier.

"There's a very large, white predator here," Toro concluded. "Some type of cat."

"Does it have fur?" Stella asked.

"Probably," answered Toro, extracting a tuft of white fur from the remains of the buffalo.

"We'll follow it," said Stella. And the next moment she was gone.

Four hours later, she finally stopped. The men were exhausted trying to keep up with her. The trail of the beast had been easy to follow. The gigantic paw prints were unmistakable, but the group was never close enough to actually see the animal. Toro dreaded nightfall, but it was coming upon them quickly. The air chilled as the sun descended. Toro hadn't anticipated that Stella would want to camp out on the plain. He was hoping they'd find the animal she was looking for quickly and then return to the supply ship. As the sky darkened, they saw a red glow in the distance, not from the setting sun, but from the fire Stella had started. If nothing else, the diversion had worked. They had seen no sign of human presence the entire day.

CHAPTER 42

— 119,502 —

When Risto was unfrozen, he was still unconscious, suffering the effects of the EMP blast from Stella's weapon. After several minutes, however, he opened his eyes and saw the familiar display of lights from the interior of his magnetocryogenic chamber. With growing awareness, he understood that his one chance of survival would be to overcome the first person he encountered upon his exit from the cylinder. Thus, at the same moment he released the hatch, he kicked it with all his strength, simultaneously pushing himself out with sufficient speed and force to surprise anyone who might be present. He was astonished to find no one else in the capsule. That meant his captors had unfrozen him remotely. There was still a chance he might escape if he could take command of his vehicle, but why would they have unfrozen him without first locking him out of the navigation system? Perhaps they unfroze him just to ensure his slow death trapped inside a capsule with limited oxygen.

He floated to the seat in front of the command console, a practiced movement he'd performed dozens of times as a galactic explorer. With a quick scan of the monitor he found that he'd been unfrozen by a high priority message, one that used a code that only a few supply ship custodians knew. He'd been lucky. It was the one event that could have saved him. His captors apparently didn't know about the code and had done nothing to ensure he wasn't prematurely unfrozen by such a transmission.

Risto read the message. It was from Benjamin Mizello, who was on the planet named Happiness. He reported that Stella and her gang were attacking the planet and had already started a fire that threatened the entire population. He warned that Stella probably had a supply ship and was using it as a base of operations. He advised Risto to be extremely careful in dealing with the gang. He believed, but wasn't certain, that they were intending to land on the planet in an area that had been set aside to protect animals. Benjamin provided the coordinates of the game preserve.

Risto snorted. He didn't have to be reminded to be careful. He'd been a victim of Stella's violence already and he didn't ever want to be in that situation again. Still, he knew that they'd all be at Stella's mercy as long as she had control of the supply ship. For the third time in his life, he was placed in a position of having to commandeer a supply ship. His first attempt had been successful; the second had been a dismal failure. How would he try it this time?

With a feeling of dread, Risto glanced at the oxygen gauge. There were less than two hours remaining in the capsule. Whatever he chose to do, he would need to act quickly.

He activated the capsule's radar system. Several seconds later, the monitor displayed the locations of all the solid objects in the capsule's vicinity. A rotating line of luminescent green moved against the black background, clearly showing two nearby objects. One was very large, obviously the supply ship. The second was much smaller—another space capsule.

Directing the vehicle's telescope toward the supply ship, an image of the larger vessel appeared on the screen against a brilliant field of stars. At the docking ports were two capsules. Someone was aboard the ship, but Risto couldn't tell who.

He turned the scope at the other object. It was indeed another space capsule. Risto decided to dock with the other capsule and board it. If the occupant was frozen, it would be easy to take control of the vehicle. Perhaps it had more oxygen than his, or even better, weapons. If the occupant wasn't frozen, it would be easier to overcome one opponent than to attack a supply ship with at least two people on board.

Even though the other capsule was close by, it still took thirty minutes for Risto to dock with it. Many years earlier, Risto had manually opened the hatch of a vehicle he had docked with to rescue Ilsa Montgomery. He used the same procedure, and within ten minutes he was on board. As he expected, someone was frozen in the capsule's magnetocryogenic chamber. He was glad to see that the other capsule must have had more oxygen than his because now, with the two vehicles connected, he had an extra hour of breathable air. That was true as long as the other person was frozen. He had no intention of unfreezing the person in the chamber, but he was curious to know who it was. He activated the capsule's computer and displayed the image of the occupant. Risto recognized him immediately. It was the giant who had tried to rescue him while he was paralyzed and at Stella's mercy.

Risto recalled the old warnings about sleeping giants. Nonetheless, he decided to unfreeze the man. It took thirty minutes before the indicators turned green. Risto opened the hatch on the chamber and floated away expecting the man to emerge, but he didn't. Risto drifted back and looked inside. The giant was still. Risto wondered if he was dead, but the life support alarms would have gone off, if that was the case. He grabbed the man's boot and pulled. The large man fit tightly inside the chamber. Once Risto had him completely out, he pushed him over to the command console and secured him to the chair, fastening the straps around his waist and shoulders.

Risto waited, unsure of what to do. He saw no visible signs of injury. He floated to one of the storage cabinets that held the first aid kit. As he was extracting it, he heard a groan. He turned and saw the man beginning to move, struggling to free himself from the restraints.

"It's okay," Risto said. "It's only a safety harness."

The man stopped abruptly and looked at Risto, blinking with confusion. His mind seemed to be overcome by reality.

"She shot me," he said.

"Ahh," said Risto, finally understanding. "You were unconscious when they froze you and still unconscious when unfrozen."

"Where is she?" the man asked.

"I'm not sure." Risto floated over and offered his hand to the man. "I am Risto."

"Theonius," the man said.

Risto told Theonius everything he knew, or thought he knew. Theonius could add little, except right before he was shot, he'd heard Stella and Toro talking about landing on a place on the planet where there were animals.

While they were talking, Risto was scanning the indicators on the control panel of Theonius' capsule.

"Your vehicle has no fuel," he said.

"What does that mean?" asked Theonius.

"It means you're at the mercy of the large woman and her men. There is nothing you can do but wait for their return.

"Can't I land on the planet?"

"No. Landing requires fuel to fire the rockets that will prevent the capsule from crashing."

"What choices do I have?"

Risto considered this. He regretted having unfrozen the man. Had he not done that, he could be landing on Happiness already and searching for Stella and Benjamin. Now, he had to worry about the fate of a complete stranger.

"You could return to your magnetocryogenic chamber and wait."

"Wait for what?"

"For the pirates to return and bring you back onto the supply ship. Or for me to return to rescue you."

"Return from where?"

"From the planet. If Mizello and I are successful in overcoming Stella, I'll come back and take control of the supply ship. Once on the ship, I'll guide your capsule to the docking station and unfreeze you."

"And if you're not successful in defeating Stella?"

"Then the pirates will probably return to the supply ship. What they will do with you at that point I cannot say."

Theonius was visibly disturbed by this. Risto wondered whether he had miscalculated by being too honest with Theonius. The man could easily overpower him and take his capsule. Then again, Theonius knew nothing about piloting a space capsule. He wouldn't know what to do with it, even if he did take it from Risto.

"If you don't mind, I'd rather take my chances crashing

on the planet. Please, show me how to land the capsule. I prefer to perish on the surface of Happiness than die in space at the hands of those people."

Risto nodded. He would have made the same decision himself. However, he was unable to send the man to his death. Risto made a decision that might cost him his life, but his honor and pride allowed him no alternative.

"Take my capsule," he said. "I'll program it so you will land safely on the planet. Once there, you must give me your word that you will do everything possible to defeat Stella. If you do, please look for Benjamin Mizello. Tell him I'm frozen in a space capsule with no fuel. Tell him I've set a course to his father's supply ship. He will know how to help me."

"Why are you doing this?"

Risto didn't know. "Because I have a better chance of surviving in a crippled space capsule, and you have a better chance surviving on the surface of the planet. Please convey my apologies to Benjamin that I couldn't be of more help to him."

Theonius looked troubled. "Thank you for this, but I must refuse. I cannot condemn you to an uncertain fate. Please, I will land in my own capsule."

Risto shook his head. "I won't send you to your death and then land my capsule next to the wreckage of yours. It's impossible for me."

Risto unbuckled Theonius from the seat at the console. "Follow me. I'll give you instructions on how to land. It's all automated, but I'll prepare you for what will happen."

To Risto's relief, Theonius argued no more. He pushed off from the control panel and floated behind Risto to the opening separating the two capsules. Risto took a seat at his control console and programmed the computer for the reentry sequence. Theonius watched in silence, unable to comprehend anything Risto was doing. When Risto was done, he moved out of the seat and motioned Theonius to sit. As Risto was fastening the constraints, Theonius grasped his arm tightly and said, "I will succeed in overcoming Stella and deliver your message to Mizello."

"Yes, I know you will."

"We will meet again," said Theonius.

Risto didn't answer. He propelled himself back through the opening. Moments later, the hatches of both vehicles closed and the two capsules separated. Risto returned to the control console of the capsule Theonius had occupied. Grimly, he scanned the displays. He was on a space capsule with hardly any fuel and barely enough oxygen to last one hour. He knew he should set a course to Arthur Mizello's supply ship and return to the magnetocryogenic chamber, but he remained concerned about Stella's supply ship, still orbiting Happiness and capable of inflicting unlimited damage on the planet. He entered commands into the computer to intercept the supply ship. The two vehicles weren't far apart, but the low thrust of the capsule's propulsion system made it an agonizingly slow process to close the distance between them. Risto watched the progress on the capsule's video monitor. The supply ship grew larger. He was approaching from a direction that was nearly perpendicular to the long axis of the ship. The massive structure rotated about its axis to create the artificial gravity on the interior surface of the hull. The rotation took several minutes. Once during each spin, Risto saw the communication antennas rotate into view. He maneuvered his capsule to point his forward directed EMP weapon toward the antennas, and then waited. With the next rotation, the antennas would be close enough to be fired upon. If all went according to his plan, the electromagnetic pulse would strike the antenna and be conducted into the ship's electrical system. Without the gas-filled cylinder, it could destroy a large part of the electronic circuitry that powered and controlled the supply ship.

He fired. There was no way to tell if he had succeeded. Nothing changed in the appearance of the ship. He reversed the thrust of the capsule's rocket motors and narrowly missed colliding with the larger vehicle. The maneuvers had exhausted almost all his fuel and he was down to his last ten minutes of breathable air. He hastened to the magnetocryogenic chamber and initiated the freezing sequence. Inside the chamber, he waited for the bang

that would be the last sound he'd hear until he was unfrozen—
hopefully at Arthur Mizello's supply ship. He'd done everything
he could do. The rest was up to Theonius now on the planet
below.

CHAPTER 43

— 119,502 —

Toro was awoken by a distant roar. It was still dark, but in one direction he saw the crimson glow from the fire Stella had started. In the opposite direction, the first faint blush of dawn was extinguishing the starlight. Stella was awake, too. He could barely make out her silhouette against the pre-dawn sky.

He walked toward her with intentionally heavy footfalls so as not to surprise her. "Did you hear something?" he asked.

"Yes. It sounded like the entry of a space capsule."

"Who could it be?"

"I don't know. I tried to contact your men on the ship, but they didn't respond."

"Maybe it wasn't a space capsule."

Stella snorted. "It was a space capsule and I don't like it. Take the men and head back to the landing site. We should have left someone there standing guard."

"What will you do?"

Stella nodded in the direction of the rising sun. "If I'm right, the capsule landed there. I'm going to find it."

"Do you want to take one of the men with you?"

"I don't need any of your men to handle one person on a space capsule. Besides, none of your men can keep up with me."

Toro nodded. Stella was right. He turned to wake the men.

Alone on the plain, Benjamin had an opportunity to view the sights more slowly and carefully. Just before noon, the Tattoo People had left him with a small rowboat he could use to return whenever he was ready. He thanked them and wished them well in their continuing fight to extinguish the fire.

Even after so many years living on Happiness, there were times when he had to convince himself that he was no longer on

Earth. The plain he traversed reminded him of the high chaparral country of western America. The climate was semi-arid, with cold, snowy winters and hot summers. Under cloudless skies, little heat was retained after sunset. The trip along the waterways had been chilly, but now at noon on the open plain, Benjamin felt the full warmth of the sun.

The herd animals were easiest to spot. They meandered across the flatter expanses of the region in large groups easy to discern against the surrounding landscape. Benjamin steered clear of them. He understood from previous visits to the plain to keep away from the grazing animals because they also attracted predators. In the 25 years he and Xyla had lived among the Tattoo People, he had visited the plain only a few times. They had an agreement with the Tattoo People that the existence of the animals on Happiness should remain a secret from the humans. To honor that and avoid putting the Tattoo People in an awkward position, he and Xyla had decided not to ask for special privileges. Whatever the approach the aliens were using to protect the plain and the animals had worked well for thousands of years. The only opportunities they'd had to go there were when Xyla was escorting Tattoo children on field trips and Benjamin accompanied them.

Benjamin had brought his EMP weapon, even though it upset Xyla. He explained that it was to protect himself from encounters with hungry carnivores, but Xyla worried he planned to confront Stella and her gang. He hadn't been very clear about just exactly what he planned to do. He hadn't been very clear because he himself had no idea what he was going to do.

More insects seemed to thrive on the plain since the last time he'd been there. They were all crawling, hopping, or low-flying types that moved about his legs as he walked. Correspondingly, he saw more small rodent-like animals and lizards than he'd ever seen before. It was fascinating to observe the abundance of life forms, especially knowing exactly how many years since they'd been brought from Earth. On Earth, the fossil record gave an indication of how life proliferated on the scale of millions of years, shaped by evolutionary forces. But the changes that take place over thousands of years are subtler, and probably dictated more by genetics than evolution. The unfortunate consequence of restricting access to the plain was that it prevented the new knowledge that could be gained. A team of well-trained biologists would have a field day, so to speak, studying the species that thrived on the plain of Happiness.

Xyla wasn't more than an hour behind Benjamin. She'd convinced the Tattoo People to bring her to watch after Benjamin. She knew he wouldn't allow her to go along with him, so she'd arranged for a separate escort to the plain. The Tattoo People agreed, with the understanding that they couldn't stay with the human couple because they had to return to help fight the fire.

Xyla had decided to follow Benjamin after she saw him retrieve his EMP weapon from where he kept it stored away. That had convinced Xyla that he planned to find Stella and help mitigate, in some way, the danger she brought to Happiness. When she found Benjamin struggling to don the blue jumpsuit he'd worn during his days as a galactic explorer, she had to chuckle. Somehow, Benjamin was using this crisis to resurrect the life he'd given up when he agreed to remain with her. She felt a twinge of guilt. Had she really taken him away from a richer, more fulfilling life? They'd been happy through the years, or so she thought, but perhaps Benjamin was just very good at concealing his discontentment. At any rate, they'd grown extremely close, and there was virtually no way Xyla would wait for Benjamin at home, while he went to the plain to look for hostile visitors from space.

The Tattoo People who brought her to the plain were in constant radio wave contact with those who'd brought Benjamin. When Xyla disembarked at the boat left for Benjamin, they pointed her in the direction he'd set out. Once on his path, it was easy to follow because the footprints stood out clearly against the sandy ground. She walked with her eyes downward, careful not to miss even one of his steps, but she also stayed alert for the sounds of nearby animals that might threaten her. Unlike Benjamin, she carried no weapon.

As usual, Toro preferred not to walk with the rest of his men as they made their way back to the space capsules. While they trudged through the dry washes and gullies, he traversed the ridges and elevated areas, which afforded him a broader view. Occasionally he lost sight of the others, but he was always able to intercept their path again at some point. It meant he walked much farther than they did and changed elevation more often, but that didn't bother him. All of them, including Stella, had radios by which they could communicate, but they only worked within a distance less than five kilometers. Being from a time on Earth where communications satellites were as ubiquitous as the stars in the sky, he'd been spoiled to believe that radios or phones could connect two people regardless of where in the world they were. Without those space-based systems, however, radios were only a little more useful than two tin cans connected by a string. Nevertheless, he kept his radio turned on in case Stella or his men were close enough to transmit or receive a message.

The return trip to the space capsules went faster than the previous day's journey, perhaps because they'd proceeded rather haphazardly before, following Stella's manic drive across the plain looking for animals to shoot. Just after noon he could see the flat area where they'd landed. All the capsules appeared to be undisturbed. With so much daylight left, he decided to explore the plain on his own instead of assembling with his men at the landing site. He radioed them and instructed them to secure the capsules and wait for his arrival. He then began a purposeful trek in a large circle about the perimeter of the landing site.

Theonius had been walking for hours on the plain, but hadn't seen any sign of Stella and her men. Upon emerging from the space capsule, he'd spotted herds of wild animals in the distance—a vista that reminded him of his prior life on Earth watching over the wildlife preserve. He was so excited to see the animals that he almost lost interest in finding the large, violent female who'd kidnapped him from Earth, but he remembered his promise to Risto. He strolled among the herds of buffalo and antelope, marveling at their gentle, trusting nature. Theonius could read the signs written into the ground telling of the presence of living creatures, and he kept mental notes of the various types he encountered. He wasn't surprised to see evidence of predators on the plain, but he hadn't actually seen one yet.

Just as he was wondering how long he might have to walk before he ran into Stella, he came upon a patch of ground clearly disturbed by the passage of many animals moving quickly. He recognized the telltale signs of a stampede, and from the nature of the destruction to the surrounding foliage could easily determine the direction from which the animals had run. Knowing that herd animals stampede to flee from a threat, Theonius followed the path back to whatever the source of the panic had been. It might have been a predator, or it might have been a group of men led by a trigger-happy woman.

He didn't have to go far before he came upon the blood stains from a slain animal dragged across the sandy plain, the scarlet streak of the massacre disappearing over the adjacent ridge. It was the obvious cause of the stampede, but out of curiosity Theonius followed the bloody mark to see if he could find a clue to what manner of beast had been the predator.

Before long, he found the buffalo carcass, foul-smelling and covered with insects. Theonius bent to examine it more closely. With his experienced eye, he could tell that a large feline carnivore had made the kill. The claw marks were unmistakable and the jagged remnants of flesh indicated chunks of meat torn away by extremely sharp incisors. There had been carnivores on the game preserve and Theonius appreciated how well such an animal could grow and thrive where the source of food was virtually endless. How many such creatures populated the area?

As Theonius mulled over that thought, a slight breeze carried to him a premonition, an undeniable feeling, that something or someone was watching him. Instead of looking around to confirm his instincts, he rose casually and set off in the direction the predator had gone after its meal. Theonius suspected that whatever was watching him didn't want to be seen, and therefore couldn't be seen. He walked with the frightening certainty that he was now the prey.

Before leaving Xyla, Benjamin studied a topographic map of the plain to narrow down the possible landing sites for Stella and her gang. All space capsules used similar algorithms for determining the optimal locations for landings. With the extra constraint that Stella would want all the capsules clustered together, that limited the number of possibilities to three locations. Benjamin's first destination was to the best of the three. He was rewarded by success. Eight capsules sat randomly distributed over a large flat area, looking as incongruous in that setting as a locomotive might be.

Seeing no one about, he approached the nearest of the capsules and walked around it, letting his hand glide across its metal surface as if confirming its reality. The capsule was of the type used by Carl Stormer's army. They'd been refurbished and modified by the Arilians during the years after the failed invasion attempt. Though he admired the Arilians, he had to question the wisdom of allowing members of Stormer's army to join the Union. They'd naively thought the men had been rehabilitated, and perhaps they had, but now some were part of Stella's gang bent on exercising their own brand of galactic terrorism on the new worlds struggling to survive.

"Drop your weapon," a voice commanded.

Benjamin started in surprise, confused by the mention of a weapon. He'd forgotten he had one. He did as told and looked up to see first one man, then a half dozen , step out from behind nearby capsules, all with weapons aimed at him. He recognized the men as those he'd confronted on the island of Nucleanis.

"You came back," he said to the first man. "Still looking for something?"

"None of your business," the man said.

Benjamin scanned the group. "Where's Toro?"

"None of your business."

Benjamin shrugged. "Okay. What now?"

The man seemed uncertain how to answer. He looked at the others as if seeking help, but found only blank faces. "We wait," he said finally.

He motioned for Benjamin to walk toward an area of tall shrubs. In the space formed by the vegetation, the men had created a crude camp with equipment and supplies from the capsules. In a small pile off to the side was a pile of bones—the remains of something the men had eaten.

Benjamin sat on the ground with his back against a boulder. He'd been captured by Stella's band, but somehow felt satisfied that he'd successfully found them. This was as far as his plans had taken him, and he had an inexplicable sense of accomplishment. With the sun descending, and the situation requiring him to do nothing more than wait, he idly considered the possibilities for the inevitable encounter with Stella. Strangely enough, none of them offered any chance for a successful outcome.

———————

Toro was close enough to the others that his radio received the crackling message reporting that they'd captured Benjamin Mizello. To Toro, it wasn't good news at all. It was a complication that brought uncertainty. What was Mizello doing here? Did the people of this planet know they'd landed? Were others on the way? His last encounter with Benjamin convinced him that the man would not yield information easily. Toro hoped that Stella would return soon. She'd been confident she could handle Mizello and Toro believed it.

He was about to turn back toward the landing site when a movement in the distance caught his eye. Using his digital binocular, he saw that it was a woman, walking rapidly through a gully on a course that would eventually lead to where the capsules and Toro's men were. His eye instinctively traced a route along the connected ridges that would intercept the woman's path. He set off in that direction, quickening his pace.

Xyla was daydreaming. Tracing Benjamin's steps through the dry washes of the plain was effortless. She mused over the irony that after so many years living with Benjamin on Happiness, she now found herself once again following him. He'd been the driving force for her to leave her home planet, to join the galactic explorer fleet, and to come to Happiness. She was intrigued by the process of imprinting, where young organisms become bound to the first image they're exposed to. She'd even seen it among the Tattoo children, some of whom she knew from infancy. They remained attached to her through the years almost as much as they were to their parents. On Aurora, had her limited existence made her an infant in the universe? Had Benjamin appeared from space and been imprinted on her primitive psyche to the extent that she could never find true contentment without him?

It was at that thought when a man stepped out before her, carrying a weapon and sporting a rude smile.

"Nice day for a walk," he said.

Xyla jumped in surprise. She looked about her trying to put the unexpected appearance of the man into some understandable context.

"Who are you?" she asked.

"I'm Toro. Who are you?"

"My name is Xyla."

Toro waited, following Xyla's gaze as she scanned the area about them, showing her that he also knew how alone the two of them were.

"Where are you going?" he asked.

"Nowhere."

Toro glanced down. Benjamin's footprints were obvious in the sandy floor of the gully.

"You're following Benjamin Mizello."

Xyla gasped. "Where is he?" she asked, fear and dread in her voice. Her distress amused the man. His smile didn't waver.

"He's with my men. They're taking good care of him." He paused, then added, "I think."

"Take me to him."

The man said nothing. Xyla felt uneasy under his glare. She was in her fifties, but still in excellent shape. The clothes she wore did nothing to hide the womanly figure she'd had all her life. She recalled her encounter with Steven Nutley on his supply ship after she and her son had first left Aurora. The man before her seemed made of the same stuff as the depraved supply ship custodian.

"Take me to him," she said again. This time she made it sound like a command instead of a request. She stared back into the man's eyes with a look that left no room for compromise. He shuffled his feet nervously in the sand, weighing his options.

Finally, he stepped to the side and waved her forward with his weapon. "After you."

Xyla hesitated momentarily, then strode resolutely past him brushing defiantly against the muzzle of the gun. Toro fell in behind her.

"Are you looking for animals?" she asked, without turning back toward him.

"Not any more. There's plenty here."

"What do you want with them?"

"We like animals."

"They're protected here. Treasured. Almost sacred to the people who live here."

"What people? We haven't seen any people other than you and Mizello."

Xyla changed the subject. The last thing she wanted was for these men to become curious about the Tattoo People.

"What do you want with Benjamin?"

"Just his help. After we get what we came for, we'll leave."

"Help with what?"

"You'll find out soon enough. After you meet Stella."

The trail of footprints they were following turned abruptly and angled up an adjacent ridge. The climb was strenuous and Xyla spoke no more. She could hear Toro behind her. He was younger and stronger and easily kept up with her. Finally, at the crest of the ridge, they stopped. Before them was a broad flat plain upon which eight space capsules sat glistening in the late afternoon sunshine.

The remainder of the trip was downhill. Once at the landing site, Toro took over and led Xyla to a clump of trees. There she saw the other men Toro had spoken of. Rising to greet her was Benjamin, with shock and alarm written visibly on his face. She ran to him and they embraced, with full awareness of being watched by Toro.

They moved off to where Benjamin had been sitting. The sun was setting and the air growing cold. Benjamin wrapped his arm around Xyla. They spoke in low voices so as not to be heard by the men nearby.

"Why did you come here?" Benjamin asked.

"I was worried about you. I couldn't let you go alone."

"You shouldn't have."

"What do they want?" Xyla asked.

"Animals."

"To eat?" Xyla asked, looking at the remains of the antelope piled in the camp.

"Maybe, but there's more, I think."

"What can we do?"

"I don't know for sure until Stella shows up."

The name caused Xyla to shudder. Toro had said the same thing. She tried to control a rising panic within her. Toro's men seemed to have invented a game designed to torment their captives. They sat around an artificial light that emitted an iridescent, green-tinted glow. One by one, they approached the couple huddled together on the ground and circled menacingly before returning to the others. Each return was followed by muffled conversation culminated by rude laughter. It was suggestive and demeaning, and all Benjamin could do was draw Xyla more tightly against him, regretting that he'd ever decided to confront Stella and her crew.

———————

Theonius suspected the canyon he was walking in would dead-end eventually. The walls, about fifty meters apart, were getting higher and steeper. He was familiar with the topology. Carved by rushing water from higher elevations, the wash had created a depression in the surface of the plain that would terminate at some point. When he reached it, whatever was following him would show itself. He was intentionally walking into a trap because that was probably the only way he'd find what he was looking for—what was looking for him.

Rounding a turn in the canyon, he was confronted by an area with a stand of trees surrounding a shallow pond. The surface of the pond buzzed with insect life, and the muddy shore was pockmarked with the tracks of animals of various types and sizes. They were indistinguishable from one to another, even to Theonius' trained eye.

He approached the pond and bent to scoop up some of the water. He splashed the cool liquid on his face.

"I should kill you right now," said a female voice behind him.

He stood and saw Stella, standing with the dreaded EMP weapon aimed at him.

"Go ahead," he said. "It wouldn't be the first time you shot me with that damned thing."

"I was just playing with you those other times. I'm not playing anymore."

"Sure you are," Theonius said. "I've seen you when you're not playing. You wouldn't be talking."

Theonius could see the rage in Stella's face and knew in the same instant she would fire the weapon. He dropped to the ground. It was most certainly the first time Stella had ever missed, and she quickly lowered the muzzle of the weapon to follow the motion of her target. But Theonius was now moving laterally away, just ahead of the electrified pulses which, though potentially lethal to him, produced only little puffs of sand after missing their human target.

Theonius would have been hit had Stella not been interrupted in her attack by a white blur that seemed to come from the air itself. It bowled her over as if she were a twig. Theonius halted his rolling momentum and looked back to see Stella lying prone beneath a gigantic albino cat. Her hands were gripping the fur on each side of the beast's neck in a feeble attempt to keep its mouth from completing a determined descent toward her exposed neck. Theonius launched himself from the ground and covered the distance to where the struggle was taking place, barreling into the side of the cat, his head taking the full force of impact against the animal's rib cage. It was sufficient to enable Stella to scramble to her feet and lunge for her EMP weapon, lying in the sand where she'd been standing a moment before. She fired three rapid shots at the cat as it was turning to charge again. This time the animal executed an amazingly graceful pivot and leapt into the underbrush by the side of the pond, disappearing as quickly as it had appeared. Theonius and Stella stood in mutual paralysis and shock, their minds slowly catching up with the events that had transpired so quickly. Three streaks of blood oozed through tears in the side of Stella's jump suit.

"What was that?" Stella asked.

"A very dangerous predator," answered Theonius. "We need to get away from here."

Stella turned and stormed off with strong angry steps in the direction from which they'd come. Defeat didn't sit well with her, and Theonius could tell she was already planning her revenge on the big cat. He was baffled by what to do next. Not having anticipated this circumstance, he could think of nothing else to do than follow Stella. Even injured, she was difficult to keep up with.

Benjamin heard footsteps approach the camp. He waited. After hearing about Stella for so long, he was almost anxious to finally meet her. Toro and his men stood and pointed their weapons in the direction of the approaching sound. In the next moment, an enormous, 500th Century female stormed into the emerald light of the camp.

"Someone, get me a medical kit," she roared. She was injured and obviously in pain, but it didn't seem to diminish the power and vitality in her presence. She paced back and forth glaring at the men, stopping finally to look at Xyla and Benjamin.

"Who are they?"

"Benjamin Mizello and a woman named Xyla," answered Toro.

"What are they doing here?"

It was disconcerting that Stella wouldn't address them directly—as if it were beneath her.

"They won't really say," said Toro.

"Kill them," Stella said, and stormed away.

Just then, another enormous figure appeared out of the darkness.

"Don't listen to her. She's just angry because a cat almost killed her."

Xyla and Benjamin were transfixed by the bizarre performance being enacted before them. In the spherical glow cast by the camp light, unlikely demons appeared to deliver unpredictable dialog as if on a supernatural stage. It could have been one of the shows the human actors on Happiness would perform were it not so gruesome and terrifying.

Stella reappeared, confronting the giant face to face.

"Just because you saved my life doesn't mean you can take over. Stay out of my business. Toro, shoot those two."

"How did Theonius get here?" asked Toro.

"Who knows? Who cares?" raged Stella. "Shoot them, and then shoot him. And then get me a link to the supply ship. I want them to set fire to this whole damned planet!"

The large man standing before Stella suddenly reached out and grabbed her about the ribs. Stella screamed in pain from the pressure the giant applied on her open wound. The two of them fell to the ground. Tumbling over one another, they crashed into the camp light, plunging the area into absolute blackness, through which the agonizing groans of the two combatants were gut-wrenching and visceral.

Benjamin stood suddenly and pulled Xyla up next to him. Stumbling, he led her away from the camp. It was impossible to see in the darkness. They fell multiple times, tripping on roots and boulders, but each time rising and moving farther away. When the sounds of the struggle at the camp diminished, Benjamin slowed, trying to avoid additional falls. He knew they were leaving tracks in the sand that would be easy to follow, but he hoped he could get far enough away to avoid being recaptured. If they could last until dawn, they had a chance to find their way back to the waterway and his boat.

Progress was slow. Both were exhausted from the events of the day. The terror they'd felt when Stella had ordered their execution left them spent and emotionally drained.

"I'm sorry," was all Benjamin could say to Xyla as they made their way, cautiously reaching out with arms extended to anticipate obstacles.

"It's not your fault, Benjamin."

"I should never have come here."

"Benjamin, it's good that we came. We need to get back and warn the Tattoo People that Stella aims to set the whole planet on fire."

"I'm not sure what can be done to stop them."

"We have to think of something," said Xyla.

"Stop!" said Benjamin suddenly.

They froze and caught their breath. Benjamin squeezed Xyla's hand. Above the ensuing silence was the unmistakable sound of someone moving toward them, closing fast. They couldn't outrun it. Benjamin moved in front of Xyla and peered into the darkness, waiting. Whatever it was stopped several meters from them. They could hear it breathing in the depth of the darkness.

A blinding light came on, illuminating the giant who'd attacked Stella. He held the flashlight to his face so they could see him.

"I will help you. I won't hurt you."

Benjamin stepped forward and attempted to look into the dark behind the man.

"Are they following you?"

"They're coming after us all. The big woman is very angry."

"You've a light," said Benjamin. "It'll help us move faster."

"Perhaps," said the man. "But it will also show them where we are. Let me lead. I can see better in the dark." He walked past them. "Follow me."

"Who are you?" asked Benjamin.

"I am Theonius. A man named Risto helped me. He sends his regards."

And with that, he plunged into the night, flashing the light every few seconds so Xyla and Benjamin could follow.

The light carried by Stella, Toro, and the other men clearly illuminated the path taken by Benjamin Mizello and his two friends. Stella lost no time in pursuing them. Theonius had pushed her away and disappeared into the night too quickly for her to react. She was enraged, but not so much as to sacrifice the efficiency with which they undertook the hunt for her prey. Stella didn't let haste interfere with the calculated measure of her pursuit. She told Toro and his men to spread out on each side to ensure no one slipped through the net she was casting. It was just a matter of time before she overtook the fugitives. She cackled with delight, momentarily forgetting the pain caused by her wounds.

Toro was on the flank, as usual. Before departing the camp, he retrieved Stella's weapon, which she'd dropped after being attacked by Theonius. He holstered his own weapon and carried Stella's. He'd admired the weapon from the first day he'd seen it. Now he looked forward to the opportunity of using it. In typical fashion, Toro drifted off away from the track his men and

Stella were following. Before long, he was well away from them. The lights they carried were easily discernible against the blackness of the surrounding region. As the distance separating them increased, his eyes became better adapted to the dark. For that reason, he was first to catch sight of the blinking light that must be Benjamin, Xyla, and Theonius making their way through the darkness. Toro moved to intercept them. When he was close enough, he'd fire Stella's EMP weapon at the light and the game would be over. It had gone on far too long already.

For some time, Benjamin had been looking back at the row of lights pursuing them. He refrained from calling attention to it. Theonius was already moving too fast for Xyla and him to keep up. There was nothing to do but follow him and hope that at some point Stella would lose the trail.

At that moment, a blue streak split the darkness and Theonius fell to the ground with an abbreviated cry of pain. Xyla ran to where he'd fallen, kneeling next to him, and searching the inert body for signs of life. Benjamin slumped down next to his companions in defeat.

Toro was first to appear, followed closely by Stella. The light from their flashlights stung Benjamin's eyes. He saw Toro's weapon aimed at him and waited for the end to come.

Just then a new light appeared in the night, accompanied by an eerie humming sound. There was a blue glow, emanating from the surrounding darkness, encompassing them with an otherworldly radiance that grew steadily brighter. The humming sound became stronger as well. It was a disconcerting, threatening sound, like the buzzing of angry bees or the warning rattle of a snake. It produced an unsettling vibration that permeated the air. Stella and her men looked about in confusion. Their weapons were primed and ready for firing, but there was nothing to shoot at.

Only when the first Tattoo man emerged from the darkness did Benjamin and Xyla understand what was happening. They were surrounded by hundreds of Tattoo People, their bodies emitting the characteristic nighttime glow that Benjamin and Xyla were so familiar with. The humming noise was coming from their audio transponders, which were converting radio waves into audible sounds tuned to a frequency evoking an innate, almost primitive, fear that made the humans cower in fright. Even Stella covered her ears to ward off the foreboding sound. When she dropped to her knees in surrender, the men about her dropped as well. Several of the Tattoo people stepped forward and took the weapons from the men, who yielded their arms without resistance. With that, the humming sound abruptly and simultaneously ceased.

Theonius stirred. He sat up and looked about, dazed and helpless. Xyla tried to comfort him with reassuring pats. Benjamin rose and took a tentative step forward, unsure what to do. The Tattoo People had formed a circle around the space, diffusing it with blue illumination. There was a stir in the line of aliens and their ranks parted. From the resulting gap came an enormous white cat, padding its way toward Stella and her men, their eyes displaying unmitigated terror. The animal was followed by one Tattoo man, walking beside it with confidence and purpose. They made a complete circuit about the paralyzed group. The beast was easily larger than four men put together. Upon its second circuit, the cat turned and walked up to Stella, who was visibly trembling. No one had ever seen her so frightened. The cat sniffed at her, ignoring the panic in her face. Then it walked past, close enough that its body brushed against her. It reversed and walked by her again, this time emitting a low throaty rumble from its throat. The cat was purring. Stella's expression was transformed from panic to confusion. On the animal's next passage, she reached out and ran her hand through its fur. The animal stopped and Stella passed her arm over and around its neck, caressing it tenderly. It sat beside her, still purring. At last, Stella had gotten what she always wanted—real animal fur.

Ten days later the fire was finally extinguished. Ostinia's machine had worked continuously night and day to cut a wide firebreak that surrounded the blaze and kept it from spreading any farther. The alien vine within that perimeter was completely destroyed, but the Tattoo People reassured Benjamin and Xyla that it would grow back.

The cat was out of the bag, so to speak, and the existence of the plain with animals from Earth was finally divulged to the humans of Happiness. They were excited to see real animals. For them it was like beholding imaginary creatures from legends and myths come alive again. They admired the diligence and patience with which the Tattoo People cared for the animals and their habitat, and they promised never to intrude on the plain or do anything that might threaten the health and safety of the animals living there. Stella and her gang of space pirates weren't allowed to leave Happiness. Their future on the planet was to be as bizarre and unexpected as the circumstances that brought them there in the first place.

Admiral Chase followed the false trail planted in Stella's robot until he realized he'd been deceived. He reversed course and headed back to Prosperity, but as he approached its planetary system his command ship detected a distress signal from Druix, frozen in a reconstructed space capsule with critically low levels of power and life support. Although he realized diverting to rescue Druix would delay his pursuit, Admiral Chase didn't hesitate.

After the capsule had docked, Druix told the Admiral about the Tattoo People on Happiness and the inadvertent destruction of the space capsules that left Xyla and Benjamin stranded on the planet. When he heard about the hidden treasure, Admiral Chase diverted to Happiness, reaching the planet more than forty years after Stella. Upon his arrival, he found all was well on the planet even after Stella's attempt to set fire to it. However, he was appalled that Stella and her gang hadn't been punished for their crimes.

He sought out Benjamin, who was well known to the people there. Admiral Chase found him walking in the replica of the Arilian Memorial Park, where the statue of Captain Warner and his colleagues stood, surrounded by flowers grown from seeds descended from those the Captain had brought back with him from Supply Ship 5. The seeds were a gift from Aril to commemorate the creation of Happiness.

At 94 years of age, Benjamin was just barely recognizable to the Admiral. The two men shook hands. It was a strange meeting. For Admiral Chase, the accumulated time he'd been unfrozen since he last saw Benjamin was no more than a year. The man before him was elderly, with only the vaguest resemblance to the young man Admiral Chase had known. For Benjamin, how bizarre was it to see Admiral Chase after more than seven decades, little changed from the way he remembered him?

"Have you heard from Druix?" Benjamin asked anxiously

"Yes, he's fine. He told us everything."

"He's my son."

Admiral Chase nodded. "He told us that, too. And Xyla's."

"I wish she had lived long enough to know that he's safe. She died two years ago."

"I'm sorry," said Admiral Chase.

Benjamin stopped and sat at a bench surrounded by lush landscaping with flowering bushes and tall shade trees.

"How about Risto? Have you found him?" He asked.

"No. Where is he?"

"He was captured by Stella. He rescued a game warden from Earth named Theonius. Theonius said Risto was on a space capsule with very little fuel. He was heading for my father's supply ship."

"I'll get word out to my fleet. They'll make sure he's okay. All we found in space when we got here was a supply ship with no power."

"That was probably Risto's doing. Stella left two of her men on the supply ship, but they had to abandon it after all the electrical systems inexplicably failed. They landed on Happiness to meet up with Stella. She and the others had already surrendered though."

"So I understand," said Admiral Chase. He seemed disturbed. "It doesn't seem that Stella and the rest of them were punished at all for their crimes." His tone conveyed disappointment.

"No, not in the traditional sense. The humans and the Tattoo People made sure they couldn't escape in their space capsules. Without a means to leave, their punishment was that they were all doomed to live out their lives on a planet called Happiness."

"One of the attractions here is called Stella's Wild Animal Park and Petting Zoo," said Admiral Chase derisively.

Benjamin chuckled. "Ironic, isn't it? She and Theonius started it. He knew Stella was the kind of woman he had to keep in furs, but the furs didn't have to be from dead animals. Amazingly enough, animals took to Stella very easily. It melted even her heart."

"And the rest of the gang?"

Benjamin laughed again. "They got the worst punishment. They were forced to stage a wild-west show in the amusement park, performing a fake shoot-out three times a day. They did that until they were so old it looked ridiculous. Then they turned it over to younger actors. It's still one of the most popular attractions."

Admiral Chase was shaking his head. "Doesn't sound like severe enough justice for a gang that terrorized the galaxy and almost set fire to a whole planet. We're still trying to find the custodians of Supply Ship 3."

"True. But remember. The men were just following Stella, and she wasn't really that bad."

"That's hard to believe," said Admiral Chase.

"Can I see your weapon?"

Puzzled, Admiral Chase removed his EMP weapon from its holster on his belt. Benjamin examined it, turning it over in his hands. "This is the same kind of weapon Stella carried. There's a button on it to switch it to automatic mode."

"Yes," said the Admiral. "We keep it on automatic unless we're in combat."

"What does automatic mean?"

"Because these weapons are extremely powerful, back when we were on Earth, manufacturers were required to incorporate a special chip into them called the Omega chip. The handle of every gun is equipped with sensors that detect blood flow, sweat production, skin temperature and other properties that directly or indirectly indicate the mentality of the person firing the weapon. The chip automatically adjusts the power level of the pulse based on the real intent of the shooter, which even he or she may not know. You have to be really frightened, or really intent on killing someone, for it to emit a lethal pulse. Otherwise, it emits a lower energy shot. All the weapons manufactured in those days were smart weapons like this one. It prevented a lot of accidental and unintentional deaths."

"Right," said Benjamin. "And did you know that Stella always kept her weapon on automatic?"

"No," said the Admiral, hesitantly.

"Theonius told me later that he was shot with Stella's weapon four times—three times by Stella and once by Toro. He survived all four. He's a big guy, but as I understand it, these weapons can bring down a giant like Theonius and a dozen more just like him."

"So you're saying Stella never really wanted to kill him?"

"Yes. According to Theonius, Stella shot Risto twice with the same weapon and he survived both times. Stella also shot an antelope, but didn't kill it. Toro had to finish it off with a more conventional weapon. Later, she shot the big cat three times, and it just ran away."

"It's significant that she didn't take the gun off automatic. That's easy enough to do."

"Right. Not that she didn't have a temper. When Xyla and I were being held captive, she stormed into the camp in a rage. She'd just been mauled by the cat. She told Toro to kill us. She told him to do it because she knew her weapon wouldn't work."

"Who would have thought?" said Admiral Chase.

Two Tattoo children ran past them carrying a rubber ball.

"I suppose you know how Stella was defeated?" Benjamin said.

"It was the aliens. When hundreds of them showed up, Stella and her men surrendered."

"That's right," said Benjamin. "But do you know how they came to be there?"

Admiral Chase considered this for several moments. "No. I haven't given it much thought."

"She called them."

"Who?"

"My wife. Xyla. Bria."

Admiral Chase looked confused. "She was with you. Right?"

"Yes. She followed me to the site where Stella and her gang landed their capsules. She was alone. The Tattoo People were in the forest, fighting the fire."

"All of them?"

"Every last one of them. That fire was out of control. It threatened to spread and destroy the vine that's their lifeblood."

"Then how did they come to rescue you?"

"It puzzled me for a long time, but I think I know now. A few weeks later, I went to visit Xyla where she was teaching the alien children to read and write. I noticed that many of them weren't wearing their translating medallions. I mentioned it to Xyla. She just shrugged. She hadn't even noticed. She was having no problem communicating with the children."

"How could that be?" asked the Admiral. "I thought they only communicate by radio waves."

Benjamin sighed. "Xyla's people on Aurora grew fur to protect themselves from the cold. It was explained in terms of gene expression—stimulation of a gene present in the human genome, perhaps one that became inactive because of changing climate conditions. What if Xyla's people, the Malanites, had the unique ability to easily activate genes in response to external stimuli? What if the human genome has a gene for communicating via radio waves—some kind of mutation in our evolutionary past that was never favored by natural selection? That gene would just sit there waiting for some stress to activate it. I believe the many years Xyla spent with the Tattoo children created the right conditions for reactivation of that gene. And when we were threatened by Toro and his men, Xyla drew on that ability. She transmitted a message to the Tattoo People and they came to help us. Katru confirmed it later. He said they received a distress call. Collectively, the Tattoo People decided to leave off from fighting the fire because we were in trouble."

Admiral Chase was staring at him. "She was quite a woman," he said.

"Yes, she was. But they all were. My life has been blessed. I've been surrounded by beautiful, strong, intelligent women."

Off in the distance, a number of colorful balloons appeared, rising above the trees.

"Before Druix left the planet, I gave him a letter," Benjamin said. "I asked him to deliver it to Ilsa."

Admiral Chase nodded. "He's on his way to your father's supply ship. We made sure his fuel tanks were replenished and the capsule was functioning properly."

"Thank you," said Benjamin. "He's a special young man. And because he's Xyla's son, he may also have the ability to call upon long suppressed genes when he needs to. Watch over him. He's the last of the Malanite breed."

"I will," said Admiral Chase. He shielded his eyes to watch the balloons drifting closer now. "It must have been very hard for you after Bria died."

"I miss her terribly. I wish it had been me to die first."

Admiral Chase shuffled his feet, not sure how to speak the next sentence. "I can get you off the planet. It's not too late."

Benjamin shook his head. "No, thanks. This is my home. I can't leave."

"What about Ilsa? You have a daughter? What about your father and Krystal? They'd love to see you again."

Benjamin stopped and turned to face Admiral Chase. "A daughter," he said wistfully. His voice broke. "I have no doubt they'd love to see me again, but that's a different Benjamin. That Benjamin is long gone."

"Give them some credit. Do you think they'll love you less because you're old now?"

"Age has nothing to do with it. It's all the things that happen through the years that make a person different. Believe me. I'm not the same Benjamin they think they know."

"Maybe not, but it wouldn't diminish their love for you."

"Nor will me dying of old age here on this planet."

"You're not thinking straight, Benjamin. You're depriving people who love you from the joy of seeing you alive again."

"Perhaps, but I've given this a lot of thought. I can't leave Happiness."

"You gave it a lot of thought when there was no hope of leaving the planet. You were mentally adjusting to the hopelessness of the situation. Now there's hope. You can escape the planet. You have to rethink your decision."

Benjamin sighed long and deep. "I could have left anytime."

"What do you mean?"

Benjamin was looking into the sun. He was squinting and tears glistened on his cheek. "After the aliens overcame Stella and her gang, those space capsules just sat there. I could have left years ago."

"Then why didn't you?"

"Xyla—Bria—didn't want to. She loved being here. I could have left her, but that would've been much harder. I couldn't and wouldn't have done that."

"How about after she died?" asked Admiral Chase. "You could have left then."

"Yes," replied Benjamin. "I could have, but I didn't. "

"Why?"

Benjamin sat forward and rested his chin on his hands. "As people age, they view the world differently. Children have the tendency to give life and personality to inanimate objects. They personify everything because it animates the lifeless. We lose that through the years as reality overwhelms us. But we get it back again as we get older—in a different way. I see life in everything—planets, stars, the clouds, the statue over there, even a space capsule has life. I even see life in concepts. Love, hate, anger, compassion, hope—also have life. Once they exist, they have the will to survive, just like any organism. Evil, destructive, ugly emotions should die. After they're born, we have to destroy them. But the good emotions—love, happiness, curiosity—once they come to be, we should protect them, nurture them, keep them alive. My life on Happiness and my feelings for Xyla were like that. If I left Happiness, I'd have destroyed the beautiful life we'd made together. Does that make sense?"

"I can see some sense in that," Admiral Chase admitted.

Then he added with a smile, "I must be getting old."

"Could you do me a favor?" Benjamin asked.

"Anything."

"I've written a journal of my time here. Would you take it—make sure it gets into the right hands?"

"Of course."

"What's her name?" Benjamin asked.

Admiral Chase hesitated, not sure who Benjamin was referring to. Then he answered, "Elsenia."

Benjamin smiled. Above them, seeds descended from the balloons onto the landscape below. Admiral Chase stood and helped Benjamin to his feet. The two men resumed their stroll through the replica of the Arilian Memorial Park, their feet crunching on the fallen seeds.

CHAPTER 45
— Century 1232 —

Krystal could never quite come to grips with the discordant emotions she experienced upon reviewing the messages and data she'd recorded while frozen in her magnetocryogenic chamber. Unless interrupted by an emergency message, or the arrival of a galactic explorer, one hundred years passed between freezing and unfreezing sequences—one hundred years during which the supply ship received tremendous amounts of data, all automatically screened and mined before passing into a permanent archive with multiple back-ups. The highest priority messages were displayed first, followed by the more routine transmissions from galactic explorers and other supply ship custodians. Finally, came the data that carried housekeeping information on nearby vehicles and the stellar environment around the supply ship. The computer produced various visual displays that showed the status of the vehicles, with color-coded symbols, making it easy to identify quantities out of normal range.

A hundred years earlier, Arthur and Krystal had received the message from Benjamin that he was landing on Happiness with Druix and Xyla. Now, Krystal scanned for the messages that would almost certainly contain a report from Benjamin about his visit to that planet.

The first few moments Krystal reviewed the data always filled her with dread. She was sure the human psyche wasn't emotionally or mentally prepared to cope with the looming imminence of disaster, heartbreak, or death, communicated so effectively by advanced information technology. When she and Arthur had left Earth in the 22nd Century, information was everywhere, and the mechanisms by which humans acquired data were pervasive. Even then, the effects on humans of this continuous barrage of information undoubtedly produced a variety of human neuroses ranging from mild anxiety to openly psychotic behavior. As rational as Krystal was in carrying out her duties on the supply ship, each time she sat before the computer and gazed at the new data received, she couldn't ignore the inevitable knot in her stomach and lump in her throat. If that wasn't enough to bring her to the brink of sanity, there was always the possibility that at long last, news would arrive of the discovery of other intelligent life in the galaxy. To Krystal, this was the ultimate thrill that made the roller coaster ride worth taking.

Krystal would wonder later why Arthur had decided at that particular moment to join her as she reviewed the messages. Why hadn't he let her read the messages first, as he had always done countless times before? If he'd followed his normal routine, checking out the greenhouse gardens while she downloaded the data, she'd have been the first to learn that Benjamin was no more—dead for thousands of years, the time it took for Admiral Chase's message to reach the supply ship.

Had Krystal found out before Arthur, she'd have been able to prepare him for the devastating news that Benjamin had never left Happiness—that while Arthur, Krystal, Ilsa, and Elsenia were frozen in their magnetocryogenic chambers, Benjamin had lived out the entire remainder of his life on a distant planet. And why had Admiral Chase not flagged as high priority the message that Benjamin never left the planet? Perhaps because he knew that by the time Arthur and Krystal read the message, Benjamin would be long dead anyway. There was nothing that could have been done.

Krystal read the passage an instant before Arthur: "Your son was unable to leave the planet." She sensed Arthur's breath catch, and he reached for her hand. He continued reading for a few moments more. The message went on to say that he was attaching Benjamin's journal, which would explain everything.

Arthur breathed a long sigh with the grim realization that he would never see his son again. An instant later, he stood, as if he were lifting a huge weight, and left Krystal sitting before the monitor, her face cast in blue, her eyes unfathomably sad. Krystal knew Arthur was on his way to tell Ilsa.

———

Arthur found Ilsa in the galley. He didn't have long to consider how to break the news to her. He'd grown close to her during the time she and Elsenia had been on the supply ship. As he entered, Ilsa turned toward him with a radiant smile, filled with admiration and respect.

"Where's Elsenia?" Arthur asked.

"She's in the greenhouse, as usual."

Arthur sat in the chair across from Ilsa and took her hands in his. He saw awareness cross her face, and her abalone skin turned ashen. Before she could speak, Arthur said gently, "Benjamin is no more."

Ilsa brought her hands up and covered her face as if protecting herself from a glaring light. She uttered a cry, and then a second sound that was a muffled scream. Then she sobbed uncontrollably, interrupted only when she moaned the word, "No"—long, drawn out, and achingly sad. Arthur hugged her, unable to cry himself. That would come later.

Krystal joined them. She had scanned enough of Benjamin's journal to know what had happened.

"His capsule was damaged," she told Arthur and Ilsa. "He couldn't leave."

Over the next several hours, the three shared comments, speculation, and questions that provided a means to hold onto Benjamin. Even the news that Benjamin had discovered an alien civilization didn't mute their sadness. They talked, reminisced, cried, and gradually transitioned to resigned acceptance of the fact that Benjamin was gone from their lives forever. The conversation faded and the three were lost in their own personal thoughts. Finally, Arthur said to Ilsa, "Would you like me to be with you when you tell Elsenia?"

"No," said Ilsa, weakly. "I'll tell her." She sobbed again, uncontrollably. "She never knew her father."

The Elsenia who first arrived on Supply Ship 6 would have been angry and bitter upon learning the father she never knew was dead. That Elsenia was only concerned with the life she'd given up on Aril. The new Elsenia, reborn on the supply ship as a result of finding a fragile and unlikely frog in the greenhouse garden, had a much more respectful attitude about life. The new Elsenia hugged her mother, wept with her, and tried to console her.

Sometime later, they departed from the supply ship and began the journey to Happiness. Ilsa had an irresistible and inexplicable urge to see the planet where Benjamin had lived his life. What she and her daughter would do after that, neither of them knew.

———————

Arthur and Krystal sat on the bench in the greenhouse of the supply ship. They missed Ilsa and Elsenia. The ship seemed too empty, too devoid of life, without them. And they missed Benjamin, too, even though he had not been a physical presence on the ship in the way Ilsa and her child had.

Arthur put his arm around Krystal. She was inexplicably cold in the greenhouse. The temperature was mild, but perhaps knowing that empty space lay just centimeters away on the other side of the crystal windows created the chill.

"If you were to decide to give up being a custodian of the supply ship, what planet would you want to live on?" Krystal asked.

Arthur answered with another question. "Where do you think?"

"There are only four to choose from: Earth, Aril, Prosperity, and Happiness."

"Right. It's one of those," said Arthur teasingly.

"You're not going to tell me, are you?"

"Nope. You have to guess."

"I don't have to guess. I know. It's one thing to read about the wonderful new planets that have been established, but there will only be one real home for you and for me. Earth."

"Right," said Arthur, with a smile.

"When do we leave?"

Arthur sighed. Somehow they had both independently and simultaneously decided it was time to retire.

"We have to wait for our replacements."

"It could take thousands of years. Can I send the request to Aril now?"

"Yes. I'm ready to go home."

"Me too," agreed Krystal. She shivered once more and Arthur tightened his grip on her shoulder.

AFTERWARD
by Elsenia Mizello
— Century 1310 —

My Mom and I landed on Happiness almost eight thousand years after we left my grandfather's supply ship. It was my second experience with the shock and disorientation of interstellar space travel—third, if you count the time I traveled from Happiness to Sparil in my mother's womb.

Even though I had prepared myself for the trip to Happiness, I still resented the loss of so much time. Sure, I was frozen for the duration, but I regretted all the life experiences I might have had during those lost years. I didn't want to live a long time if most of it was spent frozen. I wanted to live a long time unfrozen! I wanted to experience everything!

Going to the planet where Benjamin had lived his life was something my Mom felt she had to do, but she didn't anticipate that everywhere we went there'd be reminders of him and the woman he lived with. They were both idolized and highly respected for the role they played in uniting the alien and human civilizations. I'm not sure how long she might have endured the visit. How could she deal with the simple truth that Benjamin had made a conscious decision to remain on Happiness with Xyla and abandon her and me forever? She'd read my dad's journal many times. She knew all the extenuating circumstances, but it still must have been hard for her. She was on the verge of tears most of the time. It was my step-dad who saved her.

On most planets, the business of life and living is the highest priority, while the arts are secondary—activities undertaken after all other requirements are met. On Happiness it was the opposite. The arts were foremost in the hearts and minds of the entire population. Creative expression was more important than food and water. It's probably what sustained the people after the asteroid struck. It's what established the bond between the humans and the aliens. It was the common language by which the two species communicated. For my mom, Happiness was the ultimate experiment into what makes a successful civilization. She wouldn't miss it for the universe, and even though it caused her great pain, she stuck with it.

As for me, I became fascinated by the Tattoo People. Although they lived in harmony with the humans on Happiness, they still kept to themselves, thriving in the protective and nurturing habitat carved out of the alien vine. The only place in the forest humans were allowed to go was the island replica of Prosperity's single continent Nucleanis. A path had been formed through the thicket allowing visitors to get to the lake, where they'd be transported by boat to the island. I visited there often, just to gaze out at the endless expanse of forest where the Tattoo People lived. Though I saw no more than a carpet of green foliage, I was aware that it pulsated with life, alien life, where communication among individuals was so fast and efficient they behaved as one. I was a self-taught student of biology, and I spent many hours pondering the lesson that could be learned from the Tattoo People. I knew a secret existed beyond my cognitive abilities to comprehend. I was anxious to go to Aril, where I could continue my studies in the more formal setting of Arilian universities. I just had to wait until my mom was through tormenting herself over Benjamin.

Then one day she came with me to Nucleanis, and while strolling among the pyramids we saw a man walking toward us, a strange smile upon his face. He was about the same age as my mom, thin with pale complexion and graying hair. I kept walking, but my mom stopped. I looked back at her and there was a mixed expression of curiosity and terror on her face.

The man walked past me and stopped in front of her.

"Ilsa Mizello?"

"Yes," my mom said. I'd never seen her so nervous.

"My name is Druix. Benjamin was my father."

My mom expelled air, folding her arms as if she were cold.

"Is this my sister?" he said, turning to look at me.

"Who are you?" I asked.

"I'm your half-brother."

"The hell you are."

He laughed. Turning to my mother again, he said, "Can we talk?"

"Okay," said my mom, grabbing my hand. "How did you find us?"

"I was on my way to Supply Ship 6 to see you. My mother told me to go to Aril, but I felt I needed to meet you—explain to you what happened. On my way, my capsule received the message from Arthur Mizello saying that you and your daughter were on route to Happiness. I was able to turn around and arrive here at the same time as you."

Druix and Mom strolled and talked for the remainder of the day. She wanted to learn everything she could about the time Benjamin and he had spent together. Before leaving us for the evening, Druix gave my mom the necklace containing the letter that Benjamin had asked him to give to her. Later, alone in her room next to mine, I could hear her crying.

The next day, I asked her what was in the letter.

"An apology, an explanation, an expression of gratitude, a wish for the future. Everything you'd expect your father to say given the circumstances. For me, it was the last sentence of the letter that was most important."

"What did it say?"

"It said, 'At the end of the day, I'd like to think that if you'd been able to know the things I did and said during my life here, you'd forgive me and continue to love me as much as I continued to love you.'"

"Nice," I said.

"Yes, he was."

Druix joined us for the remainder of our tour of Happiness. He told us all the things left unsaid in my dad's journal. It was what my mom needed. I still think that somehow or other she knew what she was looking for on Happiness and she had found it. She and Druix became very close and he returned with us to Aril. That's where they were married. It was the end of one story and the beginning of another. Druix helped get me into an Arilian university. As a galactic historian, he reappeared on Aril every few thousand years. He's a legend there. He also helped us publish my dad's journal, which became hugely popular. Many believed it to be a fable, but I know it to be the truth. Perhaps all fables are truths made wonderful by the passage of time.

Investigaciones

Deslizar

Patricia Whitehouse

Traducción de Patricia Abello

Heinemann Library

Chicago, Illinois

Customer Service 888-454-2279
Visit our website at www.heinemannlibrary.com

Designed by Sue Emerson, Heinemann Library; Page layout by Que-Net Media
Printed and bound in the United States by Lake Book Manufacturing, Inc.
Photo research by Beth Chisholm

07 06 05 04 03
10 9 8 7 6 5 4 3 2 1

Library of Congress Cataloging-in-Publication Data
Whitehouse, Patricia, 1958-
  [Sliding. Spanish]
  Deslizar/ Patricia Whitehouse.
      p. cm. – (Investigaciones)
Includes index.
Summary: Presents simple hands-on experiments that demonstrate the properties that make sliding easier or more difficult.
  ISBN 1-4034-0941-2 (HC), 1-4034-3458-1 (Pbk.)
  1. Friction–Juvenile literature. 2. Surfaces (Physics)–Juvenile literature. 3. Friction–Experiments–Juvenile literature. 4. Surfaces (Physics)–Experiments–Juvenile literature. [1. Friction. 2. Friction–Experiments. 3. Experiments. 4. Spanish language materials] I. Title.
  QC197 .W4518 2003
  531'.6–dc21

                                        2003042311

Acknowledgments
The author and publishers are grateful to the following for permission to reproduce copyright material:
pp. 4, 6, 7, 8, 9, 10, 11, 12, 13, 14, 15, 16, 17, 18, 19, 20, 21, 22, 23, 24, back cover Que-Net/Heinemann Library; p. 5 Mug Shots/Corbis

Cover photograph by Que-Net/Heinemann Library

Every effort has been made to contact copyright holders of any material reproduced in this book. Any omissions will be rectified in subsequent printings if notice is given to the publisher.

Special thanks to our bilingual advisory panel for their help in the preparation of this book:

Anita R. Constantino
Literacy Specialist
Irving Independent School District
Irving, TX

Argentina Palacios
Docent
Bronx Zoo
New York, NY

Ursula Sexton
Researcher, WestEd
San Ramon, CA

Aurora Colón García
Literacy Specialist
Northside Independent School District
San Antonio, TX

Leah Radinsky
Bilingual Teacher
Inter-American Magnet School
Chicago, IL

Unas palabras están en negrita, **así.**
Las encontrarás en el glosario en fotos de la página 23.

Contenido

¿Qué es deslizar?

Deslizarse es un modo de moverse.

Tú te deslizas cuando bajas por un resbaladero.

4

Es fácil deslizarse en unos lugares.

En otros lugares es difícil deslizarse.

¿Dónde es mejor deslizarse?

hielo

Pon un **ladrillo** sobre hielo.

Dale un empujoncito al ladrillo.

El ladrillo se desliza por
el hielo duro.

Es fácil deslizarse en el hielo.

Pon el **ladrillo** sobre arena.

¿Se desliza?

El ladrillo se queda entre
la arena blanda.

Es difícil deslizarse en la arena.

¿Se desliza mejor algo liso o áspero?

Este piso es **liso**.

Los calcetines también son lisos.

Los calcetines y el piso son lisos.

Pueden deslizarse uno sobre otro.

Las suelas de estos zapatos
son **ásperas.**

¿Se deslizan por el piso **liso?**

Las cosas ásperas no se deslizan
bien en un lugar liso.

¿Se puede cambiar algo áspero a liso?

Este bote pesado es **liso**.

¿Se desliza por la madera **áspera**?

Dale un empujoncito sobre
la madera.

No se desliza.

Échale a la madera jabón
para platos.

¿Qué pasa ahora cuando
empujas el bote?

El bote se desliza.

El jabón hace que la madera **áspera** sea **resbalosa.**

¿Cómo ayuda el agua a deslizarse?

Tu traje de baño es **liso**
y el plástico seco es liso.

¿Te deslizas?

Te deslizas por el plástico, pero
no mucho.

Échale agua al plástico.

El agua hace que el plástico
sea **resbaloso**.

Es fácil deslizarse en los lugares resbalosos.

¡Ahora puedes deslizarte!

Prueba

¿Cuál de estos lugares es más **resbaloso?**

Busca la respuesta en la página 24.

Glosario en fotos

ladrillo
páginas 6, 7, 8, 9

áspero
páginas 12, 13, 14, 17

resbaloso
páginas 17, 20, 21, 22

liso
páginas 10, 11, 12, 13, 14, 18

Nota a padres y maestros

A través del juego, los niños examinan el mundo físico y las diversas fuerzas de la naturaleza que lo afectan. Este libro amplía el juego infantil a experimentos sobre la física de la fricción. Estos experimentos exploran si dos superficies se deslizan entre sí. Los experimentos emplean materiales caseros y del salón de clase con el fin de que los niños repitan el experimento sobre el que han leído.

Cada capítulo contempla las características de dos superficies y su interacción. Lea cada capítulo, repita el experimento y comente lo que han aprendido. Por ejemplo, después de leer las páginas 10 y 11, pida a los niños que se deslicen por el piso liso en calcetines. A continuación lea las páginas 12 y 13 y pídales que traten de deslizarse por el piso con los zapatos puestos. Anímelos a pensar en otros lugares en los que se deslicen con facilidad, como un resbaladero o una superficie con hielo. Haga notar que deslizarse en esos lugares es como deslizarse sobre el piso en calcetines.

❗ ¡PRECAUCIÓN!
Todos los experimentos se deben hacer con el permiso y la ayuda de un adulto.

Índice

Respuesta de la prueba

El piso mojado y jabonoso es **resbaloso.** ¡Ten cuidado!